Praise for
Our Hearts Will Burn Us Down

"Anne Valente is a sorceress, conjuring a story of sorrow and suspense with characters so real we feel their heartbreak, their bewilderment, the horrible chills down their spines. . . . This is a gorgeous book full of mysteries. It scorches with truth, and sings with hope. Valente writes like all of our lives depend on it."

—Diane Cook, author of *Man V. Nature*

"Written in the collective voice of the community, à la Jeffrey Eugenides's *The Virgin Suicides,* Valente artfully employs short chapters on arson and anatomy, as well as diagrams, newspaper articles, and biographies of the victims on the way to an unforgettable ending, with fire serving as a powerfully fitting metaphor for grief, loss, and our inability to comprehend the nature of fate."

—*Publishers Weekly*

"Valente has written a poetic page-turner that explores how we grieve in solitude and grieve together, and what the human body endures when that grief overwhelms. Quizzical, melodic, and unforgettable, *Our Hearts Will Burn Us Down* breaks new ground on issues of mass violence, communal loss, and the act of remembrance."

—*Ploughshares*

"Valente takes us straight to the heart of the horror in this shocking (but tender and cerebral) book."

—*Buffalo News*

"*Our Hearts Will Burn Us Down* is a beautifully written, lyrical book wrapped up in a compelling mystery with shades of Stephen King. Gripping and profound, a terrific debut."

—Kate Hamer, author of *The Girl in the Red Coat*

OUR HEARTS WILL
BURN US DOWN

OUR HEARTS WILL BURN US DOWN

A Novel

ANNE

VALENTE

WILLIAM MORROW

An imprint of HarperCollins*Publishers*

HarperCollins
PUBLISHERS
—— Since 1817 ——

HarperCollins books may be purchased for educational, business, or sales promotional use. For information please e-mail the Special Markets Department at SPsales@harpercollins.com.

A hardcover edition of this book was published in 2016 by William Morrow, an imprint of HarperCollins Publishers.

FIRST WILLIAM MORROW PAPERBACK EDITION PUBLISHED 2017.

Designed by Fritz Metsch

Illustrations by Nick Springer and Noah Springer, copyright © 2016 Springer Cartographics LLC.

Library of Congress Cataloging-in-Publication Data has been applied for.

ISBN 978-0-06-242914-8

17 18 19 20 21   LSC   10 9 8 7 6 5 4 3 2

For Josh

OUR HEARTS WILL
BURN US DOWN

WHO WE WERE

THREE DAYS AFTER Caleb Raynor opened fire, the first house burned to the ground.

Three days after he entered the school's east doors during second period, after we heard screams and running and faint popping in the hallway, after our English and chemistry and mathematics and history teachers huddled us away from the doors and into storage closets and underneath laboratory tables, halfway to safety before doors burst open and shots ripped across blackboards and desks and overturned chairs, we awoke to the news that Caroline Black's house and everything inside of it had disintegrated in flames.

Caroline Black, who had once shared an elementary school with us.

Caroline Black, who had been in the hallway, on her way back to social studies from the bathroom.

Caroline Black, gone alongside twenty-seven of our peers within the walls of Lewis and Clark High School.

When we first heard the noise we imagined bang snaps, the white-papered firecrackers we once threw to the pavement every Fourth of July. We imagined nothing more than powdered paper and a quiet spark until we saw our teachers' faces and heard their strained voices, *Get down, now,* until we crouched beneath our desks and heard the firecrackers growing louder, until they became something other than fireworks entirely. And when we saw the news three days later about Caroline's ravaged house, a fire beyond gunfire, we imagined other sounds: the sound of swirling sirens, the approach of fire trucks. We imagined Caroline's neighbors standing in their yards wrapped in blankets against the fall Midwestern air, awoken by the blaze and by their own lack of being able to do anything as flames climbed the siding of the house and licked an expanse of overwhelming sky. We imagined their children padding down staircases and onto the lawn bleary-eyed, children clutched close against the growing heat, a glow alighting their faces and stinging their cheeks.

And when we learned that Caroline's parents had died in the fire, we felt a wash of relief and envy, and then guilt for even feeling it.

That they were gone, that they would no longer live with this.

And that we were still here, and that we would.

WE: 1,193 STUDENTS at Lewis and Clark. One hundred eighteen teachers. Six administrators. Three counselors. Twelve support staff. Two librarians.

We: The Lewis and Clark Trailblazers. State-champion dance squad. Members of the 2003 Chess Club, the Key Club, the National Honor Society, the Eco-Act Alliance.

We: Nick Ito. Zola Walker. Matt Howell. Christina Delbanco.

We: The junior staff members of the Lewis and Clark High School yearbook, waiting since freshman year to design the perfect book for our graduating seniors, our school's one lasting tradition, a gift to bear them away to college and toward the future.

Him: Caleb Raynor, another junior who once shared our playground. Who attended Des Peres Elementary with us so many years before we moved onward to Lewis and Clark High, who sat upon the magic carpet with us during story time, who never raised his hand in class, who only occupied his desk unseen and sketched shapes into its wood. Quiet. Reserved. A loner, but never picked on. A boy who some of us might have been friends with, who we might have dated if he'd ever moved to speak a word, if he'd thought to join the Art Club or Mock Trial, if he'd ever taken off the head-phones that became his armor once we entered seventh grade.

Caleb Raynor: a boy most of us knew nothing about. No one except Eric Greeley, his best friend, who was not at school when Caleb entered the east doors.

9:04 A.M. Wednesday. Early October. The air beginning to tinge with the crisp of autumn. Homecoming two weeks away, the marching band practicing beyond the football field each day after school. The sun already high in an eggshell sky when Caleb burst through the doors carrying a sawed-off shotgun and a handgun and sixteen magazines of ammunition, when he kicked open the door to the principal's office and gunned down the administrative assistant, Deborah Smalls, a woman who handed us hall passes on mornings we showed up late, and then moved on to Principal Jef-fries, shot dead as she reached for the PA system that would have alerted us, an alarm, an emergency.

We heard nothing in our classrooms, our pencils to paper, our ears trained upon our teachers. Not until Caleb moved down the hallway, reloaded, rattled his guns against the railings. Not until he charged into the art studio and shot Mr. Nolan, alone in the room, on planning period between classes and drawing up a lesson and snapping the sugar-free gum we knew he always chewed, listening to KSHE 95's classic rock on a transistor radio. Manfred Mann. Styx. Blue Oyster Cult. Gone in only seconds.

We heard it then. The popping. The faraway screams. Of ad-ministrators, counselors, cafeteria workers entering the hallways. Of librarians and custodians coming to realizations, of testing exit doors and finding them barred.

We have tried to gather and transpose. We have tried to rear-range this.

We have tried to catalog the details.

We have tried to set this right.

This: a record. What it means to archive, to set down disaster.

What it means to commit it to memory, to create a book, to catalog what we were to one another and what the school's halls were to us. A single book: as if we shared the same memory, as if every student at Lewis and Clark bore the same witness. As if we all beat the same heart within the hallways that morning and in the following days and weeks, as if we all understood what was happening, as if we all split apart the same way. As if a book could contain this in photographs and in words, a book meant to capture the best, to bear us away toward the future with a comfortable wistfulness.

This: an attempt to archive. An attempt at futility. An attempt to gather and collect and piece together and put away, an assemblage of articles and documents and reports and profiles. An archive of record, that this happened. An archive of moving on. An archive of prisms, of refraction, of looking at the same light from an endless stretch of angles. An archive that evaded us, that still evades us, an archive of pressing on regardless of evasion to put everything back together, to reassemble parts, to create a perfect whole from a scattering of fragments. To create a history. A laying down of testimony. An archive of a year. And an archive of the four of us, classmates since elementary school and since freshman year colleagues as well, a word we used with irony to describe our collaboration as the junior yearbook staff and a word that would hurt only later when tossed around in distant workplaces, a word that would return us always to an autumn morning and the breaking in of gunfire, to a single October day.

October 8. 2003. 9:04 A.M. A single minute, a split second, an ending.

Nick sat in English class, bent over the pages of *Moby-Dick* and listening to Alicia Hughes read a passage out loud. Alicia Hughes, who'd worn the same pair of green sneakers since freshman year, who'd once told Nick at a seventh-grade dance that she thought he was cute. Alicia Hughes intoning *That unsounded ocean you gasp in is life* and Nick imagining nothing of a windswept sea but only the curve of his girlfriend Sarah Reynolds's neck, how his breath caught and sputtered when he pressed his mouth into the bend of her throat. Sometimes in her bedroom before her parents came home from work, sometimes in the back of his Honda Civic when he took her home from school and they detoured to Midvale County Park. His girlfriend for more than a year now and both of them still virgins, Sarah pressing always for more beneath the breath-damp sheets of her room's twin bed and Nick pulling away because he was older, because he didn't want to take advantage of her, his mouth seeking air instead of the sea salt of her skin. Sarah a girl he'd first noticed at a basement party when she was a freshman and he a sophomore, how her laugh carried across the Solo cups and the bass of the stereo's speakers. Sarah downstairs in the school's music wing practicing choir when the popping in the hallway crescendoed above Alicia Hughes's voice and everyone in the room looked up and Mrs. Menda glanced toward the closed classroom door.

Nick saw his teacher's face change, a recognition. *Get under your desks,* she whispered harshly, *get under your desks right now.* She motioned everyone toward the back of the room and began pushing her bulked desk against the classroom door and John Sommers, a Trailblazers basketball guard, broke from the group to help. He grabbed one end, Mrs. Menda the other. Nick heard the gunfire approach. He felt himself iced and immobile, the same as when Sarah unbuckled his jeans sometimes and he whispered *don't,* but he pulled himself away from the wall where his peers were gathering their desks into a collective barrier and grabbed an end of Mrs. Menda's desk. He hoisted its weighted wood toward the door, a screech against the floor. He heard Mrs. Menda's shallow breath, rapid intakes rising toward hyperventilation, and thought of Sarah terrified in the school's choral room practicing vocal scales cut to a gunfired halt. He heard the sounds of his classmates: some of them crying, his own breath silent and still. He heard the groan of John Sommers's voice as he lifted the heft and together they pushed the desk flush against the classroom door. John on one end, Nick and Mrs. Menda on the other. As they slid the desk into position, a heavy blockade, Nick peered through the door's narrow rectangle of window and saw Caleb Raynor pass by in a hooded sweatshirt carrying two guns.

Christina crouched beneath her desk in French class when she and her classmates heard the shots, a rapid banging above the pronunciation videos they had been watching all week. *French in Action,* a PBS series, today an episode on ordering lunch: the difference between *des* and *les,* whether to order *some* escargots or *every* escargot in the world. *Vous avez choisi? Je vais prendre du jus d'orange.* The check: *L'addition, s'il vous plaît!* On-screen the glow of an outdoor café flickered across the faces of everyone in the room, the lights dimmed, the classroom door closed. When they heard the shots Mr. Broussard stood from his desk. He motioned everyone beneath theirs, Christina shocked by his lack of emotion, his quick economy of action. She huddled beneath her desk and Mr. Broussard let the videotape continue playing through the dark and through faraway gunfire. *Combien coute? À la carte.* Christina closed her eyes and felt shame only later to not have thought of her boyfriend, Ryan Hansen, or her brother, Simon, both elsewhere in the building, but instead of swimming practice after school and that it would surely be canceled. The team's major fall meet coming up in three weeks, practice she needed to keep her arms and legs muscling through chlorinated water. The popping of ammunition sounded down the hallway and Christina opened her eyes and let them fall on Henry Park, her speaking partner, crouched across the row beneath his own desk. *Du fromage.* The video droned. Henry a boy she knew from class but more acutely from the Midvale County Community Center's pool, where they sometimes shared swimming lanes, Henry on the men's water polo team, Christina on the women's swim team. Christina took her brother home every afternoon on her way to practice at the community center, Simon a freshman, so new at Lewis and Clark that she barely knew his schedule. Christina imagined him in one of the physical science classrooms huddled beneath a table with whoever his lab partner was, some other freshman who would shield him. Keep him safe. Christina stared at Henry Park across the thin aisle between their desks and a woman's voice accentuated syllables. *Je n'ai pas faim.* It was only then that she imagined Ryan in the gymnasium downstairs, a senior and state tennis champion, gym an easy elective while applying for the many college scholarships that had shortened his temper since the beginning of the school year, so many sent SAT scores and applications and not once had he double-checked their location or proximity to St. Louis, where she'd still be at Lewis and Clark for another year. *Je n'ai pas faim.* A pronunciation of words she would associate always with Henry's drained face and the sound of guilt and gunfire, of how easy it was to think only on swim practice and the feel of water sliding against her skin.

Zola was in the library, a study period every Lewis and Clark student had throughout the day, an academic lab planned once into the seven periods of the day. She sat at a long wooden table alongside a scattering of other juniors randomized into her study lab. Derek Wilson, the Trailblazers punter. Alissa Jankowski, vice president of the National Honor Society. Alexander Chen, a quiet kid known for his variety of food allergies: wheat, dairy, nuts, mangoes. Soma Chatterjee, the founder of the first Lewis and Clark High community garden. Zola sat beside her peers reviewing last-minute trigonometric functions before her third-period test. Slope definitions. Rise over run. Mnemonic devices: *sine is first, rise is first.* The same kind of mathematics needed for understanding apertures and scales and ratios, the photography work she did for Lewis and Clark's high school yearbook. A photo shoot scheduled that afternoon at the Math Club's weekly meeting, another shoot later in the week with the school's marching band in the end zone of the football field. Zola had closed her trigonometry textbook and pulled out graph paper and begun to sketch sample lines for her test when the first shots sounded from the hallway, an echo through the library that stopped her pencil short, a streak of graphite halted midway across the paper's boxes and lines.

When Zola looked up, everyone else in the library had also stopped. Every student in her academic lab, and in other labs scattered across so many wooden tables. Groups of freshmen, sophomores. A class of seniors gathered around Mr. Eckstein, one of two librarians, listening to proper methods of capstone-paper research. Everyone in the library fell silent and stared blankly at one another as the sound of gunshots approached and grew louder, the only sound ricocheting off the library's high ceilings and through its book-filled stacks. The librarians and teachers did what so many others did. They told everyone to get down, to climb under the tables. To hide, to tuck themselves back into the stacks. Zola dropped her pencil and ran for the stacks and hunkered down behind the science books while her peers ducked beneath the wood table. She heard the gunfire approach from the hallway, as loud as explosives, growing louder and stronger until it was in the library, until it was upon them. She heard people screaming: the voices of her peers, the voice of a lone male ordering everyone to *get the fuck down* then the hoarse rasp of Mrs. Diffenbaum, the other librarian, shouting *no, no, no, please, no*. Zola didn't think of siblings. Of boyfriends or girlfriends. She had none within the school. Though she never admitted it later, not out loud to herself or to Nick or Matt, she didn't think of Christina, either, in her French class, didn't think of meeting as they always did in the hallway between second and third period to determine where they'd congregate in the cafeteria for lunch and whether they'd brought sandwiches from home or needed to buy salads or sodas. Zola thought only of her mother. How Zola had left the house first that morning, her mother still standing in the kitchen. From her hiding place in the stacks Zola heard the sear of bullets shattering glass, cracking wood, splitting the surface of human skin. She kept her eyes trained on the one book before her with the largest font, *A Graphic History of Oceanic Biology,* its title typefaced in bold down the book's breaking spine, a book she had never read and would never read though its Garamond font and its name would billow through her brain for weeks that would become months and then years. She kept her head down, her hands clasped over the coil of her ears, and watched the book until her eyes glazed and she closed her eyes and thought of her mother by the stovetop griddling pancakes. Blueberries and banana. Maple syrup. A kiss to the forehead before Zola walked out the door.

Matt was the only junior yearbook staff member not in class. He was in the men's bathroom instead on the second floor, just past the main stairwell from the ground floor, his mouth pressed to his boyfriend Tyler's mouth in the farthest and most hidden stall from the door. Tyler Cavanaugh, a sophomore: a boy only some of us knew Matt was dating. A new relationship of four months, one Matt held as close as he could to the chest, as close as he guarded the particulars of his own sexuality within a high school that housed the LGBTQ Spectrum Alliance but also manifested unexpected slurs scrawled occasionally and artlessly across lockers. Matt's family knew he was gay. Tyler's family did not. In waiting for Tyler to grow comfortable and come out, Matt had allowed alternatives to fooling around in the absence of Tyler's house or his. Matt's hatchback Ford Fiesta. Nights in the surrounding cornfields, the sky washed above them like a dome, like starlight, like nothing they'd ever seen. And sometimes the second-floor bathroom, skipping class to meet in the farthest stall but always in the morning, low traffic before lunch, first or second period. Just the week before, the last stall, Tyler's mouth tracing the curve of Matt's ear and Matt had felt breathless, had almost whispered three words teetering dangerously on the edge of his tongue before his eyes shuttered open and he pulled them back, their relationship far too new. And here, the same stall, the same words pushing hard against his teeth, Matt held them down safe inside the lockbox of his throat. He had just pressed Tyler to the tiled wall, his hands traveling from his face down toward his belt buckle, when they both heard gunshots and opened their eyes. The shots traveled closer. They held each other's gaze, so close Matt could see the perspiration on Tyler's forehead. Matt forgot the words. He quieted the breath quickening in his lungs and pushed Tyler up onto the toilet seat to make his feet invisible below the stall and followed him up onto the other edge of the lid. They stood across from one another, the door of the stall locked. They watched each other. Matt held a finger to his lips: *stay silent, Tyler, stay silent*. Tyler focused on Matt's face until the shots grew louder and a female voice screamed beyond the door and Tyler looked down and began to weep and Matt pressed his hand across Tyler's mouth, the same mouth that had skirted his ear.

What Matt and Tyler heard, we knew later, was Caroline Black's scream as she left the women's bathroom next door. As she entered the hallway. As she came upon Caleb. As she may or may not have had time to understand what was happening before three bullets from his handgun ripped through her right shoulder, her stomach, then through the frontal lobe of her brain.

Matt would remember the slump of her body against the hallway carpet when the shots finally stopped, when he and Tyler lowered themselves from the toilet and emerged from the bathroom and saw Caroline's body first, her blood washed across the carpet. Matt would remember her unblinking, her gaze aimed high to the hallway ceiling.

He would remember it always but most acutely when he first heard, three days later, that everything and everyone in her house had burned to the ground.

WE WERE ACCUSTOMED to uncertainty then. We lived in an era of ambiguity and the numbness of television and news, strange days we witnessed but barely understood. We'd watched our country step that year into the light of a Baghdad dawn, a morning in March when we woke to the news of air strikes booming across the city and marking the beginning of a war we knew nothing of, a war that felt faraway and distant and numb. We watched streaks of fire and blazed missiles make their way across the Iraq sky, a grand display of shock and awe. We watched night-vision images grained in green from the foreign ministry, fires burning near government buildings and the west bank of the Tigris River, two locations we were told housed Saddam Hussein's palaces. What else we were told: that Iraq housed weapons of mass destruction, a violation of the United Nations and peace treaties and human rights. That Saddam harbored links to Al Qaeda, the terrorist group responsible for the attack on the World Trade Center.

We watched the news with our families, who tried to help us understand, who knew little more than we did, we could see, parents full of their own doubts and sorrows and strained distance from the world. The same sorrow we had intuited in their faces two years earlier, the lined tension in their jaws, when they tried to answer our questions about the twin towers, buildings so removed from us as freshmen. They'd tried to help us focus instead on starting high school, starting yearbook, our first football games and after-school meetings and Homecoming dances. They tried to make familiar a world we fell asleep in one September night that the next morning became another place, another realm entirely, a world no longer ours.

But we had forgotten. We intuited an iceberg but only saw its tip. We forgot the twin towers and their billowed smoke through the tumult of two high school years, a roil of exams and team tryouts and pre-SATS and erupting acne. And then we watched raids and air strikes through the summer before our junior year, a noise on television that blared between meals and trips to the public pool and night drives zigzagging across back roads and cornfields with one another, Pavement and Jay-Z blasting through the car stereo. We heard in July of Saddam Hussein's sons, their home invaded and both of them killed, a haze of information amid summer jobs at Applebee's and upon the lifeguard stand at the neighborhood pool, among midnight movies and ice cream stands and the pages of *Seventeen* magazine. By the time we returned to school in the fall and the air began to cool, the death toll had already reached nearly four hundred soldiers and citizens.

We paid attention in our social studies classes, a media awareness that rarely transcended the classroom. We lost ourselves to the new year, to being upperclassmen, to already putting stories together for the yearbook, to at last driving ourselves to school. And then just three days into October, across the news, everywhere we looked: that there were no weapons of mass destruction found anywhere in Iraq. That the search was ongoing, that nothing was conclusive. That at $300 million already, the search would require $600 million more.

How many lives? Christina's father screamed at the television. *How much money, how many lives until this is over?* Christina told us of his weekend outburst at our weekly junior staff meeting that Monday after school, the fall semester's pre-planning stage before we met with the staff of other classes in the spring semester. We were in Christina's bedroom, her father still at work, the late afternoon sun spilling through the curtains.

But your dad's always so quiet, Matt said. He sat on the floor of Christina's room and thought of past meetings at her house, her father in the living room, the sound of the television traveling down the hallway sometimes the only noise in the house.

He wasn't quiet this weekend, Christina said. Maybe it's still the divorce.

He'll get over it, Zola said from Christina's bed, where she fiddled with the camera folded into her lap. My mom's just fine without my dad.

Hey, can I see what pictures you've taken? Nick asked from the bedroom floor, a notebook tucked behind his head, a notebook Zola saw was still blank of notes or ideas.

Only if I develop them first, Zola said. It's a manual. I don't have much at all yet. I'm going to a few after-school events this week.

Christina leaned against the wall beside her bed and sipped the can of Coke in her hands. These meetings often so unproductive, the bulk of their work saved for the crunch at the end of the school year, when they at last met with the other class staff and their faculty advisor, Mr. Jenkins. She and Matt: the yearbook's junior staff writers. Nick: the junior staff researcher. Zola: the yearbook's photographer. Mondays and Fridays the only afternoons of the week when Christina didn't have swim practice and she wished regardless that she was at the pool, her arms cutting circles through the water. Her brother somewhere in the house, either in his room or out in the living room playing video games, what he'd turned on over the weekend after their father's voice finally rose in anger toward the television, after he'd slammed the remote to the couch cushions.

An anger Christina couldn't comprehend. An anger none of us fully understood.

An anger we would understand only two days later, when Caleb Raynor entered the east doors.

How many lives? *How many lives?* We would remember the words of Christina's father, what she'd told us nothing more than an anecdote. We would think of his question again and again as we put together a yearbook, something impossible, a task beyond what we'd imagined at the bright start of a new academic year. How many lives? How many lives could we possibly account for in the pages of a book? We would think it every time we imagined the shots in the hallway, across the library stacks, outside the second-floor bathrooms. And we would think of it beyond guns, beyond bloodshed, when like kindling the fires began to erupt.

WHEN THE GUNFIRE stopped, when the sirens approached and swirled beyond the windows of Lewis and Clark, when the police surrounded the school and a bomb squad waited on standby and

SWAT teams finally stormed the building nearly two hours after Caleb Raynor walked through the east doors, we emerged from classrooms, from storage closets, from beneath toppled desks and chairs and tables.

SWAT members pushed open the doors of every closed classroom, an easy task for Christina's French class but not for Nick's English room. After pushing Mrs. Menda's desk against the door, after watching through the door's small window as Caleb walked down the hall, Nick helped John Sommers push a bookcase and a filing cabinet and a storage tower to the door to fortify the desk. The floor of the classroom was littered with books, with torn pages and broken spines they'd ripped from the shelves in their haste to build a barrier. Classroom videos and student files. Grades and tests fallen open across the floor. Textbooks and twenty-six copies of *Crime and Punishment,* the next book in the junior year curriculum. A SWAT member punched through the glass, a door he assumed was locked from the inside, only to find a tower of classroom furniture stacked against the door, a tower apart from another pile of desks and chairs on the opposite side of the room behind which twenty-four students crouched, Nick and Mrs. Menda included.

Christina removed no furniture. A black-clad officer merely opened the door, a tall figure she first thought was the shooter until she saw the badge, the helmet, heard a female voice shout *all clear* from behind the helmet's visor. *Is anyone hurt?* the officer called to Mr. Broussard, hidden behind his desk. He looked up and shook his head and raised his hands above his head, a gesture Christina would commit to memory as though her French teacher had done something wrong, as though he were guilty and not simply reacting immediately to the officer's drawn gun. The officer waved them out: *Follow me.* She told everyone to keep their eyes closed. Christina would remember the static white noise of the television, the vocabulary video long over, receding behind them as her class moved single-file into the hallway and she tried to keep her eyes closed but slid them open anyway and saw a custodian, Mr. Rourke, splayed across the carpet, his legs askew, a dark flood beneath him.

Matt and Tyler had already vanished from the hallway. They had not received instructions, had not been in class, had not been waiting for an all-clear but had only waited silently in the bathroom stall until the gunfire at last ceased. They had waited ten minutes in the silence, a wait that felt longer than the four months they'd known one another. They had stepped down from the toilet's edge, unlocked the stall, and slipped into the hallway. They had stood only moments above Caroline Black's body before Tyler took off running down the hallway, away from Matt, either in shock or not wanting to be found and questioned with Matt, not even in crisis, leaving no chance that they would be asked what they'd been doing together away from class. Matt watched Tyler disappear down the stairs, then knelt down beside Caroline's body, her eyes open behind her glasses, a ruby-stained radius behind her head widening across the carpet. He watched her for only a moment, long enough. He leaned forward and lifted her glasses. He let his hands close her eyes. Then he followed Tyler's path, away and down Lewis and Clark's central staircase but with an afterimage coiled forever in the fractals of memory, a reiterated image that burned back as a spiraling, that rewired his brain.

Zola was the only one of us who did not exit Lewis and Clark through the hallways and then through the school's entrances. When the SWAT teams arrived at the library they found the doors blockaded and impassible. Not by bookcases or by desks, not by storage units pushed against the door as barriers, but by a convergence of bodies collapsed behind the doorway where Caleb Raynor had entered firing. Zola stayed huddled within the stacks. She focused on the racks of titles and their blocks of lettering to drown away the sounds of crying, of sputtering blood, of rasping voices calling for assistance. She wanted to help them. She could not move. She waited immobile, her hands over her ears, until she felt a solid arm grab her around the waist, until she screamed and the arm spoke, *It's all right,* until her body at last let go and her weight fell away and her jeans dampened with a wash of urine and the arm pulled her up and out of the stacks and toward the library's high windows.

Zola saw only broken chairs and splintered tables, only people slumped into the ground as if they were sleeping before the officer pushed her through the window and down a makeshift pulley to a cluster of officers waiting on the ground, officers who wrapped her in blankets along with thirty-three other students and teachers, thirty-three shuttled outside on a system of levers though they left twelve behind in the library, what would be the location of heaviest casualties in the entire school.

We stood in the parking lot, a chaos of students and police, of parents who had been alerted in the two hours that had passed since Caleb first walked through the east doors, parents who pushed through the lot searching each face for the certainty of their children. Parents who did find their kids: a shocked freshman, a quiet senior sitting on the curb holding his head in his hands. Parents who did not, who shoved through the parking lot, who searched and screamed and looked toward the school, who watched a stream of faces continuing to emerge, none belonging to them. A chaos of teachers, of more and more students flooding from the doors and the library windows, of wounds and weeping and the splattering of blood, some of it ours, most of it from others stained across our clothes, an answer their parents would never find.

We carried them with us upon our jeans, upon our sweaters and T-shirts and sneakers. We carried this answer, what remained. We gave them to police officers, to investigators, what evidence was left of them upon our clothes. As if spatters could speak. As if clothing bore a voice. We left them in the parking lot with police, and we also carried them home. On socks, on the tips of shoes. On the edges of belt buckles and earrings and upon the knees of our jeans. We wanted to wash them away, a swirling of pink down the drain, a stream we would watch until it ran clear as if the flow of water could circle us back. And we wanted to keep them, this stain. A mark that they were here, that all of us were. That what we were had been permanent, that this fraction had been whole, what we needed in those first hours after we returned home and then again in the coming days, when Caroline Black's home incinerated, when the first of the fires began.

TERROR IN THE HALLWAYS

Lone Gunman Kills 35 and Self at Local School, Devastates City

THURSDAY, OCTOBER 9, 2003

ST. LOUIS, MO—A student opened fire yesterday at Lewis and Clark High School in Midvale County, killing 28 students, three teachers, three staff members and one administrator. The student, identified as Caleb Raynor, 16, entered the school's east doors at 9:04 a.m. on Wednesday armed with a sawed-off shotgun, a 9mm handgun, and 16 rounds of ammunition. Though Raynor's path through the school is not yet known, police have confirmed that he first entered the principal's office and the art room on the first floor before proceeding to the second floor.

"We heard shots down the hallway," said Ben Bacaro, 17, a senior who was in a physics classroom on the second floor. "I looked out the class window and saw someone in black walk by and our teacher told us to get under our desks."

Raynor killed 35 people and wounded 22 in a rampage that lasted less than one hour. The death toll was announced this morning, though investigators are still in the process of identifying the victims and notifying their families. Police are retracing Raynor's movements through the school, a shootout that ended in his suicide. Raynor's body was discovered late yesterday in the school's gymnasium.

"He walked into our classroom and there was just nothing," said Kavita Thaman, 15, who was in a biology class on the second floor. "No anger, no laughter, just nothing. He stared at us blankly. Then he shot a boy next to me in the chest."

One hundred fifty law enforcement officials arrived on the scene at 9:22 a.m., along with five SWAT teams that later entered the school at approximately 10:09 a.m. after cell phone calls from inside the school reported that gunfire had stopped. FBI officials are also investigating the shooting and its cause. No motive has yet been determined though police are questioning Eric Greeley, 17, a close friend of Raynor's who was not at school during the shooting.

"So far he's not a suspect but we have some questions," said Midvale County Sheriff Albert Corcoran. "Right now we're just trying to deal with the magnitude of what has occurred."

The scene outside of Lewis and Clark High School was one of pandemonium when students were finally evacuated late morning. Parents waited for news of their children while students and teachers streamed from the building, some stained with blood. Law enforcement officials later corralled parents to the local public library to wait for news of their children, and to make room at the high school for ongoing investigation. Each high school student signed a register as they left the building to account for their presence. Medical helicopters and ambulances arrived on the scene to take the wounded to nearby hospitals.

Meanwhile, a search warrant has been authorized to investigate the suspect's home.

"It's just unbelievable," said Betsy Carraway, an employee in the school's cafeteria who hid with coworkers in the kitchen's walk-in freezer when she heard shots fired. "These are just kids. This is a school. This is meant to be a safe place."

Amid widespread news this week regarding the war in Iraq, President Bush held a press conference sending prayers to the community of Lewis and Clark High School and the city of St. Louis. The rampage occurred just after the state of Missouri passed a concealed-carry bill this year, legislation that Governor Bob Holden vetoed before it was overridden by the Missouri General Assembly and Senate. Governor Holden held a press conference last night that

called for prayer, care and healing in addition to continued consid-
eration of gun responsibility, mentioning specifically the recent bill.

"In the coming days, we're going to need our community," said
Jeremiah Olson, a Lewis and Clark parent who at 7 p.m. last night
was still waiting for news from his child. "We're going to need every
last shred of empathy and love and peace that still exists on this
earth."

A BRIEF HISTORY OF MEMORY

FLASHBULB MEMORY: A fixed location, a moment stilled in time.

Where we were when x happened. Solve for x. Capture. Click.

Synapse: the brain's bridge where nerve cells touch.

Neurotransmitter: an electric impulse, a firing of new data between cells.

Dendrite: feathered tip. A waving of cilia at the ends of cells that connect, that jump synapses and transport fact. Sight and taste. Sound, touch. Sensory perception of how the light fell or how the television crackled or how the spine of a book curved firing between tendrils, catching data like an outstretched hand.

Fear: the amygdala. Cortisone release. A stress response to threats, the animal brain. A quickening of heart rate and blood pressure. An intake of breath and air. A flooding of neural synapses to remember fear and to self-protect, to create connections that rewire the brain entirely.

The mind a malleable thing, a mold of plasticity. A collection of 100 trillion synapses that rearrange and transpose. A critical mass of impulses that bury trenches, that germinate and take root in the cortex. Overturned chairs. A wall of desks. The sound of popping and screaming. An assembly of pale faces crouched to the floor.

Flashbulb memory: the firing of so many synapses at once, a braid of cells.

A strengthened cord. An imprinted image.

A seed. A fractal. A road.

LOVE IS PATIENT, LOVE IS KIND

OUR PARENTS MONITORED what we knew, what we saw on the evening news. They closed our front doors to the swarming of police and the FBI and to the intrusion of reporters, local affiliates, and national news teams surrounding the school and its neighborhoods. Our parents placed signs on the porch pleading privacy, signs that told visitors to refrain from ringing the doorbell, a sound so unlike the ricochet of gunfire but still so startling, an earsplit. They presided over breakfasts and dinners without television, the phone off the hook. Homemade pot pies, chicken casseroles, trays of lasagna they accepted from neighbors. Some of our parents stayed home from work to be with us, school suspended until further notice, while others immersed themselves in their jobs, a means of coping and forgetting. All of them whispered behind their bedroom doors when they thought we had fallen asleep, some on the phone, some to one another, their voices low and terse. Despite their efforts we saw the newspaper anyway, a deluge of stories and sub-stories and so many photographs. Photographs of students pouring from the building, of response teams and ambulances, of parents gripping their children, of our peers and teachers fleeing the school marked by dark slashes of red. Photographs that were graphic but nothing of what we'd seen ourselves, images we tried to blink back and force away every time we closed our eyes. A black hooded sweatshirt walking past a window. A stain soaking through browned carpet.

An exodus of faces from the doors of the school. And the sounds: gurgling. The warbling of a droned television. Shouts calling out to us, a chorus of strained voices we could not move ourselves to answer. The muffled pound of our own blood as we held our hands to our ears.

We lay in our beds and combed through the times we'd ever spoken to Caleb Raynor, if there'd been any brief glimmer of menace or motive. Christina remembered square dancing with him in her seventh-grade gym class, his grip limp and weak. Nick thought of sharing a lab table with him in sophomore year biology and how he'd tuned out the classroom for the spiraled drawings of his note-book. Nick remembered no violence in the sketches, only a graphite menagerie of whales and skateboards and cartooned stick figures. Matt recalled standing beside him in the lunch line only once, how he'd bought a small carton of milk and nothing more, and Zola thought over and over about the one time she'd ever spoken to him during freshman year when they'd both been at the 7-Eleven near school and she was paying for a watermelon Slurpee. He walked in, head down, hair curtained across his eyes. She offered a small wave and said *hello* but he only moved toward the refrigerated cases of soda.

We searched for grudges and found none, what the hell had made him do it.

We thought of placement. Of timing. An obsession of reiterating where we were, where everyone else was, where Caleb had been. How one library table was not another table, the proximity of the stacks. How our bladders sometimes filled, how we might have caught ourselves passing between class and the bathroom when Caleb made his way through the hallway with a shotgun. How we might have been near the stairwell, how we might have been at the water fountain, how we sometimes forgot textbooks in our lockers and traveled back from class to retrieve them.

We turned off the television, a swirling guesswork of determin-

ing Caleb's motives. Though we ignored the local and national news
as best as we could, we couldn't shut out the list of names printed in
the *St. Louis Post-Dispatch* that Friday.

So many names. A wave we intuited, a tide that when it arrived
washed in and overcame us. A list we had begun to piece together
by what we knew of the school, who we saw fall, where we thought
we heard gunfire. A list we checked off by elimination, by who
we'd called to make sure they were okay, by who we'd made contact to speak only the briefest of *thank Gods* and the faint sound of
tears before replacing the receiver, before exchanging nothing but
confirmation. But when the list emerged Friday morning, in the
newspaper and across national televised news, we felt the last of our
once-lives ebb away.

Matt saw it on TV and rose from the living room couch. He
receded to his basement bedroom and closed the door. His father
remained on the couch, a forensic specialist for the Midvale County
Police Department, an official who'd been granted reprieve from
the Lewis and Clark case due to the sensitivity of his son's involve-
ment. His mother glanced away and made her way down the stairs
to Matt's bedroom, where she knocked and no one answered. Matt
sat on his bed. He regarded his hands in his lap. Hands that were
still here. Hands that had leaned over and closed Caroline Black's
eyes. Hands that should have threaded the strips of 35mm film the
night before, a Thursday shift at Midvale Cinemas that always lasted
until midnight. A late shift to build films for Friday premieres, one
he agreed to at least twice a month, his only time alone in the projection booth in the eerie blue of the movie screen, the theater dark,
everyone gone home. Tyler sometimes met him there late after the
manager had left for the night. *Finding Nemo. Pirates of the Carib-
bean.* Movies they'd watched together, the projection booth theirs
alone and the movie theater empty below them. Tyler's hands on
his face. Tyler's hands on his belt buckle in the bathroom stall. Caroline Black. Tyler leaving him behind in the school hallway. Matt

heard his mother knocking on his bedroom door. He couldn't open it. There was nothing in the world to say. His manager had called the night before. He wouldn't work until the following week. He knew he'd sit at home, a list of names and his parents worrying over him in a waiting wide stretch, so many days of time with nothing but names and no words and the hard fact that Tyler had left him in the hallway.

Christina, still in bed, watched the newscast on a small television in her room, curled into the womb of her covers. Her brother had been holed away in the storage room of his science classroom with his teacher and peers. She'd been right that he was safe. Her boyfriend, Ryan, was not on the list of names though she didn't know it until late Wednesday evening, long after her father had fled his work as a parts specialist at Boeing and found her name on the signed registry at the public library and waited until police brought her and her brother to the library's parking lot. The broken relief in her father's face enough to make her crack at last. When he at last took them home, she called Ryan's phone again and again, the deadpan sound of his voice on the outgoing greeting growing more maddening the longer she called and he never picked up. She learned past dark, when Ryan's mother telephoned her house at last, that Ryan was okay but in the hospital, that he'd been shot in the right leg in the school's gymnasium. Christina had stepped past her father and her brother and her mother, who'd come immediately to the house from her own new home in Edwardsville across the Mississippi River and stood in the front yard beneath the dome of darkened sky and took in the sharp knife of crisp October air, a welcome shard, something that let her know she was still alive.

And now the list of names on the small television in her bedroom: the same bedroom where she and Zola and Matt and Nick had met only days before, as if a yearbook and the capacity to plan were still imaginable. Only one name on the list pierced her more than any other. Elise Nguyen. A junior who'd shared the swimming

pool with Christina on the women's swim team since freshman
year. The girl who often shared lap lanes with her during practice
at the Midvale County pool, their strides matched stroke for stroke
as they glided through the water. The girl Christina drove with to
swim meets, windows down, the speakers of Elise's car blasting the
Strokes and Sleater-Kinney and the humid Midwestern air blowing
back through the front seat. The girl who'd played piano accompaniment in the school's musicals, a production of *Godspell* she'd
seen with Ryan her freshman year when they first began dating.
And Ryan: still in the hospital, where she hadn't yet visited and told
herself it was because she wasn't family. She watched the list popu-
late the screen and felt her lungs shut down, the air of her bedroom
currentless and stale and letting her forget for a moment what it was
to still breathe.

Nick was in the kitchen with his parents when he heard the list
of names on the morning broadcast, a list that forced a half gallon
of orange juice from his hands to the floor. He'd spent the previous
night researching, the only means of coping he knew: how to forget.
What the brain retains. How it reiterates and maintains the detail
of disaster. Research he knew would never make it into the yearbook, research he couldn't stop himself from culling from his bedroom computer regardless as he sat awake beneath a moon pooling
down through the window beyond his desk. Sarah was fine. She'd
hid beneath a stand of risers with the other chorus members in the
music wing, a section of Lewis and Clark that Caleb Raynor never
entered. Since Wednesday, Nick had barely spoken to Sarah, hadn't
thought to call her as she hadn't called him. He barely knew anyone
on the list, their high school a small community yet still so large,
and even still the list staggered him, a length of names and faces
scrolled across the television as the orange juice carton tilted on its
side and split open across the floor.

At her own kitchen table, Zola fled to the bathroom and barely
made it to the open toilet, her face against its porcelain. Her mother

followed her in, held back her hair. Made sure Zola was okay, her hand on her daughter's forehead. It was not the photographs printed in the paper, a skill Zola knew, how angles and light captured the contours of their faces. It was the names of so many peers and teachers she'd seen in the library before she fled to the stacks. Connor Distler. Jessica Wendling. Alexander Chen. Mrs. Diffenbaum, the librarian. Every one of them a memory she could recall before she heard the looming sound of gunfire. Connor across the wooden table, headphones on though he should have been studying, head bobbing softly to the sound of his own silent stereo. Jessica two chairs down, eyes trained on the small print of an enormous world history textbook. And beyond the library, in total: the names of twenty-eight students and three teachers plus the names of Principal Jeffries and her administrative assistant, Deborah Smalls, and of Mr. Rourke, the second-floor custodian.

Twenty-eight students, three teachers, three staff members, one principal.

The paper did not print Caleb Raynor's name, a name we already knew, a name we did not need to know again.

We'd known the number already. Thirty-five. A number printed the day before that did not include a killer. But we did not know the names. A list of faces. A list of lost handprints and first dances and ways of understanding a St. Louis summer. Thirty-five ways of watching lightning bugs, of eating soft-serve, of bracing against the first November winds and of watching rivulets of rain climb down a windowpane. Thirty-five styles of dress. Thirty-five mixtapes. Thirty-five baby books of first words, first steps, first songs sung in the bathtub among rubber toys. Thirty-five hearts that beat the center of a countless number of blinks, of twitches, of kicks and laughs and orgasms and flinches, all of them unknowable now, all of them lost indeterminably to the halls of a high school. Jacob Jensen: a Lewis and Clark soccer forward, a boy Matt had first seen kick a ball across the fields in sixth grade, a twist of the torso that sent a shock through Matt's body, an electricity that first jolted inside of him an understanding of desire. Mr. Bennington: a teacher who had been in the library, an earth sciences instructor that Christina had as a freshman and whose lecture on echolocation she still remembered, how bats find one another through the dark. Kelly Washington: the first girl that ever flamed a crush for Nick, back in kindergarten when she sat beside him in class, though he'd never spoken to her once. Alisha Trenway: a girl who lived down the street from Zola, who sometimes waited with her at the corner for the bus.

We sat with the names. We closed our eyes and saw only a fractured view. What small corner of terror we had seen within the school's hallways, what shots we heard and what blood we saw burrowed into the fabric of our clothing and into the threading of the carpet but none of it ours, none of it lasting, not even what clothing we took home and held. Home: a guilt. That we were here, in our beds and at our tables. A folly of randomness, of chance. That there was nothing that separated our bodies from a list of names scrolled in the newspaper, a list of nothing but the whims of a gun's attention, a gun aimed from an unimaginable place.

We knew the police were working, that they sought a motive. We knew they had let Eric Greeley go. We knew from the newspaper that even though he'd been Caleb Raynor's best friend, he claimed they'd grown apart in recent months and that Caleb had retreated into himself, a withdrawal that according to Eric was alarming and hurtful but came with no signs of violence.

Eric knew nothing of the guns. Knew nothing of the ammunition or the hooded sweatshirt hiding rounds of bullets or the two additional assault rifles found in Caleb's bedroom when the police searched his home. And he knew nothing of Caleb's plans but had merely been absent due to a bad cold, a virus he was still battling that Friday.

We knew nothing of Caleb's family, either: only that, according to the newspaper, they were grieving. That his younger brother was in eighth grade, not yet a student at Lewis and Clark High, that his mother was a social worker and his father an insurance salesman. That their home had been searched, that they'd cooperated fully with the police. That they'd issued a statement of grief and prayer for the community, that they asked only for the respect of privacy.

We tried not to think of it. We wanted anger. Anger that would rip through the fog of our numbness. But when we looked across the table at our mothers and fathers over lasagnas and casseroles we could barely eat that neighbors had brought by, what trace of rage we could summon dissipated in the worry lines that creased our parents' faces, faces that so easily could have been those of Elise Nguyen's parents or Mr. Rourke's family, faces trenched by an unconscionable weight that blanketed our entire community.

At night, we huddled into our sheets and watched the empty ceiling above us. Spackled ceilings, ceilings with stilled fans, ceilings with glow-in-the-dark constellations, ceilings burdened by shadows. We watched the darkness pervading our bedrooms and thought of nothing but the palpable hole sunk deep into our chests, a lack as dark as space, an emptiness that had swallowed all light.

SATURDAY NIGHT, THE night after the *St. Louis Post-Dispatch* printed the full list of names, our township of Midvale held a vigil. A community-wide ceremony open to anyone: to those who had been there, to those who had known someone, to those in St. Louis who knew no one but felt sorrow all the same, who wanted to excise a welled grief that if locked tight would overwhelm them. We stood upon the lawn of the public library, four blocks east of Lewis and Clark, the same library where police had gathered students and parents just three days before, the school a crime scene and an open investigation and roped off entirely. A vigil largely left to privacy by the media, local and national news outlets that had filled our streets for three days, though some of us saw a lone news van parked at the edge of the library's parking lot, lights extinguished, a reporter standing beside it. A vigil for the students, our peers. For their families and their friends. For the teachers and staff lost inside the building, for their fathers and sisters and daughters. A vigil of names spelled across thirty-five white signs planted in the dewed grass, names lit by the glow of staked candles, names we held silent inside our mouths. Principal Regina Jeffries. Caroline Black. Alexis Thurber. Nafisa Fields. They were a flame each of us spoke nothing of, their names caught beneath our tongues. We stood close to one another, apart, the light of our candles a heat against our cheeks in the autumn air.

Nick stood beside his father, his mother at home with his younger brother Jeff, nine years old but too young to understand fully what had happened. Sarah at home in her bedroom, still too shocked to leave the house though the chorus room where she hid never saw gunfire. Nick hadn't seen her since Wednesday. Christina stood with her father, her mother working a rare weekend shift across the river though she'd called six times through the afternoon. Her brother, Simon, a freshman, stood next to her and watched his candle blankly. Her boyfriend, Ryan, in the hospital after hiding in the shower stalls of the boys' locker room, where he and his classmates fled when they heard gunshots in the gymnasium. Stalls that could not hide him, in the end, each of which Caleb opened with his shotgun raised and took aim and fired. Ryan told her on the phone from the hospital that he heard one last gunshot beyond the locker room before he passed out in the stall bleeding, a gunshot we would later learn was Caleb's final aim to his own mouth in the center of the gymnasium. Christina looked across the crowd of parents, community members, friends. She noticed Callie Rhodes, another member of the varsity women's swim team, and knew they'd postpone practice for another several weeks despite Christina's muscles itching to move beyond the confines of her bedroom, one of their teammates lost. Her bedroom. She wondered if she and Zola and Nick and Matt would meet again at all, what could possibly be committed to paper about a vigil like this, what glint of candle Matt could document and what shade of sky she could write down as night descended around all of them, what anyone would want to remember in a yearbook.

Matt stood near Christina between his parents, each holding a hand across his shoulders. He looked at Christina and couldn't imagine saying it: that their task was to write and that they'd both fail to acknowledge it. He knew Nick was home free, that there was no research for a vigil but that he and Christina, the junior staff writers, should be taking notes if nothing else. He hadn't brought a pen. No paper. He'd brought only the vast ocean of his own brain filled with Caroline Black and her vacant eyes and Tyler fleeing down the hallway and Tyler nowhere on the library lawn. He glanced around the crowd and saw Russ Hendricks, Alexis Thurber's boyfriend. Another junior. His face a steady wall of stoicism though Matt knew he must have been breathless. He looked for Zola, unable to find her. He wondered if she'd brought her camera, if there would ever be a right time to photograph grief.

Zola stood at the edge of the crowd, eyes closed, beside her mother, who held an arm around her, a grip palpable in the strain of her fingers. She'd left her Pentax manual at home, a gift her mother had bought for her when she joined the yearbook staff freshman year, a camera Zola knew was discarded somewhere on the carpet of her bedroom floor. There was nothing here. Nothing at all on this peopled lawn to commit to memory. Only faces illumined in light, tear-dried cheeks, so many parents and family members constellated together in the darkening night. Zola spied Eric Greeley, also standing at the perimeter of the gathering, wiping his nose not from crying but from the lingering remains of a cold, Zola knew from the newspaper. She couldn't remember any interaction she'd ever had with him to know whether he'd been lying to the police or not, another face in the dense crowd of Lewis and Clark's thronged

mass of teenagers, so many faces she'd never noticed until they
became pixels in the paper, photographs of students fleeing school.
Eric stood alone in a gray hooded sweatshirt, the profile of his face
blank beneath the jersey-knit covering, a face he hid away from the
crowd though he was deemed not guilty or responsible, a grieving
he came to shed alongside everyone else.

We listened as people rose before the crowd, a gathering of hundreds standing around the row of white signs beneath a light-stolen
sky disseminating prayers and hymns through the air, a cool that
descended as stars slowly appeared. Alisha Trenway's father spoke.
Elise Nguyen's mother. Then Josh Zimmerman's sister, a senior
who'd hid in the girls' locker room, a choice we imagined she cruci-
fied herself for in hiding somewhere away from her brother, a sophomore, where she could not protect him. Mr. Bennington's partner,
through rasping breath: *Above all, love one another.* Benji Ndolo's
mother, midway through speaking, lost her composure and stepped
away from the crowd. And the minister from the United Methodist
Church on Bethel Road, who did not have children at Lewis and
Clark but who knew some of the victims and their families from
his congregation, spoke as if shedding great wisdom: *Love does not
delight in evil but rejoices with truth.* He looked out across the crowd,
a gathering of faces tinged by candlelight. *Love is patient,* he whispered to all of us. *Love is kind.*

We considered love. What was kind in it. What love meant if it
meant to kill. What would move a boy to enter the school's doors
and take everything away, so many classmates and teachers and
what love had meant for them, what love became for us when we
saw them splayed across the floor soaked in blood and bullet and
bone. We listened to the minister regardless upon the darkened
lawn of a library where so many of us had once gone for summer
reading and story hour. A library that had become a holding pen for
fear, for parents not knowing if they'd ever see their children again.
When the minister lifted his candle, we lifted ours. We raised our

candles to the Midwestern sky, a span of black with only the faint
hint of stars. We watched the night fill with a million points of light,
so much light that our vision flared in burned afterimage when we
looked away.

We glanced across the crowd. Crisp air, the scent of flame and
melting wax. We averted our eyes from the faces of so many parents
of twenty-eight students, their cheeks streaked with candlelight and
grief. We recognized parents who had volunteered, who had baked
cupcakes, who had once led Girl Scouts and coached Little League,
who had overseen field trips to the St. Louis Zoo. Alyssa Carver's
mother. Missy Hoffman's parents, turned quietly into one other.
Greg Alexander's father, who had chaperoned the Homecoming
dance in the gymnasium our freshman year. And Caroline Black's
parents, their eyes closed, their mouths moving softly in prayer.

Matt watched them across the crowd, their daughter engraved
into the folds of his memory, an image that had kept him awake
and staring out his bedroom window across the past three nights.
He'd watched the moon to block out her body. He had not slept
since Tuesday night. He looked at her parents standing in the crowd
and felt the weight of his mother's hand upon his shoulders and felt
his knees dissolve though he managed to stay standing. He scanned
the crowd. He knew Tyler wasn't anywhere in the cluster of faces
but he looked for the mohawked tuft of his hair poking up from the
crowd and couldn't find him, hadn't spoken to him, hadn't heard
from him at all since they'd stepped from the second-floor bathroom and fled.

The vigil lingered after the minister spoke, then thinned, then
gradually began to disperse entirely. Christina stood beside the
white signs with her father and brother, signs illumined by the faint
glow of the distant moon. She closed her eyes and prayed to believe
in prayer for the list of names and bore silent gratitude to no God
in particular that Ryan Hansen's name was not among them, even
if she hadn't seen him since he entered the hospital. Nick found

Sarah's mother in the diluted crowd and let her gather him in an embrace, her hands gripping his sleeve, a mother who had come in her daughter's stead while Sarah's father stayed home. Zola watched Eric Greeley at the periphery, how he gazed at the white signs and how in profile his eyes glistened wet. She watched him turn away alone, heading down the dark sidewalk until he disappeared.

Candles: extinguished and kept, tucked away into purses and backpacks. Cheeks kissed. Chests crossed. Carnations and lilies and small teddy bears left beside still-glowing tea lights. Parents holding one another. Parents holding their teenagers. Parents gathering their children all around them, constellations of families moving down the sidewalk toward the haven of their cars.

In the backseat on the way home, Nick leaned his forehead against the glass of the car window and watched the ink-spill of the Midwestern sky. He thought of Sarah at home, surely curled up in the twin bed where she'd tried so many times to make him give in at last, a roll of condoms tucked into her bedside drawer. He thought of Kelly Washington, his first crush. How he'd never once spoken to her despite admiring her from afar. How he thought her face was beautiful in kindergarten beneath a shock of dark hair and small barrettes and how he knew she'd joined the cheerleading squad at Lewis and Clark and how her older brother had been at the vigil alongside a woman who must have been Kelly's mother. How both of them looked too stunned to weep.

In the passenger seat of her father's Ford Taurus, Christina reclined the chair and leaned her forearm across her eyes, her brother in the backseat. Her father stayed quiet and in the silence she thought of Elise Nguyen, her mother and father and sister at the vigil, how they'd come so often to swim meets and cheered from the sidelines, how they were surely driving home to the echoed walls of an empty house. She thought of Mr. Bennington, how she'd been only fourteen when he taught her about echolocation, how bats and dolphins find one another across spans of dark too wide to imagine and how this had comforted her somehow, her parents just divorced, making one's way home without light. How Mr. Bennington would not, his name etched into the starkness of a white sign, his partner alone at the vigil and straining to speak. How Mr. Bennington had disappeared from the earth only yards away from where she'd crouched in French class immobile beneath a desk, as useless to him sputtering on the library floor down the hall as she was to Ryan hidden in the stalls of the boys' locker room.

Zola moved down the street on foot with her mother, their house close enough to walk. Zola's mother ran her hand down Zola's back, a comforting weight, and pointed her other hand to the sky, the jagged line of Cassiopeia. Her mother knew the stars, a backyard astronomer, her telescope standing firmly in the grass every autumn until the first snowfall of the year. Her mother whispered Andromeda and Cepheus, two stars that flanked the constellation above them. She said Cassiopeia would be brightest in November. Zola watched the stars above her so she would not have to look at Alisha Trenway's house as they passed it on the way back to their own, a house of darkened windows and drawn shades that had not been raised since Wednesday.

Matt rode in the front seat of his parents' Chevy Impala, buckled on the upholstered bench between them though the backseat was empty and full of room. His mother drove and his father sat with his arm tucked around him, a relief Matt leaned into as he watched the October landscape pass through the panorama of the windshield. He tried to latch his brain on to the view but saw the athletic calves of Jacob Jensen instead. Calves that held no sexual charge, no allure but only a symbol of lack. Of energy, of force, what could no longer move them. Matt closed his eyes to erase them and imagined Tyler instead. Nights that had been theirs alone across the summer, the headlights of his Fiesta hatchback cutting lines through the dark and low fog. The sun gone, the heat still heavy. Beyond the movie theater's projection booth, a summer of late-night drives, the radio droning, their speed whipping hot air through the car's open windows. The heat had been a blanket. Thick and warm. As hot as the hood of his car once they'd parked, the engine calming down, a ghost of heat pooling beneath its surface as Matt pushed Tyler back against the metal and ran a hand beneath his shirt and held the other against his face. He opened his eyes. The warmth of the engine. How quickly it became the heat of Caroline's blood still warm on the carpet. And Caroline's parents. He didn't want to think it but couldn't stop himself: what blankness they must have returned home to as he rode through the streets safe between his parents, a home where the walls rang silent and still and where a bedroom's emptiness pushed into them like a dagger.

And though his eyelids sagged with the deprivation of sleep, he lay awake that night in his basement bedroom and watched a water stain at the edge of the ceiling. Caroline's blood soaking the carpet, his clothes. Her gaze fixed. Her body slumped, a position he'd seen that her parents had been spared, a mercy. One that flamed guilt through him, spreading across his limbs like a growing fever. A strange intimacy. Something awful. Something he never should have seen. Matt watched the stain, his eyes open so they wouldn't see her body when he closed them. He fell asleep anyway sometime after 4 A.M. when the shade of his ceiling began to grow lighter by degree, only several hours of reprieve from a world that had pulled away what grounding he knew, a world that shifted again in the morning when he awoke to the news that Caroline Black's home had disintegrated in the night, that her parents standing bowed into one another at the vigil had gone home and closed their doors and turned off the lights and burned.

HOUSE FIRE KILLS TWO

Parents of Slain Lewis and Clark Teen Found in Home

SUNDAY, OCTOBER 12, 2003

ST. LOUIS, MO—Early Sunday morning, just hours after a community-wide vigil was held at the Midvale County Public Library for the victims of Wednesday's shooting at Lewis and Clark High School, a house fire claimed two lives within the 1300 block of Westminster Court in Midvale County. Firefighters responded at 3:38 a.m. Sunday morning and observed flames engulfing the two-story residence. The blaze, which required at least 50 fire personnel, including police officials from nearby Hamilton County, was finally extinguished around 6 a.m.

According to police officials, the victims have been identified as Jean Black, 45, and Arthur Black, 47, the parents of Caroline Black, 16, who was killed in the Lewis and Clark shooting.

"We just can't believe it," said Janet Wallace, a neighbor who stood on her porch with her two toddlers as officials doused the flames. "First the school and now this. It's inconceivable. They were all such good people, the two of them and their daughter. This week has been devastating for all of us."

As of sunrise this morning, firefighters and police officials were combing through the debris in search of clues. Though foul play is not suspected, investigators hope to gather a clearer picture of what caused the fire. No other residents were found in the home, and neighbors heard no signs of struggle within the house.

"The streets were silent last night, especially in light of the vigil," said Jason Novitsky, a next-door neighbor, whose daughter is a freshman at Lewis and Clark. "We just came home and went to bed and heard nothing until the sirens came."

Officials say that another neighbor, David Ramos, first saw the smoke and called 911.

"I couldn't sleep," said Ramos. "You know, with these kids and the school. I happened to look out the window and saw smoke coming off the roof."

Initial examination from fire officials indicates that the fire began on the second floor. The cause is under investigation.

A BRIEF HISTORY OF WHAT WAS LOST
(OR, EVERYTHING WE IMAGINED)

PICTURE FRAMES. PHOTO albums. Family portraits, snapshots, matte prints.

Knit blankets. Embroidery. Pillowcases and sheets.

Dishes. Wedding china. Flatware. Antique silver, ladles, cutting boards, spoons. Magnets collected from family travels: Nashville. Yellowstone. Bar Harbor, Maine. Sarasota, Myrtle Beach, the Wisconsin Dells, the Grand Canyon.

A pantry of boxed cereal, dried pasta. Canned tomatoes and beans and beets. A spice rack of cinnamon, curry powder, turmeric, paprika. A refrigerator impervious to burning, left standing and full of half-spoiled milk, plain yogurt, hardened cheese, a half-dozen mottled eggs. Wilting lettuce, jars of mayonnaise and mustard and pickles, apples and potatoes and pears still intact, untouched by flame. Furniture: coffee tables. Couches. The recliner where Caroline watched *Merry Melodies* after school in fourth grade. Inherited side tables and buffets passed down from grandparents, great-grandparents. Bookcases full of children's books, reference books, classics of literature, Caroline's baby book. A catalog of firsts: first smile, first steps, first words (*Mama? Mine?*), first day of preschool. Drapes, curtains, window blinds, doorknobs. Light fixtures and lightbulbs, a crackling hiss as their glass heated and exploded. Ironing board. So many clothes. Stockings, leggings, wool socks, corduroy pants, jeans, sweatpants, collared shirts, a cacophony of tees gathered from sporting events, thrift stores, marathons, vacations. Sports sweatshirts: Cardinals baseball. Rams football, the team still so new. Knit hats and mittens and gloves, scarves and earmuffs and swimsuits and beach towels. Electronics: a television, a camcorder, family videos, old filmstrips. Caroline's parents on their wedding day: a brief Super 8 film, one minute and fifty-three seconds long, a film Caroline had seen twice in her life when her father draped a white sheet against a wall and her mother dragged the projector down from the attic. Videos of Caroline: violin recitals, school plays, freshman year Homecoming with her girlfriends, all of them giggling in the thin sunlight of the front yard. A stereo and receiver, two tall speakers, a record player and a six-disk CD changer. A stack of LPs that Caroline's parents collected through college: the Moody Blues, the Beatles, Elton John, Janis Joplin. *Every Good Boy Deserves Favour, Are You Experienced?, Beggars Banquet, Surrealistic Pillow, Sgt. Pepper's Lonely Hearts Club Band,* what Caroline listened to over and over again the year she turned thirteen to find a way to play it backward, to hear the coded messages, to discover in the ridged grooves of spinning vinyl whether Paul McCartney's death had been wrongly foretold. CDs and cassettes, the first Caroline bought with her own allowance at the end of elementary school. Mariah Carey, Michael Bolton. Albums she hid in a box beneath her bed. Also in boxes: folded notes, movie ticket stubs, bottle caps, blown-out birthday candles, school photos. Diaries with tiny keys, journals of drawings, sketches of teachers and peers and turning maples beyond the classroom window. A miniature box of porcelain kittens, tiny owls, small books, a minuscule gumball machine. A jewelry box: emerald earrings. Collected necklaces. Small pins gathered on family vacations and from childhood, pins of Cabbage Patch Kids and Michael Jackson's Captain EO. Textbooks wrapped in brown grocery bags. Tarot cards. A Ouija board slid beneath the bed. Posters of movies and Monet paintings and a vintage cover of *Catcher in the Rye*. Posters adhered to the wall that went up like kindling.

WHERE WE BEGAN

WE HAVE ARCHIVED so many articles: these, the first. The first printed that week and the first we saved, now tattered and browning in the boxed corners of our basements. We have gathered newspaper articles and reports and photographs, an assemblage of texts meant to reconstruct a whole. Meant to guide us, what task of journalism we took on as our own beyond the static linearity of a yearbook, a year that lost us in the end to some understood register of shared history. We began to collect after the first fire. After the disaster of an entire high school. We knew only to act, to do something, to do what we knew how to do by saving articles and timelines, clippings hoarded in jagged newsprint.

We'd sat in our homes through a week that became a weekend, the days indistinguishable. We sat taking in the news: local news. National news. Radio broadcasts. *St. Louis Post-Dispatch* special sections on memorials and weapons, on gun control, on cancellations and chronologies and school plans and where we could possibly go from here. The newspaper tried to reconstruct where Caleb had been and when, what hallways he moved through before traveling to other hallways and classrooms, a trail we hadn't thought to replay. Matt asked his father why it mattered and *you can't imagine the destruction* was all he said, an indication that it would take time. We awaited news of funerals. We triaged our options. We considered whose we would attend, whose we would not, who among

thirty-five we'd release in our own way from the quiet privacy of
our homes. We hadn't thought to contact one another until we saw
the broadcast of the Blacks' home.

Matt was the first of us to see the news, after only three hours
of broken sleep. He drifted off past 4 A.M. in a bedroom that had
already begun to lighten, a dawn that spread through slatted blinds
when he got out of bed and crawled from the basement to the living
room, where his father watched the morning broadcast, already in
his police uniform on a Sunday. His father stood from the couch
and moved toward him, a gesture meant either to embrace him or to
shield him from the news. Behind him, Matt saw the grained faces
on-screen of Arthur Black and Jean Black: faces Matt recalled from
school-wide assemblies and holiday parties at Des Peres Elementary, faces turned away from the crowd at the vigil. Matt listened to
the newscaster speak it, not local news but already a national affil-
iate, *both died in a house fire late last night.* Matt didn't have to ask.
He knew his father would be called upon for forensics. He knew his
father had been granted a reprieve from the investigation at Lewis
and Clark High but that he would be needed for this.

Are you going to the house? Matt asked.

The only thing he could think to say.

They have fire scene investigators for that, his father said. I've
been called to the station. Chemical analysis of the debris.

Debris. A word that pulled the breath from Matt's body, that allowed him the indignity of a single thought: that nothing remained.
That a fire had razed not just the walls or a roof but the entirety of
a house.

Zola awoke to find her mother seated at the kitchen table, her
elbows bent in a triangle, her hands folded. The newspaper spread
across the table beneath her arms, a front-page headline screaming house fire. A half-page photo of the house's collapsed frame,
a home Zola recognized immediately by the barn-shaped mailbox
included in the photo's vantage point to illustrate the only thing left

standing. Caroline Black's house: a home Zola had visited countless times for playgroup in kindergarten. A group of four children
that included herself and Caroline and two twins, Amy and Althea
Robinson, a group formed by their parents when they began school
at Des Peres Elementary. Zola remembered the rooms of Caroline's
house. Her kitchen. Her small bedroom. Her living room carpeted
in green shag. Her basement where the four of them once played
with Barbies and board games and My Little Ponies, a basement
with a Ping-Pong table and a pullout couch and so many lamps and
side tables, all gone. Zola's first thought: suicide. A burden too vast
for a parent to live with, fire its only reprieve.

Nick's parents had already left for church when he woke, leaving
behind a scrawled note on the kitchen counter, *Wanted you to rest*.
They'd taken his brother with them, he knew, Jeff's bed empty and
already made. Nick noticed the newspaper missing, usually folded
on the dining room table once both of his parents finished reading it. He searched the kitchen and the recycling bin and found it
folded and placed near the trash can, its contents hidden away and,
Nick later understood, purposefully misplaced by his parents so he
wouldn't see the headline: *HOUSE FIRE KILLS TWO*. So he wouldn't sit
in the silence of a house. So he wouldn't pull the scissors from the
kitchen's utility drawer and clip the article and place it in his nightstand drawer, the beginning of an archive, so he wouldn't spend the
morning until his family returned sitting in front of his computer
researching fire and smoke and grief.

Nick read of the neighbors and the emergency and the two hours
it took firefighters to douse the flames, a blaze that left only the faint
blueprint of a home. He glanced at other news: the findings of the
Iraq Survey Group, a multinational team organized to determine
whether Iraq housed weapons of mass destruction, that after six
months of searching Iraq there was no evidence of any kind. That
although the team would keep looking, no nuclear or chemical or biological agents had been found but only remnants of long-dormant

activity from the First Gulf War, a war Nick barely remembered, a war that began when he was only three years old. He flipped back to the front page and let the scissors glide through the thin film of newsprint. He placed the clipped article in his bedroom's nightstand and lay on his back, his computer off. He heard the whirring of sirens beyond the window, a sound that had become constant across the past days. Reporters filled the streets. Local teams. CNN. FBI officials who hadn't left Midvale County since Wednesday morning. He focused on the stilled blades of the overhead fan and thought of how only neighborhoods away the Blacks had entered their home after the vigil and disintegrated.

Christina sat curled into the armchair beside Ryan's hospital bed at St. Mary's Medical Center. After waiting several days beyond visiting hours for immediate family only, Christina had gotten up early and left her father and brother in the house and driven to the hospital to be in Ryan's room when he woke. He was already awake and barely acknowledged her when she walked in, the first time he'd seen her since Wednesday, but she told herself it was distraction from determining how to still complete college applications for tennis scholarships. She held his hand as he drank water from a plastic cup and clicked the remote toward the small television mounted in the room's corner. MSNBC. Christina grimaced at the coverage, a constant stream of news replaying over and over across the weekend, national affiliates buzzing through Midvale County to interview students, eyewitnesses, teachers. *Turn it off,* she whispered but Ryan kept the television on, his leg cast in plaster and elevated. Milking the injury for its worth, she thought, though she said nothing and let the television drone on until an anchor interrupted with breaking news. Christina sat forward in her chair. Squinted at the television, so small in the corner. Despite its distance and Ryan's calling to a nurse for more water that drowned out the sound of the speakers Christina recognized immediately whose house had caught fire and burned.

That's Caroline Black's house, Christina said.

Who? Ryan leaned back in his hospital bed.

Caroline Black, Christina said again, her voice carrying above the television.

Who the fuck is Caroline Black? Ryan said and Christina got up immediately from her armchair. *Hey, where are you going?* she heard him shout as she made her way down the hospital corridor. Her legs moving. Brain hazed. She located the nurses' station and laid her hands on the counter and one of the nurses looked up with concern, a young woman who'd brought Ryan a tray of scrambled eggs an hour before.

Your boyfriend okay? the nurse asked.

I need to use your phone, Christina said.

The nurse smiled. It's only for emergencies.

I need to use your phone, Christina said again and watched the nurse lose her smile and hand her the receiver.

CHRISTINA HAD BARELY spoken to Zola since Wednesday, had only acknowledged her and her mother across the crowd at the vigil. Zola answered on the first ring and said nothing of the Blacks' house and Christina wondered which of them would break first.

How is he? Zola asked when Christina told her where she was.

He'll be released from the hospital this afternoon, Christina said. Her voice even, as calm as she could keep it, the nurse listening behind the counter. Zola asked how bad it was and Christina told her the shot to his leg had just missed a major artery and that they'd discussed nothing else, not his college applications or how the injury would affect his chance of scholarships. Christina watched a man shuffle past her down the hallway, wearing a cloth gown and pulling a wheeled metal stand holding an IV bag. Her anger softened. Ryan's reaction was forgivable given the circumstances. He'd been a state champion his junior year, readying this fall for a final spring season in both singles and doubles. His record of excellence was ex-

actly what had attracted her to him two years ago, both of them ath-
letes, her JV teammates encouraging their relationship as a given.
He'd attracted college recruiters as well, a full ride he'd planned on
taking before a bullet ripped through his leg.

Has he talked about it? Zola asked.

Not really. Christina glanced at the nurse and lowered her voice.
There were other guys there. He says that's where Will Isholt and
Sam Scott were. I can't even imagine what he saw or heard.

Will Isholt and Sam Scott: two names on the list of thirty-five.
Christina said it before remembering that Zola had been in the
library, where the news reported the most gunfire. That her best
friend could easily imagine what Ryan had seen and heard.

Zola was quiet for only a moment. Is he acting okay?

He's been distant, Christina said carefully. He didn't even call
me after it happened. His mother had to call me late Wednesday
night.

He was probably just in shock, Zola said, and Christina heard
in her voice the subtle catch, what she knew Zola felt but never
said: Zola didn't like him. Hadn't liked him since Christina started
dating him as soon as they entered Lewis and Clark. Back when she
was a freshman on the junior varsity swim team, Ryan a sophomore
and already playing varsity tennis. Back when she and Zola had
thrown Tootsie Rolls and Double Bubble from the freshman float
in the Homecoming parade, candy Ryan caught as he rode ahead
of them on the sophomore flatbed. Christina had called Zola late
at night sometimes when they fought, Zola listening without judgment. When Ryan said something terrible. When he stonewalled
her for two, sometimes three full days. She'd told Zola about losing
her virginity that summer, a July night after they'd gone mini-
golfing and it started to rain and they stayed parked in Ryan's car.
She'd told Zola sex had become habitual, that after nearly three
months in Ryan's backseat or at his house when his parents were
at work she still felt nothing close to orgasm. She'd stopped her-

self sometimes from saying too much, a widening gulf between the
initiated and uninitiated, Zola who'd never been in a relationship
beyond a three-day stretch in seventh grade that involved Carter
Johnson and her first kiss and the only time a boy had slid a hand
beneath her shirt. Christina sensed in her listening what at times
felt like silent judgment, that Zola didn't want drama, every phone
call and complaint Christina made about Ryan pushing her further
toward her resolve to be alone.

Zola alone. Christina watched the man with the IV bag disappear down the hallway and wondered if anyone had been beside her
in the stacks of the library.

I'm sorry I didn't call sooner, Christina said.

It was nothing. I'm fine. I wasn't hurt.

Did you see the news? Christina finally asked.

Caroline Black's family, Zola said. I can't believe it.

I know. I can't even imagine.

I wouldn't blame them. I wouldn't blame them at all if they
chose this.

Christina let her eyes lose focus down the hospital corridor. Suicide: what Zola meant. What she herself hadn't considered. She'd
never been in the Blacks' home but had known Caroline since their
first days together in kindergarten. Christina hadn't joined Zola's
playgroup with Caroline and the Robinson twins, hadn't lived near
enough to really know them, but her budding friendship with Zola
in their first-grade classroom had pushed a permanent distance between Zola and the group. Christina remembered Caroline's feisti-
ness. How when a group of parents suggested Margaret Atwood's
The Handmaid's Tale be banned from their sophomore year English
curriculum last year, she'd circulated a petition around the school to
make sure it stayed included. How she'd always been the first girl
at their annual Des Peres Elementary roller skating party to grab
a boy during slow songs as the lights dimmed and the mirror ball
glittered above the rink.

Come over this afternoon, she said to Zola. A statement more than a question, one she hoped would not sound like a demand.

Don't you want to be around for Ryan when he goes home?

Christina glanced down the hallway toward his hospital room. *Who the fuck is Caroline Black?* Her anger flickering again toward ignition.

I'm sure he'll be busy with his family, she said. Please, just come over.

ZOLA TOOK HER bike to Christina's, a habitual two-mile ride. Her mother out with the car buying groceries for the week, the only window Zola had alone across the days since Wednesday. Her mother watching over her like a night nurse on call. Her mother knowing she'd been in the library. Despite her mother's vigilance and care, Zola had been unable to speak a word of it. The day shone bright and crisp, the sun a high disk in a cloudless sky, the leaves a shock of yellow and copper. The sun's light hurt her eyes: a light she'd waited for, fall her favorite season, every color alive. A light that broke over her as she pedaled fast past Alisha Trenway's house on the corner, her legs spinning to outpace the choked lump of her throat. Christina had asked about the library. The first thing Zola had thought: not screams or the rasped gasping for air or the metal of gunfire but the urine stain that had darkened her jeans, and whether any of her classmates had seen what control she'd lost. At times across the past days she could think of nothing else at all, an awful vanity, what she couldn't tell Christina or her mother or anyone else who asked.

Christina answered the front door before Zola could knock and led her past the living room where her brother, Simon, was on the couch reading a book and down the hallway to her bedroom, her small television glowing through the darkness, her bed unmade. Her father out running errands, Christina said, and Zola noticed their freshman and sophomore yearbooks open on her bedroom carpet, books they'd assembled together, meetings that seemed like a separate lifetime.

Why do you have these out? Zola asked.

I don't really know. Just passing time.

We don't have to do anything yet. Don't even think about it.

I know. I wasn't looking for ideas.

Zola kneeled to the carpet, the sophomore yearbook open to a photograph of the women's swim team. Through the haze of the library and the dark stain of her jeans, Zola had forgotten other rooms in the high school, other gunshots. Other pinpoints of loss.

Elise, Zola whispered. Ran a hand across her classmate's face and Christina's teammate, so small in a group photograph beside the community pool.

Her mother was so sad, Christina said. At the vigil. She was so sad.

Zola didn't want to ask. Do you know where she was in the school?

I have no idea. I don't know where anyone was. I clipped the list of names from the paper. It's in my nightstand. I didn't know what else to do until you arrived.

Are you doing okay?

Same as everyone else. I'm doing fine.

Zola thought of the week's photo shoots that never happened: the Math Club meeting, the marching band practicing on the football field. She turned to the yearbook's section of celebrations and events, photographs of last year's Homecoming dance she'd taken. Students spilling across the dance floor. Strobe lights and crepe paper streaming down. A picture of Caroline Black smiling in a pale blue dress, one Zola had snapped just before Caroline helped crown the winners of Homecoming Court.

I can't even believe it, Zola said. Caroline Black's house. Her entire family.

On the small television upon Christina's nightstand, a reporter stood in front of the Blacks' home. Zola hadn't turned on her own television that morning, hadn't seen the home's ruin. She couldn't pull her eyes away from the blackened dust and the broken foundation and the stream of firefighters behind the reporter, the legs of their suits darkened with ash. She remembered Caroline's white bedroom furniture, a set that had probably long since been replaced. A trundle bed pulled from beneath Caroline's bed when Zola slept over, two twin mattresses side by side. A koala teddy bear placed always on her pillow. A Sega Genesis console in the cool damp of the Blacks' basement, video games they played while drinking Juicy Juice boxes and eating Nilla wafers. Zola watched the coverage and tried to imagine what it was that Caroline's parents had last seen. If this was suicide. The horrible possibility that it was. The sad tragedy if it wasn't. What dark ceiling they watched from the insomnia of their beds as some outlet sparked, as a stove knob neglected in the ocean of their grief ignited a flame that jumped the counter, that climbed the stairs to their bedroom and up the mattress and across the sheets.

I wonder if Matt's dad is there, Christina said. I wonder if he knows anything beyond what they're telling us.

Have you talked to Matt? Zola asked.

I haven't talked to anyone. Have you?

Just my supervisor.

You're actually going to work?

She's giving me time, Zola said. I can go back when I feel like it.

Christina looked back at the television. The coverage terrible and even still, Zola felt a flame of irritation bubble up beneath her skin. She had so few frustrations with Christina but if one was her asshole boyfriend, the other was work. Christina didn't have a job, worked as a lifeguard only in summers, her father's work at Boeing and her mother's career at a small university in Edwardsville enough to pay for her college outright. She didn't need to save for the possibility of tuition, nor did Nick, whose father was a doctor, his mother a lawyer. Nick had summer jobs, same as Christina. Matt was the only other one of them who'd had a worker's permit since fifteen, a single-income household like hers that made him start shifts as soon as he could at Midvale Cinemas. At fifteen, Zola chose the Local Beanery, a coffee shop within easy biking distance from home and school where she learned quickly how to make lattes and cappuccinos and flat whites, where she learned how to make money. Her father gone since she was three, a man she remembered only in the soft focus of bedtime stories, a disembodied masculine voice lulling her to sleep. Her mother's salary high in pharmaceutical management but challenged by the rising cost of college. Christina understood Zola's job only to the point of balking when it interfered with their weekend plans and of coming in sometimes for free hot chocolate when Zola worked after school, shifts full of bused dishes and slanting sun and the scent of burned coffee.

You're lucky, Christina said. I could use a distraction.

You can take care of Ryan. Zola's smile thin. Make sure he's okay.

Christina glanced at her bedside clock. I wonder if Matt and Nick are at home.

Zola hadn't thought to check in with either of them beyond knowing they'd made it out safe. They were alive. That was all. Everything she needed to know.

Call them, Zola said. They're home. Where else would they be?

WHEN CHRISTINA CALLED, Nick lay in the soft down of his bed. He'd clipped the newspaper and heard his parents and brother return from church sometime late morning, but he'd left his bedroom door closed. Though he'd called Sarah and tried to coax her to venture out of her house, he'd barely moved beyond his own room. He hadn't seen blood. He hadn't looked on as his classmates and teachers expired. But he'd seen a face through the glass, the passing of an armed figure, a face that haunted him into stasis if he imagined where it went and who it shot after moving beyond his English class.

Nick didn't want to leave his bedroom. But he was happy to hear Christina's voice on the other end of the line. She asked first about Sarah. Only the particulars Nick had let her know about their relationship. Christina knew only that Sarah was shy, a year younger, that she sang soprano in the Lewis and Clark choir. That Nick was still a virgin, that he was afraid of getting Sarah pregnant, that her choral scholarships would be risked if they made mistakes. Not much but more than Nick knew of Christina's boyfriend, Ryan, someone who ran in other circles, who Christina seemed to only talk about with Zola. Nick said Sarah was fine and when Christina asked if he would come over, that Zola was already there, Nick felt the exhaustion of the entire week encasing his limbs. He didn't want to move. But he didn't want to stay in his bedroom and watch the news or be tempted to scroll through refreshed articles on his computer. He sat up. He said he'd pick up Matt on the way and pulled a pair of jeans from the floor, jeans he'd thrown off after the vigil that still smelled of smoke.

In the car, a 2000 Honda Civic hatchback he'd paid for across four summers of mowing lawns, Nick rolled down the driver's side window and let in the sunlight and moved along the grid of Midvale County's streets. The days were still sun-warmed and bright blue but the nights were cool, the humidity and sweltering heat evaporated. Summer seemed far gone now, a span of months spent sweating in backyards and visiting Sarah at the custard stand where she worked and lighting off M-90s toward a hazy sky, a stockpile of firecrackers he'd kept long after the Fourth of July had come and gone.

Nick let the October air dishevel his hair through the breeze of the open window. Fall banners swayed from flag holders fastened to the porches he passed. Homes that seemed boarded up, yards bereft of children or people walking to their own mailboxes, houses closed off to the police patrols and FBI vans that filled so many once-sleepy streets. Nick watched the wind litter maple leaves across the panorama of his windshield. He'd once loved autumn in St. Louis. Born and raised in the outer stretches of the city, a landscape he'd known his entire life, he waited every August for the oppressive humidity to burn away to the clarity of September. He anticipated the turn beyond Labor Day, the pools finally closed and the summer thunderstorms gone for the promise of new teachers and new weather, an opportunity each year to begin again. He waited for the tangled foliage of poplars to strip away their green for crimson and orange, colors he watched beyond the windshield and wondered whether he'd ever see them the same way again.

He knew Matt would be home. He didn't think to call. He knew Matt rarely did anything but play video games and smoke pot in his basement bedroom when his parents weren't home, the window cracked for the smoke to escape. His mother probably home. Everyone home, shielded inside from the heavy scrutiny of reporters, hiding out in their living rooms or basements or backyards. He hadn't spoken to Matt but knew Tyler hadn't come to the vigil. He didn't know what had happened. He knew only that Tyler was safe. Nick pulled into Matt's driveway and saw his Ford Fiesta parked alone, his parents' Chevy Impala gone, an absence he knew meant his father had been called into work.

Matt's mother answered the door when he knocked. She set a hand on his shoulder and asked *how are you* and drew him into the house and shut the door. Nick tried to smile and she nodded toward the basement door, said *he's downstairs*. Nick made his way down the stairwell off the kitchen to the basement, where Matt was sitting in the alcove of his bedroom window and Nick knew right away by his face that he'd seen something terrible. He knew that somewhere in the halls Matt had witnessed what Nick had not: a scattering of blood, a gunning down, something lost to the walls of a high school. Nick said only what he could, *it's okay*, though he knew it was not.

My father's there, Matt said. Not at the house, but he's out there. For the fire.

Nick knew immediately in the tenderness of his voice what Matt had witnessed.

Caroline Black, Nick whispered. You saw her inside the school.

Matt nodded and Nick imagined Caroline's glasses and sheen of long dark hair, hair he once recognized by the back of her head from sitting behind her in their shared third-grade classroom wondering what it was like to brush something so long. He tried to imagine her bleeding, her glasses shattered, and found that he could not.

I'm fine, Matt said.

Are you?

Really. I'm fine.

How's Tyler? Nick asked.

I don't know. I haven't talked to him.

Nick moved from the doorway and sat beside Matt in the window.

We were both there, Matt finally said. The second-floor bathroom. That's where Tyler and I found her. He just took off. He didn't even stay to see if she was okay.

Nick put a hand on Matt's shoulder. I'm sure he didn't know what else to do.

Matt shrugged off his hand. I'm fine. I'm just so fucking angry. He left me there with her. So he wouldn't be caught with me.

Are you doing okay? Nick asked.

I said I was fine.

Christina wants us to come over. Zola's there, too.

Matt looked up at him, something tired in his face.

I don't want to talk about it, he said. Not yet.

Nick knew then that he meant the yearbook and not Caroline Black.

We don't have to talk about it, Nick said. He didn't know what else to say, what wouldn't be a lie: that he hadn't thought about the yearbook yet, which he had, during the hours he'd spent in his room watching the patterns of paint on his ceiling. That he hadn't researched how memory fires as synapse, how trauma tunnels into the human brain. That he hadn't started clipping newsprint to configure somehow into a record. That he hadn't already wondered how they could possibly put a book together, anything of significance to archive a year already fractured apart.

I have no idea how we're going to put this together, Matt said.

None of us do, Nick said. Let's just forget it for now. We have time.

Do we?

Nick looked at Matt. Are you sure you're okay?

I haven't slept in three days. I'm sure I'm not alone.

What you saw, Nick said. I looked it up. It changes the structure of the brain.

Researching already?

Not really. Not anything we could use.

I keep seeing her, Matt said softly. Every time I close my eyes.

That's how memory works, Nick couldn't help saying. It latches on to anything that bears a resemblance to what you saw.

Matt said nothing and Nick wondered if he'd disclosed too much. If research was his comfort alone, a means of knowing in the face of so many unknowns.

You don't have to ask your dad what he saw today, Nick said.

Matt looked at him. You're a good friend, he said. His eyes shone in the window's weak light. Nick wondered what made him say it but only nodded and looked away.

I'll go, Matt said. But only if we don't talk about it. It's too soon to plan.

We don't have to go, Nick said. We can just stay here if you want.

No, I'm fine. Let's just go. Please. Let's go.

CHRISTINA HEARD MATT and Nick walk in from her bedroom floor, where she lay sprawled with Zola, the front door unlocked, a habit of past meetings after school. Simon asleep on the couch in the living room. Her father returned from errands, she knew, by his knock on her closed bedroom door and his voice asking if they needed anything, far calmer and quieter than his yelling at the living room television just days before. Christina's bedroom carpet littered with past yearbooks. Matt walked in and saw them open-faced and told her immediately that now wasn't the time. That there was nothing to plan. Not yet. That their lone task was to sit with the names. That he would stay only if Christina packed up the yearbooks and put them away.

Christina met his eyes. Saw them hollowed out. Something empty beyond the shock she'd seen in his face at the vigil. Nick nodded hello but said nothing and Christina closed the yearbooks on the carpet and slid them in the drawer of her nightstand and Matt stepped forward only when she flipped the television station away from the news.

Christina sat beside Nick on the carpet and said nothing of the newscast. Said nothing of Simon asleep on the couch, safe because of a storage closet within the high school's science labs. Said nothing of Ryan heading home from the hospital, how he had no idea who Caroline Black was. She glanced at the red digits of her bedside clock: 4:46 P.M. She knew Ryan should be home by now and that he hadn't called. She knew Matt's father's job. She wanted to know if he was there. She wanted to know what he knew, whether the fire was deliberate or an accident, whether Zola had been right to guess suicide. She wanted to know what police had found in the debris littered across the lawn, the ashes of photos and report cards and elementary school artwork, the remains of what had once been a home. She wanted to know if there was an answer yet, a reason why Caleb had done what he'd done. A reason for hiding beneath her desk, Henry Park crouched across from her as the French video blared. A reason for Ryan's leg torn in half, his classmates gasping last breaths in the locker room stalls. A reason for Mr. Rourke pooled on the hallway carpet, what she'd seen when the officer ushered her French class away from the building. A reason for Elise, what room or closet of Lewis and Clark had claimed her away from the water, a swimming pool that would never buoy her weight again. But Christina didn't ask. She didn't know what Matt knew, if he knew anything at all. She only flipped the television away from the news and toward a mindless Sunday marathon of afternoon movies, a double feature of *The Breakfast Club* and *Sixteen Candles*. She lay on her bedroom floor and watched so many high schoolers on-screen and tried not to think of an elsewhere of teenhood, some confusion of hormones and angst and a relationship that had seemed so much more important only days before, sex in a fogged car or the adrenaline of fighting, the only remnant the sting of Ryan not calling as an afternoon wore on.

My dad's there, Matt said at last from Christina's bed, where he sat beside Zola. At the station, for forensics and fire analysis.

Christina glanced at Zola, who looked blankly back. The television mumbled behind them, a movie no one was watching. Christina seized her chance to ask.

Will he be able to tell you anything? she asked.

I don't know, Matt said. He usually doesn't tell me anything.

He might tell you something about this, she said. This is different.

What time did your dad leave the house this morning? Nick asked.

I don't know. Early.

Has he been there all day? Zola asked.

Christina recognized the opportunity and took it, grabbed the remote control and switched the channel from the afternoon movies to the ongoing newsreel, CNN and local stations alternating between the Blacks' home and continued coverage of Lewis and Clark. Matt didn't stop her. Neither Zola nor Nick moved to protest. Christina knew each of them wanted to know: stories about each family, each shot student. Speculation as to when school would resume. Roundtable pundits discussing gun legislation and mental health reform, an indefinite break from the war in Iraq and weapons of mass destruction. Just talking heads. Christina wanted information. Christina turned up the volume and threw the remote control to her nightstand.

We can't pretend this isn't happening, she said. She looked at her bedside clock: 5:54 P.M. Ryan was home, she knew, had probably been home for some time. She felt her eyes smart and she bit her lower lip to keep her frustration at bay.

I saved the article from this morning's paper, Nick said. I couldn't help it.

I clipped the list of names, too, Christina said. God. So many fucking names.

I saw Caroline Black, Matt said. I saw her on the carpet.

On the carpet? Christina asked. What do you mean you saw her on the carpet?

Christina glanced at Nick, who didn't meet her gaze, who kept watching the news.

You were there, Christina whispered to Matt. In the school. You saw her.

Matt nodded and Zola's face fell and she moved closer to him on Christina's bed, put her hand on his hand, and Christina tried to contain the mess of herself, the guilt welling up from her gut to her throat. She'd seen Mr. Rourke. An image she could barely remember. Blocked from her brain in the haste of exiting. She'd seen nothing, heard nothing but a French video droning over a classroom of empty desks, everyone tucked beneath them. She hadn't heard the last wheezing breaths of peers who'd no longer walk the length of the hallways when everyone returned to school, a point in the future that felt as far-off and inconceivable as growing old. No images burned to her brain, no sense of where Elise was or how she had died. Only imagination, not the same as what Zola had seen in the library that she wouldn't say or what Matt had witnessed on the carpet, not the same as grief transforming the wiring of her brain. Only Henry Park's face across the aisle, only a classroom that Caleb never entered. Only a boyfriend shot in the leg, one who hadn't called all afternoon. Christina had no right to feel the way Matt or Zola did but couldn't quiet the lack of stillness rattling her body, the need at once to shake every muscle off inside the resistant waves of a swimming pool, her arms gliding through the water, or else the need to set her pen to paper and start writing, the start of an archive.

She pulled the yearbooks from her nightstand. Laid them on the floor.

We said we wouldn't talk about it. There's no way we can't.

I can't do this right now, Matt said. Really, I can't.

No one's saying you need to write, Nick stepped in. Not yet. What would there even be to document at this point? But we need to talk about it. We're all here.

What do you want us to do? Zola said. There's nothing we can do.

Nick opened their sophomore yearbook to the block of photos that gridded the entire class. We at least need names, he said. The names of every junior, every person in our class that we lost. We're going to have to profile them eventually.

Where will we put these profiles? Zola asked. The front of the yearbook? The back? Somewhere in the middle? How do we even decide something like that?

I don't know, Nick said. Do you? Do any of us know how to do this?

Christina pulled the list of names from her nightstand, a folded piece of newsprint clipped and saved from the morning paper. Ryan at home, surely worrying about tennis scholarships and not her. She knew he wouldn't call all night. Matt looked away as she grabbed a pen and began circling faces in the block of sophomore year photographs.

Zola stood from the bed. Don't draw on that—

I don't care, Christina interrupted. We need to know what we have to handle.

She circled the faces. Every junior. Caroline Black. Alyssa Carver. Alexander Chen. Connor Distler. Jacob Jensen. Elise Nguyen, a drawn ring that made her hand shake. Alexis Thurber. Kelly Washington. Jessica Wendling.

Nine names, Christina said. Nine profiles. Matt, can you help me handle these?

Matt stayed soundless on Christina's bed, his eyes fixed on the front lawn through her bedroom window.

You can't put Jessica's and Alyssa's profiles next to each other in the yearbook, Zola blurted. Jared Hirsch cheated on Jessica with Alyssa last year. Remember?

Zola's objection, one that would have felt natural only days before. Christina looked from Zola to Nick and back to Matt as the room fell silent.

You can't put Kelly next to Connor, either, Matt finally said. They were both in the top ten. It will look like a list of National Merit scholars instead of a memorial.

We'll put them in alphabetical order then, Christina said loudly, her voice harsher than she intended. Does that work? Does that work for everyone?

The television buzzed. No one spoke. On the TV screen an entire community, a radius of grief.

Where do we go from here? Nick said at last.

He didn't mean the yearbook. The beginnings of an archive we would have to plan by duty, a yearbook wholly different than the one we'd envisioned just days before. A book none of us knew how to make. A testimony to what, we couldn't imagine. Of wanting to forget. Of wanting to go back. Of knowing only a counting of days, the growing distance from Wednesday to so many more Wednesdays that meant the past would only recede and become incrementally lost.

We'll do what we can, Christina said. When we're ready. It's an impossible task. We can only do our best and nothing more.

We were imperfect, she meant. We were faulted in willful forgetting. Our best: the careful placement of photographs and articles in the glossed pages of a book to square away, to close off, to place in the past and forget. We were human, she meant. We would leave behind who we had to, in order to break ourselves. In order to move on.

CAROLINE BLACK

Lewis and Clark High School

Class of 2005

November 7, 1986—October 8, 2003

Caroline Black, a junior at Lewis and Clark, was a magnetic force in the hallways of our school. Known for her humor and liveliness, she was a straight A student, her favorite subjects English and Art. She excelled at drawing and painting and had two recent pieces in the 2002–2003 Lewis and Clark High Art Show. Her favorite book was Joyce Carol Oates's *Foxfire*, and her favorite book as a child was *Charlotte's Web*.

She loved animals and often visited the St. Louis Zoo, an institution she said was the best in the world because it was free to anyone in the city. She also loved St. Louis winters and thought it was good luck to catch snowflakes on her tongue during the first snowfall of the year. She was a fan of folksingers, especially Joan Baez, Judy Collins and Bob Dylan. She was on the Lewis and Clark varsity soccer team, having played since freshman year on the JV team, and she was also a member of the National Honor Society and Key Club. She loved trying new foods—sushi, kimchee, papaya—and her favorite place in the world was the Outer Banks of North Carolina, where her family traveled every summer.

She wanted to attend the University of Missouri and study veterinary science. She was a firecracker. We will miss her energy and light.

A BRIEF HISTORY OF
CONTAINMENT

ERASE YOUR FAMILIARITY. Erase what you knew. Erase this as where you first learned the particulars of locker combinations, glances of flirtation, seven minutes of passing time between classes. Erase your heart. Shut down its valves. Think of this only as crime scene, as investigation. As a site of evidence, nothing more.

Survey the scene. Make sketches. Take photographs. Map and measure everything. Record and document where physical evidence was discarded. Search for fingerprints, for left-behind weapons. Analyze ballistics, evidence of range. Identify the residue of gunshots, trace evidence of hair, of fibers and dust. Allow first responders to take notes, allow a coroner to take over, allow crime scene investigators to arrive. Record the time. Leave everything as found. Barricade the perimeter with yellow tape.

Note the weather conditions. A wash of blue sky.

Restrain the arrival of reporters.

Place identification cards beside everyone found. Make note of eyeglasses. Earrings. Torn clothing. Skewed shoes. Place belongings in a bag. Mass disaster: contain everything. Steel yourself. Erase what you were.

PAPERWEIGHT, APRON, BEDSIDE LAMP

MONDAY MORNING: WE awoke to a mass-emailed notification sent to every student and parent at Lewis and Clark that we would take the week off for mourning, that we would resume school the following week. School as abstract. A learning how, the education of moving on. School as collective, school as process. Not the bricks and mortar of a building.

We would resume school, the email told us, but not at Lewis and Clark.

We were told that the school was a crime scene, a term our administration avoided for *still under investigation*. That the district had arranged for us to return to the Timber Creek center, an administrative building for the Midvale County School District that we knew only through D.A.R.E. programming and special events, a building available for use by every school in the district but more often empty, a building sizable enough to contain our classrooms for the duration of the academic year. That our bus routes and driving routes would change only slightly, the building just two miles from Lewis and Clark. That Homecoming would still be held at Timber Creek, a dance we'd forgotten across the length of a long weekend. That it would be held the Friday after classes resumed, almost two weeks away, to reclaim a sense of normalcy and what our lives had been.

We didn't know what to do with ourselves, the first day of a gaping, cracked-open week. A first day that would span to five, sprawling and unscheduled and impossible to fill. We walked through the rooms of our homes and felt a weight pressed to our chests as if the air we took in was nothing but water, our lungs drowning on land. We sat on the swings of our porches and listened to the wind whistle through the dry leaves. We pulled our sweatshirts tighter around us, the air still warm but harboring an edge. We tucked our knees to our breastbones, our palms folded against our hearts. We leaned back and watched a wheel of turning sky, blue and endless and aching.

We couldn't imagine a new building, a new high school, a forked route from the life we'd pictured: a junior year of dances and finally being upperclassmen and Halloween parties and SAT preparation, a year funneled down to the strange hallways of a new building that would remind us, every day, what had run off course. We couldn't imagine driving past Lewis and Clark, its hallways empty and vacant, hallways we couldn't envision walking through again as readily as we couldn't stand to not know them the way we once did. And a Homecoming dance, a celebration we'd just days before anticipated: swaying beneath streamers and balloon arches and a darkness that would no longer conceal our trembling, a trembling of harsh light and loss instead of the trembling of nearness, of standing so close on the dance floor to someone else's human skin.

Before the dance, a week off for quiet and mourning.

We knew what mourning meant: that funerals would begin.

We also knew what administrators wouldn't name in the sterile typeface of an email, that alongside the clear absence of our teachers' and our peers' detailed names there was the void of Caroline Black's parents, a fire, what no one had words to address.

Matt hadn't slept. Nick had driven him home from Christina's house past dark, cicadas all around them singing the night into being. A sound so strange in his ears, what he'd always known of a Missouri fall but had forgotten across the past days. He heard it as

Nick pulled into his driveway and they sat in the car watching the squares of his house's front windows pool light on the yard. The sound of late Little League games, a chill descending with dusk as his teammates left the diamond and the field lights flooded on. The sound of summer dying off. The sound of driving Tyler home late across the past weeks, night falling in waves of droned sound all around them. The sound of a terrible nostalgia inside Nick's car, his house waiting just past the windshield. He'd walked inside and found his parents reading on the couch. His father thumbing through a *Sports Illustrated* article on the American League Championship Series between the Yankees and the Red Sox. His mother, a new biography on President Bush and the War on Terror to know what was happening in the world, Matt knew, and with what dose of skepticism she should approach the news. She set down her book and asked how everyone was, Nick and Zola and Christina, and he'd said they were fine and turned immediately to his father and asked what he'd found out at work. His father kept his eyes lowered. *So far nothing's conclusive,* he said. Matt knew he was lying but didn't push. He'd turned from the living room toward the basement stairs and felt his parents' eyes following him, a tightness piercing his chest to walk away from them.

In his bedroom, he kept the lights off and lay down on his bed fully clothed. He listened to the silence of the house: the pings, the cracks of a house settling. Sounds he once thought were ghosts until his mother told him houses breathed and shifted. In the dark he tried not to think of Tyler, the rough texture of his face where stubble grew in. He lay there until he heard the television's volume through the floorboards above him, the muted shows switched to the ten o'clock news. He lay until he heard his parents finally turn off the television and move down the hall to their bedroom, the weight of their footsteps echoing overhead. He waited another ten minutes. Twenty. He thought of a house without sounds, what it must have been for Caroline's parents to hear no footsteps. No television, no humming radio, no creaks or doors opening that told them their daughter was there, what sounds they'd grown accustomed to across sixteen years that had vanished in the quick second of a high school hallway. Matt waited in the pitch dark of his bedroom, illuminated only by a single streetlamp beyond his basement window. When he knew at last that his parents were asleep he crept from his room, up the stairs, into the study beside his parents' bedroom. He sat at his father's desk and ran his hands across the mahogany surface then over the keyhole of the drawer just below the chair, the only one his father locked.

Matt knew this was where his father kept anything confidential. Anything of police proceedings that couldn't be left at the department, anything he had to work on overnight that was sensitive or unsuitable for adolescent eyes. Matt remembered certain nights from his childhood when his father holed himself away in this office all night. He remembered lying in his bed imagining photos of dead bodies, of blood spatters and used knives and the hollows of bullet holes. He knew how to pick a lock. He'd long ago confiscated his mother's bobby pins, had once jimmied the desk lock in sixth grade to know what his father knew but had found nothing, just the black text of indecipherable incident reports.

But as he sat at his father's desk, the urge leaked from him and his hands fell away from the keyhole. He didn't want to feel dirty. He didn't want his father to look at him in the morning and know by his face, impossible to conceal, that he'd read the reports and knew what his father wished he would never know. He sat back in the chair. He tilted his head to the ceiling. In the patterns of paint he saw only whorls of blood upon high school carpet. He wouldn't sleep. He would do nothing but watch the darkness and yearn for dawn. He thought of Caroline Black. A girl who'd once stood next to him on the risers during their second-grade class play at Des Peres Elementary, both of them chorus members without speaking lines. How his parents had asked their music teacher, Mrs. Mayhew, that he not have an acting part, that he was too shy, too filled with stage fright to be anything but a nonspeaking evergreen. How the girl standing next to him knew, a quiet peony. How his voice wavered the chorus notes and how she grabbed his hand to help him sing, her palm damp and warm.

What did you love? He wished he could ask. *What was it when you were small that made you so fucking brave?* He pulled a pad of paper and a pencil from the desk's unlocked drawers. He knew he'd told Christina it would take time. He gripped the pencil in his left hand regardless and began to write. He took breaks to close his eyes and force the air into his lungs. He did not stop writing until the streetlamp beyond the window flickered off and the walls of the study began to lighten with dawn. He traveled back downstairs from the study before his parents awoke, the profile in his hands. He set it on his dresser and lay in his bed and watched the sun crawl up the dark shades of his window. He thought of what he'd written, everything he knew and remembered of Caroline Black, so much of it inadequate, only anecdotes, words he was sure revealed nothing but how little he knew of her. His mother opened his bedroom door past sunrise and padded across the carpeted floor, his father already gone for work, footsteps Matt had heard tracking overhead from the kitchen to the front door.

Honey, Matt's mother said. She sat at the edge of his bed. He could smell coffee on her breath. Sweetheart, are you awake?

He could see the faint lines of her face, ridges that had become more pronounced as the week's news had settled into her skin.

School's canceled this week, she said. You'll go back next Monday.

To Lewis and Clark?

She looked away. No. That other facility. The one you went to for D.A.R.E.

Matt recalled Timber Creek: a cavernous building where he'd gone to a one-day retreat, where he should have learned about pills and marijuana and Missouri's growing meth problem but in the end all he remembered was fluorescent lighting and more Little Debbie's snack cakes than he should have comfortably eaten.

That shithole? He found himself angry.

Matt, his mother said.

This is fucked, he said.

I know, his mother whispered. You're just tired. You need to sleep.

He knew this. They both knew this. But he also knew what she wouldn't say, that what was between them and around them was not insomnia but a ripped-open universe, one tilted far beyond kilter by a surge of bullets and fire.

Come upstairs, she said. I'll make you eggs.

He watched the light filter through the curtains and could not look at his mother. This woman who'd taken care of him. Who had listened. Who for so long he'd considered soft, just a housewife who packed his lunches while his father charged into Midvale County and solved cases. This woman who in the end had enveloped him in her arms when he let the words gut him, when they spilled from his mouth and pooled at his parents' feet and his father only watched him without expression before walking away to their bedroom, to a door closing. He was young. He was fourteen. He was old enough to know what did and did not move him. He'd spent junior high shoving his tongue into the mouths of so many girls to push back a needling spark and freshman year losing his virginity at a basement party to a girl named Misty, a girl from another high school whose last name he never learned and whose face he never saw again, all of it to feel nothing but some pulse of normalcy, a deadening his mother absorbed at the start of high school when he at last made himself tell them by pulling him to her chest.

He'd heard her heartbeat, his father down the hall. A drumming that drowned out the television, the hum of the refrigerator. An anthem he still heard. She was here again, at his bedside. She was here. She would always be here. He pulled the covers back and stepped to the floor and followed her upstairs, his mother who said nothing of the jeans he still wore from the night before.

At the table, he scanned the headlines of the front page while she cracked eggs into a glass and whisked them with milk. Continued coverage of Lewis and Clark, of the victims and families, of who had really known Caleb Raynor. A follow-up story on the Blacks' home, a subheading blaring that information was still sparse. An article on Iraqi sovereignty, a UN-enforced timeline for establishing a governing council by mid-December. Matt looked away. The sound of sizzling eggs filled the kitchen.

What did Dad find? Matt asked.

Your father doesn't like to discuss his cases, his mother said. She tilted her head to the ceiling. God, I'm sorry, she said. I know this isn't just a case.

Did you ever lose anyone in your high school class? Matt asked. He thought to ask but stopped himself: *did anyone die.*

Janet Tillman, she said. She was in my algebra class. She died in a car accident my junior year.

Matt tried to imagine his mother at sixteen: her golden hair, a short bob he'd only seen in photos. He tried to imagine what it meant for her to sit in a mathematics class with the seat beside her empty, someone missing. He tried to imagine the classrooms of Timber Creek and how cavernous they would feel, how many absences he would sense despite how deliberately the administration would change the atmosphere and seating.

He would still know. They would all know.

There was nothing an administration could do.

His mother set a plate of scrambled eggs in front of him. She didn't open the *Post-Dispatch* like she always did, first thing every morning. She sat beside him at the table with her hands resting on top of the folded newspaper.

She was a friend, his mother said. Janet Tillman. She was on the cheerleading squad with me. She had the loudest laugh. Infectious.

She wanted to work for Amnesty International. This was the early seventies. She hated the war.

Matt ate his eggs. His mother reached across the table. It's okay, she said. It's okay to admit this hurts. She hesitated a moment. I saw what you wrote, she finally said. What you left on the dresser. Caroline Black. Is that for the yearbook?

I'll need to revise it. I barely knew her.

But we all knew her. We knew her parents. We watched you grow up together in Suzuki concerts and homeroom parties at Des Peres.

Matt looked up and saw in his mother's face that she knew. What he couldn't bring himself to say when she and his father located him at last in the library parking lot though his jeans were stained, what they could have known by the blood on his clothes.

I know you saw something, she whispered. It's okay. You can tell me.

Matt set down his fork. He was surprised just how easy it was to stay hard. But his mother knew him. This woman. This woman who'd pulled him against her, who'd held him when his father would not. How his father had come to his room later that evening and set a hand against his cheek and pulled Matt into his chest and how Matt had come undone in that moment but even still it was his mother he remembered, his mother who laid down her guard when he first spoke three impossible words.

I couldn't save her, Matt whispered. Caroline Black. I couldn't save her.

She wasn't yours to save, honey. She was already gone.

Her blood had soaked the knees of his jeans. He'd left them with the police, a change of clothes they gave him, a V-neck Hanes T-shirt and a colorless pair of sweatpants though she was still on his shoes and his hands. As if leaving anything behind would help.

I wrote about her, Matt said. I wrote about her and I barely knew her.

That's what you're supposed to do. It helps.

We have to write profiles eventually, Matt said. Of every single one of them. If I can do nothing else, at least I can start. Even if I barely knew her.

You did know her. You shared a history.

Not one that was long enough.

His mother grasped his hand. Whatever you write, it's going to be beautiful.

Matt felt the grip of her fingers and wondered what about her would always be unknowable to him. How there had been a Janet Tillman his mother carried with her since the moment of his birth. How under any other circumstance, his mother might never have told him, an entire history Matt would never know.

How there was so much of everything beyond knowing.

The empty pan on the stove. So many yellowing cookbooks. A Peter Rabbit tea set, a flowered apron, a hutch that held his father's glass decanters. Every item in the kitchen held a history. A series of moments he'd never seen. How his parents must have purchased the hutch together sometime before he was born. How they might have been laughing, a joke, an odd name for a store, Tom's Trunk of Treasures. How the sky might have darkened with rain or else the beginnings of a sunset. How much younger they must have been, whether they remembered carrying it to the car—which car? which car in the line of vehicles they had owned together?—or whether it was an outing lost to the scattered record of time. Or what might have been gifted: a tea set. What might have caused a friend or his mother's mother or his aunt Catherine to pick up a teapot while browsing the aisles of a thrift shop, to carry a piece of porcelain to the checkout counter. What items bore witness to his parents' history: what books or trinkets were picked up on vacations, against seasides, so many isolated moments that made up a life.

I don't know her history, Matt said. I feel like I know nothing about her.

You do your best, his mother said. That's all that you can do. You have a heart, a brain. Those things will make a profile she would have wanted.

Matt pulled his hand away. His mother glanced down at the newspaper on the table beneath her hands. *What she would have wanted.* As if anyone could guess. A girl who just days ago had taken in the scent of wet leaves, the sharp coolness of October sun.

I can't believe this sovereignty council, his mother said, her finger on the headlines, skirting those of Lewis and Clark. As if we can go in and upend a country and expect anyone to know where to go from here.

Matt pushed his plate away and leaned back from the table.

What did Dad see? he asked again. What did Dad find at the Blacks' house?

They don't know, she said. No one knows. But things will move quickly at their house, I imagine. We should be prepared for a memorial service. That's all I know.

CHRISTINA SAT IN her car on the street outside of Ryan's house, the windows rolled up and fogging with her breath, her hands clenched on the steering wheel. She still wore sweatpants. Her brother was at home. Ryan had finally called that morning, the first he'd called since returning from the hospital, and told her to come over, that his parents were both back to work, that his father would only return over the lunch hour to check on him.

He was in bed. He said he'd leave the door unlocked for her. Christina checked her makeup in the car's rearview mirror, a slick of mascara she swiped on regardless of wearing pajamas. She hadn't wanted to appease him, hadn't wanted to come immediately when summoned, but here she was, the feigned casualness of sweatpants, looking away from the absurdity of herself in the rearview mirror. She glanced down the street toward Benji Ndolo's house, a freshman who'd lived six houses down from Ryan and whose mother

had spoken at the vigil. A house she'd sometimes passed on her bike
when she'd ridden from her house to Ryan's on the wooded path
that connected their neighborhoods. A kid neither she nor Ryan
knew aside from seeing him on the sidewalk waiting for the bus
sometimes when she'd picked Ryan up in the car for school. She
thought of Benji's mother, the way her face broke when she tried to
speak at the vigil. Christina opened the car door and made her way
across Ryan's front lawn.

Ryan's house was the scent of cinnamon and air-conditioning
and stale smoke and vanilla sugar candles. She slipped her shoes
off in the foyer and padded softly down the hallway carpet. Ryan's
bedroom door was cracked open, a sliver that revealed his shape
resting in bed. The sound of a television buzzed from the room,
a late-morning game show. His foot elevated on a pillow. His leg
wrapped in a hardened cast. The same as the hospital room, the
covers stretched over his legs and up to his bare chest.

Christina stood at the foot of his bed. His gaze drifted to the
standing figure of her shape, the television emitting the sharp ping
of bells and whistles, contestants winning prizes. Christina watched
him, then crossed her arms at the bottom edges of her shirt. She
pulled the fabric over her head and let it drop to the floor.

What are you doing? Ryan said.

Christina ignored him and pulled off her sweatpants. Beneath
her pajamas spanned a length of shaved skin. Her legs, her abdomen. Swimmer's calves. Swaths she'd run a razor across the night
before to eradicate every bump and hair, every imperfection she
could find. To not think of a pool's waves, Elise nowhere within
them. To not think of a phone silent at her bedside. She stood before
him in the bright red of a laced bra and walked to the bed and
straddled Ryan's body and placed her hands on his chest.

What are you doing, he said.

Taking care of you, she said.

Ryan pushed back her shoulders. I'm hurt.

I know. She leaned in close, ran her breath against his neck.

He pushed her head away. A shove more violent, one that carried an acute pain.

No, Chris, I'm hurt. I was shot. Don't you fucking understand?

She sat back on her knees. Of course I understand, she said. She pushed herself off him, away from the bed. She gathered her clothing from the floor and clutched it against her chest.

I didn't mean—he started to speak, his voice softer but she was already pulling her sweatpants on, already yanking the T-shirt back over her head. She backed away from him, stood near the safety of his dresser. She kept her eyes on the floor.

It's just that my dad will be home soon, he said.

Is that it?

Yeah, that's it.

Then why did you call? Why tell me no one was home?

Because it's true. No one's home.

The television whirred and buzzed, a cacophony of chimes.

Look at me, Ryan said, his voice hardened. Look at why I'm here, why we're at home. Why we're not at school like we're supposed to be.

Yeah, we're home, she said. And you won't even touch me.

What, you want to fuck, Chris? You want to feel better? You think my dick will make the gunman go away?

She grabbed a framed photo from his dresser and threw it. The frame hit the wall beside his bed and glass shattered and rained down on the carpet. A photo of him on the tennis court, racket held high. Slipped from the frame to the white down of the carpet.

Ryan looked up at her. He didn't have to say it: *You crazy bitch*. His face screamed it instead though he'd already said it once before, what she would never tell Zola, the time last spring after a party when he'd been drinking and driving home 20 miles per hour too fast, when at a stoplight she'd stepped from the car and slammed the door behind her and started walking home alone, the roads deserted and the streetlamps blinking and he'd pulled up next to her and rolled down the window and yelled, *Get in the car, you fucking bitch.*

He hadn't even asked her across the past days what she recalled from inside the school, as if knowing she'd been in French class was enough. His pain the sun. Everything about him the center always of their orbit. How she'd been to every one of his tennis matches and watched him lob the ball across each net of singles and doubles. How she'd listened to him complain for two years that Chad Stapleton wasn't as serious about tennis scholarships as he was, a doubles partner he claimed brought down his performance. How he'd been to only one of her swim meets, the first one she'd completed freshman year right after they began dating. Elise among the members of her 200-meter medley relay team, how they'd finished second and how she'd placed first in every other women's freestyle and relay competition that year and even still he hadn't been to a single one of them, had only told her at that first meet when her relay team placed second that her stroke could have been stronger. His mouth curved into a smirk.

How she should have known then.

Christina fled into the hallway, the television and his voice shouting after her. She pushed her way out the front door and into the light of late morning, a torrent of cold air, a crispness her skin absorbed in the absence of soft hands. She pushed herself into the car. Her fists slammed the steering wheel. She exhaled into the sealed interior. She pressed her palms into her eyes and only then let tears come.

ZOLA SAT ON the swing of her back porch. Chamomile tea. The softness of an afghan her grandmother had knitted. The sun filtered down, a winking glow. Pinholes of light and shade, nothing she felt moved to capture on camera. Zola's mother had taken one more day off from the pharmaceutical company where she worked near

Lambert International Airport. Express Scripts, Zola knew, though she knew nothing else of her mother's job. She understood certain words—consulting, clinical research—but she couldn't say what her mother did. She only knew that her mother made more money than Zola imagined she herself ever would, a salary that more than compensated for her father leaving but still necessitated Zola's after-school work. Her mother was inside at the computer, returning emails, finishing tasks from home, checking on Zola frequently. Zola's supervisor had called: she wouldn't return to the Local Bean-ery until Wednesday, two more days off. Zola pulled the blanket around her shoulders and felt the porch swing rock beneath her, the sound of late afternoon cicadas surrounding the backyard.

Caroline Black's funeral: that evening. Her mother had shown her the notice in the *Post-Dispatch* that morning. A memorial ser-vice at six, a private burial following. No visitation. No donations in lieu of flowers. Until the service, Zola wanted nothing but to sit and be still. She hadn't thought of the yearbook. She'd seen the news-paper, its wave of listings. She knew her neighbor Alisha Trenway's funeral would also be held that evening. She hadn't known Alisha, a freshman, and her mother didn't know Alisha's parents but only exchanged pleasantries with them when passing along the side-walks of the street they shared. Zola had stood with her sometimes at the bus stop on the corner before she began biking to school. The neighborhood connected them. Zola couldn't say what else it was that bound them to one another. She hadn't seen Alisha's parents come or go from their house since Wednesday, the blinds shut, the lights dimmed.

Zola watched the line of oak trees in the backyard and tried to imagine what it was to die. Where Alisha had been inside the school. What resolve could make a boy she'd only said hello to at a 7-Eleven charge into a school wanting to kill and to perish himself. Her heart murmured. That there was no way out. That there would be a last breath one day, that this was fact by simple math. To cross a border. To scale a ledge. To freefall into wide-open nothing. That she could have died inside the library, her heart beating hard against the stacks. That an officer found her instead of a bullet, her jeans darkened with piss and not blood. There but for the grace of God: her peers at the table of her academic lab. Alexander Chen. Jessica Wendling. Connor Distler. What had they seen? What beyond had they lunged themselves into? What vision, what sensation, what cluttered black or closing in? The sound of choking and the gargled cries the last shred of earth they'd claimed, a bearing away more terrible than anything Zola could imagine.

The sound of a sliding door opening. Her mother's footsteps on the porch.

You have a visitor, her mother said. She doesn't look so good.

Christina appeared behind her, mascara streaking her cheeks. Zola had no time to ask what happened before Christina curled herself into Zola's blanket.

He's an asshole, Christina whispered against the afghan. Zola looked up at her mother, who lowered her gaze and stepped back into the house.

What happened? Zola asked.

He didn't even call yesterday.

Did you go over there?

I tried. He didn't want to talk. He didn't want me at all.

Maybe he's just grieving, Zola said. Like every single one of us.

That's not it. He's always been like this. I can't believe it took this for me to see it.

Zola didn't pry. Didn't make her explain. Didn't say that she'd thought Ryan was trouble since Christina began dating him freshman year. They sat in a silence broken only by songbirds until Christina pulled away and sat up, wiped a hand beneath her eyes.

This is so fucking stupid, she said. Everything happening, and this is what I choose to cry about.

Caroline Black's funeral is tonight.

I know. I saw it in the newspaper. My father, all of us are going.

We are, too. My mom and me.

How is this happening? Christina asked. How the fuck did this happen?

Zola watched Christina's hands bunch the afghan, clutch the yarn into the core of her fists. She knew this had happened by the hand of a boy who remained inscrutable to her beyond a gas station hello, a boy who walked into a high school's doors knowing he and so many others of his choosing would die. Zola wondered if he'd had a plan beyond a shotgun. What was random. What was deliberate. If he'd known which classroom doors he would open, if he'd made his way to the library or the gymnasium for a reason. If she could have died by forethought or if he'd only zigzagged his way from room to room, rattling guns against the railings. Zola wanted to respond to Christina, to offer some word of comfort, but there was nothing, no utterance or solace, no sound but the hum of cicadas and the rustling of the trees.

NICK READ THE newspaper at the kitchen table, both of his parents at work though they'd called to make sure he was okay. His mother phoned from the car, a public defender for the city, her voice strained as she moved through the streets of downtown St. Louis. Nick's father's call was much quieter, a phone call placed from the solitude of his office, which overlooked the eastern edge of Forest Park, from Barnes-Jewish Hospital, where he worked as an obstetrician. I am fine, Nick told both of them. His brother in the living room watching cartoons, the sound traveling into the kitchen. He didn't know what else to say. He'd stayed up late in front of the blue glow of his bedroom computer, researching the construction of crime scenes, though in the end he'd found nothing of consequence.

He'd called Sarah's house that morning, her mother claiming

she was asleep and unable to talk. She still hadn't called back, still hadn't left the walls of her own home. A girl who'd spent hours after school in the choir room only days before, who'd planned to try out for the spring production of *Pippin*. A girl who chastised him for coming home by himself every day after school, no extracurriculars or clubs, except yearbook with his closest friends. A girl who claimed once across the summer during their most heated argument in her bedroom that they hadn't had sex not because he worried about her welfare and future, but because he was always too much in his head and never enough inside the center of his own body.

He flipped through the continued *Post-Dispatch* features on gun safety, on updating school policies, on ongoing public memorials. Donation sites for the victims' families: where to offer money for medical bills of those who had survived with injuries, even where to donate frequent flyer miles to bereaved family members who would travel to St. Louis. A list of business openings, resumed events, what would return to regularly scheduled activity. The St. Louis Blues starting a new season, an away game against Denver, where the victims would be honored. The St. Louis Rams playing the Arizona Cardinals that evening, a *Monday Night Football* home opener that would air as scheduled but would hold a memorial before the game. Nick turned to an extended section of obituaries: a list of longer write-ups beyond what the *Post-Dispatch* had already printed, write-ups that included the most basic of information about each funeral service.

Jacob Jensen: Tuesday. Mr. Rourke: Wednesday.

Deborah Smalls: Thursday. Kelly Washington: Tuesday.

And tonight, six this evening: Caroline Black and her parents, Jean and Arthur.

Nick flipped back to the front page, its headline announcing the ongoing investigation of the Blacks' home. Information still sparse. Indicating only that burial would happen quickly, that no bodies would be held for investigation. The orchestrations of a cartoon's introduction resounded from the living room, his brother watching another episode of *Tom and Jerry*. Jeff only nine years old, dismissed from Des Peres Elementary, the entire district shut down. Caleb Raynor drifting past the window of Nick's English class: a synapse firing inside his brain. He tried to imagine Caleb at nine, whether he'd watched *Tom and Jerry* or *Merry Melodies* or kept the television off for the wilds of his backyard. If there was any indication in his behavior that he would one day become a killer. Nick listened to the television warble down the hallway, his brother curled into the couch. He picked up the telephone and called Matt's house.

MATT SAT IN the recliner of his family's living room reading *Slaughterhouse-Five,* a novel he continued for English class though he didn't know if the assignments would change, the schedule altered. His mother sat across from him on the couch, the book on President Bush in her lap. She looked up when the phone rang.

I'll get it, he told her. He anticipated the cinema's manager, that he was needed for a shift though he'd already spoken to her midmorning and agreed to return tomorrow. When he picked up the phone Nick asked without pause, Have you heard from your dad?

I'm going downstairs, Matt told his mother. Can you hang this up? He moved down the basement stairs to his bedroom and closed the door behind him.

Have you seen the paper? Nick asked when Matt's mother hung up.
I saw it this morning. I didn't read it.
Caroline Black's funeral is tonight. Her parents', too. Nick paused. It just seems soon, he said. If they still don't know what happened.
My dad's at work. He's told me nothing.
Are you going? Nick asked.

Matt sat back on his bed. Of course he was going. They would all go.

I asked my dad about the fire last night, he said. He didn't tell me anything.

Maybe there's nothing to tell, Nick said. Maybe they know it was an accident.

I wrote about Caroline last night, Matt said. A profile. I couldn't sleep.

What did you say? Nick asked.

I said nothing. Nothing important. I have no fucking idea what I wrote.

I was up, too. Nothing we can use in a yearbook. Just crime scene stuff. How they handle an investigation involving so many victims.

Did you find anything?

Not really. Nothing you probably couldn't find out from your dad.

Matt heard Nick's breath halt on the line. A pause he recognized, one preceding a question. Does your dad know anything about motive yet? Nick asked.

About the fires? I told you, he didn't tell me anything about why it happened.

No, I mean Caleb.

Matt closed his eyes. A name he hadn't spoken, a name some newscasters were avoiding to privilege a list of names and their lives. He hadn't wanted to think of motive, as if there were a reason that could explain. Caleb in the cafeteria line grabbing a carton of milk. Caleb at his desk in the back of the room, his hand unraised. Caleb someone he never thought about until it mattered, someone who confronted Caroline Black in the hallway and left her on the carpet outside the second-floor bathroom for Matt to find.

My father's only working on the fire investigation, he said. But you read the newspaper. They say they don't know. Does it even matter?

I don't know, Nick said. Does it?

It won't change anything, Matt said. He imagined what the in-vestigation entailed. Ransacking Caleb's room for journals, plans, schematics of the high school. Reviewing his computer if he had one, what files he'd deleted or online rants he'd posted. Receipts for ammunition, gun sales. When purchases were made. How a boy could buy a shotgun and a handgun and stockpile two other assault rifles beneath his bed, how a catastrophe in the making could slip so easily through so many cracks.

It won't change anything, Nick echoed. But it might help every-one move on.

Like a yearbook will? Matt said.

It's the only thing we can do, besides pretending none of this happened.

Matt sighed. What are we doing?

What he wanted to say: Can we even do this?

We're putting together a record, Nick said. An archive. As fuck-ing impossible as that's going to be.

But why? Matt watched two oak trees sway beyond his window. Why would anyone want to remember this?

They won't. But they'll want to remember them.

Them. Everyone scattered like confetti across the industrial carpet of a high school. That there was a them, that something awful bound a random group together and without their consent, something a boy in their school had made happen. A binding they would never know, recognize, see, understand. That Nick was comfortable assuming what everyone left behind would want. That a future was possible. That they would live with this. That there was no alternative but to be those left to know this.

Do you want me to read what you wrote? Nick asked.

No. I'll probably just end up throwing it away.

We'll need to start something soon. Beyond just listing names for profiles.

Overhead Matt heard heavy footsteps, a trail from the garage door through the kitchen to the living room.

My dad's home, Matt said. I should go.

I'll see you tonight.

Matt replaced the phone and bent his head to his hands. His brow hurt, an ache splitting the space between his eyes. His gaze fell on his dresser. The profile. Crumpled on the wood's surface. He stood and grabbed the notebook paper, folded it four times, and slid it into his back pocket.

His father sat in the armchair by the window upstairs. His mother on the couch, the book on the War on Terror closed.

The department let us out early, Matt's father told him.

For the funeral? Matt asked. Why is it so soon? Her parents. They're barely gone.

We couldn't find anything, his father said. We did the autopsies. There was nothing to find.

Matt looked at his mother, who was watching his father.

Tell me, Matt said to his father. You both know something.

Matt, his mother said.

No, I'm tired of this, he said. His voice rising. Do you know what I saw? Do you? Do you have any fucking idea?

Matt's father closed his eyes. We know, he said. His mouth a firm line.

You know? Matt looked from his father to his mother. What, you told him? Did you call him this afternoon? Tell him what I saw?

Believe me, his mother said. We just want you safe and okay.

By keeping things from me? By lying? Just tell me! Just tell me what you saw!

There was nothing, his father said. Let me tell you this: there was nothing at all. I sat in the lab all goddamn day and found absolutely nothing, no hint or clue, no suggestion of what the hell happened at that house. There weren't any autopsies. There was nothing left. Nothing left to examine or understand.

Matt felt something escape him. He didn't want to hear any more.

I'm not a fire investigator, his father said. But I know there's always something left, something to investigate. Something that helps us determine a cause. Son, there was nothing left. No bodies. Nothing but burn and ash.

Matt looked at his father. What does that mean?

It means there was no trace of Caroline's parents. I've never seen anything like it. We don't know what it means. All we know is where the fire originated.

His mother was weeping. It's just awful, she whispered.

I'm sorry, Matt said. To his mother, and to his father.

We're just trying to protect you, his father said. As best as we can.

Of all the things his father could have said, five words that crushed him. As best as we can. He understood in his father's voice that he meant more than what a police force could do, that his parents ripped themselves apart for not being in the hallways where they could have never known to be and for not knowing when he was a child to buy another house, in another district, for not being there at the men's bathroom door to turn him away, to not look upon a carpet that would disfigure him.

Where did the fire start? Matt asked.

In the bedroom. His father looked at him. In Jean and Arthur's bedroom.

Matt recalled what Zola said. Was it suicide? Could they have done it themselves?

Matt's father was quick. It's possible, he said. We still don't know what started it. We're looking at the electrical wiring of their entire house, to rule out the possibility that they did this themselves. As far as we can tell, the fire started where they were sleeping.

Matt didn't want to imagine them: the bodies of Caroline's parents, bowed by hurt. Bodies that wouldn't be at the funeral beside their daughter, only the empty shells of caskets. Bodies that had dis-appeared completely, leaving nothing but smoke and ash. Bodies curled into one another only nights ago in the softness of their sheets, sheets that would catch a flame and burn every last thing in their house to the ground.

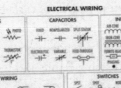

ELECTRICAL WIRING

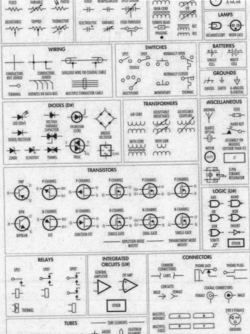

A BRIEF HISTORY OF FATAL FIRES

CARBON DIOXIDE AT 6 percent: headache, dizziness, drowsiness, illness, coma.

Carbon dioxide at 10 percent: breathing threatened.

Carbon dioxide: heavier than air. Forms pockets of lethal concentration.

Carbon monoxide: percentages at 0.01 cause no effect for four hours. At 0.04, no effect for one hour. 0.06: headache, fatigue, queasiness within one hour. Percentages at 0.1: life-threatening within one hour. Percentages at 0.35: death within one hour.

Oxygen levels below 14.6 percent: collapse and unconsciousness.

Oxygen levels below 6 percent: suffocation, death.

Investigation: victim. Establish physical background, mental state, emotional state prior to the fire. Determine cause and origin of the fire. Secure medical records. Obtain fire reports from chief officers, establish the condition of a found building. Leave the body in place, moved only in the possibility of further fire damage before a medical examiner arrives. Inspect for bruises, broken bones, any sign of struggle. Make maps, diagrams, sketches. Check the burn pattern around the body. Note a pugilistic position. Note a charring of the skin, indication of death at the time of fire. Note what remains.

Note split skin. Bone fractures emanating outward. Loss of tissue. Protruding tongue. Steam blisters. Soot inside the mouth and nostrils. Deep red to the skin. Indication of carbon dioxide in the bloodstream, lividity in colored patches as blood settles. Note particular damage to the head, indication of malicious intent. Note visible bite marks, cuts, claw marks, stab wounds, bullet wounds, defense wounds.

Cigarettes: the leading cause of fires in the home.

Bedding: the most common fuel source for home fires.

Night: the majority of fire deaths between 8 P.M. and 8 A.M.

Wrap the body in a cloth sheet. Preserve the clothing.

Remove any dentures, bridgework, false teeth.

Circulate the body before removal with the use of photos. Canvass the exterior fire scene for witnesses.

Preserve what surrounds the body.

Preserve all artifacts, everything saved.

WHAT TRAIL OF LIGHT
WE LEAVE BEHIND

PEWS. ORGAN HYMNAL. Two pillared candles guttering at an altar. A slant of light falling through the stained glass of chapel windows, the sun casting us in blocks of coral, turquoise, honey. We sat with our families. We sat apart. We watched so many faces we knew file in, the faces of our classmates alongside those of adults and children and elderly men and women we'd never seen, every resident of Midvale County who had known Caroline Black's family. We watched them take their seats. We averted our eyes to the pipes of an organ, to the wood graining of pews, to the lightbulbs of lanterns that dotted the rows of a congregation. We bowed our heads. We concentrated on our shoes, worn holes, scuffed spots upon our heels.

Zola sat with her mother at the edge of a back row, her hands folded in her lap. Large photos of Caroline and her parents stood on easels before three coffins. Zola watched her hands so she would not look at the gleam of cherrywood caskets, all three of them solid as fact at the altar. All three of them polished. All three of them closed. Her mother lined an arm along the pew's back and wrapped her fingers around Zola's shoulders, as if just looking at the caskets reminded her of how close she'd come to losing her daughter in the library, a violence of sound and grief that Zola still hadn't found words to speak out loud.

Nick sat with his parents, his brother, Sarah still at home, still unresponsive. He'd stopped by her house just before the funeral, had driven separately from his family just to see if she'd come. She'd opened the front door, her hair a mess, had shaken her head no. He knew she was hurting and afraid but even still, looking around the church, Nick couldn't believe she hadn't come. The church a cold hollow, Sarah nowhere inside of it, the summer's dense humidity long gone. How she'd been someone else entirely when they'd set off firecrackers in her backyard on the Fourth of July, the remnants still sitting in the trunk of his car outside the church. Black cats and smoke bombs, roman candles, sparklers Sarah had held at arm's length until they sputtered out. How he was the one then who'd needed guidance, Independence Day a holiday he'd never celebrated robustly, how she'd lit off fireworks with her family since she was small. How her slender fingers moved along his skin. How she tilted his hands to the sky. How he felt the timed release of roman candle detonations, quick balls of light, through the intervals of kickbacks radiating through his body. How he could have watched her confidence all night, her hands so close to the flame as trails of light spun out into the dark beyond her.

She was younger. She'd never known Caroline's mother or father, never known Caroline herself. But Nick had. He'd been Caroline's lab partner in seventh-grade biology, had dissected a worm and then a frog under the supervision of her care. Her fingers precise, her handling of a scalpel and pins far finer than his. How when they opened the frog's heart Nick turned away while Caroline forged ahead, her eyes upon the three chambers, the atria, the ventricle. Nick thought of the research he'd done, hours at his computer looking into fatal fires. How skin burned. What was left. What it was that Matt's father had investigated. He looked at the closed caskets and wondered what they could possibly contain and his brother fidgeted beside him and kicked the pew in front of them and Nick felt a hot flash of anger: Sarah at home, her refusal to carry a weight.

Christina crowded into a center pew with her mother, who'd

driven in from Edwardsville. Her father at home. Her brother pre-
served for funerals to come, for those lost in his freshman class.
Their mother: every other weekend, a settlement based solely upon
location. An admissions coordinator for Southern Illinois University, her mother had commuted to Edwardsville since Christina was
in second grade, and after the divorce had simply moved. Christina
had been twelve when they sat her down. Seventh grade. Braces
and acne, bad teeth, her bangs growing out. The start of the school
year, early September, still a hot, humid day. The living room couch
where Christina felt nothing but the faint pressure of her brother's
weight beside her as their parents told them they were divorcing,
the outside seam of his jeans scratching her thigh. Christina be-
grudged her mother nothing but even still she missed her proximity, an ache she regretted for its triviality in the church. As trivial as
hoping Ryan would call her, even still, long after she'd stormed out
the front door of his house. His leg propped up on pillows. Television droning. His lack of presence at every swim meet. His car
edging along beside her on the sidewalk. *Get in the car, you fucking bitch.* Christina lowered her eyes and they fell on a family of
five sitting quietly beside her mother, three children Christina had
never seen. All blond, a stairstep of ages, kids Christina imagined
attended the Blacks' same church or a volunteer organization. Aged
two, maybe three, up through seven or eight. They crowded into the
pew and the smallest stood on the wooden bench and Christina's
mother huddled closer to her and placed a palm on her leg.

Matt sat near the front with both of his parents and watched a
gathering of people file in and occupy the first rows, what he assumed were Caroline's aunts and uncles: the siblings and nephews
of Caroline's parents, cousins and family members who had pep-
pered their daughter's life. She had no siblings. He watched how
the church's light fell on the caskets. Rectangles. Empty boxes. Tyler
running through the hallway. Caroline's empty gaze. He wanted
to tell someone what his father had told him. He wanted to hear

himself speak it, that nothing was left, not a trace of hair or skin. He wondered how many people knew that two of the caskets were fully vacant. How only ten feet and the cherrywood finish of a box separated him from Caroline's body, a body he'd left upon the floor.

I'm sorry, he wanted to whisper.

He wanted to place his hands upon the wood.

He wanted to pull the scrawled profile from his back pocket where he'd left it stuffed all afternoon and throw it to the flame of the altar's candle, to watch it ignite and dissolve. His father shifted beside him. His mother sat still, her back straight against the pew. Matt thought of Tyler and how they still hadn't spoken, a thought that felt small inside the church's walls, a thought silenced by a minister stepping to the altar.

We heard the organ's hymnal diminish as she stood, the soft scramble of people taking their seats, a hush falling across the congregation.

Where to begin, the minister said. Where is there to begin, to offer words of comfort?

Zola looked above the minister to the light falling through the central stained-glass window. There was nowhere to begin. There was nothing to be said in the span of thirty minutes, forty-five, an hour. There was nothing in the world that a minister could claim, no word pulled from the ether to the grounding of a congregation, nothing proffered or extended or tendered that could change or reverse what was. Zola closed her eyes. Caroline's basement. The cold of a sweating can of Coke. My Little Ponies. Althea and Amy Robinson. A playgroup of four. The cool damp of a windowless cellar in the middle of a St. Louis summer, the heat bearing down upon the house's edges and all four of them inside, protected, safe.

Blessed are those who mourn, for they will be comforted.

The minister spoke words of solace. We listened to proverbs and prayers, a making of meaning from the sharing of nothing. Nothing but bowed heads, eyes gripped shut. The sound of quiet weeping. *The Lord is my shepherd, I shall not want,* but there was so much of everything that we wanted. The gasped air of breathing. A clock unwound. Custard stands and midnight movies. The burn of birthday candles. The flicker of a mouth upon ours, a first nearness. Clear blue swimming pool. Slick steam, humid sweat. A flatline of sun sinking into the Midwestern sky above a flutter of cornfields, tassels running for miles, our cars parked within them and the taste of watermelon Schnapps sugar-sweet on our lips. And a voice among ours: a damp palm extended on elementary school risers to help us sing. A trundle bed. A frog's aorta, the urgency of reading Margaret Atwood. A peer, a playmate. A study partner. A friend. The minister spoke and we heard none of her words but only the lost voice of a girl who'd been ours.

That the past was something. A noun. A thing that was.

A woman from the first row took the minister's place at the altar. Caroline's aunt. *The apple trees when we were young,* she whispered of her sister. *How you always climbed the highest.* Eulogy as memory, as valediction. A requiem impossible to hear. We listened until the woman's voice failed her, until her hands shook as they gripped the edge of the podium and a man came to the pulpit beside her, a man we assumed was her husband, who brought her back to the pews. The minister stood and extinguished the candles, a flame our chests ached to watch sputter out.

ZOLA STOOD WITH her mother in the churchyard until Christina emerged from the wooden double doors with her mother. Zola stepped forward and grabbed her hand, their mothers greeting one another in embrace, Christina's palm drained of heat and her face empty of any expression at all. A pale-marbled sky and the sun's afterglow already setting, speckled in tendrils across a wisp of autumn clouds. The trees burnt brown and eggplant, even in the faded light. Zola glanced at their mothers talking quietly, two parents who'd been closer when Christina's mother still lived in Midvale County.

Their daughters best friends since elementary school, a camaraderie Zola knew her mother had always valued and yet she wondered watching them what it was to be a parent, to make friends with the parents of your children's friends only to watch them disappear. By moving away. Zola glanced back at the church. By a home taking to flame. Matt emerged from the crowd and gathered Christina into a hug. Zola scanned the churchyard until she spotted Nick and his family across the entryway, his dress so formal, a suit two sizes too big. He looked like a child wearing his father's clothing and for a moment Zola understood their age, how young they were. Sixteen, seventeen. How old were they supposed to act? He walked over and took her hand as the sun disappeared and the coming night brought the cicadas' hum.

That sound, he said. Such a St. Louis sound.

A Midwestern sound, Zola knew. A sound that had marked every year of her memory. A wave of noise as August burned off into September, then louder still as autumn deepened into October. Zola looked cicadas up once, the summer when she was eleven and they had emerged in droves. They were everywhere. On the news, in the grass, clinging to the sapling branches of trees. She'd descended into the basement cool apart from the summer humidity already swelling into June and had looked them up on the computer, where she learned that they were periodical cicadas, buried underground for so many seasons, sometimes thirteen, sometimes seventeen. That the ones hugging every leaf of her yard upstairs and out the back door were a combination of thirteen- and seventeen-year broods, a concurrence that happened only once every two hundred years and had made St. Louis a spotlight of headline news. That these were separate from singular-season cicadas that came every year, nicknamed dog-day cicadas for their annual arrival in August. Zola had listened to their hum each summer, a drone stretched through the screens of her bedroom windows, a sound that summoned the coming of fall. She had learned at eleven that each year's brood of dog-day cicadas was first born underground, taking four years to grow and develop before emerging from the soil.

She felt Nick's hand on hers. The hum pressing down all around them. A sound waiting in the earth as they had entered junior high, as Caroline Black turned twelve.

They'll die off soon, Zola said. They're always gone by November.

I've always loved the sound, Nick said. His hand tightened around hers. A trail of lanterns led the way from the church entrance down a set of stone steps and Zola looked beyond them, to the quiet street, circles of pavement illumined by the glow of streetlamps.

I don't want to go home, she said. Not yet.

Home was an emptiness. A quiet bedroom. Home was the soft terror of her mother turning in for bed, a silent house and so many dark hours.

Then let's stay out, Nick said.

And do what?

Anything. We'll find something.

Zola pulled a sweater from her bag. The day warm, evening descending cold. A biting chill that carried an edge, a certainty that the droning sound around them would be gone in weeks. Nick's Honda waited at the curb. Zola's mother hugged her goodbye when Nick promised to drive her home safe, and Zola watched as Christina's mother looked after her daughter wistfully as Christina stepped into the backseat of Nick's car. Matt followed. A row of oaks swayed above the car in the faint light of the streetlamps, casting speckled shadows across the hood. Zola climbed into the front seat.

Where do you want to go? Nick asked.

Christina shrugged in the seat behind her. Beside Christina, Matt looked out the backseat window. Nick turned on the engine and navigated a labyrinth of streets, a planned neighborhood built in the 1960s. Houses with siding. Manicured lawns. Pumpkins and gourds beginning to appear on porches. Streets Zola had driven through so many times with Christina or Matt or Nick, a neighbor-

hood they'd cut through on their way to Christina's house for yearbook meetings after school. Zola knew who lived in every house
the car passed: Josh Weintraub, Caitlyn McMahon, Alexander
Antonov. The trees swayed above the street. The low static of the
radio billowed through the car, news talk of the Iraq Survey Group
that Nick switched for the quiet notes of a jazz trio on community radio. KDHX 88.1. A radio station they'd grown up with, an
independent stream that connected every home by filtered waves.
The car moved through winding streets and past houses, so many
lit squares of windows, so many families inside. And beyond the
homes lay the back roads: how easily Midvale County slipped into
cornfield. A once-haven for teenage drinking and stargazing, now
only a reprieve from the scrutiny of reporters and the hum of FBI
officials and police officers on every street. Back roads Zola knew
well enough, two-lane paths connecting farmhouses and intermittent mailboxes, where they'd come so many times to sip wine cool-
ers or escape their own homes. Back roads Zola assumed Christina
knew far better, cornfields concealing the backseat of Ryan's car.
How quickly a suburb gave way to the central plains, cultivated
land, and fields of crops. Dense forest edging the fields.

Zola felt the engine drone through her body as the Honda navigated the slope of the roads. She glanced back at Matt and wondered if he too knew the contours of these roads, Tyler beside him
in the passenger seat across the summer on darkened nights. Christina sat beside him, her head leaned back, her neck cupped by a
small headrest. The sky a wash of immobile black through the back
windshield behind her. A half-moon. Polaris. The arced slope of
the Big Dipper, every star Zola's mother pointed out on their back
porch though Zola never remembered, the slats of the deck's wood
cold beneath the socks of her feet. Pinpoints of stars Zola couldn't
believe were actually moving. She couldn't believe the earth turned
at all. That the wheels of Nick's car rolled across pavement, a softer
momentum than the earth's rotation, a velocity spinning away from

a library, the sound of screaming, the halls of an empty high school. How her mother could identify a pinwheel of constellations, every sign of the zodiac. How Zola looked to the sky and saw nothing but a scattering of isolated points. Nothing she could capture on a camera's film. She imagined her mother arriving home, a darkened house, her heels echoing through the front entryway. How she'd have driven past Alisha Trenway's house, the lights extinguished, Alisha's parents at their daughter's funeral.

Nick pulled the car off the back roads and onto a dirt path between cornfields, a flat landscape of dust marked by the tire marks of tractors. The radio fell away. In its place, the drone of crickets and wind and the singing of corn silk. Nick opened the driver's side door, for only moments illuminating the dome light, and then Zola found herself standing beside Matt and Christina beneath the black. Nick pulled at his suit jacket, the only fabric he had to block the cold. He keyed the latch of his trunk and swung it open and Zola saw a bag of fireworks amid jumper cables and discarded soda bottles and textbooks, alongside a bottle of whiskey. Kentucky bourbon. A bottle she knew he'd bought weeks ago with a fake ID, a handle he'd hoped they would share the night of Homecoming. He pulled the bag of fireworks from the trunk and dropped them to the dust and dirt beside the car. He opened the bottle and took a drink. Zola pulled the bottle from his grasp and tilted back her head and swallowed two shots' worth of bourbon, her face unchanged by the liquor's burn down her throat.

Zola knew Christina didn't drink anymore. Not since sometime last spring when she'd stopped all at once and never said why, a party Zola barely remembered leaving on her bike but knew Christina had left with Ryan, her face etched into the grimace Zola had come to recognize as a sign that they were fighting. When Nick passed the bottle to Christina, she angled it to her mouth. The first time Zola had seen her drink in months.

Nick opened the bag of fireworks slumped in the dirt. Sparklers.

Roman candles. A single lighter. He pulled the lighter from the bag and flicked the small metal wheel and a flame sparked up and guttered near his face. As if he held a flashlight, as if they were assembled for ghost stories. No campfire. No gathered sticks. No faint scent of firewood. Only the hum of cicadas lost to the night. An indifferent moon. A dove cooing in the far trees. The soft rustle of stalks and the sour aftertaste of bourbon, a bitterness Zola held in her mouth.

Fine night for fireworks, she whispered.

I've never shot off a roman candle, Christina said.

Tonight's your lucky night, Nick said. He leaned toward the bag, pulled out a roman candle, placed it in Christina's hands. Go for it, he said. Have a field day.

She looked at him. I don't know what to do.

Nick held the lighter. The crickets droned. In the distance, Zola heard the faraway murmur of the highway's hum. Nick placed his hands around Christina's hands, her fingers tight along the candle's cylinder. A ten-ball roman candle, markings snaked up the firework's tube. Zola leaned beside Matt against the car's trunk as Nick guided Christina's hands away from her body.

There'll be ten shots, he said. He rotated Christina's hands up, above the cornstalks. He lit the candle and Christina held it out and pulled her other hand across her eyes and the paper tube sparked and ignited, a small hiss and then a flame.

Zola watched the light shoot above them. Whirling spheres. How they spun away like small planets, a constellation of timed emissions. She saw Christina pull her hand away from her eyes and examine the light leaving a trail of smoke. Curled strands settling above her, a clouded haze dissipating across the sky. A popping that broke the silence of the stars. Zola counted down the flames, three bursts, then two, finally one. When the last rupture fired, Zola stood beside Matt in the wake of its stillness.

Nick stooped to the bag and grabbed a slender box. A box he held to the moon's light to read the packaging and unravel the plastic encasing. He pulled out a handful of sparklers and passed them around in a circle.

For Caroline, he whispered.

He flicked the lighter. He held the flame to the tip of each wand. Matt held his raised above his head. Christina and Nick followed. Zola extended her own until it touched theirs. She watched the slow burn down the length of each raised stick, cinders creeping toward the metal tips in their hands. She ignored their extinguishing. Watched instead how every sparkler burned against the dark. Caroline's parents. A funeral that convinced her it couldn't have been suicide. How Caroline's mother could have been her own, breath upon her hair, arms wrapped tight around her shoulders. Caroline's basement. Her childhood bedroom. A line of rectangled boxes. Zola closed her eyes and replaced it all with the elegy of a firework's burn, an afterimage that blazed behind her eyelids when her sparkler sizzled out.

The sharp scent of dissipated gunpowder. Charred smoke. Zola held her wand until Nick gathered each of them and threw the metal stalks into the cornfields. Christina grabbed the bottle of bourbon from the ground, its glass caked with dirt and dust, grit between her fingers Zola watched crumble and flake to the ground.

I should get home, Zola said.

Her mother was waiting. Her mother would pretend to sleep, her bedroom door half-closed, left just far enough ajar to know when Zola at last crept inside.

I should get home, too, Christina said.

The inside of the car felt stale, more brisk than the open ground of the back roads. Christina took the front seat. Matt shivered beside Zola in the backseat and she crossed her arms tight across her sweater. Beyond the car, Nick stood and watched the cornfields. *Click.* The first photo Zola would've taken if she had her camera, an archive to keep.

NICK DROPPED CHRISTINA off first, the light of her brother's window still illuminated in the uppermost corner of the house. Zola knew the floor plan of her house well, every room, wondered if she'd always know it well into adulthood and beyond. She watched Christina walk up the driveway, stumbling only once before she walked into the waiting mouth of her front door. Only two shots. Enough to stagger her steps if she hadn't had a drink since spring. Nick pulled away and turned the car toward Matt's house, Matt still in the backseat and neither of them climbing into the front.

You can just go to Zola's, Matt said. I'll walk home from there.

Nick drove them through quiet streets past so many illuminated lampposts, small lighthouses in every yard keeping watch over a spread of lawn. He turned on the radio, a soft buzzing. NewsTalk 1120: KMOX. That three more U.S. soldiers had been killed in Iraq during separate incidents. That the World Series would begin on Saturday, the New York Yankees hosting the Florida Marlins. Information Zola knew Nick cataloged, that he was listening to the radio with intention while she barely remembered that the Cardinals had finished third behind the Cubs and Astros, the National League Central the only division of baseball she ever cared to notice. The newscast switched to a brief spot on Columbus Day celebrations and protests across the nation before turning to St. Louis, to the promise of an in-depth look at Caleb Raynor after a brief commercial break. Nick turned off the radio, glanced briefly at both of them in the rearview mirror.

When Nick turned onto Zola's street, Alisha Trenway's house stood silent and dark on the corner and Zola imagined her family inside, awake in their beds, the impossibility of sleep beyond lowering their daughter into the ground. She thought of Alisha's father again, his cracked voice trembling across every raised candle at the vigil. Zola mouthed a small prayer for Alisha, only fourteen, only two years younger but still so unfathomably young. Nick pulled into Zola's driveway, the asphalt crackling beneath the car's tires, the lights in every window out though Zola knew her mother was still awake.

Nick shifted the car into park. Matt reached up and squeezed Nick's shoulder.

You both should know, he said. My father said they didn't find anything.

At Caroline's house? Nick said. You mean a cause for the fire?

I mean they found nothing. There was nothing left. No bodies. Nothing to indicate what the hell even happened.

Zola felt the engine idle. Felt lost. Whatever they were talking about, a continuation of some conversation she hadn't heard.

That's impossible, Nick said. Fires always leave behind evidence. I looked it up today. Something always remains. That doesn't make any sense at all.

Does any of this? Zola heard herself say. A wave of exhaustion, her house so close.

There has to be something left behind, Nick said. Some indication of cause.

They're working on it, Matt said. That's all my dad said.

Thanks for the fireworks, Zola interrupted, and pushed open the back door. She didn't want to hear any more. She only wanted her bed. Matt hesitated inside the car, then climbed out behind her. They stood in the driveway until Nick's taillights faded down the street.

Look, I'm sorry, Matt said. I know we shouldn't be talking about that tonight.

Zola looked at him. Sure you want to walk? It's at least a mile. You can borrow my bike.

Zol, he said.

She waited for him to speak. She watched him just long enough to see his eyes shimmering in her house's porch light.

Inside the school, he whispered. Please. I need to know what you saw.

It doesn't matter. It won't change anything for you to know.

Please. I can't stop seeing what I saw. I can't push away the image.

Zola watched the dim pulsing of stars, constellations her mother would have known. She knew what Matt was asking. Something mutual. An unburdening to share a burden. But she didn't want to tell him what she'd seen, didn't want to hear it become words beyond her mouth. She'd seen crumpled figures, broken bones ripped through the thin membrane of skin. She'd seen thick stains of blood too heavy to sink into carpet. She'd seen blasted-open wounds, the inert slumping of peers who'd sat beside her at the study hall table only minutes before. She'd smelled the blood's metal and the stench of spilled shit, the residue of gunpowder and fire and the gamey scent of her own urine. She'd seen the overturned chairs and splintered tables, the prostrate shape of Mrs. Diffenbaum, her paisley dress bunched and soaked around her waist. She'd seen only seconds, a brief moment before the police officer pulled her away from the library and out the window.

She grasped Matt's hand. There was nothing else she could do. She felt the rough texture of creased paper in his palm.

I wrote about her, Matt said. A profile. I couldn't sleep last night.

A folded piece of notebook paper in his hand. Something Zola knew he'd carried with him all night. She held it to the streetlamp's light. Its edges worn, its graining damp. Whatever it was, Matt had kept it close through the duration of the funeral.

I want you to read this, Matt said. I want someone to know I saw her.

Zola didn't want to take it. She looked at Matt. To give it back would be to give him away forever. She pulled the piece of paper from his palm and slid it into her jacket.

I didn't want to start it, Matt said. The yearbook. But I had to do something.

Are you sure you don't want to take my bike?

Matt glanced up the street. I really just need to walk.

Zola stood behind him and leaned her forehead against his back, reached her arm over his shoulder, and rested her hand against his chest.

You're okay, she whispered. All of us. We are okay.

Matt said nothing and Zola felt his heart beating beneath her palm. He held on to her wrist for a moment above the fabric of his dress shirt and breastbone. Then he let go and Zola stood in her driveway and watched him walk up the street until he disappeared, lost to the trees. She stood in the October air, the neighborhood silent, the half-moon high above the street's maples and roofs.

Inside the house, she stripped off her clothes. She let them puddle to her bedroom floor. She starfished herself upon her bed covers and listened to her breath pulse and watched the rise and fall of her own skin as it moved with her lungs. I am here, she wanted to whisper. I am here, I am here. The house billowed silence back to her, only the refrigerator's hum, a sound that traveled up the stairs to her bedroom.

Zola pushed herself from the bed. She pulled the piece of paper from her jacket pocket and curled against the wall by her window. Her Pentax camera lay nearby on the carpet, peeking out from beneath her bed. She had no desire to take photos. No desire to capture anything beyond cornfields, a night already lost to her camera. She unfurled the creased paper and began to read the words Matt had written. *Caroline Black, a junior at Lewis and Clark, was a magnetic force in the hallways of our school.* Zola looked away from Matt's handwriting, a scrawl written in haste. His question one she couldn't answer, one she couldn't let herself think about at all. She huddled into the wall and closed her eyes and pulled her knees tight into her body.

She awoke to a blanket draped over her, a fuzzed softness, and to her mother shaking her shoulders. She awoke to sirens. The growing whine of an emergency approaching. *Zol, get up,* her mother was saying. *Come on, get up now.*

And then they were on the lawn. The blanket wrapped around her shoulders. Her feet still bare. Cold grass between her toes. Her mother standing at the edge of the yard while Zola stayed back by the front door. Her mother watching as a police car and an ambulance whistled past on the street, a street lined with neighbors emerging from their homes and staring bleary-eyed toward what Zola could see from where she stood, her mother looking back at her, her face immobile in panic: the corner of their street. Alisha Trenway's home. Flames rising into the night and ribboning the darkness to shreds.

ARSON?

Second House Fire Kills Parents of Slain Teen

TUESDAY, OCTOBER 14, 2003

ST. LOUIS, MO—Two more lives have been claimed in the second house fire following last week's shooting at Lewis and Clark High School, an incident that police are now investigating for the possibility of arson linking the two homes. Late Monday night, after Lewis and Clark freshman Alisha Trenway, 14, was laid to rest at Stone Hill Cemetery in St. Louis County, a house fire at her residence in the 4500 block of Quail Run Court in Midvale County claimed the lives of her parents, Jonathan Trenway, 44, and Robin Trenway, 45. Firefighters responded at 4:57 a.m. Tuesday morning to the full heat of flames surrounding the ranch home. The fire was extinguished at 6:26 a.m. The deaths of Jonathan and Robin Trenway were confirmed in the wreckage, along with a miniature schnauzer that neighbors have verified was the family's pet dog. Due to the close proximity of the house fire that claimed the lives of Jean and Arthur Black late Saturday night, police officials are investigating links between the cases and the suspicion of arson.

"I just came from Alisha's service," said Donna Brown, a next-door neighbor who stood down the street as fire officials fought the flames. "They were such an amazing family. I can't imagine anyone wanting to do them harm."

Firefighters and police officials will comb the debris over the coming days in search of clues and indication of suspects. The effects of Caleb Raynor, the gunman in last week's Lewis and Clark

High School shooting, remain under investigation despite Raynor's death by self-inflicted wound. His home was searched early this morning for indication of an accomplice and another Lewis and Clark student, Eric Greeley, 16, has been brought into the Midvale County police department for questioning.

"We can't imagine who could possibly do something like this," said Darrell Heddick, a neighbor of the Trenway family. "At any time, anywhere, but especially after what's happened in our community."

A BRIEF HISTORY OF FIRE
INVESTIGATION TERMS

Q: What is a fire point?
A: The temperature at which a substance will burn for at least five seconds beyond ignition by an open flame.

Q: What is a flash point?
A: The point a few degrees below the fire point, wherein ignitable vapors are present.

Q: What is heat?
A: The release of energy when a substance changes from a higher to a lower state.

Q: What is combustion?
A: A rapid oxidation accompanied by heat and light.

Q: What is a catalyst?
A: A substance that affects combustion but itself remains unchanged.

Q: What is specific gravity?
A: The weight of a material in reference to the weight of water.

Q: What is vapor density?
A: The weight of a material in reference to the weight of air.

Q: What is sublime?
A: When a substance has a flash point in a solid state and changes from a solid to a vapor, or gas, at an ordinary temperature.

Q: What is a true emergency?
A: A time in which a single person's actions affect all involved.

Q: What are the three stages of fire?
A: Smoldering at first, then free burning, then smoldering again, much like grief.

THE WORLD AS IT IS

WE REMEMBER THE headlines that morning. Capitalized font. Every letter screaming arson. We remember the speculations that filled the *St. Louis Post-Dispatch,* pages that have yellowed in our basements and storage bins across the years, pages we still scan sometimes as if the past were a concrete object to transpose and set right. We remember how the igniting of the Trenways' home eradicated every shred of coincidence, how the flames that stretched high into the speckled halo over Midvale County let us know at last that nothing was random, that there was fault in this, that we could point beyond ourselves and identify a reason. We remember a ratcheted frenzy of media, a shattering of numb grief: how with the taking away of so many students and teachers and now four parents of two lost children our town began to suspect an arsonist, someone carrying out a schematic we couldn't understand or know, someone with potential ties to Caleb Raynor and a plan he was unable to enact alone.

Caleb Raynor: a mystery. No trail of bread crumbs left behind him.

Caleb Raynor's family: his mother and father and younger brother pleading only privacy and solace. Their home searched floor to ceiling regardless, investigated for any hint of accelerants or explosives.

And Eric Greeley: taken into custody. Brought in again for questioning, Caleb Raynor's only known collaborator despite Eric's protests that they'd grown apart, that they hadn't spoken for months and that Eric only wanted to be left alone.

The Blacks. The Trenways. Two incidents that in their succession and similarity signified a crime we could latch on to and solve. Two incidents: a pattern. A devastation with cause. A mystery to be seized upon and unraveled, a tangibility with reason and motive. This was an opportunist, the news channels blared: local newscasts of KSDK and KDNL up to national broadcasts of CNN and MSNBC that had been circling around St. Louis for almost a week, now-constant coverage spouting accusations that someone in Midvale County preyed upon tragedy and the shared burden of our sorrow. News anchors in St. Louis and across the country speculated an accomplice with links to Caleb Raynor, some culprit skulking unseen through the ravages of our town.

And among the speculations, anger: erupted from the germ of sorrow. At the audacity of two blazes, linked by proximity and by pattern and target, and by the unashamed disregard for a period of tenuous mourning. How there were so many funerals. How they had just began. How there was nothing more we could muster in hollowing ourselves out. A rage broke out in the newspaper and on television: that someone could take away so many children and that someone else could take away again, targeting the same community and the same families in a disaster of flames.

Zola saw it in her mother's face at the edge of the front yard, where she stood as the fire stretched above the Trenways' house. Her jaw taut, her teeth clenched. The realization of a lack of coincidence. That someone caused this. That whoever it was had been here. Someone sliding down the street with a match, with a can of gasoline, a torch, an explosive. Someone who'd passed so close to her own house, her daughter inside. Someone who'd stood before the Trenways' home in the darkest tilt of a half-moon and had regarded it with purpose, had slipped inside, had lit everything on fire.

Zola walked to the edge of the lawn. She stood with her mother,

their neighbors nearby in their own orbits of grass. She saw the
fire trucks shuttle down the street, the ambulances and police cars
and news vans, a Doppler effect bending out of tune. She heard
the spray of hoses, the hiss of water. She watched the smoke rise
in sheets above the tree line as the flames diminished and the sun
slowly rose, a muted circle of light through an early haze of fog and
smoke. Her mother sat beside her on the front porch, both of her
arms around Zola's shoulders. The flames slowly went out. Their
neighbors moved between their lawns and their homes, stares fixed
down the street, eyes shadowed with lack of sleep. The newspaper
came regardless, a white van snaking as far as it could down the
street before reaching a blockade of police tape, small tubes shooting from the van's window and landing with soft weight on every
square of grass. Zola grabbed the newspaper from the front yard, a
plastic-wrapped cylinder wet with dew. On the living room couch
she unfurled the paper and stared at the headline. *ARSON.* Zola still
in her pajamas, the phantom burn of cinders still pulsing against
her cheeks. Her mother sat in the armchair beside her and turned
on the television, toggling between local newscasts and the national
reports. A culprit. Some specter that had followed Zola and her
classmates from the hallways of Lewis and Clark and spilled out
the library windows, onto the streets, into their neighborhoods and
their homes. Zola glanced out the window. She thought of what
Matt had said only hours before about the Blacks. That nothing
was left. She set the newspaper on the carpet and curled herself
tightly into the cushions of the couch, the bolded headline blaring
up at her.

Christina didn't see the headline until long after she woke, the
sun already high and intermittent behind clouds. Her father was
at work, her brother in the living room, where the sound of video
games thundered. She heard only the occasional rumbling of weapons, a combat game centered on zombies. Ryan hadn't called. She
turned the dial of her stereo louder, the same album playing in

Ryan's parked car when she lost her virginity that summer. The mini-golf course closed down for the night where they'd played eighteen holes through rotating windmills and across small ponds. His car the only one left, hidden beside a row of trees far from the parking lot's floodlights that drew curtains of fluttering moths and mosquitoes. The windows up, the stereo billowing softly through the car. The weight of his body as it pushed into her. A flash and a pain and a flood of sweat and salt, songs that scissored her to hear now in her bedroom but allowed her escape from the hallways, from the school and Henry Park's gaze and the sound and scent of detonated gunpowder. Christina heard the sudden silence of the console down the hallway. The static drone of the television flipped on, followed by the murmuring of talking pundits. She heard the padding of her brother's footsteps running over carpet toward her bedroom, the gasping of his breath telling her to come quickly, his face already lined with fear.

Nick learned the news on Sarah's doorstep. He hadn't bothered to look at the *Post-Dispatch* that morning. A cup of orange juice instead. A Toaster Strudel. His brother had read a comic book beside him at the kitchen table, his parents at work, the telephone off the hook until after breakfast, when he knew his parents might call, when they might begin to worry and check in. He'd researched fire investigation upon returning from the funeral after what Matt had told him, that there was nothing left. He'd fallen into a heavy sleep and hadn't woken until the sun pushed through his window blinds, a day already begun, a day he promised he would spend away from the computer. A day without research, though he yearned to dig deeper into what Matt had told him. A day to go to Sarah's house rather than read the news, to take her from the murk of her bedroom. Sarah's mother opened the door. She looked at Nick and before he could ask he saw the newscast behind her on the living room television, a headline and the burnt remains of a house. He stepped into Sarah's bedroom. She lay on her side beneath the sheets, her back to the door. He pushed off his shoes. He climbed under the covers in his jeans and sweatshirt. He coiled his body against hers and wrapped his arms around her shoulders and did not think of Caroline's funeral, that Sarah had let him go alone.

Matt awoke in his basement to the howl of the telephone and a disorienting lack of light. In the dark he remembered Caroline's profile, what he'd carried around in his pocket all night before giving it to Zola. He wondered if she'd read it after he'd walked home from her house, the heavy sky pressing its weight down upon him. He'd walked straight up the street's spine, no one out but the faint blinking of lampposts. He'd let the sound of his shoes striking the pavement guide him home and had fallen immediately into bed. He slept heavily, a sleep without dreams, a waking that left him confused by the thick weight of the darkness around him. The phone blared on and he heard the tread of footsteps above him. He couldn't believe he'd been able to sleep. The ringing stopped and then there was only the lack the ringing had left, and then Matt heard his father shout *God fucking damn it,* his voice permeating the floorboards.

Matt was afraid to move. The quiet following his father's voice: total and absolute. He pulled on a T-shirt and climbed the stairs and stood at the edge of the kitchen, where his father sat at the table in boxers, his head in his hands.

Dad?

His father only looked up and Matt knew. He knew his father was holding on to a moment, a silent beat in the kitchen before getting up, before pulling on his uniform and driving to the station, before facing something Matt already knew would be awful.

Dad, what is it?

His father rubbed a hand against the stubble of his chin. Matt heard his mother's footsteps approaching from the hallway. She turned on the kitchen light and blinked through the harsh fluorescence at both of them.

Jon and Robin Trenway, he told her. House fire.

Matt and his mother knew the list of names. They knew Alisha's
funeral was the night before, a listing in the *Post-Dispatch*. They
knew her father from the vigil, his voice soft and trembling across
the crowd. They knew where the Trenways lived, down the street
from Zola and her mother. Matt knew he'd walked past their house
just hours before, on his way home through the moonlit fog of an
empty night.

I have to go. Matt's father stood. He slipped down the hallway
toward the bedroom closet where his uniform waited, leaving Matt
and his mother standing in the stark light of the kitchen.

We were not angry like our parents, our community, the news
outlets of our city and nation. We lay in bed and on couches and
sprawled upon the carpet before televisions. We read the entire
newspaper. Ongoing coverage of our high school. Speculations of
criminal intent. Things we knew and would never know, a drowning out of other news. Catholic Church allegations, sexual miscon-
duct of priests. Continued coverage of the war. The Iraqi Governing
Council. Debates of gun laws and foreign policy and military spend-
ing. We sat through an entire day of taking in or else blocking out
the world, a day of silence and inertia and the intermittent racing
of sirens beyond our living room windows. We peeled oranges. We
drank coffee and black tea. We tried to read books. We read the
same paragraphs over and over again. We looked back over our
freshman and sophomore yearbooks. Photographs of everyone we'd
lost. We couldn't stop ourselves from wondering what connected
Caroline Black's home and Alisha Trenway's house beyond the obvious, what made each fire an accident or arson. We waited for our
parents. We waited for news, for any answer beyond speculation.
But past dark, past the shouting matches on every news broadcast for gun control and heightened school security and increased
police presence on our streets, we sank quietly into our sheets and
watched the sky beyond our bedroom windows and thought only

of Alisha Trenway, her parents, the charred skeleton of their house. We watched the empty ceiling above us and felt our chests cramp, the clenched fist of a muscle tightening.

NICK LAY WITH Sarah in her bedroom until he felt her fall asleep by the rhythm of her breathing. The news nothing but further reason for her to stay inside. She'd barely spoken all morning but had run her hands over his face again and again until she fell asleep, as if reminding herself that he'd made it out of the high school safe. He'd said nothing of Caroline Black's funeral. That he'd wished she were there. He slipped out of her bedroom toward lunchtime and out the front door with her mother's wish to be safe and drive carefully. He navigated the car through Midvale's streets, around the traffic of so many news vans. Above the whir of the car, the radio off, he heard the chopped sound of a helicopter circling above. An aerial view, he knew, of the damage to the Trenways' house only miles away. He imagined the house swarmed by police. He wondered if Matt's dad was among them. He assumed Zola was at home only houses away.

Nick drove without aim and wondered what Matt and Zola stored in their brains. Flashbulb memories. Their response to fear. A means of preserving aversion to danger, an animal instinct to remember harm and recoil. Caleb passing beyond the classroom windows: all the memory Nick needed for a lifetime. He couldn't quiet the image, couldn't keep himself from staying awake and seeing it on his ceiling. He had nowhere to be. He felt himself turn the car toward Lewis and Clark High School.

He hadn't passed by it again throughout the past week. He'd averted his route, the high school only a half mile from Sarah's house. He let himself drive toward it. He imagined a bird's-eye view of Midvale County: three crime scenes. Police still puzzling through the debris of Caroline Black's house. A new squad flooding the Trenway house at the corner of Zola's street. And the school, surely crawling with cops despite the news turning toward two homes on fire. He was to research for yearbook, what he'd done in past years: inclusion of current events, world news. He was at a loss. They were the current event. Their entire town the world news. He rounded the bend and Lewis and Clark High came into view past Sarah's neighborhood and Nick saw a congregation of vans parked in the lot. Midvale County Police Department crime units and police cars and vans branded by the telltale letters of FBI, an entire team of officials filing through the halls and retracing a path and cleaning up what Nick couldn't imagine lay beyond the school's brick walls.

He pulled over to the curb. The engine idled. He watched two police officers in plastic gloves duck beneath yellow crime tape and enter the school. Nick closed his eyes: a hooded figure passing beyond a window carrying a gun. Animal instinct. How the body held on to fear. How humans weren't alone, a unit he remembered on animal memory in sophomore year biology. How the octopus brain held half a billion neurons, more closely linked to humans than to the cuttlefish and snails that shared its DNA. How under pressure the octopus could transform its short-term memory to long-term recall, a response similar to human fear. How through an entire winter certain birds could recollect the specific location of up to thirty thousand buried nuts for survival. How chimpanzees memorized numbers. How captive elephants remembered one another after thirty years of separation. How wild elephants recalled water sources and knew where to dowse down into the earth. How elephants grieved as well, what hadn't been in the classroom lesson, what Nick had looked up later on his own computer. How they shed real tears. How they buried their dead. Nick watched the high school beyond the car's windows and tried to imagine so many bodies be carried away from inside its doors.

The newspaper's list of funerals: Nick knew Principal Jeffries's service would be tomorrow and that they all would go. He imagined Matt's father somewhere inside the Trenway house or at the police station in his forensics lab, poring over what little remained.

What Matt had told him: nothing left. No bodies. Only ash. He shifted the car into drive and knew he didn't want to go home. Just blank ceilings and walls. No evidence. No outline of a body chalked upon a bed, outlines he knew filled the classrooms and hallways of the high school less than a hundred yards beyond his windshield.

MATT WAITED ON the front porch all morning for his father, unsure when it was that he'd return. Matt would work that afternoon, a short shift. Something to get him back in the theater and out of the house. He'd read the newspaper already, a curled tube that had been thrown to their lawn just moments after his father's Impala pulled out of the driveway. He drank his coffee black. He read every article, every editorial on gun control and school security, and then a sports feature for diversion on the St. Louis Rams' 36–0 win the night before against the Atlanta Falcons, a *Monday Night Football* game he wondered if anyone in the city had watched. He lingered over the front page. The expansive font. A question of arson he couldn't answer. His mother had watched the news in the other room, a steady stream of commentary and vague reporting that billowed into the kitchen, on-scene coverage from the Trenways' house.

He pulled on an old St. Louis Cardinals sweatshirt and sat on the front porch and watched the light shift, the sun crawling up the sky amid puffs of thick clouds. The television's hum drifted through the front door's screen, a white noise that diminished and eventually stopped. He heard footsteps approaching. The screen door banged open and his mother joined him, the sun leaving them cold when it dipped behind clouds.

When will he be back? Matt asked.

With something like this, I don't know.

A crisp breeze scattered leaves from the trees to the front lawn, a sound like dry paper. Matt wondered what his mother's daily life was, here at the house, what it had been for her to not work through the entirety of his childhood and to wait every day for his father to come home. Matt knew his father's schedule, knew he so often went in early so he could be home by the time Matt returned from school. A family man. The kind of man Matt thought would embrace and support his son coming out. The kind of man who wouldn't walk down a hallway and close a door. How his father had never apologized but had only softened his temper in the past two years. How his father wanted to be home, to be nearby. How Matt had let his actions speak for words.

What has he told you? Matt asked.

Everything he's told you. I wish I had answers, honey. No one knows what the hell is going on.

Matt looked at his mother. She rarely swore. She let him spew as many *fucks* and *Jesus Christs* and *goddamnits* as he needed but she almost always kept her calm. The only other time she'd broken her poise and let her guard down: when he'd heard his parents arguing upstairs after he'd told them and he could hear nothing of their words except his mother's voice ringing through the floorboards, *What the hell kind of parent are you.*

I can't imagine it, she said. Their daughter, now this. Matt felt his mother's hand on his shoulder. I hope you're all right, Matt. I hope you'd tell us if you weren't.

You shouldn't worry.

We'd take you to see someone, if it would help.

Matt knew what was coming. As soon as he returned to whatever school wasn't really their school, a horde of grief counselors would descend upon everyone he knew, every friend and classmate, a line of quickly hired psychologists who'd be available if anyone needed to talk. If anyone needed to chat. Discuss. Ruminate. Feel their feelings.

Thanks, he said. But I'm doing okay.

You say the word and we'll help, his mother said.

The sun filtered through the tree line, spilling fractals of light across the porch, and Matt felt broken. That his parents loved him. That they would do whatever it took.

He pressed his fingers to his forehead. I could use some aspirin. It's on the grocery list. I haven't had the chance to go this week. He stood. I can go grab some. At the store. Anything else you need.

Matt's mother watched him rise. Maybe you should stay here, she said. Just rest. I'll go. Maybe what you need is to just sit awhile.

Matt didn't want to stay. He didn't want to sit on the front porch with nothing but the singing of chickadees and the passing of cars and an oppressive stream of cold early light. But her face was earnest. She wanted to do this for him if she could do nothing else.

I'll pick you up some mellowcremes. The candy pumpkins. I won't be gone long.

Matt watched her pull out of the driveway. He imagined his father at work and could only make assumptions: that his father was hunched over a desk in a lab that was too bright, fluorescent bulbs bearing down on so many photographs and reports scattered across a steel table's surface. The Black report would be reexamined. It would have to be. To know what linked them: another incident, an identical house fire.

Matt didn't have long. He grabbed his coffee mug and went inside. His mother would be back in a half hour, forty-five minutes at most. He dropped the mug in the dishwater and moved down the hallway to the bathroom, a medicine cabinet hiding a pouch of bobby pins. He pulled the mirror open before he could look at himself. He took a cosmetic bag from the middle shelf and drew a single bobby pin, the only one he would need. He made his way to his father's office. To the single locked drawer inside his desk. Matt let his mind fall blank as he bent the bobby pin and broke it in half. He jiggled the two halves together until he felt the lock release. He closed his eyes. He let go of the pins. He pulled open the drawer.

Inside the drawer was every document he expected.

An incident report from October 12, 2003. 3:54 A.M. Police response, fire engines. Dozens of photographs of the Blacks' house, of the carcasses of armchairs, tables, entire rooms. Photographs of what he assumed was the master bedroom, the bed frame and the mattress scorched. No remains. Nothing at all. Only the faintest outline of two figures. Two autopsy reports from the medical examiner's office, filled out even though they'd found nothing. Both reports cleared, eradicated of foul play, indicating only where the bodies might have lain by imprints in the mattress. Both reports including a diagram of the human body regardless, figures Matt pored over like the drawings of a textbook.

He picked up accompanying photographs, his fingers gliding across everything in the house that had burned. All of them photocopies. So many scans. He knew his father never risked losing originals, that everything he brought home was a facsimile of something else. Matt held them as if they were the objects themselves, as if his hands would streak with ash when he pulled them away. He drew the images close. Squinted his eyes. Made out the shapes of what were once countertops, a coffeemaker, so many broken windows. Matt sat in the desk's swivel chair and leaned back. He didn't know how to read them. How to glean from the documents an answer, something Nick would have been far better at deciphering. He saw only *no foul play* and *clean,* nothing his father hadn't already told him. The only thing he gained was another afterimage, silhouettes in the padding of a mattress, two more bodies he wouldn't forget.

Eric Greeley back in policy custody for questioning. Matt wondered if his father would see him at the station and what connection there could possibly be. Caleb's plan inconceivable and another plot beyond it, past the realm of plausibility. Far more possible: suicide, what Zola had suggested only in a whisper. Alisha Trenway's funeral just hours before her house burned, a home as quiet as any other when he'd passed down so many empty streets. Matt looked at the documents spread out before him. Wondered what he could possibly ask his father about them, files he was never meant to see. And his father, a man Matt felt he could ask anything though there was still a thin wall, a lack of apology, a storming down the hall.

Matt knew how to pick a lock but not how to refasten one. His father would come home and sit down at the desk and pull out his key, a key hidden in some place Matt had never found, a key that would open nothing, the lock already released. Matt scanned his brain. An excuse. He felt tired. There was no lie to tell. He leaned farther back in the chair, the leather creaking beneath his weight, and stayed until he heard his mother's keys in the back door then the rustle of plastic grocery bags in the kitchen.

I'm home, she called. A loud thump. The bags on the counter.

He wanted to help her but the chair held him. He wanted to say he was sorry. He wanted to gather the documents from the desk and slide them into the drawer.

She found him still seated at the desk, a plastic carton of pumpkin spice creamer in her hands. She met his gaze. Her eyes moved down and she saw the photocopies on the desk and her smile faded.

What's this?

Matt looked away.

I bought you some coffee creamer, she said. Her eyes on the desk. She lowered her hands. Turned away down the hall and he followed.

She busied herself with putting away groceries. Halloween cake mix. A jar of sprinkles he could see from the doorway of the kitchen. Mellowcremes and Sour Patch Kids. Coca-Cola. She pulled the aspirin from the last bag and slid it across the counter.

Mom, I'm sorry.

Don't tell me. Tell it to your father. Tell him when he comes home.

I needed to know. I needed to know something.

And did you find it? Her eyes flashed at him. Did you find whatever the hell it was you were looking for?

Mom. He cupped the bottle of aspirin in his hands.

We are trying so hard, she said. The world like this. We are trying so hard to protect you.

A world like this: Matt looked past her to the kitchen window, light streaming through the panes. October sun. A world like this: pumpkin patches. Haunted hayrides. Ghost walks and apple cider and the scent of firewood, what autumn in Midvale had always been, what a world like this could have meant. Matt saw it in his mother's face, in the grimace of her rage burned down to sorrow. That her anger was for him. For him, always. That the world wasn't what she'd wanted to give him. That she could come home to photographs and reports inside her own home, that she couldn't keep the world beyond its walls.

I'll put them away, he said. I'll put them back and you'll never see them.

I already saw them, she said. I already saw them and so did you.

There was nothing left to say. He moved into the kitchen. He stood next to her and felt the tremble of her shoulders trying to shut it all in, to not break down, to hold away the world though he knew there was nothing either of them could do to keep it out.

MATT WORKED THE afternoon concessions at Midvale Cinemas, his mother silent on the couch when he left. The War on Terror book in her hands. He didn't want to leave her but knew he had to leave the house. Some sense of normalcy, work an easy return, no films needing construction until Thursday night. People filed in, the crowd light. The scent of popcorn and burnt butter overwhelmed the theater lobby. *Intolerable Cruelty. Kill Bill Vol. I.* A Tarantino movie he'd wanted to see, a movie he should have built last Thursday night. He stood sipping a large Mountain Dew to keep himself awake when Nick entered the lobby doors and made his way toward the concession stand.

One student for *School of Rock*?

I'm not here for the movies, Nick said.

Matt glanced toward the back, his manager out of sight. He scooped ice into a paper cup and handed Nick a free Dr Pepper.

I can't believe this news, Nick said.

I know. I'm trying not to think about it.

Is your dad there? Nick asked. At the Trenways' house?

I don't know. He left the house early this morning.

Has he told you anything else?

Not really. He was up when I got home last night. He only said they were looking at the electrical wiring of the Blacks' house.

The paper said Eric Greeley is back in for questioning.

I saw that. My dad didn't say anything about it this morning.

It seems weird. I know Eric knew him. But Eric never seemed like a bad guy.

A customer approached, a middle-aged man in glasses and a thin sweater, and Nick stepped to the side for Matt to take his order, a large soda and buttered popcorn. The man walked across the lobby and toward the ticket taker and Nick slid back to the glass counter, his soda cup already perspiring in his hands.

I was at Sarah's this morning.

How's she doing?

Not great. She didn't see anything, but she's not great.

Is anyone? I'm only here because I can't stay at home anymore. It's too much time. Too much news.

I know. I had to get out, too. I've just been driving around. I figured you'd be here.

I'll be here on Thursday, too, Matt said. Two shifts this week.

He recalled all the times Nick had come to the theater late on Thursdays while he built the weekend's new releases, Matt still in his work uniform and Nick sometimes in sweatpants, Matt offering him the day's stale popcorn or a forgotten bag of Twizzlers as they watched the weekend's films together inside the dark of the projection booth.

You want to see something? Matt said. Free ticket. On me.

Nick hesitated. I drove past the school.

Matt felt his face change. Just now?

It was filled with police.

I don't know anything about that. I only know what my dad said. That they're working to retrace Caleb's path.

Do you know why? It seems irrelevant now.

Matt felt tired. A morning's frenzy to seek and find, long gone. The need to know drained away amid the hum of soda machines and a popcorn maker. A return to normalcy. One broken up by Nick's insistence on talking about the school and two fires.

I don't know why, Matt said. Look, I should get back to work.

Matt, I'm sorry. But I couldn't help it. I had to drive by the school.

Why?

Because I have questions. Don't you?

Matt said nothing, his palms pressed flat on the counter.

Why those houses? Why those specific families? It just doesn't make sense. And also that there's nothing left. No bodies. That seems impossible.

My dad thought it was weird, too. But what do you want me to say?

I don't want you to say anything. Really. I just hope you're doing okay.

Matt made himself smile. Thanks for coming by.

I should get home. Thanks for the soda. Let me know if your dad tells you anything when he gets home.

Matt watched Nick leave the theater, through the double doors and into the afternoon light. It pained him to be rude but he felt exhausted, far beyond a lack of sleep. He watched people walk in, most of them alone. A few faces he thought he recognized from school, teenagers in other years, a few young parents taking their children to see *Seabiscuit,* a holdover from summer. Nick driving

past the school: what Matt had deliberately avoided. He imagined
the office at home. His father would be home soon.

A man entered the theater lobby that Matt recognized: Alexis
Thurber's dad.

He was relatively young, in his mid-thirties, a man Matt recalled
from when fathers had visited their second-grade classroom at Des
Peres Elementary for Take Your Dad to Class Day. Matt didn't
remember all of the fathers. He remembered that his own father
hadn't come, one of many investigations he couldn't put on hold.
But he remembered Mr. Thurber, a man who at the time must
have been in his mid-twenties. Matt remembered that he worked
as an independent electrician, that he set his own hours, that Alexis
beamed from the desk beside Matt's when her father stood before
the room and explained what he did.

Matt watched him cross the lobby, move straight to the theaters.
No soda, no popcorn. Matt tried not to notice the sunken circles
that rimmed the undersides of his eyes. He handed his ticket to the
taker and receded into a theater. Matt thought of him alone in the
theater, a hollow cavern of sound and dark. Matt wondered where
Alexis had been inside the school. If she'd been scared. If there'd
been anyone beside her. A girl he barely knew beyond sharing an
elementary school classroom and knowing who her boyfriend was,
Russ Hendricks another junior Matt had seen at the vigil, but who
felt more real to him here, her father at the cinema, her father walking into the shelter of a theater where he could silence himself to everything. He wondered where Mr. Thurber was when he received
a phone call, when his life split in half. He thought of the fires. Two
homes. Two sets of parents who'd lost a child. Two homes with potential commonalities that none of the other families shared though
Matt couldn't help imagining more fires for a split second, the possibility of an arsonist claiming more homes in flames. He watched
the gaping dark of the theater doors where Mr. Thurber had disappeared and wondered if he was in danger.

IT WASN'T UNTIL early evening, long after Matt returned home, that his father's car at last pulled into the driveway. Matt peered at his mother across the living room in an armchair where she continued her book on President Bush. She'd said little when he returned home. Waiting for his father to come home, he knew. She glanced up but continued reading as Matt's father entered the kitchen and set his keys on the counter.

His father didn't call to them. Matt had left the documents splayed across his father's desk. He heard his father open the fridge and then nothing, no clinking of bottles or the hiss of a cracked beer. No clatter of pickle jars. No sizzle of poured soda. Matt imagined his father staring into the fridge, an abyss of choice. And then he was in the living room, boots removed, his police uniform creased. He looked at both of them, then moved down the hallway and Matt heard the carpeted weight of his father's footsteps stop in front of the office. There was no sound in the house but the rattle of the refrigerator's ice machine echoing from the kitchen. Matt's mother refused to look up from her book, even as they both heard the footsteps turn and head back toward them, even as Matt's father was in the living room standing between them.

Who opened it? he said.

Matt's mother didn't answer. She set down her book.

I did it, Matt said. I picked the lock. I needed to know.

Matt waited for the blow, the hurricane of his father's temper.

Come with me, his father said. He looked only at Matt, not his mother. Matt rose from the couch but his father was already gone, already hastening down the hallway to the office.

When Matt entered the room, his father was already seated at the desk.

Pull up a chair, he said. His voice all at once calm, though he would not look at his son. Matt wheeled a chair to the edge of the desk. He sat down next to his father.

What do you want to know, his father said. A statement instead of a question.

Dad.

If there's something you want to know, you should know it.

Matt couldn't read his father's voice. A broken barometer. He couldn't tell if within it lay a challenge or a pleading. Matt pointed toward Jean Black's autopsy report.

This diagram, he said. His index finger traced the anatomy of the drawing. I want to know what you see here. I want to know how you know this isn't foul play, especially when there's nothing left.

You can't see it here. Matt's father shuffled the papers. He pulled out an image of burned remains, what had once been a breathing body. Matt regarded the speckled shape lying on what looked like concrete, a surface he'd never seen inside a home.

Is this from the Blacks' house?

No. Stock footage from arson investigation protocol. Even without a complete body, we have their outlines. The shape of their bodies in the mattress, how they died.

Matt looked at the photograph his father held before him. He didn't know what he'd expected of burnt skin: blackened ash, the residue of cinder, the same cinders of his family's fireplace when they'd burned logs down to dust. He didn't expect the clear shape of a body. He didn't expect the lucid contours of limbs and a torso, the familiar outline of a nose and a mouth. He didn't expect the patches of pink and red, the outline of muscles and tendons beneath the char. Human tissue like gold leaf. Fine and thin. Flashes of color amid the ash, the tips of icebergs, so much more muscle and mass beneath the black that Matt did not want to imagine.

You can't see it as readily on an autopsy diagram, his father said. But look at this photo compared to the outlines on the Blacks' mattress. Compare it to what we found.

Matt wanted to close his eyes but felt himself fixed. His father held the photograph of the Blacks' mattress against the stock picture and pointed to the arms on the stock photograph. If you look here, he said, the arms are contracted. Pulled into the torso. He pointed to the photograph of the Blacks' mattress, the outlines of two figures curled into themselves beside one another. The outlines, even without physical evidence, resembled the shape of the body in the stock photograph. Matt could see the match.

Jean and Arthur Black, they died by fire, his father said. There was no foul play involved. No one tried to keep them in the house while it burned.

How do you know? Matt asked.

His father's finger traced the outlines. Unless someone rendered them unconscious, which is unlikely given the way they were found, no one tried to keep them in the house while it burned. Pugilistic stance, he said. Over time, the body curls into the fetal position when exposed to high heat. The fingers are drawn into the palms, the legs to the torso. These two died by fire. Not by something else. Nothing tied them down. They never tried to escape.

Matt leaned close to the photos. He looked between them. The curvature of the body a mirror image for the ghosted coils outlined in the mattress.

How do you know someone didn't just catch them by surprise? Matt said. Burned down the whole house before the Blacks could react?

We're still working on that. It's a possibility.

How would you know?

The origin of fire, his father said. Burn patterns. Where it started, and how it burned. He pointed to the mattress. If you look here, given the level of damage, this is the worst room in the house. The fire started here. We just need to know what started it.

What could have started it? Matt asked. And what difference does it make?

Faulty wiring, his father said. An unattended candle. Those things are blameless. We're looking for evidence of accelerants, igniters, flammable fluids in the burn pattern of the fire. We're looking for multiple points of origin, which would indicate that a fire was lit in many places. But here. His father pointed to the mattress. Here, there was just one origin. This bedroom. This bed.

Matt looked at the mattress, the outline of Caroline's parents a fairy ring upon it.

How do you know someone didn't just douse the bed with lighter fluid? Just once? Then flick a match and walk away?

We don't know that. It's unlikely. But now, with all of this, we just don't know.

All of this. Matt wanted to ask. He wanted to ask what they'd found at the Trenways' house, what was similar and different, whether there'd been anything left of the bodies and where they could lay blame. *Those things are blameless.* His father had said it. Outlets and wiring, the neglect of a candle. Matt imagined Arthur Black lighting a pillar on the bedside table for his daughter after the funeral. Matt imagined him falling asleep, the flame still held in his gaze, the last light he saw.

Anything else? his father said.

Matt hesitated to ask. Why Eric Greeley? Why did the police bring him back in?

That's not my investigation, son. I don't know. Probably just brought him in for further questioning, all of this right on the tail of what happened at the high school.

What about suicide? Is that even on the table?

Double suicides? At both homes? We looked into it initially, but it's unlikely.

Matt looked at his father. He'd been gone all day. He heard it in his voice: that this was his job, but it was not without grief. So many photographs and reports, thousands of images without answer. Documents his father would take back to work, the lock broken. Documents Matt knew he would never see again.

Anything else?

Matt shook his head.

We want you to use this time, his father said. We want you to take care of yourself. We want you to heal.

His father gathered the photocopies, images Matt knew would stay in his brain regardless of being taken away.

I'll fix the lock, his father said and Matt heard quiet footsteps in the hallway heading back to the living room. His mother had heard everything. She'd seen the photos when she came home from the store, and now she knew what they meant.

Matt wanted to ask about the Trenways' house. He wanted to keep the photographs, the documents, to take them with him and show them to Nick. He wanted to know what his father had seen. His father said nothing. Matt pulled the chair away from the desk and set it back in the corner. He left his father in the office, the photos still scattered like tornadoed remnants across the desk.

PAST DARK MATT lay in his bed, the television upstairs pulsing through the ceiling above him. He pulled a small pipe to his mouth and inhaled. He knew his parents were watching the news, a constant stream, cycles on CNN and MSNBC that would keep everyone updated and tell them nothing. He couldn't hear from the basement whether his parents spoke to one another amid the television's drone, if his mother asked about the photographs. He remembered the last time they glued themselves to the news cycle, two years ago when he was fourteen and the planes hit the towers. He'd been let home early from school. His parents had come home and turned on the television. They didn't speak. They'd watched smoke billow from the buildings, over and over.

A scratching grated at the basement window, a noise Matt barely heard above the television's indecipherable whir. A sound like a branch pulled across the panes though Matt knew there were no trees at the basement's level. The scratching stopped. The sound of knuckle against glass. Matt sat up in his sheets and hid his pipe. He moved across the room to the bedroom's small window and pulled back the curtain and saw Tyler's face.

Matt felt the seawall of his anger rise up and cage him from the window. He wanted to close the curtain. Or open the window, tell Tyler to go fuck himself. But he unlatched the window as he had so many nights across the summer: humidity pressed against the glass. A damp so thick Matt thought he could hold it. He'd pulled Tyler into his bedroom so many times and held him huddled in the night sweat of July heat before Tyler slipped back through the window once light tinged the horizon. Matt opened the window. The air was stark. Not the fluid lush of summer but a cool knife that sliced the room. Hey, Tyler said. Crouched in a sweatshirt, hood hiding his hair.

Tyler crawled inside and Matt let him and they stood unmoving in the dark of the bedroom, Tyler's face slashed by moonlight leaking through the open curtain. Matt looked at him and saw Caroline. Her heat on the carpet. Tyler fleeing down the hallway. Matt looked at Tyler and felt the impossible cage of his own skin. How he could not escape it. How he wanted to shed himself. How he ached to be new again. How he felt himself trapped in the bindings of his bones, his brain waves, the barrier of his cells. How despite his anger he felt his body preordained to forgive. To absolve, to take Tyler back, to feel nothing but desire, to be taken in. To know Tyler. To know what it was he saw, to dissolve into him entirely.

It took you long enough, Matt said.

Tyler moved toward him and Matt wanted to hit him, wanted to throw him to the ground. But Tyler touched his face and Matt let him. A nearness, unbearable. Tyler's skin. He let himself be calmed. He let a hallway disappear. He let himself be held.

OFFICE OF THE MIDVALE COUNTY MEDICAL EXAMINER
430 Westport Avenue
ST. LOUIS, MO 63132

REPORT OF INVESTIGATION BY COUNTY MEDICAL EXAMINER

DECEDENT __Jean__ __Louise__ __Black__ RACE __W__ SEX __F__ AGE __45__
     First Name   Middle Name   Last Name

HOME ADDRESS __1342 Westminster Ct. Midvale County, St Louis__ OCCUPATION: ____
     Number and Street   City or County, State

TYPE OF DEATH: Violent ☐   Casualty ☐   Suicide ☐   Suddenly when in apparent health ☐   Found Dead ☑
(Check one only)   In Prison ☐   Suspicious, unusual or unnatural ☐   Cremation ☐

     Comment __Assumed__

If Motor Vehicle Accident Check One: Driver ☐   Passenger ☐   Pedestrian ☐   Unknown ☐

Notification by __County Homicide__ Address __County__

Investigating Agency __Midvale County Police Department__

Description of Body: Clothed ☑ __Assumed__   Unclothed ☐   Partly Clothed ☐

     Eyes __BR__   Hair __BR__   Mustache ____   Beard ____

     Weight ____ Length ____ Body Temp ____ Date and Time ____
         Pounds   Feet Inches   Farenheit

Marks and Wounds ____

__No body, imprint found in bedroom__

PROBABLE CAUSE OF DEATH	MANNER OF DEATH	DISPOSITION OF CASE

Pending	(check one only)
	Accident ☐ Natural ☐
	Suicide ☐ Unknown ☐
	Homicide ☐ Pending ☑
		1. Not a medical examiner case ☐
		2. Autopsy requested Yes ☑ No ☐
		    Autopsy ordered Yes ☑ No ☐
		    Pathologist ____

I hereby declare that after receiving notice of the death described herein I took charge of the body and made inquiries regarding the cause of death in accordance with Section 38-701-38-734 Missouri Code Annotated and that the information contained herein regarding such death is true and correct to the best of my knowledge and belief.

____
Date

____
Place of Investigation

____
Signature of County Medical Examiner

A BRIEF HISTORY OF FIRE SCENE
INVESTIGATION

FIND A FIRE'S point of origin: trace the route from the least amount of damage to the most.

Windows, doors, beam structures: checked. How glass breaks, the angle of sharding, an indication of speed and intensity of fire. Glass broken in the pattern of a half-moon: signification of rapid cooling.

Smoke: a pattern documented by trace in material, a point of origin otherwise lost to dissipation. Film boiling: when vapor sifts between paint and wood and lifts one away from the other. Metal surfaces: color patterns an indication of fire temperature.

An investigator must ask: Are the walls destroyed? What is their condition? Has the paint separated away? Are there burn patterns? Are the walls pushed in or out? Are there char patterns where the wall meets the floor or ceiling?

Burn patterns on the floor: are they seamless? Do they indicate liquid accelerant, the flow of flammable fluid? Are there points of pooling? Are the floors nonporous? Is there a chance that liquid has evaporated? How deep is the grain of charring? How far down has flammability seeped? Is the flooring hardwood? Linoleum? Tile? Carpet?

Detonation: an explosion. Search for indication of broken gas lines, sewer lines, hazardous storage of flammable items or medical oxygen.

The area of heaviest burning: sweep the floors, the ceiling, every corner and every molding. Sweep the entirety for a cause, for the shifting trace of a spark.

TO BE ALONE

Slate sky, temperatures hovering in the low fifties. We awoke to nothing but the sound of cardinals and robins. The distant honking of Canadian geese flying south. No television hum, no sirens or reporters. Only the weak light of a clouded sky filtering through window blinds. We awoke to more memorials. We awoke to Principal Jeffries's funeral, every last person at school invited.

We anticipated community, a shared grieving. For our principal and for our entire school, so much like the vigil beneath starlight. So many people we hadn't seen since Saturday night, an entire county, our peers and their parents and the one time we'd all been together before fracturing across a week to separate funerals and gatherings that centrifuged us away from a center.

We knew from the paper which funerals had already occurred. Missy Hoffman, Monday afternoon. Nafisa Fields, late Tuesday. Mr. Rourke, our second-floor custodian, a quiet ceremony we heard little about for the media swarm around our peers. Deborah Smalls, the administrative assistant: her funeral equally hushed and also elsewhere, some other town, her family from a small community in southern Illinois. And today: Josh Zimmerman. Darren Beechwold. Alisha Trenway's parents, a service listed quickly. Ceremonies we had no heart to attend. A spectacle for reporters and newscasters. Most of us hadn't spoken since Caroline Black's funeral and the cornfields beyond it. We still tasted whiskey. Slow wash of bourbon. A burn in the backs of our throats that across college campuses and after-work happy hours and so many years ahead at darkened kitchen tables would remind us always of a star-washed field and the hushed scratch of wind through corn silk.

Principal Jeffries's funeral: 11 A.M. A memorial service our parents would attend to pay their respects. Not only for how Principal Jeffries rushed from her office, how she tried to stop Caleb before he moved through the hallways and into our classrooms, but how she'd guided our school for the past twelve years well before any of us ever dreamed of high school, how she'd always said hello in the hallways, how she always knew our names. How we would speak hers a last time.

Nick shuttled downtown early in the passenger seat of his father's Dodge Caravan, a fogged sun crowning due east in front of them as they traveled down Highway 40, the central artery of the city. His father had several patients through the morning but would take him to the funeral after, his mother off from the law office for the day and at home with his brother. The funeral would be held in a downtown church, not far from the Barnes-Jewish Hospital obstetrics wing where Nick's father worked. Nick said he would wait in the wing's lobby. What he didn't say: that he would try not to think of his computer at home, the information on fire scene investigation he'd found the night before. How even through a full night of searching there was still no explanation for a lack of remains. How he wondered about Matt's father and what he'd seen, what Matt wouldn't say at the movie theater. Nick found a chair apart from the waiting mothers and their partners and several lone patients, visibly pregnant. He opened a paperback copy of *Crime and Punishment,* the one book he was assigned to still read across Lewis and Clark's weeklong hiatus. To keep him busy. To have something to speak of when everyone returned to class. They'd left *Moby-Dick* behind, too long to leave across a week. Nick bowed his head over the pages and found himself distracted.

He rested his head against a window and through the glass heard the hum of the traffic below, a constant *whoosh* punctured by the din of car horns. The Gateway Arch distant beyond the buildings, a pillared portico curving above downtown, the only marker anyone who wasn't from St. Louis associated with the city. He recalled ascending the monument with his family when he was in elementary school, the one requisite trip every child who grew up in St. Louis made during their childhood. They traveled in an egg-shaped elevator that moved at right angles, an invisible staircase up the entire length of the curve. Nick's brother had cried, the egg claustrophobic, the Arch swaying in the wind when they reached the top. Nick had gazed through the monument's small windows shaped like Pez and barely visible from the street below and had listened to his brother crying. He'd looked down at the pencil-point people moving along the riverfront and was shocked with fear, as terrified as his brother. He watched a riverboat chug along the Mississippi, a toy in a bathtub, and thought *we could all disappear.*

Nick looked down at his book. The eastern sun broke through clouds and cast shards of light directly into the waiting room. He read the same lines of the same chapter over and over again and finally closed the book. In the waiting room: new families. A mother with her baby, a child Nick guessed wasn't more than six months old. The drone of a wall-mounted television running *The Today Show,* Matt Lauer reporting on a foul ball disruption in last night's National League Championship Series game at Wrigley Field. Nick watched the footage of a man in glasses and a green turtleneck reach down for the ball, a Cubs fan reporters said had cost the Cubs the game. Nick's attention moved to a woman sitting beneath the television, a worn copy of *Parenting* in her lap, a magazine she could practically balance on her belly. Nick imagined her life. Whether she had a partner, whether this was her first child, what she did for a living. Lawyer, like his mother. Social worker. Small-business owner. Whether she'd been watching the news every night thinking of the schools and its students and what would become of her newborn.

Nick slid the paperback into his pocket and moved out of the waiting room, down the hospital hallway, toward the restroom. He leaned over the fountain and wet his fingers and pressed them against the heat of his forehead. When he stood he noticed the fifth floor's only other wing beyond the special care nursery and the antepartum unit where new mothers healed. Cardiology. He peered into its waiting room, one just like the waiting room for his father's division. Panoramic windows. Wall-mounted television. A wall rack of magazines and pamphlets, a receptionist desk of opaque glass. He knew his father wouldn't be done until ten at the earliest. Nick opened the door and moved inside and sat among another group, another television. There was nothing different but the patients, one man completing a crossword with a pen and two women sitting side by side, their hands clasped in their laps. Everything else the same, the television broadcasting the same morning news as the maternity ward, but the room felt changed. Nick wondered where the neuroscience wing was and whether anyone there could tell him for certain what had happened to his brain. Flashbulb. Caleb passing by through the window of Mrs. Menda's classroom door. Whatever image Zola kept of the library, what Matt remembered of Caroline Black's body. Nick sat long enough for his father to find him there just before ten, his appointments finished early. When he felt his father's hand on his shoulder, he didn't flinch. He looked up and his father nodded and they made their way down the elevator, to the parking garage, then to the minivan, where they drove to the church in silence.

WE SAT BESIDE one another. Nick, his father. Zola and her mother, Christina and her father. Matt came without his parents, his father working, his mother at home though Tyler Cavanaugh followed him into the church and sat down beside him. We said nothing to each other. We watched a procession of our classmates find seats and await the service. Family members. Adults in the first rows we could only assume were Principal Jeffries's brothers and sisters, her mother and father. Stained-glass windows. The low dirge of organ pipes. A paper program in our hands, its edges crushed inside the damp folds of our palms. We knew what to expect after attending Caroline's service. A minister. Organ hymns. A closed casket we avoided. Pews full of Bibles and passages the minister called to attention, thread-thin pages we never opened. Our hands in our laps, fingers clasped between our knees to halt the pendulum of their trembling.

We expected the rites of a church. Stifled coughs. The soundlessness of tears. A clouded sky strained through patterns of glass. What we didn't expect were hundreds of people pushed against the pews and filling the aisles. People leaning beside the church's brick pillars. People crowding the back, standing behind the last pew. *Love is simple.* The minister waved his hands across the entire congregation. *Look at everyone who loved her. All we need is love to push out the dark.* We followed the movement of his hands across so many faces. We looked closely at the lines that edged so many parents' eyes, the way their pupils tracked downward, how their necks strained with visible tension. How we recognized Jacob Jensen's mother in the pews, her son gone barely a week. How we noticed Alexis Thurber's father by himself, sitting near the back of the church alone, Alexis's boyfriend, Russ Hendricks, nowhere in sight. How love was anything but simple. How love was the hardest thing any of us knew.

Our principal's partner gave a eulogy. A middle-aged woman, her hair frizzed, her glasses large. *You were the love of my life.* Her voice breaking. Principal Jeffries's daughter standing beside the woman, barely the height of her waist, a family we never thought to consider. A principal we only envisioned within the walls of a high school. Behind a desk in her office. Circulating the cafeteria every so often as we ate our mayonnaised sandwiches and drank Hawaiian Punch. A woman who every year closed out the Homecoming Parade riding in a borrowed convertible and followed by police cars that took away the street barricades before the football game began. A parade we wouldn't have this year. Just a game. A game we knew would be rescheduled elsewhere, at another school, a game none of us would attend.

What we couldn't have anticipated: how sorrow permeated the air of the church for Principal Jeffries but also anger, a bitterness that felt new and strange. How beyond hymns, beyond bowed heads and the carrying away of a casket, people stayed and milled through pews. How we saw Jacob Jensen's mother clasp the hands of Georgia Tarkington's mother, two peers we wouldn't have imagined to have ever known one another. Jacob Jensen a soccer player. Georgia Tarkington a math wiz who served in Mu Alpha Theta. How their mothers were cemented to one another in their loss, a bind neither asked for. How our peers' parents spoke around us. How we heard what they whispered: *arson.* Tips of culpability. Who'd been lurking at the Trenways' house and who'd been seen walking along the empty sidewalks of Caroline Black's street and who'd been taken in for questioning, the Greeley kid, what the paper mentioned and never elaborated upon. How we heard parents speak of guarding. Of tending to one another's children. Of organizing collectives, a neighborhood watch, how they swore they would protect this community and help the police do their job. Parents who knew each other from parent-teacher nights at the start of each elementary school year, from the bleachers of Friday night football games, from dropping us off at one another's homes before we knew what it was to drive. Parents who sent each other holiday cards and missives of school closings due to snowstorms, who we always imagined would gather together to celebrate our high school graduations on some warm May weekend, the future sprawled out like an unbroken highway. Parents inscrutable to us, how they'd first come to settle down in Midvale County, how it was that their choices had made us what we were, how we'd taken root beside one another because they found a house, a job, a community.

We watched Principal Jeffries's family trail from the church out into the weak afternoon sun. Her daughter's curls. How they caught the light. How Principal Jeffries's partner smoothed the girl's hair and held a hand upon her head, fingertips we could almost feel. There was no lingering this time outside the church. No time for quiet, for standing beside one another as the sky tilted away from us. No time for stars, the sky hazed, the sun sliding behind the clouds. Chilled air. A breeze with muscle.

Matt saw Jacob Jensen's mother alone at the curb smoking a cigarette, her face calm, though he noticed her hand shaking as she brought the filter to her lips. He remembered her from a fifth-grade class party when she'd brought cupcakes but couldn't stay long. How another parent had made a snide comment about her leaving. How she'd whirled back and said some mothers worked and did just fine on their own. How Matt remembered this, the first time he realized not every household had two parents.

His own mother at home. How she'd woken up no longer angry with him, how she'd wanted to come to the funeral and sit beside him. How he knew Tyler would come instead, Tyler who'd stayed in his bedroom long past the darkest hour the night held. How Matt's mother had embraced him and even still neither of his parents knew about Tyler. Matt wanted to keep it that way. He'd told her he would attend with his friends.

He walked up to Jacob Jensen's mother and stood beside her at the curb. In the city's breeze whipping between buildings, he caught the scent of her perfume. He didn't think. Your son was a good person, he said. The first words he could think to say though he barely knew Jacob, knew only the chisel of his legs from afar, the smooth curve of his calf, and once his daily schedule throughout the high school: an impossible crush he'd kept watch over in the hallways until he met Tyler.

I'm so sorry for your loss, he said.

Jacob's mother exhaled a plume of smoke that dissipated in the wind. Her face still young. Her eyes ancient. The corners of her eyes cracked, fine lines spilling down and disappearing into the gaunt stretch of her cheekbones.

I appreciate that, she said. She pulled a last drag from her cigarette and threw the filter to the ground. She didn't ask who Matt was, how he knew Jacob. She said nothing at all before turning away from Matt, the tails of her black coat flickering in the wind.

Tyler came up beside him.

She used to scream from the bleachers at our matches, he said.

You played soccer? Matt said, and hoped Tyler wouldn't ask how he knew already what kind of match, how he knew Jacob's sport without having known him at all.

Just freshman year, Tyler said. She knew all the rules, the fouls, the yellow cards.

Matt wondered how it was that there was so much about Tyler he didn't know. How dating since summer, even confidentially beyond the gaze of peers and parents, hadn't let him in much further than if they had never known one another. He slid his hand down the sleeve of Tyler's jacket. Found his palm. Tyler let his hand be held for only a moment, then squeezed Matt's palm and pulled away.

WE DISBANDED. WE left one another at the brick steps of the church. We'd thought to collect ourselves, to go somewhere for the afternoon without discussion of yearbook or fire or funeral and found instead only exhaustion. Only the desire to be alone. Zola mentioned her first shift back at the Local Beanery, that she had to report by three. Nick said he'd been gone all morning and just wanted to go home and rest. Christina let her father's car take her in with barely a goodbye, saying only that she was tired and wanted to change out of her dress. Matt stood at the curb beside his car with Tyler.

Want to go somewhere?

Anywhere, Tyler said. I don't really want to go home.

Matt started the car, Tyler in the passenger seat. They traveled along downtown streets filled with steel buildings that blocked out the sun. Matt navigated west, back toward Midvale. He didn't take the highway, the quickest route. He meandered past Union Station, the train depot converted to a mall where his parents had taken him to a fudge shop and model train store when he was small. Past the castle-like towers of Washington University, a college he'd never visited. Past streets lined with trees. Silver maples. Black maples, their leaves exploded in yellow. Sugar maples, leaves like stars washed in red. Tyler cracked the window, a burst of cold air. He pulled a cigarette from his pocket and Matt felt at once irritated.

We could go to the zoo, Matt said. It's close by. It's free.

Fine with me, Tyler said. He blew smoke toward the passing trees.

Matt steered the car toward the entrance of Forest Park, the largest city park in the country. A landscape of grass and hills and trees. They drove past the Grand Basin, the park's enormous fountain. Past the art museum on the hill, the statue of King Louis crowning its entrance. Everything deserted on a Wednesday afternoon. Matt parked the car along the street in front of the zoo and Tyler flicked his cigarette out the window.

Where to? Matt asked.

Anywhere. Really, I just need to be outside for a while.

They moved through the turnstiles and headed past a stretch of small mammal habitats Matt remembered wanting to visit first as a child whenever he came to the zoo with his parents. One reclusive red panda, its straw hut in the rear of its pen. A striped tail he always located in the trees though today, the sky overcast, the panda was nowhere to be found. A Malayan sun bear paced in the adjacent pen, one corner of the enclosure to the other. Matt watched the bear track the same path, a worn groove in the dirt.

I haven't been here since elementary school, Tyler said.

Me either, Matt said. What he didn't say was how strange it was to be here again with Tyler. Someone he'd kept hidden from his parents across an entire summer, parents who'd guided him past these same exhibits as a child. Someone who'd left him in the hallway beside Caroline, an anger he knew he was still trying to leave behind. Tyler turned to the sea lion pool across from the small mammal enclosures. They could eat up to thirty pounds a day, Matt remembered a keeper once telling the crowd. He stepped to the pool's edge and placed his hands on the railing and three sea lions darted through the water, gray submarines beneath the surface of an overcast sky. Matt tried to think of something to say to Tyler. Anything. The air stilted between them out in the open.

Tyler moved away from the railing and they passed a wall of outdoor enclosures, small alligators and a bevy of tortoises that led toward the indoor reptile center. The building was warm inside, a reprieve from the crystalline chill of October sky. Matt approached a large window where a boa constrictor lay curled and stood with his face to the glass. The footsteps of children echoed around him. He felt their feet vibrate through the floor, stepping to the glass before moving away toward the amphibians and desert snakes. Matt felt himself planted. He watched the boa and imagined being swallowed whole. A body thicker than anything he could dream, what it would feel like to pass through the walls of a snake's body and feel its muscle push in and contract.

And then Tyler's hands were against his back, breath against his ear. There's a bathroom in this center, Tyler said. Empty stalls. A place to be alone.

Matt felt his lungs grow tight. He nudged Tyler away before he could think.

What the fuck, Tyler whispered loudly. A mother ushered her

child away from them. Matt made his way toward the bathroom, Tyler behind him, and didn't stop until they reached the last stall. He'd barely closed the stall door before he felt Tyler push him against the tiled wall, his tongue in Matt's mouth. Matt felt something split inside him, a light, something aching and weightless and bright. A light broken quick by a flare, a red-hot flash of adrenaline that made him shove Tyler away. He thrust him hard enough for his body to hit the stall door, the sound echoing through the bathroom.

Jesus, what's your fucking problem? Tyler said.

You're my fucking problem.

What, because I'm here? Because I want you?

Because where the fuck were you? Matt felt his palms ball. Where were you, and why now? Why here? What makes you want me now? When you couldn't bear to acknowledge me in public at school or even at the funeral this morning?

Tyler rubbed a hand across his shoulder. Matt didn't want to say it but couldn't stop himself.

You left me there.

Tyler didn't move. It's not that simple, he said.

Do you know what it felt like? For you to leave me there? Do you know what it was like to stand there and watch her—

Matt felt his throat close. He couldn't say what it was he watched Caroline Black do. Everything she'd been bleeding away across the carpet.

You think this is easy for me? Tyler said. No one knows. You think I want to be caught with my pants down in a bathroom stall while a gunman shoots up the halls?

No one knows what, Matt said.

What the fuck are you talking about.

You said no one knows. No one knows what?

Tyler's eyes flickered across the stall.

You can't even fucking say it, Matt said. Gay. No one knows you're gay.

Before he even finished speaking, Tyler's elbow was across his throat. Matt felt his head slam against the tile, Tyler's arm pinning him to the wall, his face drawn close. Tyler's eyes swimming. An electric heat. For a moment, Matt thought Tyler would spit in his face. Then he pulled back and Matt drew in breath and watched Tyler's shoes leave the stall. I can find my own way home, he heard him shout before the bathroom door opened and whispered to a close.

CHRISTINA STOOD AT the edge of the diving board, water dripping down into the pool beneath her feet. Only a few swimmers populated the Midvale County Community Center pool, arms knifing through lanes and slick with water. Ryan hadn't called. Two days of nothing. Two days of listening to the constant hum of the television in the other room, a droning newsreel. Two days of waiting for her father to come home, her brother playing video games or else locked away in his room and her mother at work across the river and calling every day, a comfort but a ringing nonetheless that left her chest aching. That it wasn't Ryan. That he refused to call. That she'd come home from the funeral with her father and there were no messages yet again and she'd felt her lungs push against her breastbone and grabbed the keys to her car.

She'd alternated drills of freestyle sprints with laps of kickboard flutter kicks, the same practice as her swim team. She knew they wouldn't meet for weeks but her limbs were restless, in need of slicing the water. She pushed her way down the narrow lane, her goggles sealed across her eyes, and thought of the one time she'd been snorkeling, a trip to Florida in junior high to visit her mother's sister. Shallows off the coast of Destin. Her parents and brother billowing somewhere in the water nearby. She'd identified sand divers, trumpet fish, the iridescent blue of angelfish before removing her snorkel and pulsing all the way down to the flat sand of the ocean floor. She gazed up through her mask and watched light shimmer

at the surface. The water silent as a chamber, a stillness she sought
in the community center's chlorinated waters. She'd swum laps for
a half hour, the dark stripe of the lap lane visible beneath her. Her
body in motion, her flip turn the only rippling of the water's surface.
When she finished, she climbed from the water and noticed the
deep end of the pool and its empty diving board.

Despite her place on Lewis and Clark's swim team, she hadn't
jumped off a diving board in years. A lone lifeguard sat on the
stand watching the few other swimmers turn and glide through
the lanes. She'd climbed the metal ladder. The same as climbing
the water slide at Midvale County's outdoor public pool when she
was small. She walked out to the precipice and felt her toes grip
the edge of the diving board. The water deep blue and dark beneath her. This community center a place where she'd practiced
so many early mornings, so many afternoons beyond school. Elise.
The habituated routine of her swim partner sliding through the
water in the same lap lane, their bodies matched stroke for stroke,
their hands pulsing in synch with one another. Christina stood at
the edge. She shifted her weight to test the board and let herself
jump.

She dove headfirst into the pool, her goggles still on, a rippling
of bubbles she could see as her body sliced through the water. She
kept swimming to the bottom as she had in the ocean off the coast
of Destin. Silent blue. The surface of the water winking back way
above her. She swam down until her hands reached the rough base
of the pool's foundation and through her goggles she could see
the faint, far-off movement of swimmers in shallow lanes. She let
herself be still. Elise Nguyen. A lack of air. The deepest stretch of
the pool. Christina felt her lungs fill with pressure. She thought of
Ryan in his bedroom and the shattered picture frame and Principal
Jeffries and a casket she'd seen only hours before, a woman she'd
seen last week. Her lungs throbbed to resurface and she imagined a
world beyond this. The ocean floor. The coast of a state she hadn't

seen since she was a child. Another elsewhere entirely, sea salt and blue, one she could almost feel from the bottom of a pool.

ZOLA PEDALED THE mile to the Local Beanery, a stiff wind breaking through her sweater. A three-hour shift, her first back. A distraction but not enough. She relieved Marilyn, the middle-aged woman who worked early afternoon shifts, and stood behind the counter taking bites from an oversize muffin, the only lunch she thought to have in the bitter aftertaste of a funeral.

The shop was empty. Two women drank iced tea in one corner. Near the far windows, two college-aged students sat with laptops at separate tables, neither seeming to know the other. Zola looked through the window beyond them, the sky growing overcast with deep stratus clouds. She felt Matt's profile in her back pocket, a slip of paper she still hadn't read, one she'd kept hidden in her clothing through the funeral. She watched a bulk of low clouds move in thick filaments across the sky and felt nothing, no urge to capture them to film as she once had. She'd taken photographs since seventh grade, an amateur, a skill her mother had noticed that holiday season with the gift of her first camera. She'd photographed icicles, frozen pines. She'd tried to snap snowflakes as they fell to see if each one was different. As her mother trained her telescope upon the stars Zola pointed her camera to the sky, sure she could capture constellations. She felt nothing now. Her camera gathering dust beneath her bed. The world dulled to a lack of color. She finished her muffin as the front door opened, a bell dinging a customer's arrival.

Zola wiped her hands against her pants and looked up to see Beth Zimmerman walk in. Josh Zimmerman's sister, a senior. A girl who'd spoken at the vigil, whom Zola knew from Des Peres Elementary though not well, right between Beth and Josh in age though she remembered them as fixtures of the hallways, the lunchroom, the elementary school library. Beth had been in the coffee shop many times before, and her mother, too, their house not far from the storefront. She was in jeans, an old T-shirt. Zola knew from the newspaper that she'd buried her brother that morning.

Large coffee, Beth said. Her face hollow, eyes empty.

To go?

Please.

Zola pulled a paper cup from a stacked set. She didn't ask what she'd been trained. *Dark roast or light? Room for cream?* She filled the cup. Beth stood waiting. She figured Beth knew who she was, a high school of 1,200 and even still they'd shared a set of hallways for nearly ten years between Des Peres and Lewis and Clark, though they'd never acknowledged it directly the many times Beth had been into the coffee shop. Zola wanted to reach across the counter and tear the pain from her chest with a clenched fist.

Beth kept her eyes on the ground. Zola placed a plastic lid on the cup, set it down. She pressed numbers into the cash register, aware of Beth's hands resting on the counter and quivering. Zola wanted to touch them. Let her hands leave the register and surround them. She stopped herself but not before she let her mouth fall open and say the words.

I'm so sorry, she whispered. I'm sorry for your loss.

Beth nodded. I had to get out of the house.

Zola pushed the coffee across the counter. Please. Just take it.

Beth took the coffee and hastened away from the shop, the small bell of the door ringing behind her. Zola watched out the windows as Beth climbed into her car and sat for a moment in the driver's seat before pulling away. Homecoming Court. Zola knew Beth was nominated this year. The dance next Friday. A future untethered, impossible. Zola watched Beth's car exit the parking lot, brake lights lifting, and then she was gone.

NICK SAT AT the computer in his bedroom, his family in the living room down the hall watching sitcoms, a laugh track creeping through his closed door. He'd spent the afternoon researching, looking up every search term he could think to type in. The particulars of arson. Linked patterns. How the human body loses itself to flame. How it was even possible that there would be nothing left.

A knock at his door. His mother peered in. We're all watching a movie soon if you want to join us, she said.

I'll be out in a minute.

What are you working on?

Stuff for the yearbook, I guess. I know it's early. I just need to keep myself busy.

She came in and sat down on the bed. Your father said the funeral wasn't easy.

It was fine. I think people are just starting to get scared.

Nick's mother reached out and touched his hair. Are you doing okay?

I'm fine. Just tired.

Is there anything I can do?

Nick glanced at her. Have you ever defended an arsonist?

In my years at the courthouse, one or two.

Were any of those fires fatal? Cases of arson where someone was killed?

Not that I recall. Mostly just property damage. People acting out in anger, or business owners committing fraud for insurance.

So you haven't seen anything like this before?

His mother hesitated. I don't know if anyone's seen anything like this before.

What do you think it means?

I really don't know. I just want to make sure you're okay. And safe.

I'm fine. Just sad, I guess.

We all are. She reached over and held his hand. Want to come out and watch a movie? It might be good to take a break from all of this.

I'll be out soon, Nick said. In just a minute.

His mother kissed the top of his head. She slipped out of the room and Nick turned back to the computer screen, a Web page replete with information on multiple points of fire. He didn't want to tell his mother the information that hadn't appeared in the news: that no evidence of bodies had been found at the Blacks' house. Nick wondered if Matt was home and picked up the receiver in his room.

Is your dad home? Nick asked when Matt answered on the second ring.

No, he's not home yet. Take a break. Please. Just for the night.

I don't know if I can. There's too much unanswered here.

Let me guess. You're at your computer.

I've been looking all afternoon. It just doesn't make sense.

I know. But what can I tell you? My dad hasn't said anything more.

What do you think it means? That there's nothing left?

Honestly, right now I don't give a shit what it means.

Nick leaned back in his desk chair. He heard the subtle ache in Matt's voice, something beyond frustration. What happened?

Nothing happened. I'm just so fucking tired.

Tyler?

Nick heard Matt sigh.

Look, you don't have to talk about it, Nick said. Not unless you want to.

I really don't. Can we just take a break for today?

Nick paused a moment. I think we should meet soon. All of us. We should keep working on the yearbook.

Can it wait until tomorrow?

Tomorrow would be better anyway. I'm sure Chris and Zol are as exhausted today as we are. But could you call one of them?

I'll call Christina later. I'll see if she's written anything. Paul's Books?

Nick glanced out his window. Paul's Books. A nearby store he hadn't been to in weeks, the place they sometimes met to discuss the yearbook if not at Christina's house.

Paul's Books, Nick said. We can figure out a time later.

Take it easy tonight, man. Just relax. Stay away from your computer.

I'll try, Nick said. He replaced the receiver to its cradle. He heard the start of a movie down the hall, the overture of opening credits. Photographs of fire swam across the computer screen before him. Photographs of nothing but rubble and ash.

MATT LAY IN his bedroom until the cicadas beyond his window lost their teeming. He'd heard them whine a cascading symphony toward dusk, a noise rising over the browning grass and fallen leaves. He'd heard his mother come home an hour before from her volunteer shift at the animal shelter, what she'd resumed to stay busy, followed by the slow scent of cooking onions and garlic and paprika. She was making chili, he knew. An aroma that despite the day's events made him hungry. He hadn't called Christina. He'd tried not to think of Tyler. An elbow against his throat. He heard his father come home at last, the drone of the garage door vibrating through the ceiling above him. He emerged from the basement just as his father stepped into the kitchen and pulled off his jacket.

Long day? his mother asked.

He kissed her forehead. Investigation ran overtime today.

Matt sat at the kitchen table. His father opened the refrigerator, pulled out a beer.

How was the shelter? Matt asked his mother.

Slow today. We took in a cat. There's still that pair of guinea pigs in need of a good home.

Matt knew the particulars of his mother's volunteering, that two guinea pigs had been rescued from a farm out in Festus. Nearly a month ago now, he recalled. Two guinea pigs neglected by their owner, found alongside three skeletal horses and four goats, all of which had gone to a rehabilitation facility in the Missouri hills.

Matt's mother glanced at him. How was the service today?

Fine, he said. A brief pang in his chest that he'd told her not to come.

You didn't go? Matt's father looked at her.

He said not to. I wanted him to be with his friends.

It was fine, Dad. A funeral. There wasn't much either of you could have done.

We could have been there for you.

Lots of people were. Almost the entire school was there.

Matt's mother turned back to the stove. We'll go with you if there are others.

Matt didn't want to think it. Others. Other funerals he didn't have any energy left for. He turned to his father. What happened today?

Matt's father smiled and leaned against the stove. I knew that was coming.

Can you tell us anything?

We don't know much. Not yet, at least. We're still comparing the two fires.

What about Eric Greeley?

I told you, that's not my case. But I know he's still being questioned.

So they're just holding him at the station? Matt's mother asked.

They can't really do that, not without evidence. He's being brought in at shorter intervals for questioning, and beyond that, we're keeping watch on his house.

Matt imagined cop cars winnowing down the street past Eric Greeley's front door.

He said he didn't know anything, Matt said.

We know that. But it's the only thing we've got right now.

What else? Matt asked. Did you find anything at the Trenways' house?

I wasn't there today. I was at the station lab, the entire day.

He doesn't need to know, his mother said. Just for once, can we have a nice dinner without all of this?

Matt saw it in his father's face. Something. Dad, what is it? Tell me.

The autopsy report I showed you. From the Blacks' home.

Jim, his mother said.

What happened? Matt said. What do you know?

The Trenway house. His father glanced at his mother, her fists curled tight against the kitchen counter. I got the report back today. The same thing.

The outlines?

We found nothing. Not a single trace of a body.

Is that even possible?

It's unusual. I've never seen anything like it before. No evidence of foul play. The exact same as the Blacks' house. We're checking outlets and wiring. But they're still holding the Greeley kid for questioning. We're still looking into the possibility of arson.

Why, if you know there's no foul play?

Can we stop this? his mother said.

Because it's the exact same—the same origin. The same stance. The same maddening lack of physical evidence. Nothing left.

Goddamnit, enough! his mother shouted. I said enough.

The chili bubbled on the stove. Matt glanced across the table but his father wouldn't look at him. Matt's mother at a breaking point, a curse she let slip, a day of funerals that would only be followed by more. Matt wanted answers and there was nothing but questions. The funeral for Alisha's parents that afternoon: wooden boxes containing only air. The same as the Blacks. Empty caskets. No indication of cause. No suspicion of foul play. Only a replication of conditions, the same origin, what his father had said without saying it directly: that the Trenways had burned in their beds, just like the Blacks, that they'd curled into their sheets and let the moonlight flood their windows and closed their eyes to a night that had seen their daughter buried, a night that broke through the panes and consumed every fiber of their bedroom in flames.

A BRIEF HISTORY OF CREMATION
(OR, HOW THE BODY BURNS)

THE FIRST TO burn: human hair, illumined in blue flame as crematorium jets heat.

The head snaps back, the body goes rigid. As temperature heats to 700 degrees bones within the body hiss open and explode. Rapid heat reddens muscle. Skin turns black then slowly divides. Flesh reduces into molecules, carbonizes, splits even smaller still into the atoms of oxygen. The body then exposed to 2,200 degrees Fahrenheit for at least ninety minutes, muscle and organ burning away from the bones, a continued hissing, a series of perpetual detonations. The crematorium's temperature lowered, bone smoldering for two hours longer, simmering down to ash.

What is known: that house fires rarely exceed temperatures of 1,200 degrees.

What is known: that even at 2,200 degrees, a crematorium leaves behind recognizable fragments of human bone.

JACOB JENSEN

Lewis and Clark High School

Class of 2005

September 12, 1986—October 8, 2003

Jacob, a junior at Lewis and Clark, played center forward on the varsity soccer team. Known for his athleticism and his camaraderie on the team, Jacob began playing for Lewis and Clark High School as a freshman. He played junior varsity for only one year before advancing to varsity due to his talent and goodwill.

A scholar-athlete, Jacob also maintained straight A's in all of his classes including honors and AP courses. He was particularly skilled in biology and hoped to declare pre-med in college while also continuing to pursue soccer. At the start of his junior year, he was already entertaining scholarships from universities and colleges across the country. In addition to playing on the soccer team, Jacob was involved with the National Honor Society and with Students for Humanity, a charitable organization. His most recent work of community service was to organize a safe driving event with the local police department for new teenage drivers.

Jacob was known as friendly and fun-loving. He was never without friends in the cafeteria or in the hallways, and he was always one to say hello to those he did not call close friends. His many talents and amiability will be greatly missed at Lewis and Clark.

MEMORY, RECORD, ARCHIVE

WE AWOKE THURSDAY knowing we would meet: not for a funeral or a vigil, but for the simple fact of beginning. We'd lain the night before in the overwhelming dark of our bedrooms, the television whirring down the hall beyond our closed doors. We felt the hollow of our chests fill with pressure the longer we lay there, a lonesome heat. We promised to call after dinner, after television, after our parents had gone to bed. We made promises we couldn't keep when we found ourselves spent, unable to pick up the phone beyond the exhaust of a day spent grieving.

We knew we'd meet in the morning, a daybreak that brought a continued news cycle on television spotlighting St. Louis, though our newspaper turned for a brief day to other things beyond the constant stream of reporters in our streets. In the *Post-Dispatch:* the United Nations Security Council moving for Iraqi sovereignty, a proposal pushed by President Bush and backed by the United Kingdom, Chile, Cameroon. China's first astronaut in space circling the planet in the Shenzhou 5, a twenty-one-hour trip in a shuttle that felt far-off and remote to us. The Marlins heading to the World Series, beating the Chicago Cubs in seven games. Steve Bartman: the name of the man who interfered with the foul ball at Wrigley Field, whom Chicago blamed for killing their first World Series chance since 1945, whom Illinois governor Rod Blagojevich urged to join the witness protection program. We looked at the photo, a grained image of a man sitting in the stands wearing a Cubs hat. We turned the page, toward other news stories beyond the impossibility that a man's life could be forever changed by a game.

We sat with coffee. Tea. We ate pears and yogurt and cereal. We imagined the Trenways' house, a cluster of wreckage, a ranch home we'd never entered but knew. The end of Zola's street. A corner home she could see from the edge of her yard, its burnt scent still filtering through screen windows, settling upon couches and kitchen tables like dust. We needed to get out. To leave our streets. We agreed to meet at Paul's Books, where we once met to discuss the yearbook as a change of pace from Christina's house, the small shop located in a strip mall less than a mile from each of our homes.

Nick gathered clippings: every news story he'd cut from the paper. Every story and sub-story on Lewis and Clark, on the fires ravaging both homes. A manila file folder he'd begun to organize though he spoke nothing of it to any of us. A folder he kept in the drawer of his computer desk, newsprint and photos, a record of fragments and scissored pieces. He placed the folder in his bag and drove alone. Zola brought Matt's profile, still unread, still folded in the pocket of the same pair of pants she'd worn all week. She biked to the bookstore while a mile away Christina climbed into her car, bringing nothing but her purse and a mix CD that Ryan had made though she drove noiseless through the streets, the radio off, the sky clouded for the second day in a row. Matt left his house quiet behind him, his mother reading and eyeing him carefully, his father already at work. He brought nothing to the bookstore: no reports, no photos stolen from his father's desk. He brought only the profile he'd written the night before for Jacob Jensen, the only person he could think to set down to paper in the night's darkness. He brought the knowledge that nothing remained at the Trenways' house and the silent ache that Tyler hadn't called or pushed his way through Matt's window past dark, an apology.

We gathered early in the back corner of the bookstore's café. Just past opening. Before anyone we knew would think to walk in. Nick ordered a coffee. Christina a hot chocolate, Matt a blackberry scone. Zola drank water and watched the wind rake leaves across the strip mall parking lot beyond the window. We took in the sound of being outside our own homes: the clink of café dishes. The whirring of foamed milk. The watered dunk of mugs being cleaned. Sounds the same as the Local Beanery. Sounds beyond television, beyond the soft hum of ceiling fans. We sat in a cluster of puffed armchairs and Nick pulled the manila folder from his bag and spread it across the table between us.

No more sitting. Waiting. No more lying in our bedrooms without light. No more staring across our yards, no more reading the same lines in the newspaper. We knew nothing of what to archive. We knew no schematic to make sense of the articles and photographs Nick placed before us. We were tired. Spent. We didn't want to look at the newspaper. We'd seen everything within the folder, every photo, everything on the television that leaked down the hallways into our bedrooms. We had no options left. We had to begin somewhere. We leaned forward and sifted through the clippings.

Christina picked up a photo of the remains of what had once been the Blacks' home. We can't solve this, she said. We can't solve any of this.

We're not looking to solve, Nick said.

Then what are we doing? Zola asked.

We're putting together a book. It's our job. It's what we have to do.

This isn't what we do, Zola said. We take photos of school dances, pep rallies. We research the year's world events for archiving. We write profiles of honors students.

I think we're beyond that now, Nick said. That's not really an option anymore.

Then what is? Christina asked. What the hell are we supposed to do now?

We have to make sense of this for a book, Nick said. That's all we can do.

Zola scanned the images: burned houses, so many skeletons of former homes. Photos she couldn't imagine putting in a yearbook, a record of what was.

There's no way we can print this, she said. This isn't what a yearbook should do.

Then what should it do? Nick asked. Pretend? Make a year that wasn't?

It should remind everyone of what was good, Christina said softly. It should make them happy. It should make them remember.

Zola picked up a photograph of Lewis and Clark High taken just after police response. Students she recognized being guided from the doorways, down the school lawn, and toward a line of ambulances. Their faces ashen, broken in grief.

What will anyone want to remember of this, she said. There's nothing. Nothing at all to set down in this yearbook.

For once Matt wanted to focus on Caroline and the profile he'd written, but Tyler flooded his brain. His elbow to Matt's throat. How he hadn't called. How Matt preferred to think instead of humid-damp summer nights, him and Tyler inside his car. Him and Tyler within the capsule of the cinema's projection booth, just the two of them alone.

We can make it what we want, he said. We can decide what we set down.

We can't change the past, Christina said. She meant the high school's hallways but saw Ryan. Saw a swimming pool, Elise nowhere within it. She swept a hand over the table, the scattered newsprint. We can't change any of this, she said.

But we can make it ours, Matt said. We decide what it is we should remember.

Zola picked up a photograph of Mrs. Diffenbaum, one of the two librarians, a portrait of her face printed last Friday beside thirty-five other photographs and names. Zola closed her eyes. The shape of Garamond font on a library shelf. *A Graphic History of Oceanic Biology*. The sound of human seepage. The animal scent of her own urine.

We can't control what we remember, she said. How can we?

By writing it down, Matt said, and Zola felt the shape of the profile he'd written still crumpled in her pocket. From pants she'd worn yesterday, pants she'd grabbed again from the floor though she still hadn't read Matt's words, paper now soft and worn at the edges. She pulled it from her pocket and placed it beside the photos on the table. She looked away so Matt would never know she hadn't read it.

What is that? Christina asked.

I wrote a profile, Matt said. Caroline Black. He pulled the other profile he'd written from his bag. I profiled Jacob Jensen last night, too. This is all I can do. I'm not sleeping. I'm not doing anything but thinking about this.

Nick set down his coffee and picked up Caroline Black's profile. He unfolded it, tentatively at first, giving Matt time to stop him though Matt made no move.

This is what you wrote? Nick asked.

It's all I could think of.

We need this. Profiles. Articles about each and every one of them.

Christina picked up the profile of Jacob. Scanned its lines, ashamed she hadn't written a single word. Zola gazed across the newsprint and photographs and knew their objective: not a scattering of headlines but words and photos that would make them what they were, words that would reconstitute and resurrect them. Profiles to pick them up from the carpet, from the floor of the library. A bulletproof archive. A book to beat back nothing any of them could control.

She stood and told Christina she'd be right back and made her way to the lone restroom at back of Paul's Books, where she locked the door. An overhead fan whirred when she turned on the light, an overwhelming sound. Black dots crowded the edge of her vision. Stale urine. The green vellum of a book cover. She pressed her knuckles to the wall and leaned into them and slid to the floor. *I cannot do this.* Four words splitting the cells of her brain. As if the past could be changed. As if by pen alone a goddamn thing could be changed. All of them unaware that in the forced reimagining of a high school's year they were making her remember scream-choked voices, the stench of loosed bowels, bullet-cracked wood and mothballed books and discarded backpacks splattered in spit and blood. She focused on the tile beneath her hands. Smooth and cool. A surface as placid and still as water. She breathed in. Out. Sucked in air as the fan above her droned. She pulled herself up, her heart a jackhammer, her pulse flooding her ears. She ran the faucet. Pressed water to her cheeks. Matched her gaze in the mirror. *Fucking pull it together.*

At the table, she found Nick writing notes on a legal pad. Matt sat hunched over the news articles. Christina held Matt's profile of Caroline.

This is lovely, Christina told him. It's just what Caroline would have wanted.

Zola felt a spike inside her breastbone: that she hadn't read it. That Matt had given it to her. That she'd been the only one to ignore it, to smash it inside her pocket.

That Christina thought she knew what Caroline Black could have wanted.

The paper said Eric Greeley's still there for questioning, Christina said. He was always such a fucking weirdo. I wouldn't be surprised.

Keep your voice down, Zola snapped.

Christina looked up at her. What do you care?

You don't know what you're talking about.

And you do? Christina said. You know Eric so well? You don't know anything, nothing more than I do. Christina got up and brought her empty mug to the café counter and Zola felt as if she'd been slapped.

Nick glanced at Zola. Don't take it personally. I think she and Ryan are fighting.

What, you think I don't know that?

Nick said nothing and Zola regretted the tone of her own voice and Christina returned to the table and looked at both of them. What don't you know?

Zola shrugged. You and Ryan.

What, you're all talking about me now? I get up for one minute?

No one's talking about you. Matt sighed. Jesus Christ. Can we stay on task?

No, tell me. Christina looked at Zola and felt a heat bubbling up the center of her chest. Two years of a relationship Zola had judged in silence. As if she thought Christina wouldn't notice. What do you want to say? Christina challenged her.

I don't want to say anything.

I'm the one who brought it up, Nick said. Not Zola. All I mentioned was that you and Ryan might be fighting.

And you and Sarah aren't? We haven't seen her in eight fucking days.

We're not fighting. She just hasn't wanted to leave the house.

How are you so calm about all of this? Christina said. How are you not angry?

Hey, back off, Matt said. And lower your voice. Not all of us have to feel the same way you do about everything.

I'm not saying you do. But while we're on it, I saw you yesterday. With Tyler. At the funeral. Matt, he fucking left you in the hallway. If anyone should be angry, it's you.

At least Tyler was there, Zola said.

Christina turned to her. What the fuck is that supposed to mean?

Zola met her eyes. It means your boyfriend wasn't. It means he's an asshole.

Zola expected Christina to erupt. Expected to wish she could take back the words. But it felt like a freedom to at last say what she should have told Christina their freshman year. Zola braced herself but Christina only sat down in the armchair next to Nick, the features of her face falling.

He's got a bullet in his leg, she said softly. He can't leave the house.

Look, I'm sorry, Zola conceded. Chris, I didn't mean what I said.

Of course you did. I know you've felt that way for a long time.

Zola sighed. What do you want me to say? Sometimes he's not a nice guy.

Zola expected her to fight. But she only sat there and Zola all at once felt terrible.

You know what? Christina said. You're right. Sometimes he's not.

She leaned back into the cushions, far softer than anything Ryan had said or done across the past days. He hadn't called. He hadn't asked where she was inside the school, how she felt about Elise, how she was doing given gunfire and burning all around them. He'd let her smash a frame and walk away. *Get in the car, you fucking bitch.*

I'm so stupid, Christina said. Jesus Christ. Do you all feel this way? Have all of you wanted to tell me for two years that I'm dating an asshole?

Matt wanted to tell her she wasn't alone but Nick stepped in instead.

I'm sure Ryan's just hurting, Nick said. Same as Sarah. Same as Tyler. Same as everyone in the entire goddamn school.

Zola sat back in her armchair. She felt exhausted. She didn't want to talk about yearbook, about photographs, about the pettiness of relationships. The only one of the four of them who didn't have a boyfriend or girlfriend and listening to them, she wanted to keep it that way. She gritted her teeth not to scream that compared to what was happening in their high school and community and everything beating around in her brain like a brood of bats this was all child's play, nothing but small-minded bullshit.

She glanced at the photos and news clippings scattered across the table. This is way beyond us, was all she said. What are we doing? There's nothing we can do.

We're putting together a yearbook, Nick said. That's all we can do.

Why? Who will want it? No one's going to want to fucking remember this.

Look, we have to, Nick said. We have until spring to get this right.

Zola felt her blood spike. Did he? Did he know? His English class, desks pressed to the door. His girlfriend in the choir room, completely safe beneath the risers, everyone quiet and huddled against the walls. Zola wanted to take the articles, the photographs. She wanted to claw them into shreds. She looked at Matt. *What did you see?* Zola wanted to ask him, wanted to resume their conversation from the haloed light of her driveway. *How could you see what you saw and write what you did, how can you be here talking about this shit instead of slashing your own heart out?* She closed her eyes. Breathed.

Have you taken any pictures? Nick asked.

I haven't. Not a single one.

Come on, Zol, Matt said. We need your help.

What if I don't want to help?

Zola couldn't stop herself. She'd lashed out at Nick and Christina and now she could lash out at Matt. Three for three. She knew her role, well defined since they'd first worked together on the freshman yearbook staff. The only one who knew the camera, the angles. The rule of thirds, the principles of composition. She saw Matt flinch at her voice. *You are a bitch,* she told herself. *Stop being such a bitch.*

I'll do what I can, she finally said. I promise.

Take pictures, Nick said. Anything you want. Maybe not now. Maybe not right away. But photographs of what we should remember. Pictures we need to include.

Matt looked away, his hands lingering over the photos of burned homes. Christina still held the profile he'd written of Caroline Black.

I'll try to write a profile, Christina said. I haven't gotten to it yet.

I've only done it because I can't sleep, Matt said. It's fine to take your time.

I'll keep researching, Nick said. Not *Billboard* hits or Oscar winners, he knew: all of this so far afield from the current events he'd been expected to include before.

Fine, Zola said. We'll do this.

Words she spoke. Words she didn't believe.

MATT RETURNED HOME just before lunch to his father's car in the driveway, the sun high and strained. He found his mother in the living room, sitting on the couch still reading her book on President Bush. The War on Terror. Weapons of mass destruction Matt wondered briefly if they'd ever find.

Dad's home?

He's in the office. She glanced up from her book. Came home an hour ago.

Is he working?

How are your friends? Zola, Nick. How are they doing?

We're trying to plan the yearbook.

You have time. You have all year.

Were you at the shelter this morning? Guinea pigs adopted?

I'll find out tomorrow. I've just been here reading since your father came home.

Does he know anything?

He's working. But you can ask him yourself.

Matt walked down the hallway and found the door to the office half-closed, an angle of light slicing the carpet. Matt knocked. When his father didn't answer he creaked open the door. His father sat at the desk, pen in hand, papers scattered across every surface of the wood: as much paper as the newsprint covering the table at Paul's Books.

Any news? Matt asked.

His father set down his pen. There's nothing here. Nothing you should see.

His father watched him and Matt saw in his face that he couldn't acknowledge his son had seen. The school hallway. The carpet. What he couldn't say, just like moving down the hallway and closing the door while his mother held him, the razored silence of the living room. His face pressed to her chest. The heat of his own breath against her shirt. His mother whispering *it's okay, he'll come around,* his mother telling him again and again, you are who you are and you are known.

I wish I could keep you from this, his father said.

You can't, Matt said. He sat down near the desk and his father let him.

I can't show you everything, his father said. I'm bound by my job and the law.

Can you at least tell me what you're looking for?

An arsonist. Even though the evidence we have shows a lack of foul play, we're trying to determine if this is intentional. We're comparing evidence from each of these fires and if they're connected at all to the high school.

So you do know something about the high school investigation.

His father looked at him. Not really. Just the evidence we need.

Evidence, Matt thought. He remembered the time over summer when, long after he'd locked up the theater for the night, he and Tyler drove back and watched a filmstrip in the projection booth, the theater empty below them. *28 Days Later,* something terrifying, a reason for Tyler to slide closer and closer until his tongue was in Matt's mouth. After-hours. A transgression Matt assumed his manager would never know. How the next day at concessions, the sun pulsing hot through the lobby windows, his manager walked up and said nothing but dropped a condom on the counter, what had slipped from Matt's pocket to the projection room floor.

What evidence? Matt asked. How can you tell arson from an accident?

Matt's father pulled photographs from the scattering of papers and singled out an image of the Trenways' house just after it burned. A crowd stood at the sidewalk behind a barrier of police tape. His father told him arsonists sometimes lingered with the fire engines and crowds, that they were often the ones to call 911. That neighbors had made the call at both homes, that a comparison of photographs from each crime scene revealed no match of faces in the crowd. That the deliberateness of two fires in two homes of families who'd lost a child suggested something calculated but even still, there was no evidence to suggest either had been intentional. No accelerants at the Blacks' house. No burn trace of gasoline, no residue of flammable agents in the floorboards. Chemical analysis still being done at the Trenways' house, but no faulty wiring in either home.

What about Lewis and Clark? Matt asked. What are the links to school?

We don't have any. Eric Greeley is our only lead, and he's turning up nothing.

He's your only suspect?

He isn't a suspect. A person of interest. They're polygraphing the kid today. That's all I know.

Matt looked at his father and saw the wall: the invisible force field of confidentiality. What he'd brushed up against in his questioning, what his father didn't want to tell him. He knew the language of sidestepping, of skirting, words that placed no blame and spoke of nothing. Words he'd heard in the news, a lack of weapons and a lack of reason for invasion. Iraqi sovereignty. Mistakes were made. Words to conceal information before they revealed anything of substance. And Eric Greeley: short and hunched, his pants always too high and too tight. Christina had been wrong in Paul's Books.

Eric was quiet, solitary, always alone in the back of every classroom they'd ever shared. But not a murderer, Matt knew, as easily as he recognized his father's evasion.

Dad, Matt said.

His father didn't look at him.

Dad, I saw something awful. Inside the school.

I know. His father gathered the papers and photographs into a stack. It's why we shouldn't talk about these things. You should be resting. I've already told you too much.

Matt thought of the bookstore. A fight. How it had been the worst meeting they'd had but had still opened a channel of words between them.

Why is it easier? Matt heard himself say.

Why is what easier?

Talking about all of this. Exchanging facts. Looking at photographs. Instead of talking about how either of us feels.

Matt's father looked at him. What is it, son? How is it that you feel?

He heard the irritation in his father's voice. A familiar impatience. But also something searching and honest, something else beneath a learned temper: that maybe he'd always wanted Matt to ask him how it felt. What it was to be a father. What it was to receive a phone call at the police station, to locate a child in a public library parking lot. To know no other news. To rush through stoplights believing that this was the end. Matt watched his father's face and lost the words, had no clue what to ask, had no idea how he felt. Angry. Exposed. Beyond control of his own life. Pulled open and hollowed out. Lost to photographs and reports that disfigured him if he looked at them too closely, information he drank in like water to flush out Caroline's body on the floor, Tyler vanishing down the hallway, Caleb Raynor depriving them all of a life.

I don't know, Matt said. I don't know how I feel.

His father put a hand on his for a moment before pulling it away.

You tell me when you know, he said. Even if I'm busy. You might not think it, but I'm able to listen.

Eric Greeley, Matt said.

The comfort of facts he put back on like a cloak.

What about him?

We were all talking about him today. If he's not a suspect, then who?

Matt's father rested his hands on the stack of papers.

You don't know, do you? Matt realized.

This might not be arson, his father said. Maybe it's just two unfortunate coincidences. There's no foul play yet. Not a shred of condemning evidence.

Matt glanced at his father's photographs and felt the lining of his throat burn. That what protected them, the police, was nothing but a series of smoke screens. That no one knew anything, nothing was certain. That his father was fallible, as faulted as anyone.

NICK STOPPED BY Sarah's house on his way home with a fudge brownie, the one bakery item Paul's Books was known for. He hadn't wanted to press Matt any further for details but thought nonetheless across the entire car ride about the fires, the lack of evidence. How he'd looked up cremation, how human skin burns. How high the temperature. How immense the pressure to erase bone, to leave nothing behind. How impossible it was that there was no trace of a single body. He walked up the steps to Sarah's front porch and was surprised to see Sarah answer when he knocked, her face fresh, her hair cleaned and pulled back in a ponytail.

Well, look at you, he said.

Her eyes fell to the brown bag. Did you bring me something?

From Paul's. I was just there.

She pulled the brownie from the bag.

Can I come in? Nick asked.

She left the door open and Nick followed her in.

Where's your mom?

Out. Errands. Every errand she can think of to keep herself busy. We're both going a little stir-crazy here.

Nick followed Sarah into the living room and sat down on the couch, a wide sofa facing the room's bay windows toward the back-yard woods. Sarah curled into his lap, jersey shorts fluttering against his jeans. Nick pulled his hands around her legs.

How are you feeling?

I got tired. Tired of lying in bed feeling sorry for myself.

I wouldn't call it that.

She ate the last of the brownie, crumpled the bag, and threw it toward the coffee table, her muscles moving against his chest. She tucked her face into his neck and he looked out the window above her head. Trees shedding their leaves, thin enough to see another row of houses beyond their woods. He thought of the Trenways' home, the Blacks', what made them different from any other home of families who had lost someone.

Those fires, he said. They have to be connected.

Let's just not talk about it. Only one more day before the week-end, then we go back. Timber Creek. Can you even imagine it?

Nick shook his head. There was nothing anymore that seemed unimaginable.

When does choir practice start back up? he asked.

I have no idea. But I promised myself I'd still try out for *Pippin* this spring.

Nick could barely picture the spring, if they'd be back at Lewis and Clark or still at Timber Creek. But Sarah was talking. Far better than the state she'd been in across the past days. He wanted to keep her speaking, keep her thinking ahead even if he couldn't.

I'll come, he said. I'll be in the first row if you get the part.

You'll come. Is that all you'll do?

She grinned and Nick realized she was teasing him, the question of sex. The same conversation they'd had all summer, what he'd again forgotten for Web pages on fire investigation, on cremation, on the management of crime scenes.

Maybe now isn't a great time to talk about this.

Why not? she said. I think it's the perfect time to talk about this.

Because we've talked about it ad nauseam. And you're just starting to feel better.

Then let's not talk about it then. She smiled. Let's not talk about it at all.

He heard the whoosh of water beyond the window, a creek running somewhere through the ravine of the woods. He felt Sarah's breath in the rise of her back, in and out. He felt her hair against his chin. He felt her mouth still and damp against his neck, her breath pulsing in clouds against his skin.

He felt her lips begin moving up the base of his throat.

He stopped thinking as her mouth moved. A soft suction pattering up his neck. A pressure that scaled his chin. A gravity soft as stars on his mouth, a force that pulled him to respond. He kissed her mouth. His hands running from her back to her jersey shorts. The weight of her mouth increasing, pushing against him. She moved her hands from his face, down his chest to the buttons of his shirt. One button undone. He let himself forget everything that had filled his brain for so many days, every image, every news clipping. He let himself forget every excuse he'd used. Her age. Her well-being. She was telling him what she wanted. She'd been telling him all summer. He slid his hand up the divide of her thighs. Two buttons. Her body opening. Three buttons. He slipped his hand beneath the jersey fabric and under the elastic band of her underwear.

She pushed herself against him, straddled him, pulled at his belt, and unfastened the buckle. He felt his jeans tugged open, then her hand beneath the band, her fingers skirting the crevice between boxer and skin. He let her. His hand against her skin, her shorts strewn to the carpet. This was nothing they'd never done, an entire summer back before a week that had become a separate life, everything in her bedroom or his car but sex. She pushed herself onto him. His hand underneath her. She pushed herself onto him and he stopped her, his hand to her chest. *Are you sure?* he asked and she pressed herself against him and he held her back again: *Are you sure?* She looked at him for a moment, lucid, her eyes the same as he'd always known them: not taken by heat, not clouded by the listlessness of retreating to her room but hard and clear and hers.

I'm ready, she whispered. I've been telling you. I'm ready.

She pressed herself back onto him and he let her, let her weight sink down onto him. His shirt half-undone, her hands gripping his shoulders and the cushions behind him. She lowered herself slowly, with force, a sharp gasp of breath as he felt himself push. Then she moved against him and he pulled her to him, her face, her mouth a condensation. Her breath pulsing in beats that quickened as he moved. *Wait,* he wanted to say but she clutched him against her, whispered *it's okay.* Beyond the window, above Sarah's head, branches wavered at the tree line. His body shuddered, the trees breathed.

Are you okay? he asked and she slid from him to the couch. She nodded and leaned her head to his chest and he felt exposed, his jeans open, her shorts on the floor.

Was that dangerous? he said. The only thing he could think to say.

He had no condoms, no reason to think he'd need them.

I went on the pill a few weeks ago, she said, and Nick imagined the past weeks and beyond that an entire summer of heat-soaked months. How everything he'd learned from the movies was nothing he'd ever known: sex the center of everything, a magnetic field, a looming question between every teenager. How he hadn't even known she'd started swallowing a small pill, everything about him always so much inside his head that he hadn't taken notice. How she'd been right. Nick looked at Sarah and only wanted to be near her, nothing more. He reached for her hand. She let him take it.

Why didn't you tell me? he asked.

I wasn't sure we'd need it. And besides, it didn't seem to matter to you.

It matters, he said. I'm glad you're feeling better.

She laughed. I'm feeling better. And you?

The sun pierced the bay window, an angle already on its way toward setting. The days were growing shorter, Nick knew, wind and sun whipping through the trees. Nick glanced at the mantel clock and knew Sarah's mother would be home soon.

Good. Nick traced her knuckles with his thumb. But I should go soon.

You can stay for dinner.

I can't. My parents need me to watch my brother.

Are you okay? she said. The first time she'd asked.

His brain turned back to the folder in his car, the photographs and newsprint.

I'm fine, he said. As fine as anyone else right now.

She didn't respond and when he looked up, he saw sadness in her face.

I'm fine, he said. Really. This is wonderful. You are wonderful.

She watched him.

I'm fine, he promised. He heard his own words fill the room.

CHRISTINA ARRIVED HOME to her father still at work and her brother gone, a handwritten note left on the kitchen counter: *at Brian's.* Her brother's best friend, a freshman Christina knew hadn't been at school that day, home sick and watching the events unfold on the news from his living room. Christina glanced into the garage and saw Simon's bike gone and thought to call Brian's house but the need escaped her. Simon surely knew to be home before dusk.

Christina pulled open the refrigerator door and rummaged through two Tupperwares, containers of leftover Hamburger Helper and cold spaghetti. Her father hadn't shopped, had barely cooked in the entire week they'd been home, a busy season at Boeing with third-quarter sales. She pushed past a carton of eggs, a half-full container of yogurt. She felt a lack of hunger in her gut clash with the compulsion to eat. To pass the time. To not think of what her friends had finally told her: that Ryan wasn't good for her. To not think of the photographs of each home splayed across the table at Paul's Books, news articles on the fires and the shooting and sub-articles on gun control, the legality of purchasing a lethal weapon. Articles on mental health. *Who was Caleb Raynor?* She didn't want to know anything else about Caleb Raynor, the news insistent though she could have told them who he was: nothing. Someone who had blasted all of their lives apart. She closed the fridge and noticed the answering machine blinking on the kitchen counter.

She played the message and stopped midstride when she heard it. Ryan's voice.

Christina, pick up. If you're there, I need to talk to you.

She pressed DELETE. Moved down the hallway to her bedroom and closed the door, a stone in her stomach. She knew his voice well enough across two years. She knew that tone, a calm field before a thunderstorm rolled in. She knew how his face took on a stillness before he unleashed something awful. Before he rolled down the window of his car after she slammed the door and started walking away: *you fucking bitch*. The vacancy in his face. The lack of warmth. The same lack she heard in his voice on the recording, a lack she'd have avoided by not calling back if there wasn't a knock at the front door.

When she opened it, he stood in crutches. A maroon Buick idling in the driveway behind him, Ryan's doubles partner Chad Stapleton behind the wheel.

We should talk, Ryan said.

A brief spurt of elation broke through her dread. That he was here, on her porch. That he'd made the effort in finding someone to drive him, his cast an obstruction, an obstacle he'd overcome to bridge the streets between them and talk to her.

I guess we should, she said. You haven't called in three days.

Yeah, this isn't about that.

She didn't invite him in. Dread pooling. She knew then what he'd come to say.

I don't think we should do this anymore.

Stomach gutted. Do what?

This. I can't do this anymore.

What exactly is it you can't do?

I can't be with you. It's not working.

Yeah, it's not working. Where the fuck have you been for three days?

Oh, I'm the one who was supposed to call? You threw a picture at my face. I was fucking shot, Christina. And that's what you do?

She didn't respond. The evening's cold air blew in through the open door. She glanced beyond the front porch to the Buick, where Chad sat watching them.

Look, I'll be leaving soon anyway, Ryan said. For college.

You mean in a year.

We wouldn't have lasted the distance and you know it.

Christina kept her eyes on a pine tree in the front yard.

Where do you think you're going? she said. Where exactly are you going? No college is going to want you on their tennis team now.

He didn't respond and she felt dirty. Mean. A shell of herself.

She glanced up at him. Look, I didn't mean—

Fuck you.

Excuse me?

I said fuck you, Christina. Fuck you. You don't know shit. You've never known shit, just a poor little rich girl. Go cry to Mommy and Daddy that I hurt your feelings. Or maybe just Daddy, Mommy way out in Edwardsville. You know what you are? Just a little bitch. You've always been nothing but a little bitch. Nothing but a fucking crybaby.

Go, she said. Get back in the car and get away from my house.

That's right, he said. Be a fucking baby about it.

She kept her eyes on him, the stone in her stomach a flamed rock. Kept herself from saying something awful. From being him. She gritted her teeth.

Don't ever come here again, she said.

You can fucking count on it. You can—

She slammed the front door. There was nothing but noise. The wind outside. The quiet of the house, a siren in her ears. She leaned against the door until she heard the Buick pull away and gun down her street. She didn't think to put on shoes. No coat. She moved through the kitchen and into the garage, the concrete cold beneath her bare feet. Her brother's bike gone, her father's car. Hers alone in the closed one-car garage where she'd parked when she'd come home from the bookstore, that she'd planned to move before her father came home. She pulled open the door of her car and climbed into the backseat, the silence a womb. She lay down, the same upholstery that had held her body and Ryan's so many times across the summer, nothing but skin. She pulled her hands inside her sweatshirt's sleeves and curled her knees to her chest. Exhaled thin wisps of white, the first time all fall that she could see her own breath, a phantom broken loose through the sealed air of the car.

ZOLA HEARD HER mother come home through the garage, from her spot on the living room couch where she'd watched the sun set. The clouds had dispersed through the late afternoon, leaving behind a haze of gold in their wake. Zola had watched the gold flatten and disappear against the silhouettes of trees and tried to forget what she'd said to Christina and Nick and Matt at Paul's Books.

I brought movies! her mother shouted from the kitchen. *Back to the Future. Can't Hardly Wait.* I even got a new release: *Bend It Like Beckham.* Anything you want to watch.

Zola heard plastic bags rustling in the kitchen, then smelled the sharp scent of curry. Her mother appeared in the doorway, two aluminum containers in her hands.

I got Indian takeout, too, she said. Chana masala.

Zola took a container from her mother's hands. You didn't have to do this.

Do what?

All of this. Order food. Rent movies.

But I wanted to. Long day at work. I could use the break as much as you.

No scary movies?

No scary movies.

But Halloween's only two weeks away.

I thought we should keep the scary out of our living room. At least for now.

Zola's mother sat down on the couch. She placed her container on the coffee table and hesitated. She finally set her hand on Zola's knee.

It won't always be this way, she said. This will get better.

I know.

They'll figure this out, Zola. They'll find who's doing all of this.

So you think it's someone?

I don't really know. I don't know what's going on in this town.

They took Eric Greeley in for questioning.

Did you know him?

Not really. But I'd be surprised if he did anything wrong.

Zola's mother smiled thinly, but Zola saw them anyway: hard lines of worry. The sea of anxiety her mother hid with movies and takeout. Zola saw in her face the flashed creases that vanished in her daughter's presence but would sink back past dark, when she retreated to her bed and lay awake imagining the school, the teenagers, the homes. How there was nothing in this world, no movie, no amount of love that could keep her daughter safe. How Zola threatened her mother with every breath she took by being alive, being here. By being something to take away.

It's okay, Mom. Do what you need to do. Go to work, get things done.

I will. We both will. But tonight, let's just watch movies.

Zola chose *Back to the Future* and they settled into the couch with their takeout containers. A movie Zola hadn't seen since childhood: a DeLorean. A time machine. She pulled a plastic fork to her mouth and heard a soft rustling in the kitchen. A sound like paper, then a metallic clang. She sat up, alert.

Mom, what is that?

It's nothing. Go on, eat your food.

The clanging sounded again, then a tapping.

Mom, there's something in the kitchen.

Her mother sighed, set down her container. I wanted to wait until later.

Wait for what?

Well, I guess the cat's out of the bag.

Her mother disappeared into the kitchen. Zola followed her in and saw nothing, the counter and the kitchen table as they always were. Then she noticed her mother bent to the floor beside a small metal cage.

Zola crept to the edge of the cage and peered in. A rabbit, a white baby lop. Pulling water from a dispenser, tugs that rang out a rapid-fire banging.

Who's this?

I got her for you. I wanted her to be a surprise.

Zola rested a finger against the bars. The rabbit edged toward her and sniffed.

She's only eight weeks old. I got her at that shelter where Matt's mom volunteers.

Did you see Matt's mom?

She wasn't in. But I told them to send her our regards.

Zola peeked in at the rabbit. What's her name?

You can name her yourself. I thought you could use a little friend.

How long have you been planning this?

It was an impulse. I picked her up after work, with everything she'll need.

Zola glanced beyond her mother and saw a bag of straw, cage bedding, an extra water bottle. You didn't have to do this, she said.

I know. I wanted to.

The rabbit circled the cage. Can I hold her? Zola asked.

Sure. The shelter said the more you hold her, the sooner she'll get used to you.

Zola reached for the cage door. Hesitated.

Go ahead, her mother said. It's okay.

Zola unfastened the latch and pulled down the door, a series of bars that became a small ladder. Zola didn't want to reach in. She waited for the rabbit to inspect the open door and climb out. She held her palms open. The rabbit nosed them. She waited for the rabbit to hop into her hands. When she felt the rabbit's feet on her palms, she raised its body from the cage.

See, she's not afraid. The shelter said she was friendly.

Zola secured her hands around the small body. She held the rabbit close, its nose trembling. She felt something inside herself open. She leaned her cheek soft against the fur and felt the rabbit's pulse quicken. She pulled the rabbit to her chest, its heart shuddering against her hands.

MATT CLEANED UP the projection booth alone, the only Midvale Cinemas employee left in the entire theater. It was late: past eleven. He'd waited past the final nine o'clock screening of the night to build the following day's wide release. He'd taken in the buckets of new reel, unpacked them, spliced them together with the following week's trailers, threaded them on the film platter. A 35mm print of *Mystic River*, a movie he'd watched from the booth as it blinked blue through the empty theater below. The filmstrips hummed through the platter's tiers. Everything seamless. Everything ready for the first morning screenings, a movie he wished he hadn't seen. A group of friends solving the murder of one of their daughters, all of them linked by something terrible in their own past. Matt had turned away halfway through and looked out the projection booth's lone exterior window toward a dark sky full of stars he couldn't see. Nick had accompanied him here so many times, and so had Tyler, crawling up into the booth and watching him work as he built the films, sometimes letting his hands slide beneath Matt's work shirt, sometimes sitting with patience on the floor until Matt threaded the strips and the movie began. The booth was empty, always. Space only for one folding chair at most. Space only for a projectionist and not his partner, never intended for the beginnings of love.

Matt locked up the projection booth and moved down to the theater lobby, wide-open and vacant. He wondered what he'd ignored. If he'd failed Tyler somehow. Despite his anger, if there was any space for imagining what he'd done and not what had been done to him. The same as his father, how he'd thought his father couldn't talk to him. Given the chance, how it was Matt himself who couldn't speak. Moonlight flooded the panorama of the lobby's glass windows, a half-moon expanding toward full. Matt heard the echo of his own footsteps as he secured the concession stand and made his way toward the front doors. He locked them behind him, the night biting as he stepped into its stark wind. His Fiesta, the only car left. Somewhere in the police station while he'd scooped ice and poured sodas and threaded a filmstrip Eric Greeley was being questioned. Nodes strapped to a polygraph. Matt huddled into the hatchback, the air cold inside its doors. He could see his breath. Winter on its way in only weeks. He started the car and imagined an arsonist beyond the car's doors. A book of matches. A can of gasoline. No evidence at the Blacks' house. No foul play. Everything his father had told him. No answers, not anywhere, the moon above the shape of a question.

He turned his car toward home but found himself driving aimlessly through the streets. Suburban roads he knew like the cadence of his own heart, roads deserted of other vehicles at this hour except the occasional police car passing by. Keeping watch. Patrolling each neighborhood. Looking for any telltale sign of what didn't belong. Matt passed Paul's Books and the Dierbergs where his family always shopped for groceries and the turn toward Zola's neighborhood, her quiet street. He let himself make a left. He passed by her house, the downstairs windows still illumined with light. She was inside somewhere with her mother. He thought to stop in but knew it was far too late. He continued driving toward the corner and saw the police tape before he reached the stop sign. He pulled over to the curb beside the darkened shell of Alisha Trenway's house and kept his foot on the brake. He couldn't drive past the high school or Caroline Black's house but he could let himself see this. The house was deserted, no police cars or FBI vans at this hour, the perimeter roped off against onlookers until morning. Windows broken out, the roof splintered. Everything warped by a thick layer of charring. He glanced at the backyard, visible from the home's angle on the street corner. A few trees. The moon spilling down between their branches, too sparse to obscure an arsonist. Someone would have seen something. A corner lot. Eyewitness visibility from all angles. Matt thought to tell his father but knew this was nothing the police hadn't already considered. He lifted his foot off the brake and steered the car toward home.

AFTER SIMON RETURNED on his bike before dusk and long after she'd moved her car from the garage so her father could park, Christina lay in her bed and listened to the cicadas' drone beyond her closed window. They would be gone soon. Only days. With the weather cooling and the leaves throwing themselves from the trees,

autumn would send every cicada underground until the first cro-
cuses of spring. They whined through the window. White noise. A
crescendo that had heightened at dusk before tapering off to a hum
once the sun fell. Christina lay on top of the comforter, her body
splayed, waiting for the sound to diminish once the stars appeared.

She'd made dinner for her father and brother, fajitas from the
scattered assemblage of vegetables she could find in the fridge. Two
peppers. One sweet potato. A zucchini shriveled toward expiration.
She'd told them nothing. She'd kept herself busy. She'd listened to
her brother talk at the dinner table above the sizzle of cooking. He
told her father about his afternoon with Brian, video games and
cans of Pepsi, and how the streets were flooded with police and
news vans on his way home. Christina's father kept the television
off, a background buzz they so often ate with. He glanced at her
across the table and she avoided his eyes, asked instead about work,
his schedule, when third-quarter sales would be finished.

The phone had stayed quiet all night. Christina rolled over,
looked away from the window to the notebook on her nightstand.
She'd taken notes at Paul's Books, gleaned ideas from the articles
and photographs Nick had brought. She'd considered profiles, a
series. Who she'd write about, who Matt would. How they'd divide
and conquer their assignments, a task more than an elegy. She
rolled away from the notebook and toward her wall, her bed pushed
into the corner. She pressed her hands to the wall, the plaster cool
against her skin, and thought of Ryan's body above her in his bed,
the sheets soft and the pain sharp. How stupid. How fucking stupid.
She closed her eyes and lay still.

She drifted off and when she woke, the streets were as silent as
the house. She strained her ear to the hallway for the sound of television but there was nothing, not the regularity of her father's police
shows or her brother's video games. She glanced out the window.
No cars. One streetlamp carving a circle of light on the pavement.
She sat up and checked the bedside clock: well past midnight. A

wash of stars spread across the clear sky beyond her window. The walls of her bedroom pushed in. Only silence. A lack of anything at all. She pulled on her sneakers. She crept down the hallway and grabbed her keys on the kitchen counter before slipping into the garage.

The garage door was closed, her father mindful of safety. She was glad she'd moved her car back to the driveway, the first spark of hope she felt all night. Without the garage door opening her father would never hear her, would never know she was gone. She moved to sneak around the side of the garage, to climb into her car and drive away, but her hand stopped on the doorknob when she caught sight of Simon's bike tucked away behind her father's Taurus. She imagined the streets. Empty past her house but surely full of police staking out every neighborhood. She wanted to stay unfound. She grabbed her brother's bike. She pulled up the hood of her sweatshirt and hopped onto the bike and rode it through her neighborhood's backyard, through other backyards, connected land without fencing that kept her hidden. She rode until she reached a trail, a biking path from her neighborhood to other neighborhoods and eventually to the high school. A path she'd taken certain mornings to first period. Certain nights when she'd snuck out. A path that led to Ryan's neighborhood and on to the high school eventually though she wouldn't go far, wouldn't go anywhere near Lewis and Clark. She wanted only to be outside, limbs stretched, her body pushing and pedaling and moving. The brisk October air pressed against her face as she rode, the mountain bike's velocity pushing it down her sweatshirt and against her skin, a spike of cold that left her breathless, that made her feel alive again.

Rows of homes lay visible through barren trees, leaves lost to the wind. Porches spilled over with scarecrows and sheet ghosts, a fall holiday Christina had forgotten. The sky opened above her as she rode, wide and stark beyond the afternoon's clouds. She recognized the Big Dipper through the trees, the only constellation she knew.

Nothing but a little bitch. She rode faster. Let the brisk wind rip the down of her face, let her eyes water raw. *Poor little rich girl*. Her legs pushed harder to feel the wind whip across the trail and shard her skin through her clothes, to feel only exertion and adrenaline and the shell of her own body belonging to no one. She navigated the path through the woods and felt the tires of her brother's bike roll across grass and dirt and toward Ryan's house, a circle of gravity, felt her legs humming their way toward his home.

When she breached the woods for the streets of his neighborhood, she slowed the bike and checked the road. Everything desolate. The streets abandoned. No cars, no patrols creeping along the pavement. She pulled her sweatshirt's hood tighter across her hair and set to riding along the sidewalk, in the shadows of trees in case a police car passed and regarded her with suspicion. She pedaled toward Ryan's street, her legs pushing faster. Her hair windblown, spilling from beneath her hood, legs pumping her forward until she saw Ryan's house in the distance.

She also saw Benji Ndolo's house. Three houses down.

The silhouette of a figure standing in the yard.

Christina slowed the bike. Fear carving out the pit of her gut. The possibility of an arsonist. Someone standing outside this house in the dark of night. She slid the bike from the sidewalk and pulled behind an oak tree and peered at Benji's yard across the street.

In the road's streetlamp, she recognized the figure's face from the vigil. Benji Ndolo's mother. Christina knew from the papers: Benji had been buried Wednesday afternoon. Just a freshman, a boy she only saw when she'd been at Ryan's house, in the yard sometimes with his younger brother. She watched Benji's mother across the street, standing still in her front yard. She appeared to be watching the sky, counting stars or constellations though her mouth never moved. Her expression lay indistinguishable in the dark until a lone car crept past, its headlights illuminating her grief.

The car rolled through a stop sign, its taillights flashing. Christina looked at Benji's mother, her body inert, her face passed back to darkness when the car moved on. But the headlights had betrayed her. Her eyes broken. Her face disfigured by sorrow. Christina climbed back onto the bike, a moment too private for her to witness.

When she reached Ryan's house, she stashed Simon's bike in a row of bushes along the side of the house. She stole away from the street to the backyard, where she could see Ryan's second-floor window, dark and unlit. Her anger escaped her. Benji's mother, only homes away. A quiet agony Christina shouldn't have seen, a naked moment unfolded across the yard. She stood by the family garden in Ryan's backyard and watched his window and felt the air sting her skin.

The cicadas had long stopped humming, the grass silent. Christina noticed the hammock strung between two trees, a fixture she knew Ryan's parents would take down soon and store for winter. She remembered the summer: lying against Ryan between those two trees as their weight swung the rope. His chest beating a rhythm beneath her, his arms around her, his parents inside and unaware as his hands moved from her stomach to her waistband. How he unbuttoned her shorts slow, every tooth of the zipper a lifetime. How his fingers pushed beneath her underwear, his breath on her throat. The creak of their weight. The trees. His hands calloused and rough and welcome.

What she brought on. *Fucking crybaby.* What she'd let happen, how she said nothing, how she'd taken it. A year older, the sheen of his calves and his abs, a better athlete than her. His attention a heat lamp she unfurled toward like a seedling. The weight of his body upon her. His mouth a knife. His tongue and a picture frame and a slammed car door, a silent telephone and a backseat and *get in the car, you fucking bitch.*

Christina grabbed a rock and pulled back her arm and hurled it at Ryan's window. A rock the size of a plum. A tangerine, an apple.

A rock big enough to smash the outer pane of Ryan's window and bring on a flood of lights inside the house.

Christina ran. Grabbed the bike from the bushes, pulled it from the yard, ran it along the sidewalk to the opposite side of the street. She hopped onto the seat and pedaled, her legs already burning. She pushed hard and fast and away and made herself gone. She rode despite the smoldering in her calves, the twinged ache in her outer thighs, she rode until she reached Benji's house, his mother gone, the yard vacant and desolate beneath the cold stillness of stars.

She stopped when she saw smoke escaping in clouds from behind the front door.

Christina set a foot to the pavement. The rock forgotten. She felt her blood constrict. Her limbs immobile. Her other foot still on the bike's pedals, from the other side of the street she watched the cloud of smoke build until it billowed in sheets through the closed front door and flames appeared through the living room window and their glass at last broke apart in a rain shower of smoldered shards.

PANDEMONIUM

Third House Fire Kills Lewis and Clark Parent, Places City on Lockdown

FRIDAY, OCTOBER 17, 2003

ST. LOUIS, MO—Another life has been taken in the third house fire in five days, following last week's shooting at Lewis and Clark High School that police are now linking to the fires. Thursday evening, a day after Lewis and Clark freshman Benji Ndolo, 14, was laid to rest, a house fire at his residence in the 600 block of Conway Terrace in Midvale County took the life of his mother, Andricia Ndolo, 41. Police are still investigating whether there were other casualties in the home. Firefighters responded at 1:49 a.m. Friday morning to an extensive fire that burned the majority of the home, extinguishing the fire just after 2:30 a.m. Because of the recent house fires that claimed the lives of Jean and Arthur Black late Saturday night and those of Jonathan and Robin Trenway late Monday, all parents of slain teenagers at Lewis and Clark High School, police officials have brought in federal investigators to examine the cases' connections not only to one another under the suspicion of arson, but to last week's fatal shooting at the high school that resulted in the deaths of 35 teachers and students.

"I just spoke with Andricia earlier this afternoon," said Karen Nussenbaum, a neighbor who watched from her lawn as officials fought the flames. "They just buried their son yesterday. She was doing okay, given the circumstances. I saw her as she checked her mailbox at the end of the driveway."

Investigators are still searching for leads after the release of Eric

Greeley, 16, brought in for questioning on Tuesday due to his connections to Lewis and Clark gunman Caleb Raynor. Firefighters and police officials will continue to search the debris from all three fires in search of clues and possible suspects. Residents of Midvale County and St. Louis city at large are asked to remain alert and report suspicious activity. A curfew of 6 p.m. will also go into effect until further notice due to the recent prevalence of suspicious activity past dusk. Residents of Midvale County are asked to venture from their homes during daytime hours only for necessary activities while police investigate these crimes.

BENJI NDOLO

Lewis and Clark High School

Class of 2007

April 14, 1989—October 8, 2003

Benji Ndolo was a freshman at Lewis and Clark, having just begun high school in August. He lived on Conway Terrace with his
mother and younger brother, where they were sometimes seen
playing catch. He was tall for his age. Nothing else is known
about him. His mother stood in the yard past midnight seven
days after the shooting. One day after her son's funeral. Minutes
before the entire house burned.

THE WEATHER OF OUR HEART
A STORM

WE STAYED IN. We did not move. We paralyzed ourselves to help-
lessness, our blinds closed. We feared opening our front doors to
find that the world was what we imagined: an axis beyond tilt. We
stiffened at sirens, swirled colors passing beyond our windows, the
sound of emergency. We closed our doors to police cars and reporters locusting our streets, to neighbors peering from behind curtains
and emerging only to grab their mail. We watched the news and
read the papers and awoke to our parents gone to work, the way the
world hummed on out of necessity though they promised to return
in only hours, hours that unfurled impossibly before us.

We read of Benji's mother, a woman we'd just seen at the library vigil. We read of the fire, a blaze that reached a moonlit sky
while we'd lain in our bedrooms and felt a dark ache pulse beneath
our ribs only upon waking, that streets away another house had lost
itself to flames. We read of Eric Greeley, what we gathered that the
paper wouldn't say: that he'd passed the polygraph test, that he had
no connection, that he was cleared of correlation. That police had
no leads and no suspects, no clues though the paper wouldn't report
it, no sense at all of what the fuck was happening.

A curfew: only so many hours of daylight that would allow us
to meet. Our homes turned to confinement cells, the walls crowded
and the air compact and stale knowing we would not be able to
breach the doors past dusk. We glutted ourselves on information,

a twenty-four-hour news cycle, a television that blared Midvale County from the moment we woke to the point of pressing the power off. A news cycle that never took breaks for the events of the nation and world beyond us, information we mined from the newspaper's back pages to learn that the Shenzhou 5 had made it safely back to earth. That four U.S. troops had been ambushed in Iraq. That box cutters had been found aboard flights in New Orleans and Houston. That an unnamed list of baseball players were being investigated for the use of performance-enhancing drugs, only a day before the World Series would begin. We turned off the news for other news, an emailed missive from the Midvale County School District: Lewis and Clark High would still resume school at Timber Creek on Monday despite the fires, a return to routine that the administration claimed we needed.

Nick pulled on his jeans and grabbed his sweatshirt and sneakers and keys. He ripped the latest front-page headline from the *Post-Dispatch,* an open admission that police had no clue what was going on, and shoved the clipping into his manila folder. His parents already at work, a note his father had left on the counter: *Call if you need me—had a surgery I couldn't reschedule but I'll be home at noon sharp.* His mother had left her office number at the courthouse, though he'd already memorized it in junior high. Nick gathered his things and opened his brother's bedroom door and Jeff looked at him red-eyed and Nick pushed a sweater over his head and told him to brush his teeth and then they were in the car heading east to their father's office.

Zola woke to the rabbit circling, its cage jangling her awake from the carpet by the foot of her bed. She crawled from her sheets and sat on the floor, pressed her index finger through the bars of the cage. The rabbit pushed its nose against her skin, a light tremor of cold and wet. She opened the cage door, pulled the rabbit to her lap, and felt its fur against her bare legs. *Penelope,* she thought. *You are a Penelope.* The Pentax camera lay nearby on the carpet, pictures she knew she should begin taking like she'd promised. Christina and Nick and Matt would depend on her for it, but there was nothing she could think to capture. She thought to snap a photograph of the rabbit, its downy fur. She picked Penelope up instead and held her to her face, a soft shock against her cheek when her mother burst into the room, her eyes grim, the lines of worry in her face redrawn.

Matt awoke early to his darkened bedroom well before the newspaper reached our front lawns. A light tapping at the basement window pulled him from sleep. He looked at his bedside clock: 4:46 A.M. The tapping too irregular, too insistent to be only a tree branch. *Tyler.* The same tapping of knuckles against the window, what Matt didn't know whether he could stand. The reptile center's bathroom. Tyler's shoes disappearing across the tiles. Matt hesitated in his sheets before moving across the room to the window, before pulling back the curtain to a shadow too slight to belong to Tyler.

Let me in, Christina said through the glass.

Matt could barely see her face in the dark but in her voice heard panic.

When he unlatched the window she pushed her way into the room, her hair near frozen, her clothing cold. What happened? he shouted despite his parents upstairs still asleep. He knew they'd wake up soon once the clock struck five.

Benji Ndolo's house, she said. His mother.

What about them?

I saw it. She was there in the yard. She was there in the yard and then she wasn't.

Whose yard? What are you talking about?

Last night. Tonight. I was there on the street and then their house just erupted.

Matt sat on the bed. He listened for his father. Everything upstairs silent. How his father would awake in moments and find out and leave the house for hours.

What were you doing there?

It doesn't matter.

Chris, what were you doing there?

I was on a bike. My brother's bike.

But what were you doing there? Just tell me.

Christina sat down beside him. I was coming back from Ryan's house.

And you saw Benji's mother?

She was in her yard. She was just standing there the first time I went by. When I came back only twenty minutes later or so, I saw the entire house go up in flames.

Matt tried to summon Benji's face. A kid he didn't know, a freshman he could barely recall from Lewis and Clark's halls though he remembered his mother, her soft voice and how her features collapsed at the vigil. Matt knew where Ryan lived, at least three miles away from his own house. Three miles Christina had biked through the cold wind and her own terror toward his basement window.

I thought you should know, she said. You and your dad.

You've just been riding around all night?

I went home. But I couldn't sleep. I went home and I wrote this stupid profile then I rode around some more and now I'm here.

She pulled a crumpled piece of paper from her pocket and handed it to Matt. Barely a paragraph: Benji Ndolo. A scrawl written in heavy ink. Matt scanned it, short and terse. Not one of the juniors they were supposed to profile. Not a profile at all.

There's nothing to say, Christina said. There's nothing at all to say.

Don't worry about it right now.

I couldn't help it. I didn't know what else to do with myself.

You said twenty minutes, he said. Why did you stay only twenty minutes?

I threw a rock. I broke a window.

Ryan's window?

He called me a crybaby. He said I was just a little rich girl.

Her eyes filled. Matt placed his hand on her back.

You're neither of those things.

He said I was.

Ryan doesn't know shit. He's never known shit.

What's that supposed to mean?

It means he's an ass, Matt said, knowing he should stop. He knew the rules, never speak badly about someone's partner in case they ever took them back but he felt anger sear through him regardless. Zola had already said it at the bookstore.

I wish you all would've told me so much sooner, Christina said. I've been wasting so much time these past two years.

Matt ran his hand down her back. You're not the only one wasting time.

Christina looked at him. Tyler?

Matt nodded. He's been totally absent and awful.

Ryan said I was a bitch. This summer. He called me a fucking bitch.

You never told me that.

I never told anyone. I guess I don't have to hide anything anymore.

Matt listened to her exhale the words. Felt her breath move through her back. I hope you never feel like you have to hide anything, he said. From me, or from anyone.

Christina looked at him. You know, you never told me directly about Tyler.

We haven't been dating that long. Weren't. I don't know what we are anymore.

I'm sorry what I said about him. And about you. That he left you there. Clearly, I'm no expert on how people should treat each other.

Maybe we both deserve better, Matt said.

He knew he sounded more resolute than he felt.

Tyler has better reason to be selfish right now, Christina said. I guess we all do. But Ryan's been an asshole ever since I met him.

Did he see you outside his window?

She shook her head. I can't believe Benji's mother was just standing there.

You saw her in her yard?

On the way there. She looked like she was watching the stars. She just stood still. Not moving. But I saw her face and she looked broken.

Matt imagined the expression. The same lines that had carved away the features of every other parent's face at the vigil.

And then she just went inside?

I don't know. When I came back, she was gone but the front door was smoking.

And then what?

And then the house just exploded.

What do you mean the house exploded?

Fire just burst through the front door.

Christina leaned against Matt's shoulder. He ran his hand over her hair.

What if she set the fire? Christina asked.

Matt didn't move.

I've been riding around all night, Matt. What if she set her own house on fire? She was there, and then she was just gone.

That would mean she set every other house on fire, too. Wouldn't it? Or that the Blacks and Trenways also set their homes on fire, just like her. Is that what you mean?

I don't know. Both seem unlikely. But I thought you and your dad should know.

Was there anyone else there?

In the house? I don't know. Benji had a little brother. But I don't know.

Matt heard footsteps above him, the heavy thud of someone walking through the kitchen. Past 5 A.M. now. His parents were up.

I need to go anyway, Christina said and pulled away from him. My father will be up by five thirty at the latest for work. I need to get home.

Are you sure you're okay?

Matt could see that she wasn't. A mindless question. But she nodded and pulled the hood of her sweatshirt over her hair and slipped out the window. Matt sat for a moment on his bed. Felt the cool tile of the basement floor beneath his feet. He hadn't put on socks, had barely put on pants before letting Christina in. He grabbed a sweatshirt and headed upstairs to the kitchen, where only his mother sat at the table in her robe.

Where's Dad?

Good morning to you, too.

Matt noticed thick bags beneath her eyes. She sipped a mug of coffee.

He's out on another case, she said. He left two hours ago. It's not good, Matt.

I know.

What do you know?

Christina told me. She was just here. She saw it happen. Benji's house.

She was here? His mother's face flared with alarm. And she was there, last night? What do you mean she was there?

She was out biking. She passed by on the sidewalk and saw the house begin to burn. Benji's mother was outside. In the yard, right before it happened.

Why was Christina out biking? It's too dangerous to do that right now at night.

I don't know. But she was. And she saw what she saw.

His mother stood. Your father should know this.

I know.

No, I mean he should know this right now, she said. I'm canceling today's shift at the shelter. She pulled the telephone from the kitchen's wall-mounted receiver and dialed the police station, his father's direct line.

NICK SAT WITH his brother in the waiting room of the obstetrics ward watching the sun crawl up the horizon through the panoramic windows, light piercing the steel of the St. Louis skyline. He'd acted on impulse, unable to breathe in the house, his father's office a reprieve from their television and the outpouring of news and the knowledge that under curfew he'd be locked inside all evening. He'd let the receptionist know that they'd come to see their father. She glanced away from them and dialed and spoke in soft tones. When she hung up the receiver she told Nick and his brother that their father was still in surgery but that he would be out soon, that they should take a seat.

Jeff played a video game beside him, electronic pings bouncing from the handheld console. Nick watched the sun cast a growing prism through the windows. Another day. Another fire. Three fires in less than one week. A week of sunrises that brought with them nothing but fear now for what the news would bring. A woman entered the waiting room and checked in at the front desk and sat down quietly across from them and Nick wondered if Sarah had come to an office just like this and when she'd done it, what he'd been doing elsewhere while she asked for a prescription and prepared herself for an inevitability he hadn't known. Where had he been? Somewhere out with Matt? Where was he when she'd slipped the first pill beneath her tongue? He'd barely thought of sex since he'd left her house, though his entire body felt like radiation, a neon sign. A flashing marquee of what they'd done as if he'd slipped into transparent skin, every vessel and bone exposed.

Jeff fidgeted in his chair. I'm bored.

Dad will be out soon.

Can I get a soda?

Nick felt around in his pocket but had no change. Only the thin fold of his wallet, the dollar bills inside.

Stay here for a second, Nick said. He made his way toward the reception desk, the television blaring in the corner of the waiting room behind him. *The Today Show*. Matt Lauer's voice. The last of a report on Iraq that four U.S. troops had been killed in an ambush, before he turned to the world of sports, that the first game of the World Series would begin in New York tomorrow. Nick knocked on the frosted window of the desk and the receptionist slid it open.

Do you have change for a dollar?

She rummaged through a drawer. I'm sure we do.

We'll be back in a few minutes.

Take your time. Your father will probably be another half hour at least.

Nick motioned to his brother. Jeff hopped from his chair and followed Nick down the hallway, walking with his handheld game, until they found two vending machines between the obstetrics ward and the cardiology department.

Take your pick, Nick said. You can have a soda or a snack.

Nick handed him quarters. Jeff squinted at the panels of both machines. Nick meandered down the hallway while his brother chose, back toward the cardiology wing and its waiting room. He glanced through the pane of glass at the lingering patients, a waiting room more full than it had been earlier in the week. Some watched the overhead television. Some paged through magazines. A little girl sat writing something in a small notebook with her feet dangling over the edge of her chair and Nick wondered what a girl so young was doing in the cardiology ward.

He heard the beeping of his brother pressing buttons on the machine. For the sake of brief quiet, Nick placed his hands over his ears. He peered into the cardiology waiting room through the cupped silence, the sound the same as holding a conch shell to his ear, an emulation of the ocean. The sound of a void. The sound of lack. Empty space. A hissing rush of unfilled air. He imagined the Ndolo house and wondered if Matt's father would find it the same: nothing left. Muscle burned away from bone. The sheer force of Fahrenheit degrees needed to diminish an organ to ash, what he knew by researching cremation and what must have happened inside every house. Benji's mother. The charred ghost of her heart. Nick watched the people in the cardiology waiting room and imagined the raging circuits of faulted veins that brought them here. He watched them until his own heartbeat weathered his ears, the rhythm of a storm.

MATT SAT INSIDE the Fiesta, his mother behind the wheel, the car stopped at the curb of Christina's house. The engine idling. The house a fortress beyond the windshield.

I'll wait for you here, his mother said.

She won't want to go.

No one wants to go. No one wants this to be happening but it is.

Matt stepped from the car. The sun was deceptive. The sky cloudless. Unbroken and smooth as the shell of a robin's egg but the air was brisk. Matt moved across Christina's front lawn, dappled with pinpricks of frost. Christina's brother answered the door and looked only vaguely surprised before motioning him into the foyer.

How're you holding up? Matt asked.

Fine. What are you doing here?

Christina came down the hallway in a pair of sweatpants and a baggy sweatshirt before he could answer Simon, her hair mostly dry, the tips still wet.

Hey, she said. Her face looked more startled than he'd hoped.

My mom's outside. We need to borrow you.

For what?

Not for long. Only for an hour or two.

She glanced at her brother. It's okay. Everything's fine.

Dad would kill you if he knew, Simon said. He disappeared into the living room.

He knows I was out, Christina whispered, but he doesn't know anything else.

My mom knows, Matt said. She was up when you left my room. She called my father and we need to take you to the station. You're not in trouble. I promise. He just needs to hear what you saw.

I barely have anything to tell him.

You do. You have more to tell him than anyone else in town.

I'm scared.

I know. But my mom and I will be there with you, too.

Christina glanced back at Simon. Hey, I'm going out for a little while.

Can you bring food back? Maybe a pizza?

Make your own damn lunch.

I would but there's nothing in the fridge.

Matt heard Christina's voice soften. What kind do you want? I'll be back in an hour. Two at most.

Papa John's. Mushroom. Dad left us some money on the counter.

Christina pulled on a pair of sneakers. She headed into the kitchen and came back with a twenty that she slid into the pocket of her sweatpants.

Matt let Christina take the front seat and from the back saw his mother pat her on the knee. You're not in trouble, she said. The police just need to know what you saw. They traveled toward the police station at the other end of the school district. No one spoke and Matt noticed the police cars and crime investigation units moving through the streets, their sirens quiet. Beyond them the porches of homes, steps dotted with pumpkins. Some of them carved with sharp faces and others untouched and Matt imagined the impossibility of Halloween, a once-deluge of parties and candy and costumes that felt as distant as the leaf-littered streets of his childhood.

At the police station, Christina followed him and his mother through the double doors and past the reception area to a series of small rooms without windows. Matt knew these rooms from the few times his father had let him tour the station. Offices. Meeting rooms. A break room filled with coffee and shrink-wrapped snacks. They stopped in front of a closed door marked JIM HOWELL, FORENSICS SPECIALIST. Matt's mother knocked and his father appeared, his gaze falling on Christina. He led her down the hallway to a type of room Matt remembered his father once showing him. A lone table. A camera. A microphone to take down testimony. Matt saw another officer waiting for Christina in the sliver of the doorway.

Who was that? Matt asked when his father returned to the office.

Witness services. I can't interview her as a forensics specialist.

She's scared to death, his mother said. Poor kid.

They'll take good care of her, Matt's father said. He sat down at his desk scattered with photographs and reports, not unlike his desk at home.

What's all of this? Matt asked. What did you find?

I didn't go to the Ndolo house. I've been in the office all morning.

Any news? Matt's mother asked.

They're still diagramming the house and its contents.

Benji had a brother. Matt remembered what Christina told him. A little brother. Was his brother in the house?

Matt's father was silent.

Dad, was his brother in the house?

Matt's father sighed. His brother. His father. His mother. No one survived.

Matt stood. This is fucked. Do you know how completely fucked this is?

Calm down, his mother said.

How can anyone calm down? What the fuck is happening here?

We're trying to figure that out, his father said. Believe me.

I don't know what to believe. Every day there's something else, something new, another siren or police car blazing down our street.

Matt felt the room's smallness and the air's limits before he felt the shame of screaming at his mother and father.

If you'll just sit down, his father said.

Tell me.

I can't tell you everything. I'm bound by—

Confidentiality. Please. Just tell me something. Anything you know.

Matt's father glanced at his mother. She looked away.

His father motioned to the papers beneath his hands. They're still in progress, but these are some of the lab reports. From fire debris analysis.

From which fire?

The Trenway fire. It's just too soon for today's fire, but we've had time to cross-reference the other two. We've found no evidence of accelerants. In either house.

So this is all just a coincidence. Dad. You really believe this is random?

Honestly, we don't know. We just know there's no sign of foul play. Both of them came back completely clean. We'll see what we find with the Ndolos' house.

Matt looked at his father. Why was Benji's mother standing in the yard?

That's why Christina's here, his father said. It might not matter at all.

His mother touched his knee. Please, Matt. Let's just wait and see.

Matt wanted to scream. Of course it mattered. He wanted to punch the walls.

NICK WAS IN the living room with his brother when the telephone rang. Jeff splayed on the carpet watching cartoons, their father preparing them a late lunch in the kitchen. His father had at last gotten out of surgery, a scheduled C-section, and had met them straight-faced in the waiting room though Nick could see they'd surprised him. *We didn't know where else to go,* was all Nick said. And though his father was never demonstrative he drew both of them into an embrace, patients waiting around them, the television buzzing through the waiting room the news that all of them already knew. He pulled them against his lab coat, his name stitched into the breast pocket scratching Nick's cheek. From the living room, Nick heard his father at the stove. The sizzle of a frying pan. The sharp scent of hot sauce fanning in from the kitchen. The midafternoon sun pierced the windows and warmed the room when the telephone split through the din of cartoons.

Nick answered the phone and heard Matt's voice.

I already know, Nick said. I saw the news this morning.

That's not why I'm calling. Nick glanced at his brother and carried the phone into his bedroom, shutting the door behind him.

Then what? Nick asked. His bedroom blinds were closed, the air full of visible dust. He opened the blinds and then the window, a crack of cold air blasting in.

I just got back from the police station. We took Christina there to talk to an officer. She saw Benji's mother outside her house last night just before it burst into flames.

Nick's eyes fell to the manila folder on his bed, spread open, the morning's *Post-Dispatch* article on top with its blaring headline.

Why was Christina there?

It doesn't matter. What matters is that the fire analysis has been done.

On Benji's house?

Not yet, but on the other two homes. They're still investigating, so you can't tell anyone what I'm telling you.

What? What did your dad find out?

No accelerants were involved. Nothing. Not anything that indicates arson.

That's bullshit, Nick said. You and I both know that's bullshit.

I know. I said the same thing to my dad.

Nick exhaled on his bed. Brisk air leaked in through the open window, a crack currenting through the room. He glossed his hands across the rough print of the news article. *PANDEMONIUM.* The headline screamed at him, an admission of madness.

What did Christina see? How's she doing?

She saw the house burn. But she's okay. Nick heard Matt hesitate. She and Ryan broke up. That's why she was there. I'm sure she wouldn't mind that I told you.

Is she doing okay?

Probably not. But she was mostly shaken up by what she saw at Benji's house.

What did the police ask her?

We just took her home. She seems fine, but she wouldn't say what they asked. My guess is not much, at least nothing beyond what she told me. She saw what she saw, but the police don't know what it means. My dad said it might not matter at all.

What do you want me to do?

Matt sighed. None of this can go into a yearbook. But you can look into it. Would you? You know where to search. What a fire investigation analysis means. What kinds of accelerants they look for. I don't know. None of this makes any goddamn sense.

This isn't our job, Matt. We're not going to find anything the police can't find.

Would you rather just sit here? Under curfew? Waiting for class to start?

Nick looked around his room. The bed unmade. An entire folder of articles and photographs overwhelming his sheets.

I'll look into it, he said. What are you doing today?

Nothing. My dad's still at the office. My mom's out running errands.

And Tyler? Nick hesitated to ask.

I don't know. I haven't talked to him in two days.

Everything okay?

Fine, I guess. How's Sarah?

She's fine. Nick imagined Sarah's living room, the sun pressing in, her legs straddling his lap and the weight of her pushing against him. She's finally getting out of bed and feeling better, Nick said. An evasion he was certain Matt heard.

Tell her hello, Matt said. Christina wrote a profile of Benji last night. He's not a junior so we can't use it. But I'll see what I can write today.

You can take it easy if you need to.

I should go, Matt said. Let me know if you find anything.

Nick hung up as his father called his name and the smell of cooked eggs reached his bedroom, the open window's breeze whipping the aroma through the room.

THE DAY'S LIGHT had just started to disappear when Matt's father came home from the police station, a half-eaten tray of lasagna on the table between Matt and his mother. Matt's father stepped into the kitchen and slid out of his shoes, the overhead light catching the circles beneath his eyes. Matt glanced away, speared the last of his lasagna. His father had aged rapidly in the short span of a week.

Were the streets deserted for curfew? Matt's mother asked. You should be careful coming home after dark.

No one's out, his father said. Only necessary vehicles. Only police.

There's no way everyone in Midvale County will obey that rule, Matt said.

I don't want you out, Matt's mother said. Don't even think about it.

Matt wanted to protest, just for the sake. He thought to raise his voice but found no will. There was nowhere to go.

We could watch a movie here, he conceded.

What movie do you want to watch?

Halloween's in two weeks. Something scary is probably on.

Matt's mother looked across the table at his father, who ladled a square of lasagna onto his plate. A small crack of worry fault-lined her brow.

We could watch a movie, she said. Though nothing too scary.

After Matt washed the dishes, his mother checked the television listings while his father swirled kernels in a pan and waited for the corn to pop. Matt leaned against the counter beside him. The piano trill of *Halloween*'s opening credits floated into the kitchen.

I found it! Matt's mother shouted from the living room.

Popcorn will be ready in five minutes, Matt's father called back.

Can I ask you a question? Matt asked.

Matt's father didn't shake his head no.

What's next for the police? Where's the investigation going?

Give yourself a break, son. Don't worry about it for tonight.

I'm not worrying. I just want to know.

We're working with the FBI and national agents, he said. Fire analysts and specialists. We're still pushing our way through so much debris.

Did Christina tell that officer anything?

She just said what she saw. It helps us gain an idea of what might be happening at these homes when a fire starts.

Would you tell me if it was arson? Is that why they instated the curfew?

Matt's father didn't look at him. It just keeps everyone safe. Makes things easier. All of this has happened at night. It clears the streets in case anything happens.

What's the next step?

The first kernels began to burst. We're still looking at Lewis and Clark, he said. Still retracing the kid's path through the school.

I don't see why that matters. Not now.

It's our only lead. Whatever's causing the fires, it's clear now that they're connected to the people and the kids in the school.

What about advanced arson techniques? Like ways to disguise the accelerant, to make it look like an accident?

Matt's father sighed. Why don't you go join your mother? Popcorn's almost done.

The kernels multiplied in the pan, bursting into tufts. Matt pushed himself into the living room and sat on the couch beside his mother, the lights dim. The wind threw itself against the windowpanes outside and Matt sank deeper into the cushions. The smell of melted butter filtered in from the kitchen. On-screen, an establishing shot showed a quiet neighborhood street in Illinois, the wind spilling leaves down its spine. Matt's father came into the room, a large bowl in his hands. The movie's heroine walked down the wind-whipped street with her friends as trick-or-treaters began to dot the sidewalk. A masked man waited in the bushes. Hulked behind clotheslines. Matt took a handful of popcorn and let himself be submerged between his parents and tried not to think of Christina standing at the edge of a burning house, of Nick at home in his bedroom trying to figure out what it all meant. Of an arsonist prowling through the dark, the same as a killer on-screen stalking a neighborhood's streets.

ZOLA PUSHED A wet dish towel across the Local Beanery's counter, closing up the shop before curfew when Christina walked in. Her hair pulled into a ponytail, her body obscured by baggy sweats. Zola looked around: no patrons left. No one in the bathroom, no one near the far windows. The sun dropping, a splinter of light. Nearing six o'clock, the shop's closing time and the stated hour everyone needed to be inside. Zola knew the shop would be dead throughout the afternoon. She knew she had to get out of the house, her mother at work, a long night stretching ahead of them once they both got home. She also knew Christina might come as she sometimes did, so many after-school visits for free muffins that would go stale by morning if no one ate them. She saw Christina's eyes, the whites faintly bloodshot, and knew she wasn't here for free food. Zola felt a flood of shame for the way she'd spoken to her at the bookstore.

Hey girl, Zola said quietly when Christina approached the counter.

Christina's eyes welled and Zola set down the dish towel. She forgot her shame and reached across the counter for Christina's hands.

Chris, what?

I don't even know where to begin.

Just tell me. Was it Ryan?

I was at the police station today.

Zola moved to the front door and flipped the business sign to CLOSED. She set a blueberry muffin on a plate for Christina and poured both of them the last of the decaf. Lowered the shop's music. Brought the mugs and plate to a table near the far windows where Christina sat watching the sun slip down the horizon.

Tell me what happened, Zola said.

Matt brought me to the police station. As a witness.

As witness to what?

Christina glanced up. Her face hard, her eyes the only softness. She told Zola about Ryan's visit, what he'd said. How she'd pedaled across town through the trails with the wind tearing at her face and how she'd thrown a rock and smashed his window, her rage the shape of a stone. How she'd fled on Simon's bike back to the edge of the sidewalk where she'd watched Benji's house ignite.

What did the police say?

They took me into a room. I told them everything. I told them everything I just told you, and they told me nothing.

Well, you're the one who saw it.

I don't know what I think. I don't know what I even saw.

Zola touched Christina's hand. No one should talk to you like that.

I know.

I don't mean the police, Zola said. I mean Ryan. Look, I'm sorry for what I said. I didn't mean to say it like that. But he's been talking to you that way since you met.

Christina picked at the blueberry muffin.

Chris, I mean it. No one should ever talk to you like that again.

Christina didn't meet her eyes and Zola knew, finally and with certainty, that it wasn't the first time Ryan had called her something awful. How Christina always spoke carefully as if protecting him, a deep cistern of hurt she hid like a well.

What happened at that party? Zola asked. That one at the end of the school year.

I don't know what you mean.

Come on. The one that made you stop drinking all summer.

Christina looked up. I didn't think you'd noticed.

Of course I noticed. I also noticed how tipsy that whiskey made you the other night. That's what happens when you don't drink for four months.

Christina smiled faintly. Trying to get me back in the drinking game?

No, I've just been worried. Tell me. Tell me what the hell happened.

Christina said nothing but Zola saw her lower lip begin to quiver.

You don't have to hold it in, Zola said. Just let it out.

The school, Christina said. All those homes. There's nothing I can be sorry for, nothing to be sad about.

Let it out, Zola said. It's okay, just let it go.

So Christina did. She told Zola everything. Picture frame. A broken window. The ruby lace of lingerie he'd never touched. The way the surface of water looked from beneath it, her lungs breaking inside a swimming pool. *Get in the car, you fucking bitch* and how she'd kept walking, how she'd walked for over a mile, how her slip-on sneakers had blistered her skin and even still she hadn't stopped until she reached home.

Zola listened until Christina fell silent. Kept her face impassive, rage she'd already unleashed across a bookstore and didn't want to let loose again. She knew they should get home, the sun gone, the horizon purpled beyond the coffee shop's windows. She kept her hand on Christina's hand. The store's piped-in music the only sound. *Let it go,* Zola said again and Christina began to cry.

BENEATH A SINGLE weak lamp, Nick sat at his bedroom computer, minding the curfew. He scanned every website, every article. Every shred of information he could find on chemical accelerants. Gasoline. Turpentine. Diesel fuel. A lighter's butane. The day had been a blur beyond lunch. He'd watched *E.T.* with his family once his mother returned home from work, a distraction with levity. A movie he was sure he'd seen at least a hundred times in his childhood, scenes he knew by rote memory but even still when the ship came at the end and E.T. touched his finger to Elliott's chest, *I'll be right here,* something wide and faint spread through Nick's veins, a dull but persistent ache. He'd made himself a sandwich for dinner despite his mother's protests, a lack of appetite after the lateness of lunch. He'd spoken to Sarah on the phone, her voice brighter but subdued, a conversation curled behind the closed door of his bedroom in case his parents overheard him asking Sarah if she still felt okay about what they'd done.

It was late. His entire family asleep. Slivers of moon fell through the slats of his closed blinds. Nick bent toward the screen of the computer, searching websites, finding nothing of substance. He looked up fire debris analysis. How investigators looked for accelerants in materials that were most flammable and absorbent. How they placed clothing, carpet, bits of cardboard in mason jars. How forensic chemists analyzed samples for evidence of ignition. How they distinguished accelerants from ignitable fluids, household substances that were combustible under normal circumstances. Forensic extraction. Mass spectrometry. A seeking of patterns, of ignitable liquid residues. A pattern Nick couldn't find despite two hours of searching.

He pushed himself back from the desk. Closed his eyes, clenched the bridge of his nose. The moon pressed through the window, a ghost of light. He raised the blinds and looked to the sky, clear and remote. He rubbed a hand across his shirt and felt the tempest of the muscle beneath it, the same organ he'd tried to imagine as a living thing when he looked through the waiting room window at so many people seated in the cardiology ward. So many patients, so many strikes of the heart slackening out of tune. Nick wondered if a heart could physically break. He turned off the computer and let his palm rest against his chest. The same thumping of Sarah's heart through her shirt, her body pressed against him on the couch. A muscle of ventricles and channels. The strongest organ in the body, none of them strong enough for this.

He looked to the moon. Wanted to ask it. *What is happening here?* He wanted to scream it. *What the fuck is happening?* He imagined a flame igniting the threads of a bed, licking across synthetic fiber, breaching the borders of a body. The permeability of skin, fingernails, and human hair and a line of teeth the first defenses before a flame bore down to bone, down to the faulted chambers of so many sorrowed hearts.

ZOLA STOOD ON the back porch, the house's light spilling through the windows and across the wooden floorboards. She held Penelope clutched against her sweater, nose winking, fur soft against the brisk air. Zola watched points of stars emerge among the wash of dark, names of constellations she'd never learned. The backyard was quiet. Still. The hum of the television pushed through the closed windows behind her. Zola watched the sky and imagined a stretch of flames. She wondered what Christina had seen. How a house ignited. Christina in her bedroom less than two miles away, replaying again and again in her mind an explosion, an interrogation, a smashed window.

Zola heard the back door creak open, then footsteps. She felt a hand on her back.

The Great Square of Pegasus, her mother said, pointing. And up there, that small dot—that's Andromeda.

How do you know all that?

I just do. Lots of years on this earth. Lots of gazing up and wondering.

Zola glanced at the telescope just beyond the porch, her mother's favorite autumn tool. How it would stay in the yard until November's first hard freeze.

But what made you want to learn it?

I don't know. Curiosity. There's so much about this world we don't know.

And that's a comfort to you?

Sometimes. Sometimes there's peace in the mystery of it all.

Penelope fidgeted, nudged farther into her sweater. Zola wanted to stay hard, her body impermeable, skin tough as metal. She felt herself breaking regardless. Alisha's house down the street just remains now of what a home had been. She wondered about peace. If Alisha's parents had known it. If mystery was ever any comfort to them.

How're you doing, baby?

I'm fine.

You say that, but I worry.

I'm as fine as I can be. I'm alive. What else do you want me to say?

You can talk to me, Zol.

I know.

I want to know you're okay.

Zola looked to the sky. We learned in science class that the light we're seeing up there is years old.

Look-back time, her mother said. The time it takes for light to travel that far. What we're seeing right now is starlight from the past.

Zola felt her eyes spill over. Something sudden. Something silent, choking, breathless. She felt her mother's arm enfold her shoulders,

Penelope's warmth against her chest. It's okay, her mother said, it's okay, just let it go. What Zola had told Christina. What she couldn't tell herself. *Let it go,* her mother whispered and Zola closed her eyes against the stars and saw stained carpet and the rough texture of a book's binding and the black thick of more blood than she'd ever seen.

I couldn't help them, Zola said. I couldn't do anything.

No one could. Zola. No one could. No one could do anything.

I was there. I could have.

You couldn't. Zola. Her mother's hand on her hair. You couldn't.

There was a fist inside her chest. Squeezing. Squeezing so fucking hard and at last unfurling. Zola felt herself release into her mother's arms. She felt herself small, nothing more than a seed beneath the sky's swath of impenetrable dark. She curled her arms around Penelope and felt a pulse soft beneath her fur, the metronome of her rabbit heart.

A BRIEF HISTORY OF
THE HUMAN HEART

THE HUMAN HEART: a muscular organ circuiting blood through the body, the approximate size of a closed hand. Pushes deoxygenated blood through the veins of the body to the lungs, then to the arteries bearing breath of the lung's oxygen to tissues and cells. Rests in the thoracic cavity behind the sternum, its base apex just above the diaphragm, two-thirds of its mass tilted at an angle to the left side of the body. Surrounded by the pericardium, a fluid membrane: between the heart and everything else, a protective wall. Lubricates the beating organ, preventing friction. Maintains a margin of error, a hollow space for the heart to expand when too full.

Three layers of the heart: first, epicardium. The visceral layer of the pericardium sac. Then myocardium: a middle layer of muscle, cardiac tissue responsible for pumping blood. At last endocardium: the innermost layer, the most sensitive and most protected.

Keeps blood from clotting. Lines the inside of the heart.

Keeps a guarded hand, every tight-clutched secret.

Four chambers: right and left ventricle. Right and left atrium. A four-leaf clover.

The atria smaller, receptacles for veins pumping blood to the heart. Less work than the duties of ventricles sending blood from the heart to the body's extremities, the ends of its own earth. The chambers of the right side smaller, a nearby circuit while the left pushes blood through the whole body. The reason for the left's greater size. The reason for the heart mistaken always as a left-sided organ. The reason to hold a hand to the left breast when placing a palm above the heart.

Valves: prevent blood from backtracking, from getting lost in itself.

Atrioventricular valves: in the middle of the heart. Keep blood flowing solely from atria to ventricles, a one-way route.

Semilunar valves: between ventricles and the arteries that carry blood from the heart. Named for the moon, the crescent cusps that form their passage. Controls blood flow through the body, the same as a moon, manipulating the tide of our veins.

The heart: never at rest. Constantly in flux between systole and diastole, either pushing out or taking in. Cardiac cycle: the life span of a single heartbeat. A heartbeat in three phases the eternity of a second, the movement of blood from the ventricles then to the aorta and then to each chamber. Atrial systole, ventricular systole, relaxation. All four chambers filled. The heart sated.

A fraction of second, an infinity. The only moment the heart is alone.

What we know as a heartbeat: the cycle in sound, the first long *lubb* the closing of the atrioventricular valve, the staccatoed *dubb* the subsequent sealing of the semilunar valve. Heart rate: the number of heartbeats a body produces per minute, the average human heart pushing five liters every sixty seconds through a body at rest.

The heart sets its own rhythm. The heart beats a system of orchestration and conduction. The heart holds the wand above a philharmonic of organs, a coordination of gesture and signals and synapses. The heart is electric, its own current, a system of impulses and conductive fire. The sinoatrial node: a cluster of cells, the metronome for an entire body's circuitry. A node located in the wall of the right atrium that sets the pace, the rhythm of every blood cell. A node that screams its own ticking, *I'm here, I'm here*, or else a more piercing rhythm, *You were, You were*. A node partnered to the atrioventricular node, a cluster sharing the same right atrial wall. A receiver. A transmitted signal. Carried to cardiac muscles that contract in symphonic rhythm.

What blood bears: the mark of parents. The same code of cousins, sisters, brothers. The mark of children. The trail of their lives coiled inside the shell of our veins.

What blood bears: oxygen, glucose. Proteins and minerals and carbon.

What the heart bears: a system of pulleys. A complicated language of levers. An orchestration, a sonata singing inside a chamber. A fortress surrounded by a pericardial moat that if flooded will release, a hollow space.

LEWIS AND CLARK RESUMES
AMID UNCERTAINTY
Students Return to Class; Fires Remain a Looming Question
MONDAY, OCTOBER 20, 2003

ST. LOUIS, MO—Despite concern over a rash of house fires that occurred throughout last week, killing three families of students who perished in the October 8 shooting at Lewis and Clark High School, school resumes today at Timber Creek Recreational Center, a district facility located two miles from Lewis and Clark. In order to maintain 1,120 hours of class time, the allotted amount required by the state of Missouri to complete an academic school year, the Midvale School District made the executive decision to return Lewis and Clark's near-1,200 students to classrooms today. Security will be on hand to ensure that students make it safely to class and will remain on campus throughout the day in the form of Midvale County sheriff's deputies and parent volunteers.

Police are still investigating the most recent fire, which occurred late Thursday night in the 2300 block of Conway Terrace in Midvale County. The home belonged to the family of Benji Ndolo, a freshman at Lewis and Clark whose life was claimed in the October 8 shooting. Benji's parents, Andricia and Henrico Ndolo, 41 and 47, perished in the fire alongside their second son, Daniel Ndolo, 11. Midvale County police are working with the Federal Bureau of Investigation to determine a cause for this incident as well as two other house fires that occurred last week, all afflicting the homes of student victims of the Lewis and Clark shooting. The Midvale County Police Department instated a mandatory curfew late last week due to the fires occurring after dark. Midvale County Sheriff Albert Corcoran issued a brief statement late Friday night that police are still investigating the possibility of an arsonist, though he declined to comment further on the cause of the fires. No additional fires occurred through the weekend.

Lewis and Clark students will return today to classes that resume the curriculum interrupted by last week's shooting. Counselors will be on hand for students who need additional support. David Sykes, vice principal of Lewis and Clark High School, will assume the duties of principal in the wake of losing Principal Regina Jeffries in the shooting. Students who left backpacks and personal items in Lewis and Clark High School, which is still under police investigation, will receive new school supplies upon arrival at Timber Creek.

OUTLINE, GHOST

MONDAY MORNING CAME. We knew it would. A leaving of our homes for the doorstep of school past a weekend we thought might never end. A weekend of too-hot showers, blistered water to melt the week from our skin. Of tweezing eyebrows, shaving stubble, clipping nails, everything that didn't belong. Of raking backyard piles, of standing beside dewed clumps of leaves. A weekend of the final funeral, Alyssa Carver, the last of our lost classmates to be buried. A service none of us gathered any last gasp of fortitude to attend late Sunday afternoon, one that followed a memorial that morning for the entire Ndolo family. Ceremonies we evaded to sit on our couches, to watch the start of the World Series, to see the light beyond the windows shift as dusk crept slowly down the sky. A weekend of inertia, a curfew imposed. A weekend of stealing apart from one another, a lack of phone calls, of burrowing in.

We awoke before dawn on Monday to our parents already seated at our kitchen tables, a night longer for them than our own insomnia, the giving away of their children back to the world. We sat beside them. We read the paper. We chewed the burnt crust of toast. We saw the name of our school written across the front page of the *Post-Dispatch,* a glaring limelight we never asked for or wanted. That we would return to school. News outlets squeezing what they could from a story that lacked sensation, no fires across the weekend, no reporters rushing to the scene. We learned from the paper that certain parents of our lost peers had formed an association regard-less, a barrier against the possibility: Parents for Home Protection. Their homes a target. That some had joined, others choosing to be left to their own private sorrow, those who came together promis-ing one another the certainty of a neighborhood watch, a promise taken into their own hands if everything else was beyond their con-trol. We skimmed other headlines: new Al Jazeera tapes, allegedly from Osama bin Laden. A nuclear stand-down with North Korea, the potential withdrawal of thousands of U.S. troops from South Korea. Two games of the World Series, the score tied. Marlins: 1. Yankees: 1. And Iraq: Spain pledging $300 million toward the gov-ernment's reconstruction while a roadside attack in Fallujah left a convoy burning.

We pulled on sweaters. Hoodies. Jackets. Sneakers. We grabbed our textbooks, those of us who still had them, who hadn't dropped them in hallways or beneath desks, who hadn't left our belongings behind in lockers. We climbed into cars. We stepped onto buses. We trekked down the sidewalks of our neighborhoods, the trees almost bare above us, cold morning light winking down through the spin-dles of branches. We made our way to Timber Creek. Streets we knew, but to the parking lot of a new building. A building we only knew in other contexts, classrooms unimaginable apart from the D.A.R.E. workshops and peer counseling we once attended. We couldn't fathom walking in, finding our new lockers, sitting down in classrooms that were never ours. We couldn't envision listening to teachers talk of algebra formulas and the tilt of planets as if we never stepped away from Lewis and Clark, as if we could gather ourselves back together from empty halls, as if we could forget the sound of a sawed-off shotgun.

But we did. We closed our car doors. We let our shoes find the pavement beneath our cars, our bikes, the school bus steps. We found Timber Creek's entrance guarded by sheriffs and volunteer parents. We were handed tote bags of complimentary supplies.

Nylon sacks of pencils, erasers, lined notebooks, ballpoint pens. We passed beneath hand-painted banners: *WELCOME BACK, LEWIS AND CLARK.* Signs made by parents, friends of families, a community of volunteers. We stepped into the building. We found our lockers, assignments that had been emailed from the district. We hooked our jackets, thumbed through supplies, shed the weight of our bags. We took only what we needed. A literature book. A biology textbook lined in grocery paper. We passed down the hallways, the light harsh, the walls blank except for a United States map here and a bulletin board lined with autumn trim there, hangings placed in haste to make us feel at home.

Christina slipped through the hallways quickly, though she knew Ryan was still at home, knew he wouldn't return to school for weeks and that a tutor would bring him assignments until he was healed. She wondered what her peers knew, what they'd heard of a broken window, whether everyone knew they'd broken up. She found her seat in a corner classroom where her advanced-algebra teacher, Mrs. Gornick, stood at the front blackboard writing out the quadratic formula. *Minus B. The square root of B-squared minus 4ac, divided by 2a.* Devon Leary entered the room and sat beside her, a football player who'd burned their crescent rolls in eighth-grade home economics and earned them a B-minus. He glanced at her across the aisle of desks. Hey, he said. His demeanor usually cocky but this morning his manner was somber, his eyes cast down. Christina acknowledged him and he turned away, looked toward the front of the classroom in silence. Jen Chandra filed in. Charles Pool. No one spoke to anyone else.

Matt saw Tyler stooped above a drinking fountain, his mouth meeting a stream of water. Matt walked past with his English textbook clutched to his chest, hating himself for noticing the curve of Tyler's throat and the way his eyelashes lilted above the fountain. He pressed himself into his English classroom, sterile and hollow, its walls fluorescent white. Mrs. Brooks sat at the front of the room, glancing at each student who passed through the door. Susan Waterson. Jeremy Lechaux. So many people, so many peers who had separate memories of fleeing a school, different images they worried in their brains like a bead. Matt thought of the profile he'd written of Jacob Jensen. He hadn't spoken to Jacob in years despite still knowing the schedule of his high school classes, a far-flung supergiant, knew it in the way that amateur astronomers knew constellations and phases of the moon. He knew Jacob had been in trigonometry class, second period, though he knew nothing else of Caleb's path.

Zola found the chemistry room, a basement class retrofitted into a laboratory. No windows. Beakers lining makeshift counters along the walls. Desks arranged in pairs, a system of lab partners that remained intact between schools. Mr. Albertson stood to the side of the room setting up flasks of fluid color. Test tubes. Eyedroppers. A cluster of safety goggles on the counter. He looked at Zola when she walked in, the most awkward of all of her teachers, a man who she sensed cared deeply for his students but lacked every social skill to connect or make conversation. He motioned to the seating chart he'd placed on the front desk. She found her seat near the back of the classroom and waited for her lab partner, Sejal Chaudry, another junior who was in nearly all of Zola's classes on Lewis and Clark's honors track. A girl Zola appreciated for her sense of humor and eternal good mood. A girl who shared snack bags of Cheez-Its and Fritos beneath the desk when Mr. Albertson looked away. But when Sejal walked in her expression was sober. She avoided Zola's eyes and it was then that Zola remembered: Justin Banks. Sejal's boyfriend. A name on the list. A boy Sejal had just begun dating, a boy who'd asked her to Homecoming only days before Caleb Raynor rampaged through the halls.

Nick walked into the chemistry classroom two minutes after the buzzer sounded, a temporary bell for a new school that was nothing like their former signal. A digital sound, only one of so many things that felt foreign. Nick took a seat in the back of the room beside his lab partner, Dennis Carroll, and didn't think to look for Zola. The only class they shared. *It's just the first day,* Mr. Albertson said to the room. *All of this is new. It will take everyone time to know where we are.* Dennis leaned in close, his hair unwashed. The room's harsh light bore down upon them. Nick closed his eyes and saw only the artificiality of a computer screen, the sheer frustration of finding nothing. He'd kept looking across the weekend. He couldn't help it. The classroom's PA system buzzed above them. *Attention, students and teachers.* The intercom crackled. *In lieu of first-period classes, a school-wide assembly will be held in five minutes. Teachers, please lead your classes now to the gymnasium on the ground level.* Nick looked up at Mr. Albertson, who stared back at the class, a Bunsen burner in his hands. He set down the coil and waved the room toward the door.

Pack up your things, he said. We'll start this experiment tomorrow.

Nick fell in line down the hallway beside Zola. She acknowledged him with a nod. They moved with the stream of students pouring from other classrooms into the hallway, a flood that made clear, everyone together, how much smaller a building Timber Creek was than Lewis and Clark. An improvised space: for how long, the administration wouldn't say. As long as investigation and cleanup and bagging evidence would take. And beyond that, the possibility that no one would want to return, that even with replaced carpets and windows and so many bulleted walls the entire building would have to be razed, a memory no one could keep.

Nick followed Zola to the gymnasium that had housed state tournament basketball matches, games Nick had attended with his family before he ever entered high school. Bleachers stretched toward the rafters on all four sides of the court, seating filling with students and the metallic clang of their shoes. Nick took a seat beside Zola. He scanned the gym for Sarah, knew she'd be coming from art class. Knew mornings were once her favorite, drawing followed by choir. Knew she'd surely imagined again and again what it would have meant for Caleb Raynor to breach the school during first period instead, the art classroom his first aim after gunning down Principal Jeffries and her assistant. Nick hadn't seen Sarah through the weekend, a strange distance given the weight of what they'd done. They'd talked on the phone. They'd spoken in code of their secret, *sex* and *making love* still extraordinary in their mouths. But they'd remained within the cocoon of their own homes, Sarah sounding better but still anxious, as if an interlude of lost virginity was only a brief distraction from the rising gravity of returning to school.

A hush fell across the gym. Echoing coughs. The scuffle of sneakers against metal risers. We watched as Vice Principal Sykes rose and took his place behind a microphoned podium and then his voice boomed across the gym, the volume too loud, *Good morning, everyone* followed by the screech of feedback. He adjusted the microphone. Someone shuffled behind him and checked the sound levels. We regarded him in his suit and straightened tie. We'd seen him at Principal Jeffries's funeral, head bowed in sorrow and surely imagining the duties he'd take over when school resumed. We waited for him to address us, a speech we wondered if he dreaded. A role impossible to take. He began again: *Good morning, Lewis and Clark. And welcome to your new home, Timber Creek.*

We were welcomed in iterations, so many variations of the same words. We were told that despite hardship, we would persevere in collective strength toward a better year, a bright future. We were told that counselors were on hand, this week and throughout the year, for those of us who needed them. We were reminded of available supplies, extra textbooks, copies of everything we left inside other hallways. We were told that the Homecoming game would take place at Highland Trails this Saturday, a rival school, and that the dance was still scheduled for Friday night in this gymnasium.

We sat as the lights dimmed. We watched Vice Principal Sykes light a single candle. We heard his voice break as he held its light in his hands, as he told us his job would be impossible in replacing Principal Jeffries but that he would do his best for us. We watched as a projection screen lowered, as her face appeared onscreen behind him. We watched a slide show scroll through the faces of twenty-eight students, our peers. Three teachers. Four staff and administrators. A procession without music and without the face of Caleb Raynor, his memorial absent. We heard the shuffle of clothing throughout the gymnasium, the wiping of shirtsleeves and jackets. We heard sniffling. No sobbing. A lack of open sorrow. We listened until the lights came back on and the screen retracted and Vice Principal Sykes stood blinking back at all of us.

I know there is uncertainty, he said. I know there's still so much we don't know. But we are here for you. All of us. Every single person in this administration and school. We're here to get you through this.

And though we knew by *uncertainty* he meant the fires, a threat still licking through our streets, a portent his words could do nothing to extinguish, for a moment we believed him. All together. For a moment, the gymnasium our shelter.

WE FOUND OUR second-period classrooms after the assembly. The class we'd dreaded across the entirety of a week, the same peers and the same period Caleb Raynor had interrupted and destroyed. What spun as a planet, a spiderweb, the tight threading of a loom through our brains. Threads that caught our thoughts like netting, that pulled us back in looped waves to a Lewis and Clark room where our lives divided into before and after, where we hid or trembled or quietly lost the core of ourselves.

Christina found her classroom quickly, a small second-floor room fitted to the size of her French class. She sat with Henry Park, her speaking partner, and tried not to think of watching his face as they hid beneath their desks. Mr. Broussard said nothing other than that class would reconvene with the continuation of learning to order from a menu. He wrote several phrases on the blackboard: *Je vais prendre. Des* not *les. Merci, garçon.* Christina imagined her brother in physical science class, somewhere downstairs, somewhere safe and immersed in the study of planets. Henry began to ask her questions from across their pushed-together desks: *Avez-vous choisi? Voulez-vous voir les plats du jour?* She could think of nothing to say in response, nothing related to ordering food. Henry continued: *J'aime toujours le plat du jour. Quelle surprise!* She understood him. She hadn't seen him at the pool. She wondered if he'd swum at all during the past week, if the water polo team had also postponed its practices. She thought to respond but her brain caught on the word: *toujours.* Always. That humans did this. That they made words. *Always.* Ryan at home. Elise Nguyen in the ground, a funeral Christina had been unable to make herself attend. The great madness of the human race. That we created terms for impossibilities.

Zola found herself with relief in a drab classroom for academic lab, the new library still in transition, a library that was at present no more than a room full of donated computers until books could be reconstituted. A notebook of graph paper rested on her desk beside a pad of notes she couldn't bring herself to open. Her trigonometry test had been postponed until next Monday, a third-period exam she had a week to study for. She didn't know if she would. If she could look at the lines and boxes of mathematical paper ever again. If she could graph a y-axis and the plot of its points without calling back from memory the leaving of a library desk for the cover of aisles, for the vellum of an oceanography book. Her remaining peers congregated in desks beside her, the room too large for them and spotlighting what they were missing, who was gone. Twelve casualties in the library. Three of whom had been peers in her own lab. Empty desks. Connor Distler. Jessica Wendling. Alexander Chen, sitting right across from her at the wooden table in the library. She glanced around the room. Soma Chatterjee sat on the far side of the room bent over his desk, his hair falling over his eyes. Alissa Jankowski sat beside him, ears encased in headphones, eyes narrowed to slits as her pencil oscillated in quick strokes across a blank pad of white paper, surely an assignment for drawing class though who would teach it now? Who would replace Mr. Nolan? Zola's gaze landed on Derek Wilson sitting still with nothing on his desk. The Trailblazers' punter. His hands lay flat and Zola noticed them shaking. She wondered if he was imagining the Homecoming game, anticipating the pressure. If he was thinking only of the library.

Nick placed *Crime and Punishment* on his desk in English class, a book he'd finished across the gaping stretch of the weekend. They'd left *Moby-Dick* behind. Too massive. A book Mrs. Menda conceded they could leave in the past, half-finished and stained with a barricade of desks. She stood at the front of the classroom and led them through a discussion of the first chapters, of Raskolnikov's moral compass and his plan to kill. Mid-speech, her voice halted. Nick glanced up as she pulled her glasses from her face. *I'm sorry,* she said. *Perhaps this book isn't the most appropriate.* Nick couldn't imagine what she meant until he looked around the room, saw the pinched faces of his peers. Raskolnikov's motives, a plot devised from the cramped isolation of his apartment. Not unlike another home only two miles away from Lewis and Clark, a plan devised within the quiet desperation of a teenage bedroom filled with guns and ammunition.

John Sommers spoke up: *It's the canon. It's a book we should read.* Nick glanced at the bulk of him, biceps and quads that had pushed desks and the tower of a bookcase against a classroom door. Mrs. Menda looked from John's face to the faces of every other student in the room. *Is this okay?* she asked, and everyone nodded, some reluctantly. Nick felt his heart flash. A different classroom. Caleb Raynor all the same passing by the window of the doorway. As Mrs. Menda resumed class discussion Nick imagined the steady pulse of his own chest, strong and ordered but jolted by the terror of memory, out of synch for a moment from the cadenced clockwork he'd known across an entire lifetime.

Matt sat in world history, the class he'd skipped the week before for the cool tiles of a bathroom, a cleaned slate with no stain or attached memory of violence. His eyes swam across his textbook, a chapter on the Ming Dynasty, an era he knew nothing about except that it had been considered great. He closed his eyes. Imagined Tyler's body. Imagined the ripple of his abdomen, the muscles beneath his shirt that his hands had pressed against inside the bathroom. The cool of the tile, the heat of his skin. The gun and the blast and his feet balanced on the edges of a cracked toilet and Caroline Black disappearing to the carpet and Tyler to the hallway. Tyler was here somewhere within the walls of Timber Creek, a second-period class he didn't even know, he realized. He never even knew what class Tyler so often skipped for the refuge of the library bathroom. Mrs. Albers asked Brian Meismer to discuss the expansion of European trade in the sixteenth century and Matt sank back into his seat, Brian a star pupil who would talk for the remainder of the class. Matt glanced out the window to the same browning zoysia grass that populated his own backyard. He'd sat with his father at the kitchen table through the weekend when he wasn't at the police station working overtime. He'd sat beside him in the home office, a chair at the corner of the room while his father sifted through reports, photographs, so many documents Matt couldn't name. He'd finished *Slaughterhouse-Five*. He'd wanted to be in his father's company, in the presence of something being solved even if his father couldn't tell him. He'd wanted to sit beside progress. He'd wanted to know something was happening, that something was under control. His father could only tell him what would give away nothing to confidentiality. His father and a team of investigators hadn't ruled out arson but had no suspects. They continued to retrace Caleb's path though Matt knew nothing of why this mattered, what a path of gunfire could reveal about an outbreak of house fires. But he sat beside his father anyway as he worked and pretended to complete his homework.

Brian Meismer prattled on about the expansion of European trade and the Columbian Exchange, which brought crops and plants to China, a digression Matt prayed would at once end and go on forever. He didn't want to talk. He had no reading response. He'd done virtually no homework across the weekend, only finished one book. He glanced at Jodi Hernandez beside him picking her cuticles, then to his other side at Greg Sheth, his eyes fixed out the window. Matt wondered what the past week had been like for them, how they'd filled their time at home without school. If they'd watched the walls or lain in bed, if they'd numbed themselves with hours of television and movies and newscasts. He wondered if the weekend had held fear for them: if they'd woken up each morning expecting a new fire. If they'd exhaled relief that nothing happened, that they could awake Saturday and Sunday to a cloudless sky without smoke.

Matt sank down into his seat. His mother at home, alone for the first full day since she'd first heard the news. He imagined her running errands, hands gripping the steering wheel, putting away tomatoes and lettuce and sliced cheese in the kitchen. He imagined her at the animal shelter, replacing the guinea pigs' water filters with gentle hands. He imagined his father in his office at the police station bent over so many photographs and lab reports. He'd learned only one new thing across the weekend, sitting in his father's office all of those long hours: the Ndolo house. Same as the others. Nothing left. His father in his office flipping through blank autopsy reports filled with nothing but ghosts.

WE HAD NO intention to meet. We'd planned nothing, hadn't even spoken to one another across the weekend. But we gravitated toward one another regardless during lunch, every junior eating together,

the lunch hour broken down by class in a cafeteria too small to ac-
commodate nearly 1,200 students.

Christina found Zola sitting in a corner of the cafeteria at a
table near a large window, light streaming in through the glass and
highlighting flyaway strands of her hair. A thermos sat upon the
table in front of her, black bean soup poured into a small cup that
Zola sipped. Christina had packed nothing and wasn't hungry but
slipped quarters into the soda machine for a Hawaiian Punch that
would busy her hands. She sat beside Zola and popped the can's tab,
the punch flat and thick and too sweet.

How was class? Christina asked. Peers found seats around them,
a muted chaos.

Fine. I just had chemistry, then academic lab and trigonometry and history. Nothing exciting. We barely talked about anything. You?

Same. The assembly, then French. Then English, academic lab.
Honestly, I'm ready to go home.

Zola poured more soup into her cup. She didn't know what else
to say. She glanced around a cafeteria that wasn't theirs, people
moving through the food line and the salad bar with trays and car-
tons of milk.

Did you call him? Zola asked, tired of small talk. Did he call you?

What, Ryan? I told you, I'm done.

Just checking in.

You don't have to check up on me. I'm fine.

Are you? Zola asked, a conversation she wanted to force, to
break something open between them until she saw Nick and Matt
across the cafeteria making their way toward the table. She glanced
at Christina, whispered quickly, Are you sure you're okay? Christina only nodded before Nick and Matt were upon them, their trays
on the table.

Hey, Matt said, his voice lost to the clatter of the room. He
speared a fork into his lunch, a thin slab of turkey covered in trans-

lucent sauce. No one spoke. Nick ate his salad, a mound of lettuce he'd piled with diced ham and small squares of hard-boiled egg.

How was everyone's morning? Matt asked, trying again.

Really? Zola said.

If you have something to say, Matt said, then go ahead and say it.

I don't have anything to say. I don't want to be here at all. Do you?

Look, let's not do this, Nick said. Let's just sit. Please.

Fine, Zola said. Speak, Nick. Go.

I don't want to talk about anything, either. I don't want to talk at all. I just want to sit and eat and forget that we're even here.

Come on, guys. Stop. Christina set down her punch, its aluminum clanging against the table. She reached toward Nick. How was your weekend?

Nick looked away. This is stupid.

How was your weekend, Nick? she said again. Her voice insistent. She pressed her fingers into the skin between his knuckles, pushed against the bone.

He pulled his hand away. He refused to look at Christina but his shoulders lost their tension.

It was fine, he said.

What did you do?

I watched a lot of television. I spent time with my parents and my brother. We went to the movies. We saw *School of Rock*. We went to get out of the house.

Were you working? Christina asked Matt.

I wasn't there. I already offered him a free ticket last week that he didn't take.

Christina looked back at Nick. How's Sarah?

She's fine.

Is she feeling better? Matt asked and Nick nodded.

That's all fine, Zola interrupted, but what did you really do this weekend?

Zola, Christina said.

No, really. What did you do this weekend, Nick? Because I can tell you, I spent the weekend sitting on my back porch just staring into nothing. I tried television. I tried books. Nothing works. Movies? Nothing at all works.

Christina started to speak, but Nick held up his hand.

Fine. You want to know what I did? You really want to know? I looked up fire investigation. How the body burns.

Of course you did, Zola said. As if we'd talk about anything else. You're the one who asked.

No, I asked you to say something real. I forgot that for you real means only what you can find on your computer.

I'm preoccupied, Nick said. Big fucking deal. We all are. He nodded toward Christina. I spent all weekend trying to figure out what the hell she saw outside Benji's house. And you know what I found? Nothing. Not a goddamn thing that was useful.

Christina's eyes fell to the table and her half-empty can of punch. A sweetness that bubbled back up, the taste harshly saccharine, a nausea simmering inside her and pushing against the back of her throat. She looked around the cafeteria: people clustered at tables, not enough chairs even with the lunch hour divided by class. People sitting cross-legged on the floor against walls. People balancing their lunch trays on their knees. People sitting alone. People making small talk. People spilling through a space that was never meant to house an entire high school.

Let's not do this, she whispered. Please. Let's just talk about anything else.

But when she looked back at Zola, at Matt, at Nick and his half-eaten salad, she saw it in their faces. There was nothing to say. That they were here. In this strange building when two weeks ago they hadn't been. That there had been gunfire and so many flames and a vice principal who'd broken down before them. And in their silence, a lack of disbelief: that nothing anymore in this world seemed impossible.

WE AGREED TO meet after school. To try again. To talk about anything else but school, the yearbook, every fire. To be who we'd once been, meeting at coffee shops or Midvale County Park or each other's homes after school for no other reason than wanting to be near one another. After our remaining periods of PE, we changed in bathroom stalls, those of us in gym class who'd sat through the rest of the day in our own dried sweat, the bathrooms bereft of showers and lockers. We sat through English, Spanish class, through art and business electives. We made our way home when the final bell rang, a rush of fall air that nearly choked us when we passed through the doors of Timber Creek and past the security guards and out to the parking lot, air that was fierce and angry and bracing and welcome.

We promised to meet elsewhere before our parents came home and found us accountable again, liable to speak of school and our classes and how the first day back could have possibly gone. We agreed to meet at Zola's house, Zola the only one of us with a completely empty home, Matt's mother back from the animal shelter and Christina's and Nick's brothers home from school. We agreed to meet despite Zola's reluctance, the storm of her mood unshaken. *Whatever we talk about,* she'd said at the lunch table, *I refuse to talk about yearbook or the fires.* A demand left hanging in the cafeteria's air amid the ringing of the lunch-line cash register and the hum of soda machines.

We gathered in her living room, slanted light already disappearing, the days growing shorter and the nights longer. We crowded on the couch and two recliners. Zola poured us lemonade, spiked with nothing, though Matt asked. She set our glasses on the coffee table and left out the pitcher, a hospitality without warmth.

Matt extended the leg rest on the recliner next to Christina and leaned back and asked her if swimming practice had started again.

Next week. She pulled her knees beneath her on the couch. I've been to the pool, though. I've been practicing on my own to keep up my strength.

Matt thought to ask more but knew his questions would hit a wall. Elise on the team. Christina's relay partner. Her funeral on Saturday, he knew. He didn't want to ask if Christina had gone or what her relay group would do in Elise's absence. If the team had planned a separate memorial. A ceremony apart, their own private mourning.

I'm sorry about you and Ryan, Nick said from beside her on the couch.

Christina looked at Matt. You told him?

I didn't think you'd mind. It's not exactly a secret.

I could've guessed, Nick said. From what you said at the bookstore. Anyway, I'm sorry. That you're going through it. And that I said anything about it.

No, it's fine. Christina took a sip of her lemonade. Matt's right. It's not a secret. I just feel ashamed. Like everyone knows. Like everyone at school today was looking at me.

No one was looking at you, Zola said. They have their own shit to think about. Now's not really the time for anyone to gossip.

She sat back in her recliner beside Nick's end of the couch and stopped herself from saying anything else. Anything that would sound callous, her mood still wrecked. *Now's not the time.* Anything that would brush up against the shooting or the fires.

I have gossip, Matt said. I saw Ben Kurtz and Lisa Johns together at the theater.

Over the weekend? Nick said. You worked?

A short shift yesterday afternoon. One to five.

Ben Kurtz? Christina said. The senior? Lisa's a sophomore. Isn't she on the soccer team? Ben's a drummer. What the hell do they have in common?

Who knows, Matt said. I didn't even know they knew each other, but there they were. There are benefits to working at a theater where everyone we know goes.

Do you know what they saw? Christina said.

Does it matter? I don't know. *Cabin Fever.*

That sounds about right. Nick smiled in spite of himself. Maybe they had a class together. Maybe they crossed paths in town somewhere across the past week.

His smile dissipated. *The past week.* He didn't want to see the indignation on Zola's face. What she wanted them to avoid, impossible to ignore. That they'd all been cooped up for the week in their homes, the movie's title a terrible pun. He lowered his eyes. He wanted to tell them all about Sarah and what they'd done just to fill the air but he pulled his glass to his mouth. Held his tongue. He knew it wasn't right. He knew he might tell them in his own time but that Sarah was far more private, that he didn't want to betray her just to saturate the room in sound.

No one's come into the Beanery, Zola said. Nick knew she said it to keep the subject changed. She looked at him. Not even you or Matt.

I've come, Christina said.

Tell these two what they're missing, Zola said. Free blueberry muffins and coffee.

What do I need free coffee for? Matt smiled. My dad makes coffee every morning.

What happened after that officer talked to me? Christina blurted, her voice casual enough that Nick knew she'd spoken without thinking. It had been part of her week. An enormous part. She was right to ask but Nick saw Zola tense in the recliner beside him.

Please, Zola said softly.

Did your dad talk to him? Christina asked Matt. What did they find out about Benji's mother?

Goddamnit! Zola shouted. She kicked down the leg rest of her recliner.

Christina looked at her. Zol, calm down. I know we promised. But Ben and Lisa? Who the fuck cares? Especially with everything else going on.

I care, Zola said. I care that we remember for one afternoon that there's more between us than a disaster. I care that we pretend for just one goddamn afternoon that less than two weeks ago we had completely different lives.

We did, Matt said. He sat forward in his recliner. We did and now we don't and there's nothing we can do to change that.

I wish we could, Zola said.

I wish we could, too. But ignoring this isn't going to help. Matt glanced at Christina. All my dad said is that your eyewitness account helps them determine what might have been happening at each of these homes before the fires erupted.

Did he tell you anything else?

Matt avoided Christina's eyes and she leaned toward him across the couch.

What is it, Matt? You know something.

It happened at Benji's house, too.

Nick looked up. What happened at Benji's house?

Matt looked at Zola, who kept her eyes down, arms folded across her chest.

The same as at the other two homes, Matt said. There was nothing at all left.

What do you mean, nothing left? Christina said.

I mean no remains. Nothing.

I looked up cremation over the weekend, Nick said. None of this makes any sense. It would take too much heat to burn the entire body inside a house. Too much for a single arsonist, at the very least. Unless they're using a material the police can't detect.

Do you hear yourselves? Zola sat up. This is morbid. There's nothing to be solved. Everyone's gone. We can't bring them back. All we can do is move on.

And how do we do that? Christina said, her voice rising. Really, how do we do that? How do we do that when our classmates are gone? When our school, our families, the lives we knew are all gone? How do we do that when we go to bed each night afraid that we'll wake to more news, another house burned?

Zola stood and set her glass down hard on the coffee table.

Fuck this. You know what? Fuck all of this.

She left the living room, her footsteps echoing up the hardwood stairs, to where her bedroom door opened and slammed shut. Nick held his glass sweating in his hands. Sun spilled through the windows of the room. Matt rested his head in his palms.

Christina set down her lemonade. I'll check on her.

You didn't say anything wrong, Matt said. None of us did.

She nodded. She disappeared from the room.

Nick looked at Matt. Did your dad say anything else?

Matt sighed. I sat with him all weekend. I saw him look through every file, every photograph, every report of chemical analysis. There's nothing they haven't considered. They're retracing Caleb's path through the school. That's the only other thing I know.

Who's retracing it? Nick said. Your dad's forensics team?

He's still on fire investigation. He said the high school's team is working on it.

What does a path matter?

I don't know. Maybe they're trying to figure out in all that evidence if he had an accomplice somehow. Maybe how he could have planned something like that with no one noticing, that maybe he didn't do it alone. Or maybe they're just trying to figure out how to prevent this from ever happening again.

Fuck prevention. Nick heard his own voice, amplified to a pitch as loud as Zola's. This is still happening. What the fuck does prevention matter now?

Matt looked up, his hands sliding down his face. I have no goddamn idea.

CHRISTINA KNOCKED. SOFT at first, then more forcefully when Zola didn't answer. She found the door unlocked and moved slowly into the room, where Zola was seated on the floor, back against the bed, her legs pulled close to her chest and a small rabbit sitting on top of her knees.

Zola?

Go away.

Christina closed the door behind her. Who's this?

Her name's Penelope.

Christina sat beside Zola and touched the rabbit's nose. When did you get her?

My mom brought her home last week. She thought it would help.

Christina rubbed her pinkie across the rabbit's small head and the rabbit squinted as if smiling. Christina never had pets, her mother allergic. Despite her mother moving out and living across the river, a precedent had been set. They were a family without pets though touching the rabbit, Christina longed at once for something soft.

Can I hold her?

I guess. She's not used to other people yet. As long as you're quiet, she'll be fine.

Zola lifted the rabbit from her knees and placed it in Christina's lap, a small bundle. Christina let her hands fall gently on the rabbit and couldn't believe how light its body was. No more than a pound or two. She ran a finger down the rabbit's back.

Look, I know, Zola said. You don't have to say anything.

I just want to make sure you're okay.

Zola looked up. Are any of us?

The rabbit hopped inside the circle Christina had made with her legs. Zola glanced at her camera sitting on the floor near the window.

I haven't taken any pictures, Zola said. What is there to capture? What is there to remember?

It's okay, Christina said. I've tried to write. I've tried and failed. I don't know what to say.

Nothing can explain this, Zola whispered. Nothing can bring anyone back.

But there are still fires, Christina said. At least, there were. And we don't know if there will be more.

So what?

So don't you feel afraid? Don't you want to know? Why this is happening and what it means?

Yeah, I want to know. I want to know why this, why us, what's happening, and when it will stop. Why these parents when they've already undergone so much pain. But I'm not afraid. I can't be. I can't be any more afraid than I was on the floor of the library.

Christina felt her breath catch. She forgot, over and again. What Zola had seen, what she'd heard, what she'd experienced on the floor's thin carpet. How Matt, too, had seen something awful but the danger was already gone, Caleb long disappeared down the hallway outside the men's bathroom and not blazing through the library in real time where Zola was, not moving through stacks and aiming and firing.

You can tell me what you saw, Christina said. You can talk to me.

I know. Zola reached over and touched the rabbit. I would if I could.

You can.

No, I can't. There are no words at all to describe what I saw.

Christina set her hand on top of Zola's, her palm running down the rabbit's back.

I'm sorry you're hurting, Christina said. I'm sorry this is happening to you.

It's happening to all of us. And there's nothing we can do about it.

Christina pressed her palm to Zola's knee. Wanted to provide what little comfort she could, the same as Zola had done for her in the empty dusk of a coffee shop. Zola pulled her hand away but let Christina sit with her in the fading afternoon light. Christina remained where she was, the rabbit circling against her legs.

LONG AFTER NICK and Matt left, after Christina squeezed her hand and walked out to her car and after Zola's mother came home and made spaghetti and watched reruns of *Saturday Night Live* with her on the couch, Zola watched the night stars through her bedroom window, the things her mother had tried to teach her. The sky was clear and black and a near-full moon crested above her neighbor's rooftop weathervane. Even in the dark Zola saw the unraked leaves scattered across the backyard's grass, shaken from a cluster of sugar maples that just last week had been aflame in cranberry. Penelope rattled in her cage, nibbling bits of carrot and lettuce that Zola had chopped, and Zola turned away from the window, her eyes falling on her camera. She leaned forward and let herself touch the Pentax's lens. She held the camera up, inspected its aperture. Depth of field. Distance scale. A focusing ring she'd manually adjusted hundreds of times. She remembered unwrapping the gift her freshman year, knowing already what it was by its weight. She remembered the excitement in her mother's face, the anticipation as she opened the box.

She set the camera on the carpet. Let her fingers run across its shutter release and speed dial, wiping away a film of dust. She'd neglected taking pictures. She'd ignored the duties of her position. There was nothing to capture, nothing easy, nothing as simple as words. What was it for Matt, for Christina? Words they could commit to paper from the safety of their bedrooms, a skill that could be turned off at will. A talent of imagination, nothing direct to observe or bear as witness. And Nick. Such shelter in the remove of a computer screen. Only research and compiling, a computer that could be shut down if the information bore down too hard. Only clipping articles from the newspaper. Only filing them away. But photography: what was there to do but stay immobile? She couldn't take pictures of Lewis and Clark High, couldn't climb beneath the yellow police tape and enter its halls. She couldn't walk to the doorsteps of her former peers' homes, couldn't ring the bell and ask for portraits of grief. She couldn't photograph a funeral. A home in flames. A community reduced to ashes.

Zola pressed her hands to the wall, her feet into the carpet. Her brain agitated, her body restless. She looked at Penelope through the cage's bars, her white shape a ghost. She listened down the hallway but there was nothing, only the quiet wheeze of her mother's soft snoring. Zola glanced back out the window. A wide orb of moon. She couldn't believe it had already been a week since they'd buried Caroline Black and her parents, a week since they'd cast themselves out into the wilds of the back-road cornfields, a half-moon solitary above them, the burn of whiskey, the complicated whorls of a Midwestern landscape. She couldn't believe that two weeks ago, only fourteen days, she'd fallen asleep in this very bedroom thinking only of her trigonometry exam and whether anyone would ask her to the Homecoming dance, two nights before she would awake and bike to school toward an annihilation.

Zola stood. She picked up her camera from the carpet and pulled on a hoodie. She crept down the stairs and grabbed her jacket and snuck out to the back porch, the moon radiating above her, the air seizing her lungs. November: twelve days away. She felt it coming. She leaned against the porch's railing and watched her breath cloud the air and listened to the wind sigh through the trees, gentle but brisk, a harbinger.

She pointed the Pentax toward the moon and glanced through the viewfinder. Its light filled the lens, a cardinal error her mother always told her amateur astronomers made. They always wanted to telescope the moon, the easiest signpost to locate. They thought full-moon nights were the best for stargazing, the light big and wide, and they always pulled away from the eyepiece disappointed that the lens flooded, the moon crowding out the light of stars.

Zola turned the camera toward the tops of trees, what branches the moonlight was able to make visible. The viewfinder swept across the black tips of silhouetted maples, their limbs bare and swaying in the wind. Past the gnarled stems of hickories, chestnuts, the spirals of a magnolia that bloomed only in spring. She closed her eyes and felt the breeze against her face and through her hair. She wondered if wind was capable of being captured, visible only in how it rustled branches and bent the trees. She trained the lens on the rusted iron rooster of her neighbor's weathervane. On the sag of the woodshed in their backyard, its siding splintered and frayed. On the maple leaves swirling softly in the grass, wind just strong enough to lift them. On the sound of a wind chime somewhere on their street, a tolling she couldn't locate. On her own sockless shoes, bare skin visible beneath the tongues. On the waving tree limbs. The way the moon coated them like wet paint. On the squared halo of Pegasus above her, what she'd learned from her mother.

She lowered the camera. Everything was happening.

Everything still happening all around her, around all of them, always.

She zipped her jacket and stepped from the porch and tested the edge of the yard. The grass tickled cold against her exposed ankles and she wondered for the first time if the nights had sunk yet below freezing. She moved through the grass and found herself at the edge of the backyard, the road visible around the side of the house, one streetlamp pooling on the sidewalk like a doubled moon.

The street: an edge. A curfew. The bars of a cage she would breach. Zola walked across the grass to the street, the camera still gripped between her hands.

She expected police patrols, the occasional car. Maybe a windowless van, parked and obvious, filled with FBI agents staking out the neighborhood. But there was nothing. Just the moon. She stood beneath an elm on the sidewalk and wondered what Christina had seen just nights before. A parallel sidewalk, a similarly abandoned night until it no longer was and a fire erupted. Zola made her way without thinking down the street. She made her way toward the charred shell of Alisha Trenway's house.

She'd avoided walking past the house since it burned. She'd sidestepped being outside altogether. She'd altered her route to Timber Creek so as not to bike past the blackened remains. But in the moonlight, the street deserted, her fear fell away. She quickened her pace, steps growing faster, the Pentax's strap around her neck and the camera's weight hard against her chest. She welcomed the ache, something heavy, a thudding that felt more real than her own heartbeat. She didn't stop until the sidewalk led her to the corner of her own street and to the edge of the Trenways' property line.

The yellow police tape: close enough to touch.

She reached out her hand and felt its thin plastic, a ribbon snapping in the wind. She ran her palm down its length and imagined the hands of an officer first unfurling it to stake off the property. Her eyes rose to the house. Windows blown out. The roof blackened. Brick exposed. Siding peeled to large piles of rubble. Zola glanced at the corner of the street, a busier road beyond it, but no one drove past. She looked back the way she came and saw only a line of dimly lit streetlamps. She held her breath and bent her knees and ducked beneath the police tape.

She anticipated sirens. Flashing lights. The whooping of a police car. But no one came. The hard rhythm of her heart replaced the camera's thudding against her chest. Before she could overthink it she found herself walking across the Trenways' yard. She didn't stop until her feet crunched against something other than frosted grass and she looked down where the toes of her shoes met ash. The house: so much taller and more terrible than what it had seemed from the street. Blasted windows. Jagged frames. Glass melted like a face turned down in sorrow. A broken door, collapsed ceilings, a moon she could see through the broken beams. She found no furniture in the rubble, no belongings. So much had been removed.

So much to shield from a community, from cars and pedestrians passing along the street. Everywhere the smell of smoke, even still. She tasted it in the back of her throat, a thickness that crowded the air. *What could have possibly happened here.* She blinked. She opened her eyes and the house remained. Her fingers found the camera's strap, slid down, troubled the Pentax's lens. She removed its cap and pulled the viewfinder to her face.

She pointed the lens and shot. Flipped off the flash. The camera whirred in her hands. She captured images. A house. A dream and a family lost. The light was barely adequate and it didn't matter. She rotated her body around the house and captured burnt insulation and collapsed brick and crumbling wood. She turned the camera to the ground, to the piles of plaster and siding and tile, to wood and metal and indeterminable debris. She stayed low against the ground to remain unseen in the dark. She walked the line of police tape around the house. She trained the camera on every angle of devastation.

When she made it all the way around the house she lowered the camera. She breathed in the scent of ash, almost unbearable. She could see exposed sections of the basement through the home's crushed flooring and though it wasn't the same house, Zola imagined the cool damp of Caroline Black's basement. A playgroup of four. Sega Genesis. Sweating cans of Coke. Where was everyone now? Althea and Amy Robinson: did they remember? When they heard the news did they recall themselves at age five in a basement? Zola glanced to the second floor, a tatter of floorboards she could only imagine was once Alisha Trenway's room. What ghosts lay there? What secrets were trapped in the smoke of the air? What crushes, what heartbreaks, what diary entries burned to dust?

Zola turned away from the house. She slipped beneath the police tape and across the grass, her shoes shedding ash against the dew as she moved. The Trenways' house out of sight and nothing but the full moon and a trail of streetlamps to light her way, Zola imagined

Alisha's parents lying side by side in their bed. Flames teasing the edges of curtains, licking baseboards, blackening every corner of the walls. She didn't want to think about it, what Nick and Matt and Christina seemed so desperate to know, but out here beneath a gilded moon that soaked the street in light but revealed nothing she couldn't help herself. *What happened here?* Her shoes pounding the frozen grass. *What the hell happened here?* A question beating inside her blood, a wave matching the pace of her footsteps, the camera slung around her neck and hammering against her chest.

NICK SAT IN the blue light of his bedroom, the television buzzing softly in the corner. Everyone in the house asleep, the neighborhood beyond his window silent in the curfew's wake. He'd come home from Zola's house and had dinner and sat in the living room and tried to work on chemistry homework while his brother played video games. He'd turned on the computer in his bedroom after his parents wished him good night. He'd sat before a blank screen. Fire investigation. Crime scene investigation. Burn pattern, accelerant residue. Flame color. Flame temperature. He felt himself exhausted. He'd been researching too long, through an entire weekend and now again at his bedroom desk regardless of backlogged homework he hadn't finished, a chemistry class where he'd be lost. He leaned back from the computer. He dimmed the screen and turned on his room's small television, seeking the most mindless show he could find.

It wasn't hard. Mid-October. Every network teeming with late-night *Halloween* marathons, true crime marathons, *Nightmare on Elm Street* marathons, UFO conspiracy marathons. He flipped through the stations until he came across a special on ghost hunting, what had never interested him for its lack of evidence, but the paranormal squad on-screen drew him in. A team of four investigating a long history of hauntings at the Jerome Grand Hotel in Arizona, an imposing building wedged into the side of a desert mountain.

The team stood outside the hotel, packs of ghost-hunting equipment at their feet. Night-vision cameras. EVP recorders. Dowsing rods. EMF meters. Equipment Nick knew would measure nothing, a sham investigation meant for the entertainment of television.

He leaned back in his bed and watched the team enter the hotel regardless. He glanced out his bedroom window at every house on his street illuminated by the dim glow of streetlamps. The television whirred and he wondered which homes in his neighborhood had heard footsteps in the attic. Rattling chains. Which had seen doors creaking open by invisible hands. The unnecessary energy of believing. A paranormal team so needless, he knew, Midvale County filled with so many other kinds of ghosts. What Matt had said: the police preoccupied with retracing Caleb's path through the high school. A scattered path of phantoms. Of chalked outlines, bagged evidence. A path of ballistics, of shapes where breathing bodies used to be. A heavy constellation through the hallways, police stringing lines between so many points of loss. The ghost of his classmates' voices. The ghost of a parent's body, nothing left. And fire: accelerants. Burned carpet and electrical wiring and spackled Sheetrock and wood paneling. There was nothing metaphysical about any of it. Nothing mystical. Only the hard fact of lost material and lost skin, the charring of so many homes that had held bodies that had held memories, a matryoshka of grief. Nick wondered how a path through a high school could matter now. A high school of ghosts, even Caleb's, as if fire meant he still stalked the streets from beyond the silence of a self-inflicted wound.

On television the team climbed the steps of the Jerome Hotel past dark, the screen grained in a green wash of night vision. Nick had sought distraction but he felt all at once crushed by the night's resounding quiet. Every house on his street still, everyone asleep. His only company so many chiseled circles of streetlight. Nick held a hand to his chest. A dark figure passing by with a gun. The thrumming of his heart inside a classroom matched to its pulse in

Sarah's living room, her body folded down upon him. A weight of devastation crowded his bedroom, a sensation he couldn't isolate but knew felt like suffocation. He wondered what it was about the night that made him feel so hopeless, as if sunlight was all that kept any of them from a brink. It was impossible to take so much in. Every parent, the hollow of their own dark night. His heart rioted beneath his hands. He was out of explanations. The police at a total loss. The ghost-hunting show's end credits rolled and Nick pushed himself from his bed to close down his computer. It was late. He would find nothing. There was no evidence he hadn't considered, nothing he'd find that the police hadn't found.

The computer's mouse still hovered over the shut-down key when Nick heard the opening of a new show beginning on-screen behind him. Another late-night special. Another investigation. An unsolved mystery, what he heard the host say. Strange circumstances, unexplained evidence. Nick swiveled in his desk chair and glanced at the television. He listened for only moments before he turned back to the computer screen and let himself slacken from reason, everyone asleep. Let himself entertain for one night the possibility of a cause beyond empirical evidence, the television droning in the corner behind him. He opened his browser, a new search.

He typed in a term. A term from television.

An impossible term, a phrase he barely knew.

A BRIEF HISTORY
OF STARLIT HAUNTING

THE INTERMINABLE STRETCH between twilight and dawn: a time for phantoms.

A time for creaking doors, moving shadows. A time for poltergeists, demons, residual spirits, moon-damp haunting. A time when specters feel most welcome. A time for loops of trapped energy, manifest as movement. A time for energized currents winnowing through homes and hotels, through spaces where trauma occurred.

Or else a time between dusk and daybreak when silence swallows the brain in darkness. When a body's circadian rhythm grows faint, when the brain's signals spin out of cycle. When insomnia alters cognitive chemistry and triggers depression. Sorrow sliding down the body in waves, a descending hollow. The length of a shadow across a wall. A speckled ceiling. A stilled fan. A compounded cycle, a lack of sleep. A waiting within sheets for the first streaks of light to crawl up the slats of blinds.

A game of chicken with dawn.

A dark impenetrable by light meters or digital cameras or dowsing rods.

A condition beyond phantom investigation.

A clarion call to nightfall. Come, all you ghosts.

ELISE NGUYEN

Lewis and Clark High School

Class of 2005

January 16, 1988—October 8, 2003

Elise Nguyen, a junior at Lewis and Clark, was well-known for her academic achievements. She was a three-year member of the National Honor Society and served as an after-school peer tutor. A straight-A student, her favorite subjects included biology and literature. Elise was also highly skilled in playing piano and twice served as the theater's musical accompaniment for two student productions: *Godspell* her freshman year, and *The Man of La Mancha* her sophomore year.

Elise was also a proud member of Lewis and Clark High's varsity swim team, charting school records in women's freestyle, butterfly, and medley relay. She was a powerhouse in the water, her stroke controlled and muscled with grace. She loved Sleater-Kinney and Wu-Tang Clan, what she listened to for inspiration before meets.

What else is there to say?

Elise will be so missed.

THE COLOR OF BURNING

CHRISTINA WAS THE first of us to hear the news.

She'd gone to bed just past ten, her family asleep and the house silent. But when she lay in bed, she kicked at her sheets and stared at the ceiling. Wind pushed against the double-paned windows of her bedroom and she sat up, crossed the room to her desk. She'd thought all night of what Matt had said, that there was nothing left in any home but smoke and ash. Had thought of it all evening through episodes of *The Twilight Zone* that she and her father had watched about the last man on earth, a talking doll, a gremlin on the wing of a commercial flight. Through her window a full moon rose above the roof of her neighbor's house. Her limbs felt agitated. Her hands itched to pick up the phone. The receiver so close, just on her nightstand, close enough to dial Ryan's number.

She imagined him at home, leg propped up, his picture frame shattered and his window broken. She felt no remorse. *I was here.* She'd wanted to scream it at him instead of launching a rock. *We were something.* As if it mattered anymore. Her French homework lay on her desk: Timber Creek's classrooms, the lack of light, the bare walls. French class. Algebra. She couldn't imagine doing it all over again tomorrow and on Wednesday and every day from here. She envisioned her afternoon English class, the only class that contained an empty desk. Alexander Chen. His desk vacant. Christina knew Alexander had been in the library. She knew he'd been only feet from Zola hiding in the stacks.

Christina pulled a pen from the desk drawer. First shapes. Triangles, hearts. She could have written a profile for Alexander. She knew she would have to eventually. She pressed her fists into her closed eyes and in the darkness saw the blue of a pool. Elise's funeral. What she hadn't had the endurance to attend. A profile she knew would be the worst, the hardest to write. She dragged her pen across the page and let herself spell nothing more than the letters of her own name. Elise's wet hand tagging hers in the women's medley relay. Elise on the way to meets, the stereo currenting through the car on the breeze of wide-open windows. The letters in Christina's notebook began to take the form of a sentence, the first she could think to write: *Elise Nguyen, a junior at Lewis and Clark, was well-known for her academic achievements.* The start of a profile. The blandest of openings, the staid language of formality that the yearbook required. A tone she didn't know if she could keep. A tone of decorum she and Elise had never used between them. *Had.* A verb tense strange on her tongue. A past tense that only two weeks ago had been the ever-present now, a girl keeping pace with her breathing through the water. The words came. She listened to nothing but the sound of pen pulled across paper. A gentle sound. A meditation. Nothing but the smooth ball of a pen and rough paper and the full moon and the quiet of her room.

And then a siren: faint and far, the familiar sound of a car being pulled over for speeding. The background din of the suburbs, an everyday noise, as accustomed as the constant hum of the highway beyond her neighborhood shuttling toward the heart of the city. But then one siren became two. Then three. Then a compounding of louder sirens: the approach of an ambulance, drawing nearer.

Behind it, the unmistakable horn of a fire truck.

Christina felt her body go numb. Felt every ounce of energy she'd summoned to write about Elise escape her. Felt her hand drop the pen, a thud against her desk. She looked out the window and saw nothing, just the dark of her street and the moon hanging high, oblivious. And then a single police car whizzed past, its lights dimmed, no indication of emergency but for its speed.

Christina—

Her father's voice at the cracked-open door, his face pale and stricken in the hallway. She knew he'd been asleep only moments before and knew immediately in the wake of the past week: how thin the sleep of a parent.

Something's happening, he said.

Simon? she could only think to ask.

He's already up, her father said, and motioned her from her room and down the hallway, where her brother was sleepy but awake on the living room couch, the bay window's curtains wide-open on the illumined flash of another police car racing past.

Dad, what's happening? Simon said.

Let's just stay here, her father said. Let's stay right here until we know.

He sat on the couch beside Simon and waved Christina toward him, his arm curved into the shape of welcoming. She was sixteen. She was not a child. She crossed the living room and let his arm encircle her, one around her shoulders, the other around Simon. Another police car drove by, then an unmarked van moving too fast for a residential street. Christina leaned into the warmth of her father's shoulder, his heartbeat palpable through the thin cotton of his shirt. The harsh trumpeting of a single fire truck multiplied to the dissonant chorus of two then three and they saw through the window the lights of their neighbor's house turn on then those of the house to the left and to the right, and then Christina saw Mr. Wilcox emerge onto his porch.

The Wilcoxes were their neighbors directly across the street: the neighbors who gathered their mail when they were out of town, the people her father discussed rogue thunderstorms and long winters

with. Christina had written them thank-you notes every year for
the candy apples and king-size chocolate bars they set aside for her
and Simon on Halloween. She knew the Wilcoxes still spoke of this
to her father, even now, how Christina's notes had always been thor-
ough even in the wide penmanship of first grade and how proud
the Wilcoxes were that she'd joined the yearbook staff, how they'd
always known she'd be a writer. Christina glanced out the window
as Mr. Wilcox walked across his front porch and stepped onto his
lawn, his wife visible in the window behind him.

Stay here, her father said. I'll be right back.

Christina and Simon watched out the window as their father
walked across the lawn and met Mr. Wilcox at the sidewalk.

Whose house do you think it is? Simon asked, and something
ached in Christina's chest. That in only a week they'd come to
expect this. That somewhere close, someone was burning.

I don't know, she said. She scanned her memory for who lived closest and within seconds she zeroed in on Jacob Jensen. A boy she barely
knew beyond sharing elementary school classrooms, beyond Matt
having once admitted to a crush. A boy whose mother she recalled
seeing at Principal Jeffries's funeral, a mother only two streets away.

Jacob, Christina said. Jacob Jensen. He lived on Walnut.

Echoing already in her brain: lived. Everywhere the past tense.

The soccer forward? Simon said.

The sirens grew louder. Through the window Christina could
see Mr. Wilcox gesturing down the street. Christina watched her
father nod and turn back to the house.

Richard thinks it's two streets over, he said when he returned.

Jacob Jensen's house. Christina glanced up. On Walnut. It has
to be.

Her father grabbed his coat from behind the front door.

Stay here, he said. Richard and I are going to walk up the street
to see what's happening. Lock the door behind me. And don't go
anywhere.

Can we come? Simon asked.

I don't think that's a good idea.

Christina sat forward. Dad. Can we come? I need to see.

She didn't know why she'd said it, didn't know what it was she needed to witness. She'd already seen Benji Ndolo's house. She knew what a home looked like in flames.

Her father hesitated. I don't want you to see anything.

What haven't we already seen? Christina asked.

Isn't it better for all of us to be together anyway? Simon said.

Her father sighed. Fine. Follow me closely, but if there's any danger, we're coming home immediately.

Christina pulled on her coat and they stepped out the front door, the air nipping her skin. The moon shone bright, a hole shot through the sky. Wind gathered leaves at their feet as they met Mr. Wilcox at the sidewalk.

Family outing? His voice gruff. He'd been a smoker as far back as Christina could remember. She recalled so many afternoons playing in the yard while he stood on his porch with a cigarette, a fixture of her childhood.

We figured it'd be best to stay together, her father said.

They walked down the sidewalk, Christina next to Simon, Mr. Wilcox and her father side by side in front of them. Christina pulled her coat tighter, hands stuffed into her pockets, and Simon kept his gaze down as they walked, hair falling across his eyes. No more police cars rushed past, the street empty though people gathered on porches. Some of her neighbors spilled into the street. Mrs. Skinner, a retired postal worker who lived alone three houses down, moved beneath a streetlamp toward the noise. Mr. and Mrs. Rosenstein, an elderly couple five houses down, stood near their mailbox and leaned into one another. And Mr. Edwards, a young father whose wife and two toddlers were surely somewhere inside their house, stepped onto the sidewalk ahead of Mr. Wilcox, his flannel pajama pants poking down like stalks beneath his coat.

Mr. Wilcox lit a cigarette and Christina watched the smoke escape into the air, the scent of tobacco mixing with the faint scent of ash. At the end of their street, Christina saw the reason for the lack of traffic. A flashing police car sat parked at the intersection, blocking cars from entering or exiting the neighborhood. Christina's father glanced at Mr. Wilcox, his face filled with uncertainty. They turned anyway down Cumberland, on toward Walnut, an immediate right up ahead.

As soon as they rounded the corner, Christina saw it: six fire trucks, two ambulances, more police cars than she could count, and Jacob's house in the middle of all of them. On fire. The flames rose high above the row of houses lining the right side of Cumberland. As they moved closer Christina's father stood in front of her and Simon, his body their shield. They stopped well before the intersection of Walnut and Cumberland, the street blocked off and filled with emergency vehicles. Mr. Wilcox ground his cigarette into the sidewalk. People crowded around on porches and on their lawns, some of whom Christina recognized in passing and others she was sure she'd never seen. A skinny woman in foam curlers, the kind Christina remembered her mother sleeping in when she was a little girl and her parents were still married. A teenager in street clothes, about her age, someone she'd never noticed who surely attended one of St. Louis's many private schools. A young couple who looked to be in their early twenties, not much older than Christina, the woman in a thick bathrobe and the man in a tracksuit. How was it that these people lived one street over, that she'd shared a neighborhood with them for years and never noticed them? What was it that made them a community? What drew them from their homes to the sound of sirens, to watch the flames reach the full moon, to watch a life burn?

Did Jacob have siblings? Simon asked.

I don't think so, Christina said. His mother lived alone.

A team of police officers passed them on foot, carrying barri-

cades to block off the street. Christina's family and Mr. Wilcox were
pushed back behind barriers along with everyone else in the street,
onto the sidewalk and the lawns of homes along Cumberland, but
Christina could still see firefighters. Their suits iridescent. caught
by moonlight. She saw a hydrant ripped open, water bursting down
the street's gutters. Fire trucks parked at angles, a maze of flashing
lights and sirens. Firemen spilling between them, hoisting ladders,
dragging hoses ballooning with pressure. And people pushed to
the sidelines beside her, some of them with cameras, some shouting
questions at the police. She watched the flames serrate the sky. So
much dark around them. The moon glaring back down, a puncture
wound above them.

How the hell are they going to put something like that out?
shouted Mr. Wilcox, his voice lost to the crackle of fire and the
growing surge of water. No one answered him. Christina couldn't
believe the heat, even from another street over. She took in the scent
of burning, a campfire smell but also something else: something
chemical beyond wood and paper, the burning of plastics and wire
and human hair.

Dad?

What is it, Chris?

She couldn't look at him. Do you think she made it? Jacob's
mother. Do you think she made it out?

Her father met her eyes and looked away. Another police car
edged past them, lights flashing, siren howling through the barricades.

Christina felt the fabric of her brother's shirt beside her, the rise of
his shoulders as he breathed. She watched the water rush down the
street and pool in the gutters, so much water it began to foam. She
glanced around at the faces beside her, so many people, neighbors
she'd never noticed. She wondered who lived here and who'd been
driving past and stopped to see what was happening. She wondered
who didn't belong. She remembered a police procedural she'd once

seen, a bad television drama where a witness investigator alerted a courtroom that arson suspects stayed in the crowd. Christina looked around. Blank faces standing in the grass, upon porches. She had no lens of detection, nothing within her that knew the face of arson.

She heard glass shattering and watched a firefighter on a ladder smash a second-story window. Smoke funneled out, trapped air escaping from the home. Christina closed her eyes and imagined a bedroom, the second floor of any two-story residential home. Jacob's mother settled into flannel sheets, a thermal blanket. Asleep as a flame stalked across the bedding, or else awake and waiting. Parents for Home Protection. If she'd joined, if she'd already known for days she was in danger. If they all were. Christina opened her eyes and glanced at her father. At Mr. Wilcox, lighting another cigarette.

Would they know it, if it came for them?

The flames climbed higher above the treetops and Christina watched the fire crack against the sky and wondered if it was only a matter of time, not just the families of those who had lost someone but every single one of them. A thought. A wave of guilt. Her face reddening in the dark. A high school killer. An arsonist. An entire marked community. Christina watched the firefighters aim every hose at Jacob's house, a futility she already knew, and wondered how long it would take for all of Midvale to burn.

WE HEARD THE news Tuesday morning: another headline, breaking news. A constant scroll on CNN. We heard from newspapers and from television well before we heard from Christina. Blared in headline: *FIRES RESUME.* Thick letters stamped across the front page of the *St. Louis Post-Dispatch.* The word *resume,* its implications: that this was expected. That fire had a life of its own. We barely wanted to read the article but couldn't look away. We learned that Jacob's mother perished in the fire before medics could save her. A woman we'd just seen at a funeral, wind displacing her hair, cigarette crushed beneath the heel of her pump. We learned that the fire erupted just past midnight, that firefighters fought the blaze for over an hour and that nothing had been saved. That Jacob had no siblings, no pets. That the second floor of the house undertook the greatest damage, that nothing of the upstairs bedrooms remained. That Parents for Home Protection would meet immediately to consider their options, a homegrown vigilantism. We thought of Matt's father and imagined a blank autopsy, nothing left.

We cast the thought away for other headlines, other news stories more and less imaginable. The mundane: that a man survived falling over Niagara Falls without any protective capsule. The less mundane: that a member of Al Qaeda had killed Daniel Pearl, a *Wall Street Journal* reporter. The War on Terror escalating. Human Rights Watch accusing U.S. troops in Iraq of excessive force against civilians. We turned away from the world, too tangible, too real and too sharp. We opened the sports section: the St. Louis Rams soaring on a 6-2 winning record. The World Series tied, a third game on the horizon in Miami. We gleaned only one last piece of information before we turned away from the newspaper: that Midvale's evening curfew had been canceled overnight.

A futile restriction. Everyone inside and a house still ignited. We sat in the mess of our beds and our living rooms and our kitchens and our basements, air that had long grown stale, a curfew that in the end accomplished nothing but trapping everything inside except a match and a flame. We turned off the news. We sat in the dark, the light of a clear morning pushing through the slats of our blinds, illuminating specks of dust. We pulled on our clothes, jeans and sweatshirts, pullovers and fleece sweaters. We said goodbye to our parents, embraces they held for a moment too long. A mass phone message each of them had received from the administration that school would continue, that we would stay strong. We didn't look back to see the faces of our mothers and fathers watching us from the window as we walked away. We traveled the streets of our neighborhoods, our community, our radios and car stereos and portable headsets blocking out the lingering sound of sirens, the streets a chaos of police cars and FBI vans, the presence of reporters a constant for nearly two weeks.

At school, Christina watched Simon meander up the stairwell toward his physical science class and felt her chest constrict, to turn away from him and lose sight of where he was. His breathing so close in his bedroom through the night, a sound she couldn't hear through their shared wall but knew he was within a body's length if she had to protect him. She thought of her profile. Elise. Her entire family cheering on their swim team from natatorium's metal risers. Jacob's mother gone in the night. Christina wondered if Elise's family was in danger, along with everyone in the entire school. No one spoke in the hallway. No one made eye contact. Everyone moved as if through a dream. She stepped into her algebra class as the passing bell rang and took her seat and opened her mathematics textbook and found nothing in its pages that could make her focus.

Matt moved down the hallway and imagined his father, already gone again before he awoke, already at the station reading analysis or else somewhere in the streets near Christina's house bagging evidence. Matt felt his lungs tighten. He'd barely slept. He'd stayed awake with the images of a computer echoing through his brain. What was so often only Nick's task, what he'd taken upon himself after returning from Zola's house. What he'd done to fill time before his father came home and leaned into the office and Matt made up a quick excuse that he was only checking email and would be to bed soon, and his father said there was nothing new on the investigation but confirmation that no chemical accelerants were found in the debris, that only organic materials were present.

Matt had leaned back in his father's desk chair. Organic?

His father sighed. Organic materials were all we found in the reports.

Matt blinked. As opposed to what? What the hell does that even mean?

As opposed to telltale accelerants, his father said. No fire starters. No gasoline, no chemicals. All it means is that no one tried to burn down these homes with rags and solvents. Look, Matt, I'm tired. I just wanted you to know what we found.

His father had left the room and walked down the hallway and closed his bedroom door and Matt had stared at his own reflection in the computer screen. Organic materials. No ready-made search terms. No key words. Nothing to plug into a keyboard and easily find. Proteins. Lipids. Oxygen and carbon. Words that could have pulled up anything on a browser from diet management to science reports, each of them vague and wide-open and unrefined and meaningless. Matt had shut down the computer and retreated to the basement and had slept a dreamless sleep until he awoke to the news.

Matt made his way down the hallways of Timber Creek. He'd seen the newspaper. Jacob's mother. How he'd just spoken to her at the funeral, the stupid mumblings of saying nothing to a parent in grief. The mother of a boy he'd tracked since junior high, every class and every extracurricular. All at once he felt the blank walls of Timber Creek's hallways press in, the school's air leached of oxygen, too many students and teachers crowded into a small space. He couldn't make sense of himself, this nausea, only now after two weeks of staying numb and finally falling to sleep. He turned toward his English classroom, the last door down a hallway that stretched too wide and long. He pushed himself instead into the nearest men's bathroom and dropped his textbook to the floor, his lungs seizing and his head between his knees.

Hey man, it's okay.

A voice beyond him: someone unlocking a stall door, stepping toward him. A hand on his back. Matt glanced up long enough to see the face of Samuel Winters, a running back on Lewis and Clark's varsity football team who Matt once knew to avoid. A player with a known temper, a boy who in other versions of their lives might have slammed him into a locker for nothing more than knowing he didn't prefer girls.

It's all right. I'm fine.

You don't look fine. You need the school nurse?

Matt listened and heard nothing, no one else in the bathroom stalls or at the sink. He was alone with Samuel. A quick fuse. He felt his body tense, his heart tighten.

I can call the school nurse. Samuel kneeled beside him. Not a problem.

I'll be fine, Matt said. You'll be late to class.

Panic attack? Man, sit down.

Matt glanced up at him. His chest hurt to speak. He sat on the bathroom floor.

I used to have those, Samuel said. Sometimes before games. Sometimes at home. Feels like you're seeing stars or dying.

Matt closed his eyes. Pinwheels of light.

You just need to breathe, Samuel said, and Matt felt a hand on his back again. In and out, Samuel said. Big breath in. Good. Breathe out. I'll stay here until you stand.

Matt focused on the sensation of Samuel's hand. The weight of it. What it was for another human being to touch him. Someone beyond his mother, his father, the heat of Tyler pressing him to a wall.

Good, Samuel said. Everything's all right. See, just breathe. Everything's all right.

You'll be late to class, Matt whispered.

No problem. I don't think I'll be the only one today.

Matt felt his lungs relax. He took two large breaths and sensed himself strong enough to look up. He met Samuel's gaze. Thanks, he said. You didn't have to do that.

Samuel slapped his back lightly. Hey, it's nothing. What was I going to do, just walk away?

Matt smiled and Samuel got to his feet. He pulled Matt up.

You all right? Okay to stand?

I'll be fine.

You take it easy, man. You'll be okay.

Thanks, Matt said, but Samuel was already out the door.

WHEN ZOLA WALKED into chemistry class, Nick was already seated near the far wall, with nothing open on his desk, his hands folded in his lap. There were no windows to stare through. No pictures on the wall. She took her seat beside Sejal Chaudry and wondered what Nick was thinking, whether he was replaying a house fire in his brain and calculating causes, things he'd surely spent all night looking up on his computer. Zola glanced at Sejal, who sat drawing the same lines over and over in her open notebook.

Hey, Zola said. Sejal nodded in return.

You okay? Zola asked.

Sejal didn't look up. I just don't really want to be here.

Zola didn't know what else to say. Justin Banks. A boyfriend she'd had for only weeks. She wondered if Sejal lay awake at night wondering if his house would burn.

It'll be okay, Zola said.

We were in Students for Humanity together, Sejal said. Me and Jacob.

Zola knew where Jacob lived, only a few streets from Christina. She wondered what Christina had seen, what sirens had awoken her and her family. Her brother. Her father. What smoke had blown over every home, the same scent of Alisha Trenway's house, where Zola had been standing taking pictures as Jacob's home ignited.

The passing bell signaled the start of class and Mr. Albertson looked out over the room. *Okay, everyone, let's get started.* He said nothing of the news or yesterday's school-wide assembly but only stood at the front of the room in his white lab coat, what he wore every time they conducted an experiment. He'd lined up a series of powders on the sheet-metal laboratory table at the front of the room.

Today we'll be discussing flame colors and chemicals, he said. For safety purposes, this will be demonstration-only. Get out your notebooks for observations.

Flame color. Zola glanced at Nick, obscured by the hulking shape of Dennis Carroll, his lab partner. She couldn't see him, couldn't tell the expression of his face. Zola couldn't believe Mr. Albertson hadn't thought to realign the lesson in light of the fires.

For review, he said, can anyone tell me the difference between a flame test and the temperature of a flame?

No one spoke. The last time the class had spoken of elements and flame tests, a lifetime ago in another building. She fully expected everyone to resist, to ignore Mr. Albertson's eyes and the absurdity of conducting this lesson now. So many fires in their streets. Flames they already knew firsthand without need of test tubes or powders. But Michele Theroux raised her hand in the front row, timidly at first, then higher.

The textbook said incandescence depends on the object on fire's temperature, she said. And flame tests, on the spectrum of gas excitations produced by an element.

Correct, said Mr. Albertson. And what is gas excitation?

Peter Longworth raised his hand. It's when the atoms of gases are excited by heat or electricity, when either moves from lower to higher energy levels.

That's right, Peter. And what makes them produce flame?

When they return to their ground state, they emit photons of energy.

Zola couldn't believe Mr. Albertson was continuing with this lesson plan, that despite his social awkwardness a week away from class hadn't given him time to rethink. Even more, she couldn't believe that her peers were answering him. That everyone had thought to study across a week meant for mourning. That they'd buried themselves in a textbook to keep from thinking about what they'd lost.

That's right, Mr. Albertson said. Can someone else tell me what this has to do with flame color?

Dennis Carroll raised his hand. Someone who never spoke in class. The chapter we read said energies correspond to wavelengths of light, he said. Spectrums we see as colors. Each element has its own line emission spectrum.

Good. So what we have here is a spectrum of elements, and hence, colors.

Mr. Albertson waved a hand over the piles of powders lined up before him on the laboratory table. He pulled a small torch from his coat pocket and instructed the class to take notes as he lit each pile sequentially. He held a blue flame to the first pile on the class's left, powder that ignited in a wash of crimson light.

Red, he said. Can anyone recall which element corresponds to red chemical flame?

Lithium, Claire Gallagher said. It's what emergency flares are made of.

Correct. Take notes, everyone. The colors and their corresponding elements will be on next week's midterm.

He lit the next pile: orange flame. Danielle Watkins identified its corresponding compound, calcium chloride. Yellow flame: table salt. The easiest, the one Zola imagined everyone knew. Simple sodium chloride, small crystals she could have lit up in her own kitchen. Green flame: boric acid, copper sulfate. Often found in laundry detergents, Adam Wu offered from the lab table beside hers, and in disinfectant and sometimes insect and weed killers. Zola glanced at Sejal's notebook on their lab table, empty of notes, Sejal's gaze cast away from the line of flame colors. Mr. Albertson lit the second-to-last pile, a blue burning. Blue flame: alcohol, regular fuel. Zola closed her eyes and saw nothing but the Trenways' home in flames. The Jensen home. The Ndolo home. All of them full of table salt and detergents and disinfectants, homes in flames like nothing she'd imagined: crimson fire but also cobalt, also sapphire, a rainbow of household items ablaze. Mr. Albertson lit the final pile of powder and a violet flame erupted.

Salt substitute, Zola said aloud. Potassium chloride. Often used in plant fertilizers and processed foods.

Mr. Albertson nodded. Very good, everyone. Your memories have retained a wealth of information across the break.

Zola watched the line of flares on the front table, all of them still burning, a spectrum of color she might have once thought lovely. *The break.* Nothing of what it was. Break meaning vacation, meaning leisure, meaning time off and not a stalemate, not hours of sitting on her porch watching maples shed their leaves so she wouldn't see a library and its wall of books. Mr. Albertson stood oblivious, a torch still in his hands.

I hope everyone recorded the elements in their notebooks, he said. Keep your pens out. We'll be discussing the wave-particle duality of light.

Zola looked across the room at Nick, expecting to see a visible anger. But his expression was impassive, his face blank. His eyes were only focused ahead on Mr. Albertson, his pen poised above his notebook.

PAST MORNING CLASSES, Nick walked into the lunchroom and saw Christina and Matt and Zola already seated at a round table in the far corner. The cafeteria bustled around him, loud but somehow quieter than the day before. Jacob Jensen's house and his mother. Class carrying on as if nothing had happened, the same as the resigned headline he'd seen in the paper that morning: *FIRES RESUME.* His mother had packed him a ham sandwich, one he had no appetite to eat. He'd stayed up late in front of a blinking screen. He'd dimmed the backlighting of his computer. He didn't want his parents to wake up and see the glow beneath his door. He didn't want them to worry. Didn't want anyone at all to know what he was doing, what it was that he'd looked up.

A late-night special: mysterious cases of human skin suddenly igniting.

A myth. A jokebook gag. A figment of illusion, the same as a program on ghost hunting. He'd listened to the television regardless, had opened a new browser on the screen, had quieted the typing of his keys. A program he watched until its end credits rolled for no other reason than that it provided some kind of answer, a thin explanation for unexplained fires despite the absurdity of believing. He'd gone to bed unconvinced, the flames on television only cases where even in suspected instances of self-ignition the body still remained as evidence, where every human bone and muscle didn't disappear with the burned ravages of a house.

He'd gone to bed exhausted and awoken to a new fire, another fatality.

When he reached the table, Christina was already telling Matt and Zola what she'd seen. A house on fire, a neighborhood behind barricades. How she stood with her father and her brother and their neighbor, Mr. Wilcox, a man Nick could envision from the times he'd seen him across the street from Christina's house. How she saw the fire above the rooftops, its flames snapping and bursting into the dark. How the brightness of the full moon was obscured by the shock of the fire, flickering bands Christina said she saw long after firefighters doused the blaze and long after she'd pretended to go to sleep.

Did you see anything suspicious? Matt asked. Anyone strange in the crowd?

I saw people I didn't know, but nothing out of the ordinary.

How many fire trucks were there?

I don't know. Six? Seven? There was water everywhere in the streets.

How about police cars?

Doesn't your dad tell you this stuff?

Less than you'd think, Matt said. The only news he told me this weekend was that the fires have no chemical cause. That the debris reports returned only organic material.

Nick looked up. Organic material? What does that mean?

I asked the same thing. I really don't know. All I know is that my dad says all three fires show organic flashpoints. Not acetone or butane or gasoline. Something natural.

Nick thought of human skin, self-ignition. Everything he'd looked up, everything he didn't want to hear spoken out loud in his own voice.

You mean human? he asked.

I don't think so. But at least the same makeup. Fats, carbon, proteins.

What does that mean?

Look, I don't know. I had the same reaction. I think it just means there were no chemicals, that the fires could have been started with more basic materials. The police are working with the FBI. They're trying to find answers.

This doesn't help anyone, Zola said. Jesus, Matt. Give it a rest.

Well, don't you want to know?

I do and I don't. I couldn't sleep last night. I went out and took pictures of Alisha Trenway's house. That's all I can take for now. That's all I want to know.

Why didn't you say anything? Matt said.

Well, I'm saying it now.

Did you find anything? Nick asked.

No, I didn't find anything. Just a bunch of debris. What did you think I'd find? What would I find that police haven't already found?

Nick bit into his ham sandwich, a blend of mayonnaise and stale bread. What he refused to say out loud: a lone night of rabbit-holed guessing. Web pages of photographs. Burned homes, open case files, blank autopsies. Histories of circumstances without answer, a trail of questions and only ash. Nothing worth saying in a cafeteria filled with the clatter of popped soda cans and the squeak of Styrofoam plates. Nothing he believed but for the possibilities it opened amid so many dead ends, that elsewhere homes had blazed down and left only questions amid cinder and smoke.

Zola was watching him. Don't even get me started on chemistry this morning.

Why, what happened? Christina said.

Flame tests. Burn color. An entire lesson on fire. It was as if Mr. Albertson hadn't read the paper at all, like he lives in a bubble. Like any of us wants to learn about fire right now. She kept her eyes on Nick. Except you. I saw you taking notes. I bet you can tell us every flame color.

Nick heard the tone in her voice. I probably could, he said.

Go ahead, Zola challenged. Regale us with your knowledge.

Dark red: 1,200 degrees. He felt himself grow irritated. Yellow-red: 1,920 degrees.

And what about human skin? Zola said. How the fuck does that burn?

Jesus. Nick set down his sandwich. What, Zol? What the hell is your problem?

What's my problem? My problem? That all you've done since any of this happened is hole away in your bedroom with your computer, like you feel nothing at all.

Get over yourself. There, I said it: get over yourself, Zola. You think you're the only one this is happening to? You think you're the only person? Look the fuck around you. Look at everyone here.

Yeah, well, we can't all have the luxury of having been in English class where a psychopath just chose not to go. We can't all have the luxury of seeing nothing. Of only having moved a fucking desk against a door and that's it.

Nick watched her as if slapped. What did you say to me?

Zola pushed her chair back from the table. I said fuck you. That's what I said.

She slammed her lunch tray into a trash can and left the cafeteria.

I'm not going after her this time, Christina said.

Don't, Nick said. She needs to calm the fuck down.

We all do, Christina said. She didn't mean that. What she said. She didn't mean that you experienced nothing—

It sounds like that's what she meant, Nick interrupted. He was tired. His brain a fog. And anyway, he said, it doesn't matter. We all saw the paper this morning. The curfew's been lifted. As sure a sign as any that the police have given up, that there are no rules left. That no one knows anything.

I can't even imagine the families, Matt said softly. Parents for Home Protection. Did you see that? The other parents must be scared out of their minds.

I didn't sleep at all, Christina said. I tried to write Elise's profile. It's a total mess.

Nick kept his eyes on the table. Said nothing of what he'd spent the night doing. Zola was right: he'd been interested in everything Mr. Albertson said, homework he'd forgone for a night of hare-brained searching. A chemistry lecture Zola thought was insensitive, information he'd welcomed gladly for its empiricism. Color emission. Wavelengths of light. The science of burning, the same as arson investigation. So much more tangible than unexplained cases of self-generated combustion. Christina looked at her hands. Matt ran a finger against the metal of his soda can. The room buzzed all around them, a whirlwind of echoed murmurs and plastic cutlery.

ZOLA FOUND HERSELF in the courtyard of Timber Creek, the bathroom too claustrophobic and the library, even makeshift, beyond question. She found herself without a coat, the brisk sky a knife, the school's height shadowing the courtyard and blocking out the sun. She stood apart from clusters of peers taking themselves outside for fresh air. She stood and breathed. Let her lungs let go, even as the cold of the fall air filled them. Felt her blood crazing through her veins, the adrenaline of anger.

Hey, a voice said. Zola turned to see Aurelia Lopez standing behind her.

Hey, Zola said. What are you doing out here?

Just needed some air. A minute alone.

Zola glanced through the window behind Aurelia, where students still gathered in the cafeteria. She saw no sign of Aurelia's boyfriend, Adam Wolf. A senior, a guitarist. They were inseparable, hardly ever seen apart. Aurelia's hands gripped a soup cup in fingerless gloves. Black nail polish. Her eyes ringed in coal. Aurelia had been in Zola's classes since seventh grade, all honors courses, a teenage punk who was also whip-smart.

You okay? Aurelia asked.

I'm fine. Just needed a minute. Some time outside.

This building is pretty awful. Too dark.

The small talk was a comfort, something Zola usually hated but the lightness felt necessary. Aurelia raised a plastic spoon to her mouth and Zola realized this was the first time she'd seen her since they'd come to Timber Creek. Aurelia hadn't been in English class yesterday, her presence once so obvious, someone who spoke rarely in other classes but engaged easily in literary discussion.

Did you stay home yesterday? Zola asked.

I wasn't ready to come back. I'm still not ready.

Yeah, I know the feeling.

Are you okay? Aurelia asked again. I know you were in the library.

Aurelia must have remembered, must have known by comparing the classes they shared and the few they didn't. Aurelia's academic lab earlier, Zola remembered now, though she couldn't recall where Aurelia must have been.

I was in the library, Zola said.

I can't even imagine. I was in chemistry. Pretty safe, pretty far from the noise.

Zola recalled Aurelia always entering Mr. Albertson's class as she was leaving, their academic labs and their chemistry hours the only two classes that flipped between them as junior honors students. She wondered if Aurelia had spent the morning learning about flame tests and color, if the lesson was why she needed fresh air.

It's good you were safe, Zola said.

I guess I was safe. But I don't feel that way.

I know. I've felt crazy this entire week, completely full of paranoia. And anger.

My mother sent me to a therapist, Aurelia said. They put me on Wellbutrin. It helps, I think. Are you seeing anyone?

Zola shook her head.

I didn't think I was ready to talk about it. But it helps.

I keep hearing sounds, Zola said. Gunshots. Screaming. People choking, gasping for breath. She winced as she said it, more than she'd said to anyone since it happened. But when she looked at Aurelia her face was unflinching.

You should talk about it, Aurelia said.

I don't think I'm ready.

Aurelia nodded. Everyone moves at their own pace.

How's Adam doing? Is he okay?

He's fine. He was in physics, not far from me. We made it outside with everyone else. He's just grabbing lunch. He'll be out in a minute.

I won't keep you, Zola said.

It's no trouble. It's good to see you.

I'll see you in history, Zola said.

Aurelia nodded. Zola stepped away from the courtyard and back into the building, the words bouncing back inside her brain: *It's good to see you.* That it was possible. That anything was good. That she could open up more readily to a stranger than her own mother or Christina or Matt or Nick. That it felt like a wild free fall to speak, to liberate her voice into the air of the courtyard. That something at last felt good.

WHEN MATT PULLED his hatchback into the driveway after school, he was surprised to see his father sitting on the front porch. He expected him to still be at work but he sat in a corduroy coat watching the street, a glass of whiskey on the low table beside him. When Matt drew closer, his father motioned for him to sit in the chair beside him.

How was school?

Fine. It's a little cold to be sitting out here.

I don't mind it. I needed some air.

Did you just get home?

Maybe a half hour ago.

How was work?

His father didn't immediately answer. Matt knew it was a loaded question.

Your mother's inside marinating steaks, his father finally said. We figured we'd grill tonight, even though it's so cold. This temperature dip won't last. It's still October. We'll have another warm spell before winter settles in.

Matt watched leaves whip across the yard. He couldn't imagine another warm spell. He couldn't imagine summer, the cicadas diminished now to a soft trill. He sat on the edge of his chair, his hands shoved into his pockets.

How were your classes? Timber Creek going okay?

I guess.

Things will get back to normal. I know it's hard.

None of my teachers really mentioned Jacob's house. I don't think they know what to say anymore.

Matt's father took a sip of his whiskey. There's really nothing to say. Not until we know why this is happening.

Why is it?

Matt's father looked at him. All we know is that there's a pattern. The first fire happened on October 11. Today's October 21. That's four fires in ten days. Not every other day, but damn near close.

It was so quiet through the weekend.

That's what we're looking at now. The curfew helped nothing. We thought it did through the weekend, quiet as it was. But last night proved us wrong.

A gust of wind pushed across the porch and Matt stayed silent.

In my twenty years on the police force, I've never seen anything like it. His father set down his glass. We chose this community for its safety. We chose it for you.

None of this is your fault.

Your mother and I keep trying to remember that. But we can't stop ourselves from thinking of what-ifs. What if we lived elsewhere? What if I'd worked in a different precinct? What if we'd fallen in love with a different house, in a different school district?

Matt heard his father stop himself short. *What if it'd been you in the hallway instead of that girl on the carpet.*

This could have happened anywhere, Matt said.

I know it. We're just trying to figure out why these fires are happening here.

What did they find today? What of Jacob Jensen's house? What about his mom?

Matt's father didn't look at him. The same. It's the same as the others.

What do you mean?

I mean it's the same. Nothing left. No trace of a body left.

The wind cut into Matt's skin. Dad, this is fucked.

Watch your mouth, son.

Benji's mother in the yard? What Christina saw—that doesn't mean anything?

All it means is Benji's mother was outside and then she wasn't. It could have happened at any of the other homes, too, we just don't have eyewitnesses. But it doesn't mean she's the culprit, or a suspect. There's no evidence at all to suggest that.

Then what? Matt asked. The mail truck stopped in front of their house and Matt's father waved across the yard. The mailman waved back and Matt considered the strangeness of routine, that mail was still being delivered.

Given the pattern, I suspect we'll find nothing in the analysis of the Jensen house, either. No evidence of accelerant. Nothing but organic material. No chemicals. But we're considering other leads. Other possibilities.

Like what other possibilities?

Well, for starters, nothing points to arson, even still. At least not on the level of chemical analysis. But now we're not so sure, especially after the Jensen house.

Why? What's different?

The pattern is odd. No fires through the entirety of the weekend.

What difference does that make?

Matt's father sighed. I shouldn't get into this with you.

Come on, Dad. I need to know something.

His father troubled the glass, whiskey swirling inside it. We're looking into juvenile arson, he said. I can't say specifics. But the hiatus across the weekend suggests it.

What do you mean juvenile?

A teenager. Kids. No fires over the weekend indicates supervision, the time of week when everyone's home and it's harder to slip past surveillance. It suggests maybe a kid who can maneuver around working parents during the week.

Matt sat back in his chair. He couldn't imagine that someone walking through the halls of Timber Creek or sitting next to him in class could be responsible for this. He thought of Caleb Raynor. A plan none of them knew he'd made.

That's the only thing? That there were no fires over the weekend?

Not necessarily. There are other attributes. This just makes it clearer.

What other attributes?

Well, multiple fires are an indication. Youthful fire setters tend to set more than one within a finite time span. They also use materials available on the scene. There usually isn't a lot of forethought. Since we can't find evidence of accelerants, it might mean that flammable materials weren't transported from elsewhere. That whoever did this, they used what was already available in each house. Organic materials. Like I said. Candle wax or vegetable oil. Whatever people already have in their homes. Juvenile fires also tend to be set in a small radius. Sure, some teens have cars. But most wouldn't go far. These neighborhoods are most kids' entire world.

Matt watched the mail truck retreat down the street. He thought of Christina tapping on his window in the early morning. Zola out in the Trenways' yard, Tyler sometimes in his car all night. How easy it was for everyone he knew to sneak out. He tried to remember the farthest he'd ever driven in the hatchback on his own.

Anything else? he asked.

Most arsonists set their fires late at night or early morning, Matt's father said, regardless of their age. That's the time all of these fires have erupted. And most young fire setters are dealing with high family stress. Without saying much more, suffice it to say that we're looking at kids who've been most affected by this tragedy, since all of these fires are connected to the school. Kids who might also have a history of emotional problems, academic problems. Even a history of abuse or neglect in their families.

It doesn't make sense, Matt said. Kids affected by this tragedy. Wouldn't they empathize with the families of victims instead of wanting to burn down their homes?

It depends. Grief works in strange ways. It could be that someone lost someone else close to them—a friend, a boyfriend, a girlfriend—and they want that grief to spread if they're a troubled individual. They want everyone to suffer even more.

But doesn't that take a lot of planning, especially given the police presence now?

It implies premeditation. But police have just been patrolling the streets. Every street. They haven't kept watch exclusively on the homes of those who have lost children.

But will they now?

I anticipate they will. It's something that was discussed last week with the curfew. We thought surveillance might violate family privacy, for so many people who are already undergoing enough media scrutiny. These parents are already watching themselves, too. Parents for Home Protection. But not all of them are participating.

The wind blew a small branch from the hickory tree in the front yard.

What about Eric Greeley? Matt asked. Would you bring him in again?

A third time? No. The kid is clean. Matt's father glanced at him. I can't say more, but there's a slight chance the Raynor boy had a different accomplice.

Matt sat up in his chair. A different accomplice? Dad, Caleb had no friends.

Do you know that for a fact? How well did any of you know this boy?

Matt imagined Caleb in the back of the classroom. In the lunch line, picking out a carton of milk. The only images he had of someone he'd never thought to notice.

Not well, he admitted. Is this someone at school? Someone I need to know about?

There's no someone yet, his father said. It's just another option we've reopened, given the possibility of juvenile arson. It could be that the Raynor boy had a partner in all of this, or else someone who's just very angry that he's gone. I promise, son. I'd tell you if you were in danger.

Christina lives right by Jacob's house, Matt said. She saw the fire last night.

Matt's father sighed. Benji's mother and now this.

She said last night everyone was gathered out in the streets.

People are scared. They want to know what's happening. I understand that. We all want the same thing.

Matt looked at his father. Are you sure you'd tell me? Would you tell me if you really knew something?

His father finished his whiskey. I'd tell you what was necessary to keep you safe.

NICK DROVE SARAH home after school, the wind picking up, so many leaves thrown from the trees to the street in front of them. They'd barely seen each other at school since returning. Nick knew he'd been preoccupied. He hadn't told her about anything he'd looked up, not arson or fire scenes or the process of burning. He knew she'd say he was too singularly focused, too gripped by yearbook and research, too removed from what they'd done though she'd barely spoken of it since it happened. He imagined her taking her pill, every day, the time he knew now by asking: 4:30 P.M. Just after school, before her father came home, when no one would see her slip a small tablet beneath her tongue.

How was class? he asked.

Fine. It still feels weird to be back. Weird to be in that building.

I know. I'm not used to it. The classrooms, the cafeteria. Everything's different.

But it feels good, sort of. At least it feels good to be outside of the house. I can't believe what happened. I can't believe this is still happening.

Are you scared? he asked.

I'm fine. It's scary, but I don't feel scared. Not anymore.

Nick glanced at Sarah, her shape small-seeming in the passenger seat beside him. A police car passed them, its sirens quiet but its speed accelerated.

What changed? he asked.

I guess I feel like I'm not in danger. I mean, look at so many people around us. All of these families. Their homes. I have no right to feel sad or scared.

You can feel whatever you want, he said. Yeah, it's good to be grateful. But I think it's also okay to be scared.

Are you?

Nick pushed his hands against the steering wheel and thought of everything he'd looked up. Burn patterns. Which way fires swept. Origin of incendiary, single or multiple. Diagrams, photographs, testimonies of eyewitnesses. Natural causes, accidental causes. Unexplained causes, what he'd looked up last night. Another dead end, he knew. How nothing he found comforted him. How nothing offered resolution, any sense of control.

Maybe not scared, he said. But something. I don't really know how I feel.

Nick felt her hand cross his thigh. About anything?

He looked at her. I know how I feel about you.

I'm glad we did what we did, she said.

Me, too.

He squeezed her hand to assure her he'd thought of it as much as she had, though he knew he hadn't. He'd thought of sex before, less than other teenagers, he assumed, but still there all the same through long drives and long nights and the darkened corners of movie theater dates, Sarah's body a living thing beside him. He wouldn't take it back. But he realized sitting beside her in the car: it hadn't changed his life. Not in the way movies and television shows told him it would. It wasn't what he needed. What he needed was information, puzzle pieces aligning. Some kind of pattern to connect.

I don't have to be home yet, she said.

Your mother's expecting you, I'm sure.

She's not home today. Third Tuesday of the month, her book club. They didn't cancel it, not even this month.

Where do you want to go?

Anywhere. Her hand moving higher on his thigh.

He didn't feel like going anywhere. He felt exhausted. But he didn't want to turn away from her. He deviated from the path to her house and turned toward the frontage roads off the highway. He didn't stop until they passed Lake School Park, a small public recreational area with an old schoolhouse and a playground and trails into the woods. Under renovations since they started high school, the park was always abandoned and they both knew it. He pulled into the park's gravel lot, rocks and debris crunching beneath the Honda's tires. His the only car there. He pulled into a spot obscured by tangles of overgrown branches and cut the engine and Sarah's hand traveled up his torso to the side of his face, her mouth already on him before he pulled the keys from the ignition.

He felt his pulse quickening despite himself. He opened the car door and led her to the backseat, the wind whipping around them, the car a shelter from the cold. He warmed his hands with his breath. She pulled at the button of his jeans. She unthreaded the zipper, steel teeth he felt unlock against his skin, and then her hand was inside the waistband and the wind whistled at the windows and she pushed herself onto him and then down, his jeans still halfway on. She pitched against him. He kept her fastened in his gaze, only closing his eyes when she leaned down and pushed her mouth to his. He felt his heart storming beneath the thick fabric of his jacket, felt every preoccupation trapped in his brain dissolve. He wanted her. Past a summer of waiting, past a single encounter in the solitude of her living room. Past so many nights of research, past key terms and evidence. She broke through all of it. He let himself want her, let himself escape his brain and fill his own body, the thunder of his own heartbeat. When he felt himself push past a threshold, she lay against his chest and he breathed in the soft condensation of the car against the cold glass. Over her shoulder, he could see through the windshield. The seclusion of overgrown shrubs and trees where they'd parked, knots of branches swaying in the wind. She whispered *was that good* and he nodded and spread a hand across her hair. The texture of every strand. The heat of her skin. His brain already orbiting back to his computer, his heartbeat receding. Branches knocking soft against the car's glass.

CHRISTINA LAY IN the filled tub of the bathroom she and Simon shared. The door locked, the ceiling fan whirring high in the corner, drowning out the television her brother watched in the living room down the hallway. She'd taken him to the community center after school and made him swim in the recreational pool while she turned laps in the roped-off lanes. She hadn't wanted to let him leave her sight as much as she'd needed to feel water slide against her skin, her muscles ellipsing down the pool's Olympic length. The center had been empty, only one other older woman circling through the lane beside her. Christina had swum sixty laps of freestyle and backstroke intervals, Simon's legs just visible beneath the thick underwater blue if she angled her goggles toward the pool's shallow end. She'd driven him home, her hair still wet, the scent of chlorine filling the car as they passed Jacob Jensen's street. Police cars and yellow tape. She'd drawn herself a bath before her father came home and closed the bathroom door.

She let steam fill the small bathroom. She filled the water to the bottom of the drain lever and lay back in the tub and let herself close her eyes. Pushed away a home's flames ripping tears through the fabric of a dark night. The hot scent of charring intermingled with the stale smoke of Mr. Wilcox's cigarette. Benji Ndolo's front door sharding fire and wood. Christina wanted to be nowhere. With no one. She didn't want anyone to need her, if only for the thin window of a bath. A brother who'd watched a house burn down in the night. A best friend with a grief-stricken temper. A rage she had every right to have, a library none of them had seen. A phone call Christina didn't want to make to ensure again that Zola was okay. A police officer who'd demanded answers, nothing she could give despite a questioning that had lasted more than an hour. A mother standing alone in the darkness of her front yard, what haunted Christina in the bathroom's thick steam: whether she could have done anything to change the igniting of a home and everyone within it. A mother. A father. A small brother. And only doorsteps away: a boy with a sharp mouth, a leg propped up on pillows. The satisfaction of breaking up with her first.

Christina burrowed beneath the water, her knees poking through the surface. She toed the tub's drain. She listened to the hollow sound of water leaking in slow drops from the faucet and watched them plink into the bathtub, concentric rings that rippled out across the surface. What else she'd given Ryan, across two years of sex in his bedroom or the backseat of both of their cars: a quick finish every single time. What he'd never given her. What she'd told Zola in a moment of frustration and wished she could take back: that she'd never had an orgasm, only a partner uninterested in what sex meant for her.

What she couldn't believe she hadn't tried herself across two years.

The hum of the television down the hallway. The door locked. The ceiling fan hurricaning above her. Christina let her hands slide beneath the surface, down the water-slicked shape of her own body. Past the sides of her breasts, what Ryan had once joked were too small. Across the smooth plain of a lap-chiseled stomach. Muscled thighs. A shape Christina realized she was proud of, what propelled her through the water. Her hands moving farther. Christina closed her eyes and the fan whirred and she let herself clear her brain. A police officer. An ex-boyfriend. She let every tether of need slip away. A brother. A best friend. She kept her eyes closed, the humid air of the bathroom a blanket. She let herself be alone, her own secret, apart from what anyone else required. The faucet's drip, a meditation. She let her breath quicken. She let her hands find her own pulse.

LATE THAT NIGHT, after steaks and grilled corn and long after his parents had gone to sleep, Matt sat in his bedroom with his English textbook open in his lap, a cluster of Nikolai Gogol stories he was to read by morning. He tried to concentrate. The words blurred. He imagined instead his peers. Anger problems. Trouble making friends. Those most affected by the shooting. Those with troubled home lives or a history of abuse: how was there any way to know? He thought of Russ Hendricks, Alexis Thurber's boyfriend, a junior known for so many fistfights and suspensions. He thought of Jeff Steffen, another junior who'd been Jacob Jensen's best friend. A soccer player with a temper, a known asshole. A guy Matt's manager had once escorted from Midvale Cinemas for throwing a soda at another patron, someone Matt couldn't imagine burning down a house. And Caleb Raynor: beyond Eric Greeley, Matt had no clue who his friends were. He set down his textbook. He knew he'd have never suspected Caleb of what he'd been capable of doing. But even still, he couldn't think of a single person at Lewis and Clark who could torch down a house with a family inside. He couldn't imagine returning to school the next morning wondering if someone he passed in the hallways had stalked through the streets, found household materials to set a flame, watched four houses burn.

He heard a tapping at the window. Christina again. He moved from his bed to the window expecting her face but when he pulled back the curtain Tyler's face peered back at him instead, his hair obscured by a knit hat, his breath fogging the glass.

Matt pulled open the window. What the fuck are you doing here?

Hello to you, too. Jesus Christ.

What, you don't call for days? And now you want to come in?

Tyler climbed inside and stood in the middle of Matt's room, hands balled into cold fists. His coat still on and filled with the scent of recently smoked cigarettes. Look, I'm sorry, he finally said. He glanced at Matt. For all of it. For everything.

That's not good enough.

What do you want me to say?

I want to hear you say it. I want to know what you're sorry for.

Tyler closed his eyes in frustration. He kept his coat on. Strands of hair crept from beneath his hat.

I'm sorry I left you there. He looked at Matt straight on. It wasn't my intention. I freaked out. It wasn't that we'd be caught together. It was that I didn't know what to do.

None of us knew what to do. But I wouldn't have left you there.

Do you think anyone knows how to react in a situation like that? You're not a fucking saint, Matt. We're all failing. We're all fumbling our way through all of this.

Matt felt himself soften, a slackening that made him angry.

Tyler had no right. Tyler had left him.

Tyler was human and fallible, like anyone else.

You're ashamed of me, Matt said. You can't even say what we are to each other.

Tyler stepped toward him. Have you ever even been to my house? Do you know why I'm always here, why I come to your window like this, why you're never there?

Matt thought of the number of times Tyler had found his way through the backyard, the tapping he'd grown used to across the past summer, the certainty that Tyler was waiting outside. He thought of his father's words: a lack of supervision. How his parents never knew of Tyler's tapping but would surely know it if Matt left the house, would hear him traveling through the kitchen and out the side door, would hear the ignition of his car turning. How he'd never considered why Tyler left his own house, what it was that he was leaving. How Matt's own father had turned away from him but still cared for him in the end, a kind of love that was brittle but enough.

I don't come from where you come from, Tyler said. What you want. It's not easy for me to say out loud.

You could've told me that, Matt said. He heard it already in his own voice, a sharpness rounding off, something quieting.

What is there to say? There's nothing to say. I didn't want you to know. I didn't want you to know where I come from.

Matt felt himself beside Tyler. He was there and his body fought it, a learned flinching. But he couldn't help himself. Couldn't stop his hand from gripping Tyler's coat and sliding it off. What Tyler had done, a small scarring. So much smaller than the specter of someone at school, someone capable of knifing through the heart of an entire town. Tyler pulled back his hat, his hair a shagged mess beneath.

I'm sorry, Tyler said.

Matt let the words find their place.

And then Tyler's mouth was upon his, familiar tongue, the faint taste of smoke. Tyler's mouth was on his and Matt closed his eyes and let himself go, let all of it go only hours before, according to the time recorded in the newspaper the following morning and across the news stations, Midvale County police responded to a call some-time in the night, as Tyler crept his way through the sidewalks and back to his house, that another house was burning, the emergency of Alexis Thurber's home on fire.

FIRE CRISIS

Fifth House Burns; Authorities Seek Answers

WEDNESDAY, OCTOBER 22, 2003

ST. LOUIS, MO—A house fire, the fifth in a string of residential fires across eleven days, claimed one life early Wednesday morning within the Pensacola Apartment complex in the 1400 block of Dartmouth Avenue in Midvale County. Firefighters responded to a neighbor's call at 2:23 a.m. Wednesday morning and observed smoke pouring from the windows of a third-story apartment, the top floor in the building's 32-resident complex. The fire required 25 fire personnel, including police officials from nearby Hamilton County as well as FBI representatives on the scene, and was finally extinguished at 3:14 a.m. All other residents evacuated the building, some treated for smoke inhalation though none were injured. According to police officials, the victim has been identified as Kevin Thurber, 36, father of Alexis Thurber, 16, who perished in the Lewis and Clark shooting.

"It's unbelievable," said Marcus White, a next-door neighbor who stood in the Pensacola's parking lot as fire officials battled the flames. "He was a nice guy, a good father. Losing a daughter is enough. We've all had enough."

FBI officials were on the scene to determine the fire's potential connection to Midvale County's other home fires within the past week, all linked to families of Lewis and Clark High School victims. Firefighters and police officers combed the complex for indications of arson and scanned the crowd gathered outside of the complex for potential foul play. Neighbors heard no signs of struggle within the apartment and say Thurber lived alone.

"It was just him and the girl," said Arlene McCreary, a neighbor on the third floor who called the police when she smelled smoke in the hallway. "Nice people. Always said hello. They didn't deserve this, any of this. We all just want to know what's going on."

The fifth fire occurs amid public outcry over the cause of the fires and whether malicious intent is at play. Midvale County police, Midvale County fire officials, and FBI representatives are working together to locate a cause and put an end to the current atmosphere of fear. The cause of the fires is under continued investigation.

A BRIEF HISTORY
OF HOME COMBUSTION

FIRE CHARS WOOD at a rate of 1 inch per 45 minutes on each side of exposure. 1,400 degrees: the temperature it takes to burn through grain. A minimum temperature of 800 to 1,000 degrees Fahrenheit is needed to ignite any combustible beyond wood.

Beware open windows, the drafts of which offer false points of origin. Beware wind, the pulling of air, large areas of damage made to look like a source.

Beware the kitchen. Beware oil. Vegetable, animal, fish, linseed, corn, olive, sunflower: every oil except mineral, the potential to ignite spontaneously.

Beware charcoals. Hickory. Oak. Ash. All impulsively sparked to flame.

Let a guard fall away only with gas burners, for even every burner activated full blast leaves no room for combustion due to drafts, due to cracks in windows and between floorboards and among bricks and the gaps of screened windows, all keeping gas below the danger of a flash point, all leaking air from a home, imperceptibly, all of the time.

Steer clear of thinking, for a second, that gas, oil, or oak is the cause.

Known melting points: aluminum, 1,220 degrees Fahrenheit. Polystyrene: 266 degrees Fahrenheit. Copper: 1,083 degrees. Steel: 1,400. Ethyl alcohol: 1,540. Gasoline: 1,490. Stove propane:

1,778. Magnesium: 1,995. Glycerol: 550. Lead: 3,100. Water: 212. Salt: 1,470.

    Calcium, bone: 1,547.

    Human skin: the thinnest membrane.

    Human skin: just 162 degrees between flame and disintegration.

LAMP, CARPET, CLOCK

WE LEARNED THE news early, so few of us able to sleep fully through the night.

We knew Alexis Thurber from our classes, a girl who'd run in other circles, a girl we remembered most vividly from Des Peres Elementary's school-wide production of *The Wizard of Oz* when we were in sixth grade and the kindergartners were members of the Lollipop Guild and Mark Linehan was the Cowardly Lion and Colleen Zhu the Tin Man. Alexis Thurber: the Good Witch. How we remembered this in junior high when Alexis rounded bases early, when we knew nothing else of good or bad except who attracted boys and who lost their virginity first. How we knew she harvested the attention of Russ Hendricks in high school, a boy with a temper. We knew little of her home life, only that her mother had passed away and that her father raised her alone in an apartment not far from school. We didn't realize how young he was, only twenty when she was born, his age printed so clearly in the *Post-Dispatch*.

The fire consumed the front-page headlines in thick print we turned away from after we couldn't see it any longer, headlines and subheadlines that blurred together. We knew the paper would tell us nothing, that whatever officials knew they would manage it carefully to avoid mass panic. A panic we'd already felt rising across the previous day, another fire, police out in force on the streets and FBI vans swarming through our streets, agents and officers and a flood of reporters. Women in starched suits. Men in gelled hair. All of them waiting for the slightest shred of new information.

The cicadas: gone. We awoke to silence, summer gone for good, so many chilled dusks that had at last swallowed their hum.

We awoke to other news, stories we gleaned from back pages of the newspaper. The Yankees up by two in the World Series. Elliott Smith gone by suicide at only thirty-four, songs we associated with long drives and cornfields whipping past the car windows. The War on Terror: Wall Street journalist Daniel Pearl confirmed killed by the principal mastermind of September 11. The security of Kabul unstable, according to United Nations forces in Afghanistan. Human Rights Watch accusing U.S. troops of using excessive force against Iraqi civilians.

We awoke to news that school was still on, always on, that we couldn't afford to lose any more days. But something new: that counseling sessions would be mandatory, a missive from the Midvale County School District that a team of school therapists had been temporarily hired. That during academic labs every student would see a counselor for at least one required meeting to determine if further sessions might be needed, and to manage the stress of returning to school and the tension of an ongoing investigation.

We awoke jaded. We awoke scared. We awoke fully devastated, news that even expected still fireworked through our skin. We awoke unsurprised. We awoke suspicious.

We awoke imagining an apartment, a dark night, another incineration.

NICK PORED THROUGH the latest news on his computer before school, the *St. Louis Post-Dispatch*'s online version and CNN's website, his door closed and his family in the kitchen down the hallway. The language of every news story: ever vague. As vague as the language of flame colors and flash points, what Nick had stayed up researching long after he'd dropped Sarah off at her house and before he awoke and learned of Alexis's father. The feel of Sarah's body still pulled through him, the same pull of having entered the ocean as a child and feeling the waves roll through his skin for days after, a lulling of blood and water, the same tow of the moon. But he couldn't stay away from his computer, a gnawing compulsion to follow every trail to its end. Mr. Albertson's lecture: oxidation. Gas excitation. Atoms burst to heat, a rapid shift from low to high energy. A thought he'd returned to across dinner and across a night of television, a tongue worrying again and again the socket of a former tooth. He'd stayed up late, the monitor's screen the only light glowing through his bedroom. He'd researched everything he could find that could stretch beyond the lectures of Mr. Albertson's classroom, flame temperature and flash points and when the human body first ignites. He'd also looked at what Matt had told him in the cafeteria: organic materials. Fish oil. Mineral oil. Vegetable oil. What was left behind in a kitchen, what could be thrown aflame into a bedroom. What didn't make sense at all, every home a demolition, an inferno so far beyond rags and bottles of cooking oil. Nick had let himself delve further online into the chemistry of fire, everything Mr. Albertson had said, everything surely inside the textbook he'd left inside his school locker. Line emission spectrum. Flame color. Hues corresponding to ignited compounds. Household items. Chemical accelerants, what Nick knew could be ruled out. Organic materials: canola oil. Oxygen and carbon.

The fabric of human skin.

Nick looked away from the computer and his gaze landed on the television, turned off in the corner of his bedroom. A late-night special beyond the bounds of evidence, research no one knew he'd done the night before. There was no shame, everyone asleep. No harm in bending beyond rationality for one more night. Nick leaned forward and opened a new browser and let himself call up the same websites he'd already seen, every case he could find on unexplained home fires. Conspiracy theorists and bloggers and wikis of speculation, the same kinds of sites he would've found if he'd looked up local paranormal investigation teams, ghost sightings with no empirical evidence. Testimonies thin as silk. Eyewitness accounts he could easily blast apart. But also credible sites: scientific sites. Sites using the terminology of research, the same as those explaining the process of gas excitation. Historical sites. News sites of the most recent cases. Web pages explaining the consequence of spontaneous burning.

Self-ignition: organic. No evidence of accelerant or external cause.

More than two hundred cases reported since the first in Italy in 1745, a countess drifting to bed early, the last anyone would see of her, and by morning a pile of ash but for the remaining evidence of her feet. 1806: *An Essay on the Combustion of Humans,* a treatise disseminated by French scientist Pierre Lair. Then a rash of cases taken up by American Prohibitionists as their championed cause: that alcohol was flammable, the root of spontaneous fires inside the bodies of those who drank. Most recent studies: trial experiments on the body's production of certain chemicals when ill, organic compounds that in their toxicity were far more likely to burn.

What didn't make sense: in every case, there was always something left. A pair of shoes. Human hair. The charred remains of legs from the knee down. Not absolute disintegration. Not the eradication of an entire home. A complete combustion even more implausible than spontaneous burning due to the enormity of flame temperature it would take to burn an entire body and an entire home. The human body: 80 percent water. How difficult it would be to set fire to so much liquid. Bones in particular, too brittle to burn. How even crematoriums burning at 2,000 degrees wouldn't diminish the body fully to dust. How only heat beyond 3,000 degrees could consume a human skeleton, what 250 years of spontaneous ignition couldn't account for: the body reduced to ash, incinerated. Leaving nothing but the powder of cinders.

And now, this morning: a new browser open to the morning's terrible news. Alexis Thurber's father. What none of the articles mentioned and what Nick knew the police would find: nothing left. He heard his family in the kitchen down the hallway, another day of school he felt reluctant to face. The night's research still open on his computer in three separate tabs: spontaneous igniting. Gas excitation. Atoms displaced from one level of energy to another.

Nick squinted at the three tabs of sites, still in his pajamas. Alexis Thurber's apartment. Flames piling high into the night sky, smoke billowing across the entire complex. A parent's grief. A father's atoms, an entire life displaced inside his body.

Displacement. Excitation.

Nick sat forward in his chair.

Self-ignition: an inescapable fever. Every organic compound readying to burn.

Nick heard a knock at his bedroom door, breakfast waiting down the hallway, another day of high school beyond the kitchen. He closed down every browser.

Self-ignition: heat rising beyond a bearable threshold.

ZOLA WAS THE first of us to be pulled from her academic lab, her name called by an administrator at the door. She listened to the names of her peers and watched them slowly disappear from the room in alphabetical order, one by one, a fifty-five-minute class period for every one of them to speak to someone for a mandatory half hour. Her academic lab, its fallen students: likely flagged as one of the most crucial to file through sessions. When Zola's name was finally called, she rose from her desk and resolved to stay silent.

She followed the administrator down the hallway, a middle-aged man she'd never seen at Lewis and Clark. She watched his pant legs bunch and stiffen at the ankle as he shuffled down the corridor. He escorted her into a small room, one she'd have otherwise assumed was a janitorial closet. Its door opened to a tiny space with an industrial-looking couch and a lone desk seating a woman in a black pantsuit, her face turning in welcome.

Come on in and sit down, she said. Zola sat on the couch beside a small table sparsely populated with items suitable for a therapy room: lamp, clock. A box of tissues.

Please, call me Natalie.

I don't have much to say, Zola said bluntly.

Natalie smiled. Everyone's different. Some people have a lot to say—they want to talk about everything—and others aren't sure where to begin.

I know where to begin. I just don't have much to say about it.

Well, we have thirty minutes today to determine that. Why don't we start with today's news. How you feel about that.

I don't feel anything about it. The news is the same. It's the same every day.

Does it frighten you?

It might have last week. Now I've just come to expect it.

And how does that make you feel? That you've come to expect it?

Zola met the therapist's gaze. I know what you're trying to get me to admit. So fine, I'll say it. I can't believe that this is the new normal.

I'm not trying to get you to admit anything. I just want to know how you feel.

That this is what we've come to expect? What we wake up to every day? I don't know what you want me to say. That I feel good about it? No one does.

I don't want you to say anything.

It's scary. It's frightening. It's terrible. All of those things. But after a while you grow numb to it. You have to.

Why do you have to?

Because there's no other way through it.

Natalie sat back. She held a notepad but took no notes.

Why don't you tell me about the shooting, she said.

I was in the library.

Natalie's eyebrows rose just slightly.

I hid in the stacks. There's nothing else to say.

Then why don't we talk about something else? Like the past week. What has the past week been like for you? Your time at home?

Zola told Natalie the most cursory of information: that the week at home had been spent mostly reading, watching movies with her mother, sitting on the back porch and watching autumn recede. She told Natalie about the yearbook, about Matt and Nick and Christina, that her job was to take photographs and that she hadn't been able to document anything. She said nothing of Alisha Trenway's house. She mentioned the lull through the weekend, the quiet of watching more movies and reading more books and preparing for the start of school. She mentioned her classes and the cafeteria and her vague frustration with Nick, the previous day's conversation that had exploded.

And what about him makes you so angry? Natalie asked.

Zola thought of chemistry class earlier that morning, how Nick hadn't acknowledged her across the classroom. How he'd sat resolved at his lab table taking notes and listening to Mr. Albertson.

He's just so oblivious, Zola said. These fires. People are grieving. They've lost their children. And Nick wants to focus on fire chemistry? He's so fucking analytical. Sometimes things are more complicated than that.

In what way? Natalie asked.

It's just that— Zola said.

It's just what?

Zola looked at her. It's just that if you could have heard what I heard.

Natalie waited for her to say more.

In the library. Those sounds. The sound of choking. People gagging. Losing breath on their own blood. Nick will never know that.

It's easier. It's so much easier to be analytical with nothing bouncing through your head like that.

What would you say to Nick, if you could?

I don't know. I don't know what I'm asking for. Not much. Just for him to know that this is what I saw. This is what I heard. This is what so many other people are experiencing. I just want it acknowledged.

Do you think he knows that?

I think he does. But it's easier to look at it as an equation, something to solve.

What would you want acknowledged? What specifically?

Zola looked up. She recognized that she'd sunk into the couch, her body more relaxed. I don't know, she said.

It's okay. Just say whatever comes to you first.

I guess I want a witness. To what I witnessed. I want someone to say that this happened, that it's okay to feel this broken.

Zola felt herself breathless. In the silence that followed her words, she wished she could take them back.

Natalie glanced at the small clock. Our time's up for today. But I want to see you back here tomorrow. If you're up for it.

I guess I could be, Zola said. A window of time she'd dreaded, one she couldn't believe had gone by this fast. She shook Natalie's hand and let herself be escorted from the room. She filed into the empty hallway, still five minutes before the next class. She listened as her footsteps echoed on the tile and as her own voice bounced back dumbly through her brain. *That it's okay to feel this broken.* She felt her heart catch on the sound of it inside her head. To have admitted it. A heat humming through her chest.

NICK SAT WITH Sarah in the cafeteria, her lunch-hour choral lessons canceled for the week, a window of time that allowed her to eat during the time slot intended for juniors. She was still only a sophomore, college two years away, but Mr. Dyson met individually with

choral members who planned to apply for competitive vocal scholarships. College was something she and Nick hadn't discussed: who
would go where, whether they'd align their applications even with
a year between them. People found seats and gathered quietly at
circular tables around them. Nick couldn't imagine college, a far-off
place that had felt distant and vague since the start of high school
and felt even more formless now.

How was class? Sarah asked.

Fine. Nick bit into the turkey sandwich he'd packed in the
kitchen before Mr. Albertson demonstrated wavelengths of light
and the array of colors that compounds produced, greens and reds
billowing inside a line of beakers at the front of the chemistry classroom. Zola hadn't looked at him. He'd taken notes but had trouble
concentrating.

I had my counseling session this morning, Sarah said.

How did it go?

It wasn't terrible, just not that helpful. We talked about the
shooting, about being scared. We didn't talk about last night, which
I thought was the entire point of suddenly making these sessions
mandatory.

Nick thought for a moment that Sarah meant what they'd done
at Lake School Park. *Last night.* She'd barely spoken to him of the
fires or Alexis Thurber's apartment. What was happening in their
community.

Are you going back? Nick asked.

I can go back if I want, but the woman seemed to think I was
doing fine.

My session is later this afternoon, he said. Sixth period.

I don't even know why we're here. Couldn't they have just canceled school for another week, at least until they solve this? I saw
three FBI vans on my way to school today. Six police cars. Not to
mention the news vans. One is parked right outside.

Sarah motioned through the cafeteria's glass panes toward an unmarked van just beyond Timber Creek's student parking lot, its swirled antenna giving it away. Nick had seen FBI vans on his drive to school, some clearly marked and others attempting to stay undercover though it was obvious who they were and what they were doing.

Maybe it will take a while to solve, Nick said. Are you doing okay?

I'm fine. I mean, we're not in danger. It's pretty clear by now that whoever's doing this is only targeting the families of people who were killed.

Nick thought of the group: Parents for Home Protection. He wondered if Jacob's mother or Alexis's father had joined, if anyone had been watching their homes.

It's still unsettling, Nick said. And sad. Don't you want to know what's happening?

It's not my job to figure it out. Or yours. Let the FBI and police figure it out.

Sarah glanced past him then, her eyes tracking someone, and Nick turned to see Zola standing next to their table. She held nothing in her hands, no lunch bag or cafeteria tray, and made no motion to sit. She nodded hello to Sarah, then turned to Nick.

I just wanted to say sorry, she said. For blowing up at you yesterday.

It happens, he said. We're all stressed.

I'm sorry I said that. I didn't mean it.

Sarah glanced between both of them and Nick wanted to tell Zola that he knew he'd never know what she knew, what he'd only imagined of the library. Of crouching in the musty stacks, the quiet of her own breath separating her from a gun's barrel. Of hearing rounds of gunfire and then silence and not knowing which was worse. She seemed like she wanted to say more but realized where they were. She looked at Sarah. It's good to see you, she said. Then she turned and made her way across the cafeteria to a far table where Nick could see Matt and Christina congregating.

That was weird, Sarah said. What did she say to you yesterday?

Nothing. She's just having a hard time. She's been angry about a lot of things.

You said she was in the library, Sarah said. I'd be upset, too.

Nick wrapped his sandwich in his paper lunch bag and stood. I need to finish my world history reading before next period.

Want to come over after school? My mom won't be home until five.

Nick smiled faintly but shook his head. I need to pick Jeff up from school.

He kissed Sarah and promised he'd call her later and walked away unsure why he'd lied. He didn't have history homework. His brother took the bus home every day, old enough to watch himself. But he felt a pressing need to be alone, to not be near Sarah or her house or even join Matt and Christina and Zola at their table. He didn't want to sit with them and lie that he'd been surprised to awake to the news. That he didn't know what it meant to have sex, that he saw it as a milestone instead of a distraction. That his head was full of things they'd never believe, that he himself wasn't sure he understood. He left the cafeteria and climbed the stairwell to the second floor and its makeshift library and saw two policemen escorting Russ Hendricks down the hallway: Alexis Thurber's boyfriend, not yet in handcuffs but his arm bound by the firm grip of one of the officers. When they disappeared around a corner, Nick hustled into the library and moved past the improvised stacks to a row of second-floor windows behind them. The room silent, everyone in other classrooms or downstairs at lunch, a space populated only by the thrum of several computers and the presence of a librarian temporarily hired in Mrs. Diffenbaum's absence. Nick watched out the window as Russ was led outside the building's side entrance and into the dark of a waiting police car that crawled quietly from the parking lot, no sirens or lights. No news vans followed, not the one Sarah had seen far off to the other side of the school. Nick forgot the need for research, the row of computers humming behind him. Nick forgot the need to be alone. He hastened down to the cafeteria and found Matt and Zola and Christina just as the bell sounded the end of lunch, just as he said they needed to meet after school, immediately, now.

MATT WONDERED ALL afternoon what it was that Nick could tell them, what information could possibly be worse or more urgent than another fire he'd tried his best to block out. He'd said nothing at lunch to Christina or Zola about what his father had told him: the possibility of a juvenile arsonist. He'd pushed himself through afternoon classes on high alert, thinking nothing of algebra or chemistry. He'd glanced out the windows of his classrooms, the day warmer and glossed by sun, the air stagnant and still. He'd attended his first mandatory session, spoken to a therapist. Told a woman he'd known only ten minutes that he was fine, that he was taking all of this one day at a time. He didn't want to tell her about Caroline Black. That she'd been pushed from his brain if only for one night by a visitor at his bedroom window. That Tyler had left late. That letting him in was far better medicine than any mandatory session. Matt let his gaze fall away and fixate upon the carpet, the small clock, the ready boxes of tissues. He awaited the end of the school day knowing he'd meet Nick and Christina and Zola, all of them waiting in Timber Creek's parking lot beside Nick's Honda when the final bell rang.

There was no destination. No clear agenda. Nick only said *not here* and Matt climbed into the backseat beside Zola and they traveled in silence through the streets of Midvale County, beneath so many tall trees lining the sides of the roads. Nick's car passed more FBI vans, many of them unmarked but obvious in their separateness from a suburb, then another news van not far from the Pensacola Apartments, where Alexis Thurber had lived. Matt eyed the complex as the car drove past, Alexis's apartment obscured from

view behind police tape and other apartment buildings. The scent
of sulfur and burnt wood filtered through the car's closed windows
regardless, a smell that had grown familiar across the past week.
So many homes. A small radius. No one spoke as the car drove by.
Nick turned up the volume on the stereo, anything but the drone of
news talk radio, and curved through the neighborhoods toward the
open back roads again, the edge of every subdivision, a long stretch
of shorn stalks and withering cornfields. Matt let Nick's Honda
trade so many rows of homes and the fear dwelling inside of them
for the wide-open forgetting of rolling hills and a blue sky.

Nick turned at last into Midvale County Park, a large recreational area that formed the bridge between neighborhoods and the
hills of Missouri country. He pulled into a lot by the park's lake-
front lined with shelters and barbecue pits, each of them abandoned
until next summer. He cut the engine and left the car and Christina
turned and looked at Matt from the front seat. Matt shrugged and
opened the car door and followed Zola and Christina to a shelter
against the lake's shore where Nick sat on the surface of a picnic
table, his sneakers on the bench.

What is it? Matt asked. Enough suspense. Just tell us.

I saw Russ Hendricks being hauled away, Nick said. Just before
the end of lunch.

What do you mean hauled away? Christina asked.

I mean escorted down the hallway. I mean placed into a police car.

Matt imagined Russ beside him in American history sophomore
year, the only class they'd ever had together. So I guess they've identified a suspect, he said.

Maybe, Nick said. After nearly two weeks of nothing, they've
acted pretty quickly.

Matt sat on the picnic table and watched the sun diamonding off
the lake's waves.

My father said they were looking for a juvenile arsonist. Russ
must be it.

Christina approached the picnic table. What do you mean, a juvenile arsonist?

Matt sighed. Maybe someone in our school. Someone out only at night, when no one would be supervising them. Someone who stopped setting fires across a weekend when their parents were home. Someone directly affected by the shooting, given the targeting of grieving families. Someone like Russ Hendricks.

I don't buy it, Zola said. Yeah, Russ has a temper. All of us know that. But starting a bunch of fires? Actually killing people? I don't believe it for a second.

He's practically a criminal, Christina said. Remember when he almost hospitalized Ben Worthington last year?

He just broke his nose, Zola said. Yeah, he's been suspended a bunch of times. But just because he can break someone's nose doesn't mean he killed anyone.

I didn't say I thought he was guilty, Nick said. I just saw them lead him away. Maybe they're just bringing him in for questions. Maybe they think he knows something.

Matt watched Nick, the tone of his voice faraway, as if he were daydreaming. This the exact kind of information Nick craved, a tangible answer. A suspect. And what Matt could tell him: that he fit the profile of a juvenile arsonist. But Nick only watched the water of the lake and Matt saw he wouldn't meet any of their eyes. Matt thought again of what his father had said: someone beyond Eric Greeley who knew Caleb Raynor. What else he could tell Nick.

My dad said they're going to start patrolling the other families' homes, as a preemptive strike. He also said they're looking for the possibility of a different accomplice.

Nick looked at him, what Matt knew he would do. You mean to Caleb?

Did Russ even know Caleb? Christina said. He had a pocketknife in class once, in eighth grade. He said he kept it in his backpack just in case.

We didn't know Caleb could do something like this, Nick said. What does it matter now if we think they knew each other or not? At this point, anything is possible.

Matt felt the cold of the lake push through his jacket despite the sun's warmth. He scanned his brain for some indication that he'd ever seen Russ talk to Caleb and turned up nothing. No link, though it didn't mean his father and the police wouldn't find one.

Well, at least they're getting somewhere, Christina said.

I guess, Zola said. But I think they're doing the wrong thing.

And what's the right thing? Christina asked. Yeah, this is information. But it doesn't tell us anything. Not yet. What are we supposed to do with this? She glanced at Nick and motioned to the lake. Why are we out here?

We're out here because this is bullshit, Zola said. We all know Russ Hendricks isn't a killer. She turned to Christina. Did you see him anywhere near Benji Ndolo's house, or in the crowd outside Jacob Jensen's house?

Of course not, Christina said. But that doesn't mean anything.

What about all of these parents watching each other's homes? Nick said. What about the reporters, police, everyone knowing now where to look? Wouldn't they have seen something by now? And why would Russ want to kill his girlfriend's father? Aren't these questions anyone else is even considering?

To share the grief, Matt said. To make everyone feel as much pain as he feels.

Who told you that? Nick said. Your counselor in these bullshit therapy sessions?

Matt felt all at once punched. The shock of Nick's tone. Nick not caring at all about any of the things Matt could tell him.

My father, Matt said. Thanks for asking.

Cut it out, you two. Zola glanced at Matt. Russ has problems. But he wouldn't burn down homes, especially not with families inside. Not with Alexis's father still there.

How do you know? Christina asked. You didn't know him. You didn't see those houses burn. Did you know they're burying Jacob's mom today?

Nick stood from the picnic bench. Maybe your dad's not telling you everything.

He said he'd tell me what was needed to keep me safe.

Maybe this arrest is keeping you safe, Christina said.

I doubt it, Nick said. None of this adds up.

Then what does? Matt asked.

Isn't that what we're all trying to figure out? It could be arson, sure. But do you think Russ is capable of burning down an entire home and everything inside it?

I don't know, Matt said. I guess my dad will know more this afternoon.

Nick stood and walked to the edge of the lake, pooled wide and gray beyond the shore. Matt wondered what it was that was bothering him, if he and Sarah had a fight. And if so, why he'd brought all of them out here to tell them he'd seen Russ taken away only to say it didn't mean anything. Matt waited for him to speak, to elaborate on what he'd seen, but he said nothing, eyes on the water, the waves of the lake the only sound.

WHEN NICK DROPPED them all off at Timber Creek's parking lot, Matt asked if he was okay but he only nodded and pulled away from school, said he had to get home to watch his brother. Zola headed toward the Local Beanery on her bike, Christina toward home in her car. Matt climbed into his hatchback and didn't want to go home. Russ Hendricks at the police station, where the officers had surely taken him from Timber Creek. Matt glanced at the radio clock. He felt restless. He felt angry. So much information and Nick cared about none of it. He knew where his father would be.

He'd gone into the station a million times before, knew his father's colleagues, had shadowed them at Take Your Child to Work Day at least a half-dozen times across his elementary school years. He waited in the parking lot. He couldn't saunter through the station's doors, just checking in on his father, the department managing FBI officials and arson investigators and more media attention than they'd ever known. He left his backpack in the passenger seat. Steeled himself. Made his way toward the sliding glass doors of the police station. The receptionist recognized him and led him past the secured doors, and he followed her through the buzzed-open entryway and past rooms where he could see officers and detectives bent over computers and scattered papers. His father's office door lay open. He looked up from his desk.

You shouldn't be here, he said. Today's been insane. Your mother will worry.

Matt said nothing and sat down in the chair across from his father's desk.

I have work to do. Work I'm trying desperately to finish so I can get home.

What kind of work?

You know I can't tell you that.

Fine. Then let me tell you what I know instead. I know Russ Hendricks was brought here. We saw him being taken away from school today for questioning.

His father got up and closed the door. No one knows that yet, he said. We're keeping it confidential for now. No reason to raise unnecessary suspicion.

Is he here? Did they give him a polygraph test just like Eric Greeley?

That's enough, Matt. Keep your voice down.

Matt sat back in the chair. I want you to tell me. Please. Tell me what's going on.

Matt's father looked past him toward the closed door, as if expecting another officer to push his way in. You remember what I told you yesterday, he said. About what we're looking for. Russ Hendricks fits the bill.

Matt wanted to believe him. He thought about what Zola and Nick had said at the lake. That Russ had violence in him but not enough to kill.

He's been in fights, he said. But that's it. Did you find out anything else?

He may not have an extensive criminal record, but he's got some telltale issues. A history of anger, social problems. A low academic record, evidence of past criminality in property damage. I shouldn't even be telling you that. Family problems. Looks like his father died when he was small. Single-parent household, possible lack of supervision.

Christina lives in a single-parent household. So does Zola.

It's only one factor among many. Lots of kids grow up in great homes with one parent. We're looking at the few who didn't, statistically speaking, who've displayed evidence of criminality and social problems.

But do you actually have any evidence? Anything concrete that places Russ anywhere near Alexis Thurber's apartment, or at any other house?

I can't tell you that. I'd be breaching confidentiality.

You said you'd tell me anything to keep me safe.

I would. Don't think for a second I wouldn't. But trust me when I say that I won't tell you anything unless I absolutely have to. Trust that I have your best interest at heart, and everyone else in that entire goddamn school.

Matt felt nothing but a quiet shame. To have challenged his father, so much work spread across his desk like the pages of a disheveled manuscript.

Fire's not my area, his father said. But suffice it to say that we've found some evidence at the scene, evidence that links Russ through more than profiling.

He was probably there hundreds of times, Matt said. Alexis was his girlfriend.

We know that, which is why we're not making anything public just yet. He's really just a person of interest at this point. Not a suspect. They'll probably question him through the evening and then let him go home. They can't hold him longer than that.

Matt looked at his father. Is Russ the accomplice?

We still don't know if Caleb had one. But it's a possibility.

Matt sat back in the chair and imagined returning to school in the morning.

He'll be let go if he wasn't arrested, Matt said. He'll be back at school tomorrow.

I'm telling you, don't worry about it until you need to worry. I promise I'll tell you if you do. What I can tell you is that we're still working on the scene at the school.

What do you mean, working on?

Matt's father sighed. A situation like that calls for more cleanup and investigation than you can imagine. We're working with the FBI on that. It will take time. But we're still tracing the kid's path through the school. Because it's necessary. Because even though it seems so obvious what that boy did, it still needs to be retraced. Not just for investigation and evidence but for future prevention, so this never happens again.

Matt thought of police sweeping through the darkened classrooms, a mess of overturned desks and discarded backpacks. A trail of chalk markings indicating where his classmates had been found. The echoing halls of Lewis and Clark. Long corridors lined with ghosts. A place he knew he'd never want to see again.

How could anything have prevented this? What could we have done differently?

Nothing, Matt's father said. No one could have done anything differently to change what happened. This isn't anyone's fault. But the more we know about his path, the more we know how we could have stopped him sooner.

Matt looked at his father. He wanted to believe him.

We're close, his father said. The force has dispatched a new team to keep an eye on the other homes. Just know that we're getting there. That we're on our way.

ZOLA SAT BEHIND the counter of the Local Beanery, where she'd biked after Nick dropped them off back at Timber Creek's parking lot, a notebook of graph paper resting on her lap. Trigonometry functions; x, y. Variables that swam across the gridded page. Her homework, a thin pretense: near the far window, Kelly Washington's mother and two other women sat talking quietly. Zola recognized Kelly's mother from homeroom activities at Des Peres Elementary. Handing out glue sticks. Collecting unused pipe cleaners. A woman who sat hunched now, a mug of coffee enfolded in her hands. Zola didn't recognize the other two women though she knew they were mothers of her lost peers. Parents for Home Protection. Zola knew this. Knew without a doubt that this was their meeting. She thought of Alexis Thurber's father, a parent she couldn't imagine joining in, and recalled that Matt had seen him at the movie theater alone. How parents navigated the complications of grief, each in their own way. Zola looked to the women at the table, their faces hard but without the strain of tears, and for a moment she couldn't believe that they were in the world without breaking something, without shattering the glass of the coffee shop windows, without burning down the entire city.

Can I get a refill? a voice asked from the edge of the counter. A middle-aged man motioned his mug toward Zola and she held it beneath the coffee dispenser.

Fifty cents, she said. The man pushed two quarters across the

counter and returned to his armchair when she gave him his re-
filled mug. The sun slanted down the horizon beyond the Beanery windows, nearly sunk behind the trees. Zola thought of Nick,
surely at home, sitting at the computer in his bedroom. Looking
up juvenile arson. Culprit profiling. Or else combustion and gas
excitation, what he'd clearly absorbed in chemistry class, seeking
some explanation for how nothing remained. Zola wondered if the
women in the coffee shop knew that no bodies were left, what still
hadn't been printed in the newspaper. She knew they had no idea
Russ Hendricks was at the police station at this very moment while
they met, that they could have celebrated the catching of a suspect
though Zola still didn't believe it. She imagined Jacob's mother's
funeral, another lowering away she couldn't believe had happened
that afternoon. Russ had a temper. A given. Zola knew he couldn't
have possibly burned down so many homes. She also knew the fever
for an answer. She thought of the pictures she'd taken of Alisha's
house, evidence no different than police photography, how they'd
told her absolutely nothing.

The same as what Russ could tell police.

She set down her notebook and looked at the women. She felt
her stomach roll in a wave of nausea. She realized she hadn't eaten
lunch. She wasn't hungry, muffins and scones waiting in the display
case and even still she couldn't imagine eating, these women only
yards away planning how to keep their homes from burning. Their
children gone. Zola felt her stomach lurch, the strange workings of
her own body. That it could alert her to something wrong, a flood
of queasiness. That it could turn on her, a system of pathways and
networks she barely understood.

MATT WATCHED FROM the bay window of the living room as the last
of the sun slid down the glass in ghosted light. It was impossible to
imagine such a sun bringing only devastation as it slipped away, that

dusk meant only bracing. For darkness and a flame. For the inevitability of the newspaper. That he'd come to assume this, even with Russ Hendricks detained at the station.

His mother came in from the kitchen and stood beside him, dinner near ready.

Did you know her? The Thurber girl.

Not well. I knew of her.

With any hope, this will be the end of this.

He knew his mother meant Russ, a name his father had mentioned when he'd walked through the front door a half hour ago. Police still working at the station. Russ still being questioned, Matt knew. His father had vowed he'd be home for dinner but had retreated down the hallway and closed his office door despite his mother's meat loaf warming in the kitchen's oven, the aroma of roasted beef and browned ketchup filling the house until his father finished working.

Have you been writing? his mother asked. I'm not trying to snoop, but I vacuumed your room today. I saw the profile of Jacob Jensen on your desk.

It isn't worth reading, Matt said. Christina's been trying to write them, too.

They'll be valuable. You can't know it now. But your classmates will be grateful for them, for the memories you captured. When they go back and read those books.

When they go back. Matt couldn't imagine his classmates as fully fledged adults, Nick or Christina at thirty, Zola at forty. If anything from here could be imagined, a future as impossible as so many blistering fires. Maybe that was why Nick had been so subdued. That he'd hit a wall. That the only thing left for them to do was look back. To put together a book. As if anything of this could be kept.

I don't even know what I'm trying to capture, Matt said. There are barely words.

But the words you find will be the right ones. I'm sure of it.

She touched his shoulder and they watched the roof of their neighbor's house absorb the last light of the sun and though he wanted to believe her, as readily as he wanted to believe that his father and the police team had control of an investigation at last, he knew there were no words, his task an illusion. The illusion of statement, of setting this down. Of creating a comfortable history. Of stabilizing the past. Of saying this was, in words that fixed meaning for anyone who would ever read them.

Will you write a profile of the Thurber girl?

Christina and I haven't talked about it. But I can try. Chris has done enough for now. She's seen enough in the past few days.

Your father told me she saw the Jensen house. On top of seeing Benji's mother.

This isn't easy for anyone, Matt said. Just waiting around for news to come.

I finished my book. The one on President Bush and the War on Terror.

What did you think?

His mother looked at him. He's an interesting man.

And?

She hesitated. It's easy to be certain. It's harder to admit what we don't know.

Matt followed her back to the couch, where she turned on the television, his father still behind the closed door. Matt sat on the armchair near the window, leaving the couch to his mother and soon his father once he emerged from the office. He thought to work on his history homework but gave up quickly, a notepad in his hand, the television whirring. A game show instead of news. He glanced out the window at the dark treetops, the sky heavy with new clouds that blocked out the moon. A storm was moving in. He could see it in the bend of every tree branch. He glanced at his mother, her attention divided between the television and a new book she'd started, a brief history of the world from the dawn of the Big Bang to the modern age. His blood oscillated beneath his skin, the same restlessness he'd felt in his car. There was nothing he could do. Nothing but continuing to write profiles, the best he could do, a notepad in his hands.

Alexis Thurber. His pen stayed poised above the notebook.

There was so little to write. So little he knew of her and her life. But he knew his task, the simplest of actions, something to draw his focus: a profile to set down. He pushed down his pen. *Alexis Thurber was loved.* He didn't know if it was true. He didn't know what else to write, what information he could conjure up about a girl he'd barely known. The telephone rang and his mother set down her book, reached for the side table where the receiver sat but only tolled once. She withdrew her hand but Matt could hear his father talking to someone in the office, his voice audible above the television.

Then the door opening. Quick footsteps. His father in the living room.

Jim, what is it? his mother said. Her book dropping to the couch cushions.

Fire. His father already pulling on his shoes. Another fire. God fucking damn it.

Matt steeled himself against a wave of shouting, his father's anger as terrifying as his hardened quiet, the rage of walking from a room and down the hallway and closing the door behind him, his silence a stone. But his father only grabbed his coat. He opened the front door wide, the wind gusting in. I'll be home when I can, he said. I'll call when I can. The door whipped shut behind him and Matt watched through the front window as his father threw himself into the car and pulled away from the house and disappeared fast down the street. He watched until long after the car was gone, a heat rising in his chest.

That Russ Hendricks was still at the station.

That unless there was another suspected accomplice, Russ wasn't a killer.

That Russ meant nothing.

That he also meant everything: that there were officially no answers.

It's too soon! his mother shouted. This just happened. Are we going to go through this every night? The same thing every goddamn night?

Matt didn't answer her, his mother a rock, always the rock and breaking down into rubble. He knew it as well as his mother did: too soon. A pattern broken. Not the dead of night but just after sunset, a community awake, the streets still screaming with police cars and reporters. Not a juvenile, not someone who shared the walls of his high school, not someone whose parents were home having dinner just like his were. His mother stared out the window. Weight-born sky, thickening clouds. Wind beating against the windowpanes. He closed his eyes. He saw no culprit. He saw no accomplice. The only possibility left, a trail of smoke. He saw nothing but a flame and his father racing toward it.

ALEXIS THURBER
Lewis and Clark High School
Class of 2005
March 3, 1988—October 8, 2003

A junior at Lewis and Clark, Alexis Thurber was loved. We know this now: her boyfriend Russ Hendricks was not a killer.

Alexis was active in theater, serving as a technical assistant for *Godspell* as a freshman and *The Man of La Mancha* as a sophomore. She was slated to work on lighting for the 2004 spring production of *Pippin*. Active in community service, Alexis also worked in horse stables and volunteered with the Equine Therapy Center.

Alexis was a kind soul, one who was loved by her friends, partner, and family. She will be greatly missed by the community at Lewis and Clark High School.

A BRIEF HISTORY OF
THE HUMAN BODY

THE AVERAGE HUMAN speaks 16,000 words a day, approximately one-sixth the word count of a standard novel.

The human body takes between 17,280 and 23,040 breaths, a range dependent upon level of daily activity. The rate of respiration a sine wave, in and out, the rhythm of mathematics so much like a sea.

The human body's blood travels 12,000 miles through more than 60,000 miles of blood vessels every cycle of 24 hours. 60,000 miles: more than twice the distance around the earth. Human blood, a liquid organ. A conduit that flows between lengths of entire continents, from Los Angeles to Moscow and back in the span of one day.

Each cell in the body: six to eight feet of DNA, a coiled helix sprung tight.

The body's electricity: impulses traveling between synapses at a rate of 248 miles per hour. Saliva: one liter produced every day. Human hair: 100 strands lost. The human eye: 23,000 blinks, the retina's cone cells capable of discerning up to 100 million color surfaces, more information taken in than the largest telescope on earth.

The human heart: 2,000 gallons of blood. Approximately 100,000 heartbeats every day, enough energy produced in one hour to raise one ton of weight three feet from the ground. Under stress: rising heart rate, 120,000 to 140,000 beats per day. Increased blood pressure, liquid pushing against the walls of each vessel. Palpitation. Irregular heartbeat. The strain of fight or flight. Enough energy to slacken cells from routine. Enough to break the body of order, to throw a locomotive from its track.

AS MUCH TO KEEP US SAFE

MATT WAITED UP for what felt like hours for his father, his mother's shape a fortress beside him on the couch. He closed his eyes and willed his father home. He let the sound of the television fill his ears. *American Idol*. The nine o'clock news. Then the ten o'clock news, the fire breaking at the top of the hour, camera crews at last on the scene and a reporter standing before a swirl of flashing lights. The camera panning behind her once she mentioned the address and the camera tracked toward the fire. The 1400 block of Fox Run Road. Not far from Nick, Matt realized. Only a few streets over. Fire trucks everywhere. Hoses. Water. Flames filling the perimeter of the screen. Matt imagined Nick's neighborhood and its houses and who among them lost a child and zeroed in on Darren Beechwold, a sophomore he remembered sometimes seeing at the school bus stop at the end of Nick's street. Matt hastened downstairs, telling his mother he'd be back up in a minute. He picked up the telephone in his room. Nick answered on the first ring.

NICK SAT PERCHED in the nook between his bedroom window and computer, the desk chair hard against his back. He kept an eye on the street outside, neighbors emerging from their homes to see what was happening though he knew the fire was streets away. He knew already whose home it was. Darren Beechwold. A sophomore he knew had been lost inside Lewis and Clark, someone he'd often seen riding his bike through the neighborhood though they'd only nodded hellos and had never spoken to one another. Police cars passed. Nick knew they were blocking off streets. A parade of fire trucks swarmed through, lights flashing. Heavy wind pulsed against the house and pushed the trees against Nick's window. His family was congregated in the living room. Nick had sat with them until he couldn't stand it any longer.

He knew already: a fire in the early evening. A broken pattern.

What he'd known at the lake: there was no juvenile arsonist.

Russ Hendricks easy. So much easier than the complications of the human body.

Nick sat in front of his computer. Every fact he could find on what the body was capable of doing. Every brain wave. Every heart-beat. Every electrical impulse. Everything he wasn't sure he believed but had nothing else, everything he couldn't say out loud for how reckless and stupid the words would sound spilling from his mouth.

When the phone rang late beside his computer, he knew already who it was.

I don't know anything, Nick said. The entire neighborhood's on lockdown.

Can't you go outside? Matt asked. Even just to your yard?

My parents are keeping us inside, Nick said. I would if I could.

So where are you? At your computer?

I can see out my bedroom window, but that's it.

What can you see?

Nick pivoted his desk chair. There are police everywhere, he said. There are a few people in their yards, just like what Christina described from the other night. But this isn't like that. It's so much earlier. People are scared. The police are keeping everyone inside.

There's no curfew.

I know, but it's beyond pattern. People are still out. I'm guessing they don't want to take chances in case someone's out there on the loose.

Darren Beechwold's house, Matt said.

It can't be anyone else, Nick said. He's the only person on the list of names who lives in my neighborhood. Is your dad out there?

He got a phone call a little while ago. He's probably waiting until the fire's extinguished before entering the scene for evidence.

Nick winced at the word: *scene.* This was not a scene. It was someone's house, an entire life he hadn't bothered to know beyond waving hello on the sidewalk.

Did you see any police earlier near your street? Matt asked. My dad said they'd start patrolling the families' homes.

I didn't see anything. But I've been inside. I've been inside all night.

It's probably going to rain any minute.

Nick glanced out the window, every tree pulsing with the first wall of a storm's wind. That won't stop the police, he said. And it won't stop a fire, either. I counted at least six fire trucks. They all raced down the street, one after the other.

I'll wait up for my dad if I can. I don't know when he'll be back.

Nick sighed. We both know what this means.

Russ Hendricks, Matt said. My dad told me earlier that he's still at the station.

Which means he didn't do this. We knew that. Come on, Matt. We both knew.

I didn't, Matt said. I thought my dad finally had an answer.

Nick said nothing. An answer. What he'd begun to trickle into believing but couldn't say. The science of fire: the same principles of the investigation Matt's father led. Nick couldn't speak. Couldn't let the words travel across a line, nothing more than a fledgling theory in the face of another fire upon so many other fires.

Are you okay? Matt asked. You seemed off at the lake.

Nick hesitated. I'm fine. I just don't think this is someone at our high school. The pattern's broken. It doesn't add up to someone we know setting fires.

But you were quiet this afternoon. Long before anything broke a pattern.

I'm just trying to find answers. Same as you. Same as Christina and Zola.

What are you looking at? Your computer. I know you're looking at something.

Nothing that isn't on television. My family has the local news on in the living room. The stations finally picked it up just this hour.

My mom's watching it, too. There was nothing on the nine o'clock hour.

The ten o'clock wasn't much better. I figured I'd have better luck online.

So what did you find?

Nick was careful with his words. I haven't found much.

Come on, man, just tell me.

Well, I'm looking at the chemistry of fire. Gas excitation.

Like chemistry class. I thought you'd been looking at that for a while.

I have. But when you said organic material, I thought of the human body.

What about it?

What it can do. What the body does every day to keep us moving.

Like all the amazing things we learned about in biology in junior high? Like how an unfurled intestine can stretch to the moon and back?

Nick smiled despite himself. I'm just saying that under pressure, the body responds. Just like flashbulb memories. What the brain recalls when pushed to its limits. Look, I know people experience grief all the time. They experience it without a shooting and without houses burning down. But there's been so much, Matt. There's just been too much here to even begin to comprehend.

Nick heard Matt sigh. I know.

Beyond the window, Nick watched the first raindrops begin

to fall and knew he'd said too much. That he'd done nothing but make Matt recall Caroline Black, an image he knew Matt wanted to forget.

It's too much, Matt said. All of this. It's just too much.

I know, Nick said. Believe me, I know.

There's still the chance of a different accomplice, Matt said. Beyond Russ. What my father told me they were looking for.

Nick watched rain slide down the windowpanes, small bubbles that joined other droplets. Russ Hendricks still at the station being questioned. The possibility of someone else out there, another suspect, someone who could be occupying the desk beside him in history class or academic lab. Nick wanted to believe it, wanted to shut his computer down and sit with his family in the living room and forget any need to know. The rain began to cascade in curtains. Nick wished Russ an arsonist. He wished an answer, an end.

WHEN MATT AT last heard his father's voice inside the house it was late, the rain long gone, the sky thick beyond the pulled-open curtains of the living room window. He'd fallen asleep on the couch, the notepad still sitting on the chair, Alexis's profile short and inadequate but complete. He knew nothing about her life. He would never print the sentence about Russ Hendricks. He heard his parents' voices in the kitchen, the percolating sound of the coffeemaker dripping. He heard his father's voice: *Nothing left.* Words hovering above the sound of the machine. He wanted to listen to the confidence between his parents, what they discussed when they thought he was asleep, but he couldn't make out any other words beyond murmurs. He pulled himself from the couch and entered the kitchen. They sat at the table across from one another, his father still in street clothes, his mother in her bathrobe.

What happened? Matt asked. What did you find?

Have a seat, Matt's mother said.

Want some coffee? Matt's father asked and his mother protested, said it was too late. At this point, Matt's father said, I don't think anyone's getting any sleep anyway.

What time is it? Matt asked.

Past two, his mother said.

Did you just get home? he asked his father.

Not long ago.

I'm an adult, Matt said. Please, Dad, just tell me what happened.

His father glanced at his mother across the table. It was the Beechwold kid's house, he said. Sue and Grant. You know the rest by now. There was nothing left. Surely the same: organic cause. We know it already, without need of lab reports.

Matt said nothing. Everything accelerating. So many houses multiplied like a rapid-spread virus. It had taken his father two days to tell him what they'd found at Jacob Jensen's house and now here, in the kitchen, his father could guess everything only two hours beyond Darren Beechwold's house burning.

Matt's mother reached for his hand across the table. Did you know him?

No, Matt said. We only saw him sometimes in Nick's neighborhood.

Poor Nick, his mother said. He and his family must be so frightened.

Matt looked at his father. What about Russ Hendricks?

They released him. Unless he's part of some wide network of arsonists that snuck through a neighborhood while he was in custody, he's no longer a suspect.

I could've told you that, Matt said, and regretted it. It was late. His father had done what he could.

The police are working, his mother said. They're doing the best they can.

What about an accomplice? Matt asked his father. What you mentioned before.

It's on the table. Frankly, it's the only thing on the table we've got.

But tonight breaks the pattern, Matt said. Everyone was still out in the streets. It couldn't be a juvenile arsonist. Which is what an accomplice would have to be.

Matt's father looked at him. After what happened tonight, the pattern's been broken. It might not be a teenager at all. Still a time when parents would be home, when supervision would be at its height. It could be an adult, but it could still be someone at the school. Time of day is just one of many possible factors.

The coffeemaker dripped. Matt felt exhausted beneath the harsh bulbs of the kitchen's fluorescent light, the sky a black hole beyond the small square of window above the dishwasher and sink. He thought of what Nick had said: the human body. He felt his own breaking beneath the burden of this night.

What's the next step? Matt asked his father. Cancel school? Lockdown? What?

They can't cancel school, his father said. Not any more than they already have. We'll all just keep doing what we're doing. High security. And at this point, maximum security around every house of the remaining families.

I thought the police were already doing that, his mother said. And I thought there was concern over too much scrutiny. A lack of privacy.

Matt's father sipped his coffee. By now, any question of privacy has gone out the window. Those families have as much privacy as the rest of Midvale County. None. What's more police security? They'll need it. We're the eye of the country right now.

WE AWOKE TO more news. More headlines.

We awoke to the surety that Matt's father was right.

We were the eye of the country, the center of a media storm of television and newspapers and websites. We had been for weeks. And now, a tenor reaching a fever pitch, a fire broken out every single night since we'd returned to school. We awoke to blaring headlines, to the angry shouts of reporters on television. *What about the children?* Our names invoked. *What about these poor children and their safety?* We awoke to public outrage leveled hard at the Midvale County School District for letting us travel unprotected to Timber Creek's doors.

The administration sent no cancellations, no postponements. No indication that plans for our continued education had changed. We awoke only to another terse email from the school that their thoughts were with the Beechwold family and those who knew them. That counselors were on hand. That sessions remained mandatory. That to maintain routine, classes would resume as scheduled.

The A1 front page that morning: a full-scale photo of the Beechwolds' home surrounded by flames and firefighters, the headline above challenging police officers, *WHAT NOW?* No mention of Russ Hendricks anywhere in the article. Only brief indication that police surveillance would increase and that Parents for Home Protection had gathered in force. That Alexis Thurber's father would be buried in a private ceremony that afternoon. The entire front page a demand that the police do something, that they solve everything, all of this, now.

We took in the pages. We read every word. We lost our will and turned to other pages, the back sections that let in the rest of the world: that Al Qaeda was operating in Iraq and also in Afghanistan, planning attacks on U.S. troops. That leaders of the European Union were working to release twenty-six Europeans detained in Guantanamo Bay, prisoners held indefinitely by the United States without charge or legal representation. That the outgoing prime minister of Malaysia called the United States the terrorists of the world. In sports, other pages we turned to for reprieve: that the Marlins had taken the fourth game of the World Series in twelve innings. The series tied. That the next game would include a brief memorial at the start of the game, a moment of silence for Major League Baseball's friends in St. Louis.

Our teachers couldn't ignore us or the news. They couldn't start our first-period classes without mention of Alexis Thurber or Darren Beechwold or so many fires, so close to our own basements and bedrooms within the gridded streets of Midvale County. Mrs. Menda held a moment of silence in Matt's English class. In algebra, Mrs. Gornick asked Christina and her classmates if there was anything they'd like to talk about beyond equations and formulas. And in chemistry Mr. Albertson did the best he could, a man with so little sense for the connective element of empathy but enough to set down his beakers, to look beyond colored fluids and test tubes and ask the entire class without eyeing anyone in particular, *Is everyone okay?*

We attended our counseling sessions. Academic lab. We watched the small clocks in the therapy rooms tick toward their mandated end. Christina found herself seated on a hard couch midmorning beneath the pressure of finding words that meant something, of saying anything of substance to the counselor sitting before her with a notepad. *I'm feeling okay,* she said. *I just don't know what's happening.* The woman nodded, her gaze sympathetic, her head tilted to the side, a woman who seemed too young to be a therapist. She asked Christina about the Ndolo fire and about the Jensen fire and a surge of guilt pushed through Christina that she'd have rather talked about Ryan than the homes she'd seen burning. That she'd broken a picture frame and a window and brought on her first orgasm in a single week that everyone else would remember for fire and nothing else.

Zola sat on a similar couch across from her counselor through the second period of the morning, a reprieve from chemistry and the hard data of science. *How are you feeling?* Natalie asked, a question as wide as the fields of the back roads. Zola wanted to say she was on fire, that at night she felt as combustible as the homes that surrounded her. That she'd lain awake well past three knowing a house was burning again in a two-mile radius, that the house was only blocks from Nick's house and that they shared this now, the scorched scent blanketing everything from their porches to the blades of browning grass in their backyards. That she and her mother had watched the news until her mother said that nothing about it was news but only the catharsis of watching. That her mother had gone up to bed, had asked if Zola wanted to sleep in her bedroom for the night. That Zola had shaken her head but regretted it as soon as her mother closed the door. That she'd gone into her own room and lain on her bed and felt the photographs of Alisha Trenway's house alive and pulsing on the carpet, still trapped in her camera, undeveloped and unprinted and unable to tell her anything at all but that something awful had happened here. That she'd pulled Penelope from her cage and held her close against her chest, velvet ears soft as a hymn against her cheeks.

I'm fine, Zola said to Natalie. She said it loud enough that she believed it.

And your friend Nick? What about him? Did you get the chance to talk, to resolve your fight?

I said what I could. I apologized.

Did you say everything you wanted to say?

Does anyone ever say everything they want to say?

What else would you say, if you could?

Zola looked at Natalie. Wondered what was acceptable. Wondered what was appropriate in the space of a mandatory counseling session, what she could ask of this woman licensed only to speak of grief and reveal nothing of herself.

What do you think is happening? Zola asked.

What do you mean?

I mean, tell me what you think is happening. You live here, too. You go home to your house, every day. You have your own fears, your own thoughts. Your own sense of why this is happening.

Why do you think it's happening?

I don't know. That's why I'm asking you.

Natalie set down her notepad. I really don't know.

Please. For a minute. Just pretend I'm not your patient.

It's my job. I'm here to support you.

But if you weren't. If we were just having coffee. What do you think is happening?

Natalie glanced toward the door. It's not for me to say. But since you asked, I'll admit it. I'm scared, too. I don't know what's going on.

Do you think anyone knows what's going on?

I really don't know. I'm sure the police are working on it. Does that answer your question? What else do you want to talk about? How about your family? How is everything at home?

Zola sat back on the couch. An opening sealed. The closest Natalie could come before locking herself back into the role of adult, of therapist. Zola settled back into hers. She let herself speak. She let herself talk knowing authority was nothing but illusion. That everyone she once believed knew everything was scared, even the police, that those in charge knew nothing of what was happening or what to do.

WE MET IN the courtyard at lunch. The day unexpectedly bright past the previous night's storm, light beating down on the benches and brick. A late fall warm-up as Matt's father had predicted before winter settled in, the sky cloudless and blue and the sun heating our sweaters against our skin. We met with our sandwiches, our vended sodas, our lunches barely packed.

Russ Hendricks was released, Matt said. Last night. My dad said there's no way he could have done it.

So he was still at the station? Nick asked.

That's what my dad said.

I saw Russ this morning, Christina said. Coming out of the first-floor bathroom. It's like nothing even happened.

No one knows he was questioned, Matt said. Unless someone

else saw him being taken away yesterday, though I'm guessing no one did. Everyone was at lunch or in class. The police never released the information. He was just a person of interest.

But not anymore, Zola said. What happened last night, that was way too early. My mother and I watched on TV and couldn't believe it. She glanced at Nick. Did you see anything?

The streets were blocked off, Nick said. My parents wouldn't let us leave the house. And even if we had, we wouldn't have gotten any farther than our front yard. The police had the whole neighborhood on lockdown.

You wouldn't have seen anything even if you'd made it down the street, Christina said. There were people everywhere outside Jacob's house. Too much going on. It was hard to concentrate on anything with flames like that.

Was Benji's house the same? Zola asked. Did the fires look the same?

I don't know. Christina sipped a can of Sprite. I saw that right as it happened. I didn't stand there long enough to watch the fire grow. But with Jacob's house, the flames were already sky-high. I've never seen anything like it. The sound was deafening.

I could hear the flames, Nick said. Even from a few streets over, if I opened my window.

I still can't believe this, Christina said. This is all so unbelievable.

I know, Nick said. Which makes anything possible.

Matt looked up from his sandwich, the tone of Nick's voice strange. Matt wanted to ask again if he was okay but Christina spoke before he could.

Did your dad say anything else? she asked him.

Only that nothing was left at the house, Matt said. Same as the others. That police are increasing surveillance. That they're still re-tracing Caleb's path through the school.

What difference does it make? Christina said. People are still dying and police are putting their efforts into the route a psychopath took two weeks ago?

I don't know why it's important, Matt said. But my dad seems to think it is.

It's because they don't know what the hell else to do, Christina said, her tone rising. They have to make it look like they're doing something. It's easier to go back over what they already know. She quieted her voice. I can't believe they didn't cancel class. I can't believe they didn't postpone Homecoming.

Is anyone going? Zola asked.

Sarah wants to go, Nick said. I promised I'd take her.

I can't imagine going at this point, Matt said.

I'll go if you go, Zola said. And you, Chris. You need to get out of the house. Forget what happened. We should all just be together to forget everything.

I wrote another profile last night, Matt said. Alexis Thurber. I didn't even know her but there was nothing else to do.

I didn't write anything, Christina said. I'm done. What else can we possibly say? What else is there to write or research or photograph? We're putting together a yearbook. One that no one will ever want to read.

Matt looked across the courtyard, at the faces of peers he'd shared a building with for years but barely knew. The same as Alexis Thurber. And Darren Beechwold, a sophomore he'd only seen on the sidewalks of Nick's neighborhood. The same as Jacob Jensen, a boy he'd tracked so intimately for so many years that he felt like they knew one another, though Matt realized they'd barely ever spoken. He didn't know anyone, didn't know this school, this foreign facility, this place he was supposed to create a written testimony of memories for, an entire book his peers would read far into a future that felt as impossible as finishing an academic year, a strange school surrounded by strangers.

HALFWAY THROUGH ACADEMIC lab, as Nick anticipated, he was called into his counseling session with the school therapist selected for him, a middle-aged man named Marcus. Nick hadn't decided at the end of the previous day's session if he would see Marcus again. But when an aide opened the classroom door and called Nick's name, he let himself be guided from academic lab and down the hall toward Marcus's small office.

I'm glad you decided to come back, Marcus greeted him.

I had a long night, Nick said.

He sat on the couch and told Marcus that the previous night's fire had occurred two blocks away and that he'd stayed up until the sirens receded, until the fire trucks extinguished the blaze and police relinquished their blockade of the streets. He mentioned watching out the front window with his parents and his younger brother. He mentioned the scorched smell pervading the neighborhood, the thick scent of smoke from so many types of fire: wood, chemical, electrical. Something toxic and nauseating and invisible but the only indication that anything had happened, that the fire trucks and sirens two blocks away were battling anything at all. He mentioned the reporters, how news vans had tried to navigate around the blockade. How one news team had set up camp at the end of his street, a microphone and a light Nick could see from his window.

How did that make you feel? Marcus said. What was your reaction to a news team being on your street?

They've been in our neighborhoods for two weeks. This is nothing new.

But they haven't been on your street. Does it feel different, that close to home?

I guess it doesn't feel any different. I feel like nothing can shock me anymore. What's one more news van? What's one more broadcast, even if it's from my street?

Do you feel safe? Especially given the news? I saw this morning that they're still looking for suspects. Does this particular fire make you feel anything different, or raise any new concerns?

Nick looked up. Does it raise concerns for you?

Tell me what you mean.

I mean that I know you're trained in counseling, but has your training prepared you for something like this?

Not necessarily. Grief, certainly. Anxiety and fear.

But not a shooting. Not the ramifications of a series of fatal fires.

Well, not exactly. But I'm here for you to talk about those things.

I know. But I guess I mean that we're in this together. All of us. That none of us knows how to handle this. You must be scared, too.

I am, yes. I think we all are. But I believe these crimes will be solved.

Nick watched Marcus, calculating his response. He thought of everything he'd been researching, what he hadn't even been able to tell Matt. Something spontaneous. Something organic and chemical all at once, a body's composition. Something heavy with a night's darkness. Something laden with grief. He didn't know if he could say out loud what he'd been trying to push from his brain for two days.

How do you know they're crimes?

Tell me what you mean.

I mean what if it wasn't an arsonist? What if there wasn't a suspect at all?

Well, someone is setting these fires. Just like someone held a gun to your peers.

Something's causing the fires. But how do you know it's someone?

I don't think I follow. What else could it possibly be?

Nick didn't meet Marcus's eyes. What if it was something less premeditated? Not the shooting, but its repercussions. How the body processes grief. It must be something you know about.

How the body responds to grieving? Of course. I'm well trained in physiological responses to extreme stress.

Like what? Nick asked. You'd know better than anyone I've talked to.

Beyond depression, of course, there's an increase in harmful chemical levels and hormones. The body is in a constant state of stress. Heightened cortisol. There are disruptions to biological rhythms of sleeping, eating, digestion. Even circulation and breathing. Concentration and coordination can be compromised. The immune system can be damaged. The effects are huge.

And what if the body went further?

Nick hesitated. A chemical process, he told himself, the same as gas excitation. He had every right to say it out loud.

What if grief changed the body entirely? he said.

It can. There's no doubt about that. But how does that relate to a rash of fires?

Nick looked at Marcus directly. What if grief displaced atoms to the point of starting fires?

Marcus's pen halted on his notepad. Tell me what you mean.

Think of atomic bombs. The slight shifting of a single particle. What if the body's chemistry was completely realigned? What if sorrow pushed the body to breaking?

The body isn't radioactive, Marcus said. It's not a test site for nuclear fission.

But it contains atoms. Nuclei, protons, electrons. Atoms that under pressure could split, could break themselves in two.

And do what? Burn an entire house down?

I really don't know. I'm just thinking out loud, since there's no other explanation. The body is 80 percent water. Two atoms of hydrogen and one of oxygen, over and over again. If a single molecule split apart, even just one under the pressure of grief—

Then what? Really, son, what are you saying?

Nick stopped. *Son.*

I'm not saying anything, he said. Really. Forget I said anything at all.

Go on, Marcus said. Talk it out. Tell me what you think.

But Nick knew. A gauntlet thrown. An end.

It's nothing, he said. Just thoughts you have when it's late. When you've been up for hours and you can't sleep and houses are burning down only streets away.

The mind can tell you lots of things when you're tired, Marcus said. When you're hurting and don't have answers for that hurt.

Nick forced himself to talk about other things. About Sarah. About schoolwork. His brother and his mother, his father. He let the tableside clock recede to the end of the mandated hour. He released himself from the room and moved down the hallway. He stopped midstride. He didn't want to go back to his academic lab. Five minutes left of sixth period. He didn't want to stay quiet and curl inside of himself, what he thought Marcus's reaction would make him do. He wanted to hear himself say it out loud to someone who wouldn't turn away from him.

He knew where Matt would be. He walked to the makeshift math wing and waited outside of Matt's algebra classroom until the passing bell rang and caught him walking out the door just before his chemistry class, the same lesson Mr. Albertson had taught him and Zola that morning on wavelengths of light. Matt looked at him and his face changed and Nick understood that his own face was transparent, that Matt knew something was wrong, that something had been wrong for days. *Are you okay?* What Matt had kept asking him. What Nick finally wanted to scream and hear echo down the hall. *Can I talk to you?* was all he heard himself say. Matt nodded and followed him down the hallway. Through Timber Creek's side entrance. No one guarding the parking lot. No one making them return for the day's final period. The sunlight piercing Nick's eyes beyond the building's darkness and the dim lamplight of Marcus's office. Matt following close behind him, a comfort of nearness quieting Nick's fear to say it out loud. Matt following without question, across the parking lot to the silence of Nick's car.

ZOLA BIKED TO the Local Beanery after school, a short shift from three until closing. She pulled her sweater off at the coffee shop, the afternoon far warmer than she'd anticipated, and relieved her coworker Darlene, a woman who attended night school and only worked days. Customers occupied several tables in the shop. A few people typed at laptop computers. A couple sat near the far window speaking in low tones. A lone woman sank into a stuffed armchair, a hardback novel propped on her knees.

Zola poured herself coffee from the shop's constant drip and leaned against the backside of the counter. She hadn't foreseen wanting this, a culprit. An answer and end to this madness. She'd seen Russ Hendricks in the hallway at the end of the day, had watched him come toward her walking in the opposite direction. The way he kept his eyes on the floor bulleted her heart that she'd wanted him arrested, held indefinitely by the police. He was a human being. Grieving. He was nothing but an explanation, an easy way out. Yet even still she'd wanted him as the resolution and the realization held a rabid mirror to her own hunger, predatory as an animal. She sipped her coffee. Dregs, the taste of ground beans. She closed her eyes and in the dark of them, grief welled up within her, a rolling wave.

Excuse me? Are you still open?

Zola's eyes opened and fell upon Mrs. Zimmerman. The mother of Josh Zimmerman, the sophomore who was killed, and his older sister Beth, who'd been into the coffee shop the week before. Zola always between them in age though she remembered Mrs. Zimmerman from the school's Halloween parade and the fall carnival each year, her face familiar among the parent volunteers. Zola remembered her from recent Homecomings as well, Josh and Beth both routinely on Homecoming Court, their mother and father escorting them down the football field track during halftime.

We're open, Zola said.

I'll have an iced tea, Mrs. Zimmerman said. I didn't expect today to be so warm.

For here or to go?

To go.

Zola filled a large plastic cup with ice. She placed it beneath the tea dispenser and tried not to look back at Mrs. Zimmerman standing alone at the counter. A mother. A woman she wanted to ask so many questions. *Are you scared?* The tea flooded the ice. *Are you waiting for your home to burn?* Zola set the cup on the counter in front of Mrs. Zimmerman, sealed with a plastic lid and accompanied by a wrapped straw.

How much?

It's on the house.

Are you sure?

It's our last brew of the day, Zola lied. If it's too weak, I wouldn't want you charged.

Mrs. Zimmerman smiled faintly. Thanks.

Zola watched her leave the shop, unsure if Mrs. Zimmerman knew who she was. That she'd gone to school with her children. That regardless of never knowing them well, they'd all grown up together. Zola wanted to ask what it was to lose a child. If she and her husband grieved in different ways. If only one of them wanted to know what had happened inside the school. If they both wanted to leave it behind, unknown. What they clung to, what they remembered from that morning just before they sent their teenagers to school. What Josh had said as he brushed his teeth. As he'd grabbed his backpack and stepped out the front door. What they regretted. What they took upon themselves. What they clutched tight in the darkest hour of the night, in the moon's soft light leaking through their bedroom window.

Zola watched Mrs. Zimmerman disappear from the shop until she lost her to the sun-gleamed cars of the parking lot. She felt something inside of her fissure, a crack. That no one could shield this woman, a mother. That Mrs. Zimmerman carried herself out into the streets, a city that offered no protection. Zola knew it: not

police. Not FBI. Not a critical mass of parents. Not anything in this
world that could keep her from burning.

TYLER MET MATT at his locker after the last period of class, long after
Nick had pulled away from Timber Creek's parking lot and Matt
had gone back inside. He hadn't gone to chemistry class. He'd only
stepped inside the men's bathroom and sat in a stall listening to his
own breath move in and out of his lungs until the bell signaled the
end of seventh period and the conclusion of the school day. What
Nick had said inside the sealed car: something impossible. The
wind from the night's storm still howling all around them. Something Matt would never have believed if not for how crushed Nick
looked, a revelation he'd clearly wrestled with for days. If not for
how rational his approach always was to the process of research and
evidence. If not for the lack of any other explanation, the police and
the entire community running out of answers, the thin possibility
of another accomplice the only logical lead left.

The flash point of human skin: cells sparking. Inside the chest,
the organs, the heart. A burn spreading up a throat and jumping
from a mouth to the curtains, to the thin sheets of a bed. Incineration. Nothing left. Not even fragments, a language neither forensics
nor science could speak. Matt didn't know what he believed. He
knew only that he didn't want Nick to be alone. He'd placed a hand
on his shoulder and Nick shrugged it off and said he needed to get
home. Matt had returned to his locker for his jacket and saw Tyler
waiting for him against the cabinet's metal door.

Matt thought of the evening before him: a Thursday night.
Home, then work, then home. If life would always be this way, a
circuitry of moving among safe spaces while beyond the doors an
entire community burned down. He grabbed his jacket and wallet
and stepped out to the parking lot with Tyler beside him, the school
grounds cluttered with security to ensure that everyone would get
home. Matt watched a stationed officer check IDs at the parking

lot's exit and wondered how Nick had managed to escape school so early. If he'd said he was sick. If he'd told the officer last night's fire had occurred just past his street. A news van sat parked on the main road just past the lot, police barricading the immediate school grounds from media.

Where should we go? Tyler asked.

Matt felt tired. Honestly, I just want to go home.

Won't your mom be there?

Probably. But she won't mind. She'll be upstairs reading. We can stay in my room. She won't bother us.

Tyler climbed into the Fiesta's passenger seat and they traveled toward Matt's neighborhood, windows open, the wind blasting in and the sun warming their arms. Police cars lined the streets. Police parked at the curbs of homes. Police waited with their engines cut near intersections and stop signs. Matt knew what this was, the heightened security his father had mentioned the night before, patrol and protection augmented at three o'clock in the afternoon past the previous night's break in pattern. Though his father hadn't said so, he wondered if the police were running surveillance on Lewis and Clark's students: where they took themselves after school beyond view of administrators.

This is crazy, Tyler said, nodding at a national news van parked on the street.

I know, Matt said. My dad said we can expect this. An increased police and media presence. To protect the families, the ones that remain.

That sounds so morbid. Like everyone's just expecting them to burn.

Wouldn't you be scared? If you were them?

I guess. I'd probably leave town.

Matt hadn't thought to ask his father if this was a possibility for some of the families, if anyone had chosen to leave their lives behind for the safety and solace of elsewhere. His father wouldn't have known, couldn't keep tabs on every family, though surely the FBI could. But Matt had seen in the paper this week despite the *Post-Dispatch*'s preference to keep news of Caleb Raynor to a minimum that Caleb's family had left St. Louis for an undisclosed location, for protection and for the privacy of their own grieving.

I can't believe we're even in school this week, Matt said. My dad said they can't cancel any more class after last week, but this seems too big to ignore.

Damage control, Tyler said. He pushed his hand into the window's breeze. This must be a PR nightmare. The school just wants everything to remain normal and calm.

I'd hardly call mandatory counseling sessions normal and calm. Did you go to yours?

It wasn't helpful. Was yours?

No, Tyler said. I went to the first one and just sat there. I don't feel like I have anything to talk about.

How has your family reacted to all of this? Matt asked. Have they talked to you about it?

Not really. My dad's always home late, after I've gone to bed. Third shift. We never see each other.

And your mom? Matt asked. He realized he knew nothing about Tyler's home life, that he'd never thought to ask.

She works days. She's home when I'm home but she barely says anything to me. You know the moms in commercials, the ones who bake cookies and serve after-school snacks and ask you about your day? My mom isn't that mom. Not at all.

Matt thought of his own mother. How she was. So much more than any representation of what a mother should be.

Anyway, it's fine, Tyler said. My parents don't really need to ask. I'm fine.

Matt couldn't imagine a home bereft of asking. Are you really fine?

I think so. As fine as anyone else.

A traffic light halted them, the flow of cars heavier for a Thursday: people leaving work early, police out, everyone in Midvale County seeking the safety of their homes.

I can't believe we've already been back almost a week, Matt said. I can't believe they're still having Homecoming and that it's tomorrow.

No shit. No one's going to go.

Are you going?

Tyler looked at him. Are you?

Probably not. I thought about it. Just to get away. Just to get out of the house.

Even if you did. Tyler hesitated. It's not like we could go together.

Why not? Matt wanted to ask instead: what they were to one another.

Because you know why. Yeah, it's not 1950. But people talk. People judge.

What, you think anyone cares? No one cares. Especially not now. Look around us. You think people will care that two boys are at a dance together?

Tyler turned away. I can't.

We can just go as friends.

I can't do that, either.

They pulled into the driveway, where Matt saw the Chevy Impala parked. His father was home. Too early.

Should I still come in? Tyler asked.

Of course. Matt grabbed his bag from the backseat. I just don't know why he's home. He's hardly ever home before dark.

Tyler remained in the passenger seat until Matt motioned him forward. Matt's parents knew enough of his life to accept him for who he was but they didn't know Tyler, a boy Matt had never thought to introduce to his parents, their relationship still so new, still hushed through the quiet back roads of so many summer nights. Matt's parents knew his truth, had let him stand inside it even with his father's resistance. But speaking love, the first sparks of it, was something else entirely. Matt had asked his father only of investigation, of police terms and procedures. Nothing of what it meant to love someone. Tyler followed him into the kitchen through the garage, letting Matt take the lead.

Matt didn't expect to see both of his parents sitting at the kitchen table. As if they'd never left from the night before, as if an entire day hadn't transpired between the strange light of a pitch-dark morning and an afternoon of classes and school.

This is Tyler, Matt said. His words stupid in his mouth. He motioned Tyler out from behind him, a meaningless gesture if not for the way his hand grabbed Tyler's. His mother's eyes moved from Tyler's face to their hands clasped briefly together. His father sat back in his chair and said nothing. Welcome, Tyler, his mother finally said.

What's going on? Matt asked.

Something's happened in the investigation, his father said. He glanced at Tyler. Now might not be the right time to discuss it.

I can go, Tyler said. I'm sorry. I didn't mean to impose.

Don't be silly, Matt's mother said. You want something? We have lemonade.

I'm fine. Really, it's okay. I should get home.

Let me at least walk you outside, Matt said to Tyler. He thought his parents might protest, at least his mother, but they sat at the kitchen table and said nothing. Matt followed Tyler back through the side door, away from the kitchen and his mother and father. In the garage, heavy with heat from the day's sun, Matt touched Tyler's face.

I'm sorry, he said. I didn't expect this at all.

It's fine. It's not your fault.

But I drove you here.

It's not a far walk. I've done it before.

Take my bike? Please. I'll pick it up later.

Tyler looked at Matt's mountain bike hanging on the garage's far wall.

Okay, he said. I'll ride it to school tomorrow to bring it back.

I said I'll pick it up later. Can I come? Would you let me come by later?

My dad will be home late. You probably shouldn't.

But I want to. I'll be quiet. I promise.

Tyler squinted out into the afternoon. Okay, he finally said. Okay.

Matt pulled the bike from the wall. He let Tyler take it. He watched him ride down the street until he turned a corner and disappeared.

In the kitchen, his parents remained at the table.

Was that a new friend? his father asked. The word emphasized. *Friend.* A tone that meant he knew.

We've known each other awhile, Matt said. He's just never come around much.

He can come around anytime, his mother said.

Matt looked at his father. Made himself say it. Dad, Tyler's not a friend.

His father nodded. Didn't look at him. Matt prepared himself to explain but his father's face had already changed. Look, I didn't mean to chase that boy off, but we've had a break. There's new information.

It wasn't the reaction Matt expected. His father distracted. But he hadn't yelled, hadn't stormed down the hallway and closed a door. A reaction he'd have to take, good enough. Matt let himself fall back into the language of fact and nothing else.

What kind of new information?

The school. The kid's path through the high school.

Matt looked at his mother, her eyes on his father. Whatever it was, she already knew.

What is it? Matt asked. What happened?

Nothing happened so much as what we've found.

What did you find?

Matt's parents exchanged a glance and he wanted to scream, to hear his voice rip a hole through the kitchen walls. To break open a circling of evasion.

Well, what is it? Are you going to tell me?

Matt's father placed his palms on the table. Why don't we take a drive?

Come on, Jim. You can tell him from here.

Tell me what? Matt heard himself yell.

Let's just take a drive, his father said again. All of us, let's take a drive.

Matt's mother looked away, her jaw a line, but she stood anyway as Matt's father grabbed the keys to the Impala. And then Matt was outside again, Tyler gone only minutes before, the Fiesta's engine still hot, he knew, if he placed his hand on the hood of the car. His mother slid into the passenger side of his father's car, Matt into the backseat. He let himself be guided through the streets of his neighborhood without asking any further questions, a thick silence between them. Along the sidewalks stood bare trees, stark limbs stretched toward the still-beating sun. Pumpkins nestled uncarved in yards, corn husks tied to the stalks of lampposts. Halloween: one more week. His parents hadn't even bought candy. Matt couldn't imagine Halloween night, kids in costumes, that any child would be allowed to walk the streets past dusk. Porch lights extinguished. Bowls of Snickers and Tootsie Rolls left on front decks with only a note. He saw no one in their yards as they drove past, not even venturing to the end of the driveway for their mail. Police saturated the roads. News vans snaked through every street. Midvale County's homes: locked up like the square confines of jail cells. No one out in the open but only moving from building to car to building. The neighborhoods evacuated of humanity, everyone watching the world unfold from their windows. Matt realized as they moved that the Impala was steering them toward the high school.

Dad?

It's okay, son. I just need to show you something.

Jim, he doesn't need to see it again. Does he really need to see it?

Just trust me. He needs to see. He needs to see what it is we're doing.

Matt didn't interrupt the volley of his parents' words. He only watched out the window as Lewis and Clark High drew closer in the distance. The building a fortress. A fun house. A chamber. A mass grave. What he was being forced to rewitness beyond the bounds of his own will. As they approached, he noticed police cars. Their red and blue lights killed, the cars parked, a clear attempt at anonymity though Matt recognized this police presence as something beyond routine, beyond the barricade of patrol cars and yellow tape to keep onlookers away. He hadn't driven past the school since leaving it, a purposeful forgetting. He could see that something was happening. A few officers moved beneath the lines of tape and into the school. Matt's father pulled the Impala into the parking lot and was waved in by an officer standing guard. He parked the car near other police vehicles, the windshield a wide panorama upon the school.

This is where we're working now, his father said. The school investigation has melded with fire investigation. There's no other way around it at this point. I took a break this afternoon to come home to tell your mother what we found.

Tell Mom what? Is anyone going to tell me what the hell is going on or even ask if I want to be here? Matt felt a heat creeping up his neck to the flush of his cheeks. A panic rising. The car closing in. No view but the school beyond its windshield, fixed and wide-open and suffocating.

I told you I'd tell you, his father said. Whatever it was. I told you I'd tell you only as much to keep you safe.

Matt's mother averted her eyes from the windshield's view.

Well, you're safe, his father said. That's why I brought you here, so you could see it yourself.

Matt saw nothing past the windshield. Only a lone officer making his way through the front doors of the school. Only a faint nausea bubbling through his stomach and creeping up the lining of his throat.

I don't see anything, Matt said. I don't see anything at all.

Matt's father turned in the front seat, the driver's seat squeaking as he pivoted.

We've traced the path of that boy, his father said, every step he took through the entire school. We weren't absolutely sure before. We're sure now. The sequence of when each of those kids died. It matches the exact sequence of their homes catching fire.

Matt felt the air leave him. The cavity of his lungs a vacuum.

Caroline Black first. I know you saw it. You saw it, and for that I'm sorry. But you need to know. Caroline first. Then he shot the Trenway girl. Then the Ndolo boy. Jacob Jensen. Alexis Thurber. Darren Beechwold. How that boy made his way through the school is our pattern. It fits. Not the administrators, and not teachers. Only the kids. The path of their shootings is the same exact pattern of how those houses are burning.

Matt closed his eyes. Why are you telling me this?

Based on the path, if there are to be more fires, we know now whose homes we can expect to burn. We know who and what to protect. We know how to stop this, where to find our culprit—obviously someone linked to the Raynor kid, who knows the route he took. An accomplice just like I told you. We know where to wait and watch for something. We know where to investigate what the boy left behind, where to look for links. We're ready for it to happen. We'll be waiting. We're ready to catch our killer.

Okay, that's enough, his mother said. She reached across the backseat, took Matt's hand. He's heard enough, Jim. He knows enough. Please, just take us home.

Matt looked from his mother to his father. You said safety. To

keep me safe. How does this keep me safe? How does this keep
anyone safe? Those homes will burn.

It means we know the pattern, his father said. They won't burn.
We can catch the culprit before they do. We'll be there. We'll be
there waiting.

Matt watched the school. This place he once knew. Its walls a
shield. Everything within it lost to knowing. He knew that here in
the stifled air of the car his father's explanation made less sense than
everything Nick had told him. He knew the police would retrace
and remap and still they would find nothing. That no suspect could
know the random hazard of a gun and its bullets. That there was
no accomplice. That the homes would blaze, that nothing could
keep them from burning. That his father sought a culprit, something tangible and solid, something real. His father pivoted in the
front seat, nearly touching his leg, and Matt knew there were not
enough words upon the human tongue to bridge the distance between them.

I told you I'd tell you this, his father said. I'd tell you what I
needed to keep you safe. Well, you're safe. Whoever's doing this,
their attack is extremely targeted.

How exactly does that keep me safe?

His father looked at him. You're safe because you didn't lose anyone.

His father turned the ignition. He drove them home. What he'd
told them, meant as love. He left them to the silence of the house
and he returned to the high school and his mother asked *Can I make
you an early dinner?* and Matt shook his head and said he needed
to go to work. He put on his theater uniform. He walked out the
door. He told his mother not to worry. He worked concessions and
ate nothing, no free popcorn and no stolen soda. He sat alone in the
booth until nearly eleven. He built a new film: *Elephant*. Strips he
threaded together but couldn't watch. He only listened to the projector's hum, its ratcheting a broken heartbeat.

After work he drove the streets to an address he'd never visited but had memorized regardless, a basement window where the light was on and where he knocked to be let in. Tyler's face appeared through the glass. *My mother's upstairs* but Matt shook his head, pushed past Tyler when the window opened. He wanted to apologize. He wanted nothing at all. He sat on the floor. Tyler came down beside him, placed a hand in his palm. On the thin carpet of Tyler's basement bedroom Matt knew that he was not safe, that no one was. That Nick was right. Tyler's hands. The smooth lines, the thin membrane of his skin. That he was vulnerable. That we were all vulnerable. Every one of us, our fragile, stupid hearts. That those parents were nothing if not the echo of their children's laughter, their hair catching the sheen of sun, the starlit certainty that when they drove the back roads their cars would carry them home. Tyler's hands. Their soft shock tracing the lifeline of Matt's open palm. That it took so little for our bodies to revolt, an annihilation time-bombed inside our genes. That it took nothing for our atoms to surrender. For the code of our cells to break apart.

A BRIEF HISTORY OF LOVE

COFFEE MUGS: SHATTERED porcelain. Broken pieces of Mickey Mouse's ears. Brought home from Disney World after driving through the night from Florida to Missouri, the highway's center line a flash mirrored to the sky's shooting stars. Plastic flatware melted in cupboards. Boxes of dried pasta and cereal, stored liters of Gatorade. Cups and wineglasses without stems and burst bottles of pinot noir. Puffed coats. Missouri winter. A black leather jacket stuffed in the back of a closet. Love letters. Notes saved from junior high, from anniversaries and birthdays and Valentine's Day. Bubbled handwriting dotted with hearts. The salt taste of sweat. Threads of hair still clinging to a mattress, afternoon light slanting through windows and kaleidoscoping the walls.

Baby books of inked footprints. Smudged palm prints. Small as ducklings, thimbles, beginnings. *The Cat in the Hat. Goodnight Moon.* This book belongs to. Goal netting. Soccer ball. Jersey knit shorts and dry-fit shirts and the spikes of cleats clotted with grass. Mix tapes. Videotapes. Board games. Monopoly. Candy Land. Hungry Hungry Hippos. Monkeys in a Barrel. Lincoln Logs. Tarot cards and playing cards and a Ouija board used only once, a sixth-grade sleepover when the planchette moved and so many hands flinched away.

Best to think of them as objects. Best to not think of them. Best to not even blink, to not know them as love. Best to look away, to pretend none of this mattered. Best to let all of it take to the sky in smoke. Best to let a spark catch, to let a blaze stalk a trail through a room. Best to let everything burn.

LEWIS AND CLARK HS

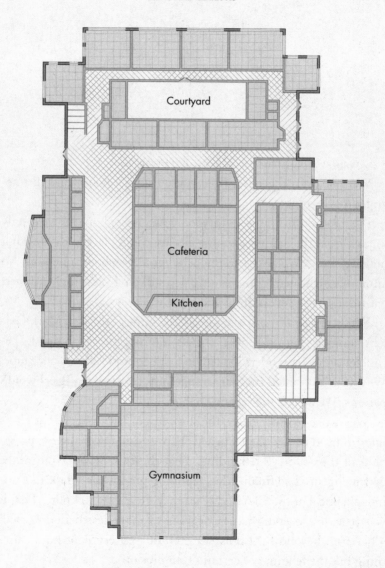

IT IS TIME

WE AWOKE UNSURPRISED. We awoke ravaged.

We awoke to the news that Mark Carter's house had disintegrated in the night.

His mother, his father: everyone gone. A sophomore we'd only known from the hallways, whose face we could place in a crowd but nothing more. We awoke to the persistence of school, an email. An announcement that Homecoming was still on. Friday night's dance, Saturday's game, everything and all of it, always, still on.

We awoke to a front-page spread, the same as the last. Mark Carter's home in charred debris, officials and firefighters circling its perimeter while bystanders looked on from behind yellow police tape. We awoke to printed funeral arrangements for Darren Beechwold's parents. We awoke to nothing changed.

We awoke to other news, the slimmest of back pages: that Iraq's interim head of state had warned the world to lower their expectations of the country's rebuilding. That the U.S. Senate Committee on Intelligence had finalized its report on pre-invasion data, its findings skeptical of the CIA and what they'd claimed to know. That it was true, in the end, that no weapons of mass destruction existed. That even beyond St. Louis not even our government knew anything but the feigning of certainty, an illusion.

Other news: that the Marlins were up 3–2 in the World Series, the next and potentially final game to be played Saturday night.

That an astral storm in outer space had caused satellite system dis-ruptions. That despite the interference, a celestial outburst scientists were calling the Halloween solar storm, the solar flares would bring the most profound aurora borealis display the northern United States had seen in years. That here in the Midwest we saw nothing but faint stars that blinked back their forgetting.

And we awoke to what Matt told us: what the police believed, what his father had revealed to him outside the school. An accom-plice. What lead of sequence the police were pursuing. What at long last, across the days and weeks that would follow, every one of us turned away from as more homes burned and the police failed to protect any of them.

We attended counseling sessions. Mandatory for everyone. No longer a means of opting out, the only policy the school changed. *How are you feeling?* the counselors asked us, an open question from a tall woman in a green dress, a thick man in round glasses. Natalie. Marcus. We watched the clock tick. We avoided their eyes. There were so many counselors that eventually we lost count.

I am burning, we wanted to say. We wanted to say out loud that we were combustible, that at night our chests felt like a heated hand had reached in and gripped our breastbone and that we were as vul-nerable as any parent. That there was nothing of safety. That as the news mounted, we felt our bodies fissure and break down. But we said nothing. We'd lost nothing. We'd lost the companions of our classrooms and the frustrations of shared homework but we hadn't lost the nucleus of our homes, everything at the center that had kept them alive. We hadn't lost those beside us on the couch, watching television, reading books, quiet but there. We hadn't lost the sound of other voices echoing against the walls. We thought of Jacob Jen-sen's mother, returned from a funeral to the pressing hollow of an empty house. We thought of the Beechwolds coming home from the vigil, their candles extinguished and Darren's bedroom vacant. We thought of Caroline and we thought of Benji Ndolo and we thought of Alisha Trenway and Alexis Thurber and we felt the storm of their absence, a tempest annihilating every single thing they left behind.

We looked up at our counselors. I am fine, we said.

We met their eyes. We said it over and over.

Then we went back to class, to the Crimean War and Raskolnikov's motives and the application of force and the speed of sound and we went home and we watched the news and we killed ourselves inside at waking each day to something new, to something no longer new, to a flood of fires that whispered nothing to the ash of our ravaged hearts.

IN THE END, every family burned.

Every parent of our twenty-eight peers and classmates, a rash of fires that took only weeks to take everyone.

A month beyond the shooting, every parent was gone.

After Homecoming, that Friday night: Josh Zimmerman's house. His mother and his father and his sister Beth, who we'd just seen slow-dancing with her boyfriend beneath the heat of a strobe flash after the Homecoming Court was announced, her dress glittering against her skin and her face pressed to his chest and her eyes closed to the light.

Then Alyssa Carver's house. Her mother inside. Kelly Washington's home. Missy Hoffman. Elise Nguyen, Christina retreating to her bed for two days. James Sharma. So many homes that we lost count, homes in Midvale County but also elsewhere. Alexander Chen's family cabin out in Innsbrook, where they'd gone to take time away. Constance Bellamy's father alone in a hotel room, a weekend business trip to Chicago. A trip to get away, we knew, to abandon the walled-in pressure of our city that followed him elsewhere. A pattern we'd anticipated from a list of names, a trail the police knew but couldn't prevent from igniting. At home, our parents let the television blare behind dinner. On low, a quieter volume, a volume all the same for them to hear. That the evidence was still inconclusive, the investigation ongoing. That a pattern had been determined and that police were drawing nearer. That they'd staked out every home, that each time one flared they were ever closer to their culprit. Our parents glanced at us across the table and muted the volume. Zola's mother watched the stars, a solar storm her telescope couldn't detect. Matt's father worked late and his mother kept her eyes on him always above her book or across the kitchen table. Nick's dad kept watch out the front window while his brother read on the living room floor and his mother worked. Christina's father awaited the mail at the end of the driveway so he could speak to Mr. Wilcox and to the mailwoman, to any other voice with an answer while her mother called from Edwardsville every day to check in. Our parents walked the tenuous line of asking us and not asking us. Of being attentive and leaving us alone. Of wanting to know whether we were okay. Their hands lingered on our backs as we helped clear dishes from the table and upon our heads as we stood at the kitchen sink.

At night, we knew, they watched us.

In our own lack of sleep, we heard our doors creak open and felt a sliver of light from the hallway redden the underside of our closed eyes. We waited in silence as our parents stood in the doorway, sometimes minutes, sometimes longer. We heard their feet approaching our beds and the rhythm of their breath beside us. We felt their hands soft upon our covers to know we were still here. And when they left, we kept our eyes closed.

We imagined a world without them.

We imagined our homes in flames.

CALEB RAYNOR'S FAMILY: the last.

The last of the homes to flame out.

His mother, his father, his brother: gone in the debris of a small rental home out in Spanish Lake where they'd sought privacy and their own healing. Nothing left but the blackened logs of an all-wood cabin the *Post-Dispatch* printed on the front page. A house looking out on the lake. Lewis and Clark Memorial Park not a mile away, our city's namesake and the name of a high school their son eradicated. The last fire to burn, early November, a blaze that drew more media attention than any of the others. And then when no more cases occurred, when a day and then two passed and the winter winds blew in for good and the sky lowered itself toward the earth, the reporters receded and the headlines changed and the police continued investigating a radius of fires that even from Spanish Lake, even from the far reaches of a Chicago hotel, was still small enough for the possibility of arson. They searched for weeks. They found nothing. St. Louis vanished from the national news, a slow wash away from a twenty-four-hour news cycle to hourly updates and then to a daily checking in. And then only brief mentions on the scroll that ticked constantly across the bottom of the screen and then nothing. Within a month, we disappeared from the eye of the national storm completely.

The only survivors: the families of our administrators and teachers.

As if their bodies had known the nearness of loved ones long enough beyond the brief spark of teenhood to come to terms, to make bargains. To comprehend the pierced ache of an ending they knew would eventually find us all in some distant bedroom or basement, a loss that even in youth we knew our cells could never accept.

Midvale County police investigated. Our city buried it. Lasting questions that eventually died away, that we knew had no answers beyond a series of reports done by fire chiefs and arson analysts, beyond a news swell that lingered and then died down and then forgot us entirely.

We remember when Matt's father and a full team of local and national investigators closed the case nearly a year to the day of the shooting. We remember their ruling in the face of a maddening lack of evidence: that given the sequence and seemingly deliberate nature of the fires, our city had seen the work of a highly skilled arsonist. An arsonist we couldn't trace or uncover. One who had range, who knew the streets, who tracked each family like a hunter. An arsonist with resources and mobility: the capacity to follow families beyond the bounds of the city, to throw off an entire trail of police. Someone who knew Caleb's path. An accomplice. Someone in one of our classrooms or else a mole within the police force, though Matt's father never spoke of it. Matt's father never spoke of anything, a case he shut tight inside of himself, a box sealed and buried in the backyard of his heart. But Matt knew, he told us, that his father still searched. Matt knew by the light spilling down the hallway well past midnight some nights, leaking from beneath an office door that blocked his father's work from view, leaving only the sound of shuffled papers and intermittent silence.

We offer Matt's father credit, even still. That even if arson was nothing but an easy answer, an understanding we sometimes believe he intuited, he got one thing right. What Matt was never able to say to him, not even nights when he knew his father stayed awake searching: that he gave us one answer. A path of destruction.

A gasoline trail, one that took nothing more than a match.

The Monday morning past Homecoming weekend, after Josh Zimmerman's home burned, the *St. Louis Post-Dispatch* published wide across the front page a sketched diagram of the entire school and Caleb's path through it. A map of Lewis and Clark's first and second floors, its wings and classrooms. A map printed next to images of Josh Zimmerman's burned house and grained photographs of his mother and father and sister. A schematic linking the fires at last to Lewis and Clark.

A dotted line indicating the route Caleb Raynor took through school.

The newspaper told us what we already knew, what we'd pieced together three days before on that Friday afternoon before

the Homecoming dance, just after Matt told us what his father revealed to him: Caleb's path and its link to the fires, how the way
he'd killed mirrored the rash of homes exactly. How police and
an entire community could anticipate next moves, how an arsonist
could be caught.

No matter a published diagram. We made one ourselves. We
made one seventy-two hours before the *Post-Dispatch* ever printed
anything. We re-created Caleb's path by what Matt said his father
had told him, by a list of names and by the way the homes had
already burned. We pieced it together through our own archives,
through the news clippings and the Web articles Nick had book-
marked. Through the profiles Matt wrote, through the eyewitness
accounts of what Christina saw at Benji's house and on Jacob's
street. We stitched it together from Zola's photographs, the ones
she'd taken of Alisha Trenway's house after dark and finally showed
to us. From what we knew of our peers, some better than others,
some to whom we'd never spoken. From where we'd seen them in
the hallways during passing time between classes. We placed everything together in Nick's kitchen, his father still at work, his brother
in the other room finishing his spelling homework on the carpet.
We put together an archive on the kitchen table and made our own
map, so far from a yearbook, less than two hours before the Homecoming dance.

We thought of what we assembled hours later as we held one
another beneath the gym's lights. Taffeta dresses. Suit and tie. We
knew Caleb Raynor entered the east doors of Lewis and Clark High
School on the morning of October 8, a Wednesday.

A sky without clouds. 9:04 A.M.

Boutonnieres, baby's breath corsages already wilting.

We knew he'd sat in his car through first period watching the
school. Hands agitated against the steering wheel. Red Bull. Three
cups of coffee. Adrenaline. The same rattling of every weapon
against the railings of a high school. We knew he'd waited in his car

through the entirety of first period before crossing the parking lot
at the start of second period. Black sweatshirt, hood raised. Pouch
hiding extra rounds of bullets. Weapons slung across his back and
hidden in his back pocket, three two-by-fours bent beneath his arm.
Thin wooden beams he slid through the exit doors of the north and
south and west entrances, circling the perimeter of the school before
pushing through the east doors. We knew he carried a sawed-off
shotgun and a handgun and sixteen rounds of ammunition into
Principal Jeffries's office, where he pushed open the glass door and
she stood and tried to block him from coming any farther into the
school and he shot her and her administrative assistant, Deborah
Smalls, before making his way back to the first-floor art studio,
where he shot Mr. Nolan. Sugar-free gum. A radio still ringing
KSHE 95's classic rock. Half-finished drawings. A still-life display
of two apples and a vase set up for third period. We knew he moved
from the art room up the central stairs.

Balloon arches. A hired DJ. A transformed gymnasium, Timber
Creek not even ours a week. Matt stood with Tyler to the side of the
dance floor, his collared shirt sticking to his neck in the gym's heat.
Couples dancing all around them. Tyler beside him, his hand inches
away but just beyond touching.

We knew Caleb Raynor met Caroline Black in the hallway outside the second-floor bathroom, just past the central stairwell. We
like to imagine she hadn't heard gunshots. That she was only re-
filling her water bottle at the drinking fountain before returning
to social studies class. That she had no idea what was happening.
In the gymnasium Matt closed his eyes, blinked away the hallway
carpet, took Tyler's hand. The dance floor. Strobe lights. Flashbulb
memory. Shoes gripping a toilet seat. Matt's hand on Tyler's mouth
pleading him to stay silent. Tyler let himself be led to the dance floor
beneath lights that were too harsh and bright.

We knew Caleb moved from the second-floor hallway toward
classrooms, a left turn. The first classroom Caleb could find. A

freshman writing course that held Alisha Trenway and Benji Ndolo. What Alisha might have thought about when she saw Caleb kick open the classroom door with a gun: first learning to ride a bicycle without training wheels. How thin so many years were that brought her to high school, to this moment. And Benji: his younger brother. Playing badminton with him in the front yard.

In the gymnasium, Matt's hand fell against Tyler's rib cage, his starched shirt. Tyler's body a breathing thing, something alive. Tyler trembling beside him, skin sweating beneath fluorescent light, but he didn't let himself drop Matt's hand.

We knew Caleb raged from the writing classroom to the math wing on the second floor. A trigonometry classroom that held Jacob Jensen, Alexis Thurber. Russ Hendricks elsewhere in the school, not knowing yet that his life would split apart. We imagined Caleb paused. That he took a breath, only seconds, a space long enough to reload. Not long enough to realize what he was doing or whether so many parents already felt something miles away in their work offices or desks or at home at their kitchen tables, a bullet piercing skin and their chests flashing, mistaken for heartburn.

We knew Caleb moved from trigonometry to the science wing, the hallway he must have passed down when Nick saw him through the small window of Mrs. Menda's classroom door. Flashbulb: *click*. Synapse, memory. Nick held Sarah on the dance floor, her arms resting on his shoulders, her tea rose corsage pricking the skin of his neck. We knew Caleb walked into Mr. Duggar's sophomore biology class, where he shot Mark Carter and Josh Zimmerman. Josh's mother and sister: patrons at the Local Beanery, their time-line sealed as Caleb drew his gun. Mr. Duggar: the third teacher killed, pulled out from beneath the lab table where he'd draped his body across Mark and Josh crouched and shuddering beneath him, all three of them shot point blank.

Nick felt Sarah lean her weight into him beneath the gym lights. He felt her heartbeat. Seventy beats per minute. The length of a song: three minutes, more than two hundred heartbeats to claim as his. Heartbeat as memory, what he could take with him. Memory stored as matter, the brain's core. Nick focused on Sarah's dress, the apple scent of her hair. Memory as aroma, a firing of transmitters. Memory as sound, speakers through the hollow rafters of a gymnasium. Memory as skin. Sarah pressed close. Memory as her body pushing into him on a living room couch, in the cramped backseat of a car parked beneath so many knots of swaying trees. Memory as forgetting a door's window and overturned desks and the faraway sound of a gun moving down a hallway.

We knew Caleb stayed in the science wing, that he walked from Mr. Duggar's biology class to a physics lab of juniors. Alyssa Carver. Kelly Washington. Missy Hoffman. Elise Nguyen. Alyssa on Lewis and Clark's dance squad. Kelly allergic to almonds, a petition circulated their freshman year for greater nut allergy awareness in the cafeteria. Elise: girl in the water. Girl joyriding through the streets, girl rolling down the windows to let out the stereo's sound. All of them gone in seconds. Eight other students injured. Everyone else in the school hidden inside their classrooms. Everyone huddling beneath desks or inside storage closets but for a few who'd been elsewhere like Matt and Tyler had been, in bathrooms or at lockers or on their way to the library during study periods. James Sharma, a near-graduating senior: shotgunned in the corridor as Caleb left the math wing and moved toward the library. Then Mr. Rourke, the second-floor custodian, a location we know by how Christina saw him when she first exited the school. A pooling circle, a darkened carpet. Then Justin Banks, a senior, shot in the hallway just outside the library only days after he'd asked Sejal Chaudry to Homecoming.

Then the library.

Zola stood to the side of the dance floor, her Pentax camera in her hands. Christina beside her, neither of them speaking. Zola taking photographs intermittently, an archive of what celebration should have meant. Photographs she would review that Sunday night, her mother on the back porch watching constellations. Samuel Winters sock-hopping with Dolores Fremont. Lindsey Cho and Adam Hunter standing in line for professional photographs. The Homecoming Court. Beth Zimmerman smiling faintly when her name wasn't announced, a relief at last to stay beyond a spotlight. Lauren Kirkland and Daniel Brown, first dance as Homecoming king and queen.

Zola didn't step onto the dance floor once.

She'd offered nothing in Nick's kitchen but the names of those who'd shared her academic lab. Connor Distler. Jessica Wendling. Alexander Chen. All of them beside her at the library's long oak table. We knew Caleb entered the library's double doors and shot at them first, the table so close to the hallway entrance, all of them crouching beneath it and Zola hidden in the stacks only yards away. *A Graphic History of Oceanic Biology*. Green vellum. Amygdala. Cortex. Memory. Peers who had shared pop-quiz tips with her across so many hours of academic lab, who had shared mnemonic devices for math equations and earbuds for Billboard Top 40 listening and snacks of dried apricots. We knew Caleb aimed at a group of seniors gathered around Mr. Eckstein to learn capstone-project research: Ilya Litvin. Georgia Tarkington. Greg Alexander. Carolina Olson. Constance Bellamy. Jake Berger. Jackson Pavey. Their names a cascade of flames, homes Zola knew from inside Timber Creek's gymnasium would burn within days.

Christina stood beside her drinking fruit punch, the taste too sweet on her tongue.

We knew Lewis and Clark's gymnasium downstairs was where Caleb moved last, where Ryan hid in the boys' bathroom while Christina curled beneath the desk of her French class upstairs. A seniors-only gym class, boys pressing themselves into the wet humidity of a locker room's shower stalls. Dan Zeller. Sebastian Holmes. Will Isholt. Sam Scott. All of them gone, a mental image

Christina closed her eyes to kill as we mapped the last of Caleb's path that Friday afternoon at Nick's kitchen table.

She scanned the dance floor. Ryan at home. The picture frame and his window splintered to pieces. He would leave for college. He would never speak to her again. She would leave the movement of his body above hers and the tangled sheets of his bed to nothing but the faded scar of memory, to photographs in a drawer, to a life she couldn't imagine she had once lived. Memory as swim partner. The blue of a pool. Memory as girl scalpeling through the water. Memory as orgasm, a tendriled wave billowing through the steam of a bath. Memory as losing the rough texture of a boy's tongue skating across her skin, the sound of her own shoes running far and fast from his car.

We knew the last name: Caleb Raynor. The last home to burn. We knew no motive, a self-inflicted wound inside the gymnasium of Lewis and Clark High, a separate gym we blinked away from the dance floor of Timber Creek.

We knew a path. Nothing else. We knew nothing more than Matt's father in the end. We knew a trail of gunfire. We knew the human body, as best as we could. We knew a path of grief but nothing of its mechanics. Of how it knew when to ignite.

We know how we held one another inside the heat of a gymnasium.

We know how even as we wished to move as far away from ourselves as we could we wanted to keep this, even still, all of us in the same walls and the same town and the same blaze of our youth and our grief before we germinated upward and out, before we left the shells of who we were and became something else entirely. We looked at one another across the gym, beyond the punch bowl, from the sidelines of a dance floor. We felt our chests torch us from the inside. We knew it was not the swelter of a gym.

We know we loved one another.

We knew only that the body knows when to burn.

WE MADE A book, by year's end. We archived what we could.

We assembled our photographs, our profiles. We submitted work that made up the 289 pages of the 2003–2004 Lewis and Clark High School yearbook, a record of action shots and smiles and sanitized silhouettes of those we lost, a witness to nothing at all that could tell us what we were.

We grew up. We grew away from ourselves. We fanned out across the country to distant colleges then to internships and big cities and to office jobs we hated, jobs we could disappear into and forget.

We come home infrequently.

Our parents visit, or we speak to them by phone. We hold the receiver to our ears and imagine them in our childhood homes, our former porches and closed-in kitchens and bay windows looking out on front yards that once held the scent of smoke and the air-blown remnants of ash and before we hang up we can still hear the soft rattle of their breath on the line, a faint beating back that remains only to hear ours.

We keep an archive, a dusted book. A record of our making that we still open, not for memory but for a question without reply. At night, when we can't sleep, we retrace our history over every news-paper we kept. We feel a palpitation. A roil we know as dormant, latent always inside us. We scour the headlines and the fine print, all of it yellowing and tattered. We search for answers in photographs of our school, of the homes, of the guns and ammunition used. We run our hands across the glossed pages of our once-selves, across pictures and profiles. We keep searching. We understand now how Matt's father shut himself off, a valve closed. We know there is noth-ing, no answer, but even still we can't stop ourselves from seeking. We search for confirmation. Something.

We search for some shred of evidence to explain this.

We imagine all of those parents and their silent homes before the flames burst and left nothing but ash. We sit in our basements alone knowing what inimitable dark overcame them. We light our own candles, votives too late, a scent of fire that burns back a vigil, a Midwestern sky. We huddle in the quiet of our basements after our partners and children have fallen asleep and we think of them curled into the bedrooms above us, their beating blood, the cadence of their lungs. How their breath rises. How it falls. How we pray that it never stops. How we're cloaked inside new lives that have taken us to coasts and mountains and so far away from Missouri plains we once knew but how sometimes even still we can't keep ourselves from a familiar ache, from the soft knife of home.

How there are pockets of memory within our bodies that light up when we pass back through our former streets. Upon the routes we took to school. Past the empty lot where Lewis and Clark was eventually demolished. How the maps of our brains blaze upon the swing set of our first kiss. Upon the abandoned pool where we climbed the fence and swam beneath a star-speckled St. Louis sky and smoked our first cigarette. Upon a full moon. A waving poplar. The sound of soft wind through corn husks. How we know the backs of our knuckles, their creases of skin, but can't begin to understand our own cells and what they contain. How we know memory bears weight, every image an ounce. How we've learned to move away, to move on. How when we return home memory erases us, tells us time and distance mean nothing at all.

How we carry this with us, a schematic. Not a school but an entire town. How sometimes when we're home we drive the back roads, streets we still know like a diagram of our own veins. How the back roads have become highways, every cornfield bisected and diminished, but the land long and flat and tasting still of whiskey and the salt of someone else's skin.

How our brains deceive us because they must.

How they tell us the past is something we've discarded. How we drive the length of roads we once thought stretched for miles to the edge of the Midwest and we think of our parents, our once-classmates, our lovers and children up through the floorboards, so close, above the piled boxes of our basements. How we know the earth as unsound. Vulnerable. Always on the edge of bonfiring. How our homes are exposed, no safer than the houses that once lined the tree-drenched streets of our neighborhoods.

How we would burn them down if the world made us.

How we would feel a flame tell us it is time.

How a spark would climb the ladder of our throats and jump the tip of our tongues. How it would catch the curtains. The bedspread. The nightstand lampshade. The wires of the walls. How we know only enough of our own cells to know they speak a language we can't hear. How our atoms slacken and slide out of tune. How they slip past one another, the slightest of friction. How they whisper insurrection. How they articulate in flame what we leave behind.

ACKNOWLEDGMENTS

THANK YOU TO this novel's earliest readers, Michael Griffith and Matt Bell, for your encouragement, feedback, and unwavering support. Thank you also to Chris Bachelder and Jim Schiff for invaluable feedback, and for so much kindness and guidance.

Thank you to Kerry D'Agostino, a wonderful person and tireless champion of this book—thank you for believing in this novel and in me. Thank you to Margaux Weisman for so carefully reading, editing, and supporting this book, and for so keenly understanding my vision for it. I am beyond lucky to work with both of you. Thank you to the entire team at William Morrow and HarperCollins for your dedicated work on this book.

Thank you to Lindsey Kurz, Julia Koets, Rochelle Hurt, and Steven Stanley (Go Orangers)—you couldn't have known it, but through the dark of writing this book you were four points of the brightest kind of light.

Thank you to the generous support of the University of Cincinnati, the Sewanee Writers' Conference where the first chapter of this novel was workshopped, and to Emily Nemens for excerpting the first chapter in *The Southern Review*. Thank you to Leslie Jill Patterson for publishing the short story in *Iron Horse Literary Review* that eventually became this novel. Thank you to the *Denver Post* for their archive of the Columbine shooting, which shaped my understanding of mass tragedy and its scale within a community.

Thank you to the Public Library of Cincinnati for providing a multiplicity of textbooks on crime scene and fire investigation. Thank you to the inspiration of my colleagues and students at Santa Fe University of Art and Design.

Thank you to St. Louis, my home and my heart.

Thank you always and forever to my parents, Michael and Maureen Valente, to my sister, Michelle, and to Jeff, Noa, and Salem. If there is understanding of family and what it means to love in these pages, it is because of you.

And to Josh Finnell, the very earliest reader, for seeing me through every step of the journey this book had to take—thank you for following me through the dark.

ABOUT THE AUTHOR

ANNE VALENTE's first short-story collection, *By Light We Knew Our Names,* won the Dzanc Books Short Story Prize. Her fiction appears in *One Story, The Kenyon Review, The Southern Review,* and the *Chicago Tribune,* and her essays appear in *The Believer* and the *Washington Post.* Originally from St. Louis, she teaches creative writing and literature at Hamilton College.